I suppose being an only child I had always made up stories in which I included brothers or sisters, also the fact that my father never seemed to be bothered about me, so I made up stories where I had a loving father. Thankfully my mum and maternal grandparents made up for what was lacking from my father.

For years I made up stories in my mind but as I grew up I began writing them down, always for my own amusement. In times of trouble or worry I would always lose myself in either reading books or writing my own stories. When my daughters were growing up and I was at home I once again began writing, but still all for my own amusement. It wasn't until I met my late husband Bob that I was encouraged to start thinking about doing something more positive about it, hence my first novel *Polerro* was born as we went down to Polperro and do some research. It wasn't until after Bob died that I was encouraged to send it off to a publishing company. (It had always been a dream of mine to become a published author.) The day I received a letter saying that a company actually wanted to publish me, I cried. *Polperro* took me four years to write, and it wasn't until eight years later that I submitted *St Petersburg*, again when I had a letter saying that this should be published. Again I cried. *St Petersburg* was a labour of love and I thoroughly enjoyed every minute of writing it. I have worked in several different jobs throughout the years from dental nursing, to switchboard and reception and then as my daughters grew up I began in sales. I even worked for four years as a Deputy Registrar in the Register Office only to return to sales again. Now I am retired and spend a good part of my life reading or writing. I hope you enjoy reading *St Petersburg* as much as I enjoyed writing it.

For my Bobert for his love and support and inspiration for *St Petersburg*. Our journey may have ended but our love will go on forever.

To Lizzy
Loads of love
Jill
xxx

Jill Wells-Wane

# ST PETERSBURG

AUSTIN MACAULEY PUBLISHERS™

LONDON • CAMBRIDGE • NEW YORK • SHARJAH

A CIP catalogue record for this title is available from the British Library.

ISBN 9781528922906 (Paperback)
ISBN 9781528926386 (ePub e-book)

www.austinmacauley.com

First Published 2022
Austin Macauley Publishers Ltd®
1 Canada Square
Canary Wharf
London
E14 5AA

Many thanks to Mum and Dad Hall, whose love and support enabled me to carry on with this. Thanks to my daughter Vicky for her help in printing off various bits and pieces and also for her encouragement. Thanks to everyone at Austin Macauley Publishers, including Victoria White and Vinh Tran for putting up with me pestering them before, during and after Covid restrictions. Many thanks.

# Chapter 1

## The Journey

I can't remember how long I had been sitting, staring mindlessly out of the train window at the winter white landscape. The snow-covered scene before me now stretched for miles in all directions, with only the dark grey of the railway track snaking through field upon field of virgin snow. The grey smoke from the engine made its way skyward to join the dark bulbous snow clouds that were despatching more and more of their fine powdery contents to the passing scenery. Only the black skeletal trees interspersed the countryside, showing no signs of humans or animals to mar it. We had already passed through the mountains into densely populated forests, tiny hamlets and villages on our journey. Above us, the dark wintry sky still hung low with more great grey, bulbous clouds, holding even more snow and threatening to dispatch its contents at any moment. Mama had told me that the next city would be St Petersburg, which was still a few hours away.

This was my first journey by train, ever and we were travelling to the great city of St Petersburg to see my grandmother for me to be launched into Russian society.

"Lia," I heard my mother speak from the seat opposite me in our private, first-class carriage. "What on earth can you find that is so spellbinding, to look at, out there? There is nothing but snow as far as the eye can see. Why not go back to reading your book?"

I sighed. "I can't read any more, Mama. I am so excited that I find myself reading the same passage time and time again. The words seem to blend into one another and still the meaning eludes me."

Mama placed the book she was reading down beside her on the seat. "Yes, darling, I should imagine you are very excited, having never been on a train before and now travelling all the way to the great city of St Petersburg to meet your Grand Mama." She took my hands in hers and squeezed them lovingly. "Our life in St Petersburg will be so very different from our life in Smolensk, my darling." She had told me this, many times, since she had received the letter from Grand Mama, just a few short weeks ago.

Already life had changed, not just for Mama and me but also Anya, who was Mama's maid, friend and confidant, since before I was born. She had been Mama's maid, even before Mama was married and living in St Petersburg. That had been Mama's home. Then when Mama married my father, Anya had travelled, on Grand Mama's insistence, to Mama's new home in Smolensk, where she had remained with us for the past eighteen years. Wherever Mama went, Anya followed closely behind in her footsteps. Sometimes I used to tease Anya about her being Mama's shadow, she used to threaten to cuff me around the ears but never carried out the threat, knowing that it was all said in fun.

This journey had held many firsts for me. It was the first time that I had ever travelled by train. (Although trains passed through Smolensk and I had seen them, this was the first time I had actually travelled anywhere by train.)

We had started our journey from my home in Smolensk and travelled, by train, through to Moscow, staying overnight in small, comfortable hotels and then onto Moscow and the Station Hotel. This was the first time that I had ever slept anywhere but in my own bed and then, in the morning getting on to yet another train, to travel from Moscow to St Petersburg. All this had been arranged and paid for by Grand Mama. It was a long and tedious journey, travelling for days on the train.

We were lucky, we travelled first class, thanks to Grand Mama, who had booked our tickets and sent them to Mama some weeks ago.

When Mama told me that we were finally going to visit my, as yet, unseen grand mama and I was to be launched into Russian society, I began dancing around in glee, until Mama told me that this was to be a secret to the rest of the household. If my father found out, he would do all in his power to keep us with him.

Outside it was freezing cold. Luckily, our carriage was relatively warm, but we still had to wear our heavy coats and, on the whole, it was reasonably comfortable with deep blood red, velvet-padded seats. In our compartment, there was only Mama, Anya and myself occupying it. We were very privileged. Not only did we have warmth in our compartment but also privacy. Those people in second-class were huddled together in seats in the long carriages. Those in third-class were even less fortunate than those in second-class. The third-class passengers were squeezed together in what could only be classed as cattle wagons. We were fortunate enough to have some kind of heating in our compartment at the front of the train. Those in second-class had a heater to heat the whole of the long carriage and those in third class had to rely upon each other's bodies to provide heat.

The windows were steamed up as the warm air of our carriage hit the cold air penetrating from the outside. I had cleared a 'spy hole' in the window next to me, so that I could watch the scenery whenever I wanted. The poor people in second-class weren't as fortunate as us. They sat on hard wooden seats, wrapped up, as best they could, against the biting cold. The air in these class carriages was nearly as cold as the air outside of them. The ice on the inside of the panes had formed pretty, delicate lace-like patterns, not that the passengers appreciated it. They were trying their hardest to keep their bodies warm in the freezing cold and the meagre heat that came from the pot-bellied stove.

We were travelling to St Petersburg, the capital of Russia, home of the Tsar of Russia and his family and also the home of my maternal grandmother, whom I had never met but, over the years, had heard so much about. My grandmother was the younger sister of the Dowager Empress of Russia, who, of course was mother to the Tsar and my great aunt.

But I am forgetting my manners. I haven't even introduced myself. I beg your pardon. I am Thalia Marguerite Titania Bobrov, the only child of Baron Rudi Ivanov Bobrov, my father and Baroness Marguerite Babushka Bobrov, my mother, who was the only child of Count Yuri Popov and Countess Ludmilla Popov. It was my grandmother Lilia that we were travelling to visit. My maternal grandfather had died the year of my birth, leaving Grand Mama to live on her own with her servants, in the years that followed. This had all happened after Mama married. Grand Mama Lilia had invited us to St Petersburg many times before, over the years but my father always refused to let us go, shouting for everyone in our household to hear, that our place was by his side, in his home.

This time my grandmother finally had her own way, insisting that we travel to St Petersburg for my debut, before the Tercentennial celebrations of the Romanov reign began. I was now seventeen and any young lady of breeding would be launched into Russian society at my age. I was to be dressed in satins and silks and paraded around certain venues to try and catch the eye of an eligible bachelor and eventually marry a suitable husband. I wasn't exactly sure how I felt about this. Any girl would enjoy being dressed in beautiful clothes and going to various balls, feeling like a princess in a fairy-tale. It was the trying to catch an eligible bachelor that worried me.

I often thought that if my own father did not like me, why should any man? I was also worried, that I might make the same mistake my mother had and marry a complete brute, (how much of a brute I didn't know, but Anya always called him a brute behind his back).

It was true what Mama said; my whole life was due to change. All of my life I had Mama drum into me about good manners, etiquette and posture and always held the fact that my grandmother was the youngest sister to the Dowager Empress of all of Russia and that one day I would have to make a 'suitable match' as befitting the granddaughter of the youngest sister to the Dowager Empress.

I was lucky that Mama and I had such a wonderful relationship. She was not only my mother but also my best friend. Anya was my confidant who, without being told, knew all that was going on, in our home, in the village, everywhere, so it seemed. Officially, I was not allowed to make friends with any of the children in Smolensk as none were equal to my position. Secretly, I had gone behind Mama's back and made some friends, from when I crept from my home to play with the local children.

My father was a different story altogether. I was only a girl. Mama had nearly died giving birth to me and our village doctor had told my father, after my birth, that my mother was not to have any more children as it could kill her, her baby or both. So as a mere girl and no possibility of a legitimate male heir, my father all but ignored me. He and my mother did not even share the same bedroom nor had done since the day of my birth. Mama's bedroom was next to mine, whereas my father's bedroom was on the other side of our home, well away from Mama and myself. I had heard staff talking, including Anya, when she thought that I wasn't listening, that my father took other women to his bed and I believe that I did have siblings somewhere in the village, but they were kept well away from me.

My father was a harsh man and as Mama had told me, with none of the refinements of the St Petersburg aristocracy that Mama had been born into. He was born in Smolensk and rarely visited the capital of our country (except when he was looking for a suitable bride). Why should he want to leave Smolensk when he had everything that he needed right there? I have seen pictures of him when he was younger and I must admit he was very handsome, with practically white-blond hair, which I had inherited from him and I had seen several children in the village with similar hair colour to that of my father and myself (all younger than me) but I had Mama's beautiful big brown eyes, fringed with long, dark lashes. My father's eyes, which I very rarely got close enough to him to see, were like shards of ice. I remember, as a child reading the story of the Snow Queen and a shard of ice got into the little boy's, Kai, heart and remained there, turning him as cold as ice, like the Snow Queen and like my father, I often told myself.

Mama had been born in St Petersburg and had lived a very privileged life with Grand Mama and Grand Papa. She was 'Brought out' when she was seventeen and met my father at her debut ball in St Petersburg. Because my father was a Baron, (his father had died a few years before he and Mama had met, and his mother had died some years before that). My father inherited his father's title and lands on his father's death. As a Baron, he was classed as a good catch for Mama and she was so pleased that she had caught the eye of such a handsome young man. They had a very brief courtship which, of course, ended in their marriage.

The day after their wedding, Mama was removed from the high-class Russian society that she had lived in all of her life, to travel to the small village in Smolensk, to live in my father's family home, which compared to the rest of our village was large and well-furnished but nothing compared to the grandeur that my mother had told me would be waiting for us in St Petersburg.

I was conceived in the early days of my parents' marriage. When my mother was in the sixth month of her pregnancy, she received news that her father was dying. Much against my father's wishes, Mama travelled back to St Petersburg, with Anya, to be at her dying father's bedside. After my grandfather died, Mama stayed on in St Petersburg, for a month, giving comfort to my grand mama, who wanted Mama to stay in St Petersburg until after I was born (needless to say, my father was not at all happy about that). Every day he wrote to Mama saying that his heir should be born in the family home. (Of course, my father thought that I would be a boy.) In the end, he came to St Petersburg to take my mother back home to Smolensk, where she would have her baby. Grand Mama argued that Mama should not travel so near to the birth (Mama was just a couple of days short of her eighth month of pregnancy by then) and that the doctors in St Petersburg were far more advanced than the young local doctor, Doctor Urvanski, in Smolensk. My father insisted that Mama return with him and as his word was law, he dragged a heavily pregnant and tearful wife back to her life in the country.

My grand mama was proved right. The journey back home was detrimental to Mama's wellbeing and she went into labour just over a month prematurely. She had been suffering pains on the final stretch of train journey home. By the time they arrived back in Smolensk, Mama was in full labour with her contractions coming every few minutes. Father carried Mama into the house, with Anya following closely behind, calling to whoever heard them, to get the doctor 'immediately'.

It was a long and hard labour for Mama to bring me into the world and when after thirty-six hours my mother finally gave birth to me, a girl, my father stormed out of the bedroom without even looking at me and took to the vodka bottle. As I was not the son my father wanted, he all but ignored me from that day onwards. When the doctor told him that Mama should not have any more children, my father moved his belongings out of the bedroom they had shared and into one of the other bedrooms at the far end of the corridor and had stayed there ever since.

It took Mama many months to recover from my birth and I was given to a wet nurse to feed, much to Mama's distress. According to Anya, Mama had very little energy anyway after the long labour, without her feeding me and sapping her strength even more.

It was left very much to Anya to take over the everyday running of the household duties, which my Mama had done as the mistress of the house, until Mama was fully recovered.

Each day I was taken, under Anya's supervision, to Mama for a short time for her to hold. If my father did, occasionally, have to address me over the following years, he either called me 'Girl' to my face (which was very rarely) or 'The girl' when he referred me to someone else. Whatever feelings my mother might have had for my father, in the early days of their courtship or just after their marriage, leading up to my birth, had dissipated. Over the years, my home seemed to be split in two, rooms where Mama and I inhabited and rooms which my father inhabited. This suited us all very well, if a little unconventional. My father hardly ever spoke to Mama these days and even then, only to shout. Needless to say, when Mama received Grand Mama's letter inviting us to St Petersburg, Father said that it would be a cold day in hell before he would let us go. With much arguing and door slamming and crying on Mama's part, Anya, secretly, packed cases for us all, hiding them from my father. Anya arranged for us all to be taken by cart to the local train station. I don't think my father had any idea about us leaving. He had gone to one of the other villages on business that day. Mama, Anya and myself quietly slipped out of the side door to a waiting cart to take us away. (We had to use someone that was not attached to our house for fear that whoever helped us to leave would be severely reprimanded and more than likely lose their position in our household). All of the way to the train station and even just getting onto the train, Mama kept looking about her, to see if my father was coming to take us all back. I realised how desperate this action was, to slip away from home without being stopped by my father. I also kept looking around to make sure that my father was not around to take us back. It was only as the train left the station and we were finally on our way did we all give a sigh of relief and settled down for the long journey ahead of us.

As the journey was so long, it gave me plenty of time to reflect on my life and on Grand Mama's involvement in it. I was excited to go to St Petersburg but was worried that because of my sheltered upbringing, I might not be as sophisticated or as well educated as the other young women, who would also be presented to the Tsar at the same time as myself. So, I was excited, but that excitement was overshadowed by trepidation.

Mama had kept Grand Mama informed of my progress on a weekly basis over the years. Mama had taken it upon herself to teach me in deportment, etiquette and embroidery. She had schooled me in all subjects until I was five years old, then Gregor Gregorovich came into our lives as my tutor. My grand mama had also hired him in St Petersburg and Gregor had travelled to Smolensk, (his ticket also being paid for by Grand Mama). Even his wages had been paid by Grand Mama, so that he was not employed by my father who could dictate whether Gregor stayed or went.

According to Anya, when Mama broached the subject of my education to my father, he just shrugged his shoulders and left the room. Gregor became an important part of, not just my life but also Mama's, who used to join in our conversations, debates and sometimes our lessons. I think if it had been left up to my father, after I was born, I would have been left out in the snow, to perish, as they used to do to girl children in years gone by. My father never cared at all about me, my education or my life. I was just a reminder of the fact that he had sired a girl child who could never inherit his lands or title.

I became fonder of Gregor than I ever would my father. How could I be fond of someone who treated me with such total distain? Over the years, as soon as I saw my father, I turned away from him so that I didn't have to extend the courtesy of acknowledging him, any more than he had of me. My hate for him increased. No matter how hard I tried in, my lessons, my father ignored me. It was Anya that told me, that no matter what I did, it was my sex that turned my father against me. There was nothing that I could do about that.

Still, I tried to succeed in all that I did; my lessons, my dancing, even my horse riding, trying to gain my father's attention, probably to prove to him that I was as good as any boy but still I failed. One day while I was out riding my horse, Kallithea, I saw my father sitting on his own horse, some way off. I thought he was watching me. I don't think he realised who I was or maybe he knew and thought that I hadn't seen him. There was a high fence in between us and at that time I still craved his attention and approval. I gathered up the reins and dug my heels into Kallithea's, body. I could feel the power in him draw up and we surged forward. My horse cleared the fence with room to spare and I still remained seated. I looked over to where my father had been but he had already left. I wondered if he had seen the jump or had he left before I had cleared the fence? Obviously, even that had failed to impress him. From that day forward, I stopped trying to impress my father and treated him with the same contempt that he had shown me. As far as I was concerned, he was dead to me. Gregor showed me more affection.

Over the years, according to Anya, my father had 'let himself go' to use her exact words. He had started drinking on the day of my birth and according to Anya, not a day went by since, without him drinking heavily. He either passed out on the floor of 'His study' or took one of the female servants to his bed. No one would dare challenge him, including Mama, for fear of a beating. All of the vodka he drank had taken its toll on him. His body had become bloated, his complexion had begun to ruddy and his hair became greasy and unkempt. In fact, his whole persona was unkempt. When I did, by chance, pass him by, which was rarely, I could smell his unwashed body and bad breath. I was glad Mama no longer shared his bed. Mama was fastidious, as I was, in our toilet.

Gregor Gregorovich had remained with us until we had begun this journey to St Petersburg and Grand Mama. I didn't know what would become of him, once we left Smolensk. He taught me reading, writing, mathematics, English, French, Latin, history and geography. He was a very well-educated man himself, with a quiet, friendly, demeanour and intelligent, brown eyes, which twinkled behind his spectacles and dark hair that looked so soft and silky that it seemed to shine when it caught the sunlight. Unlike many men of the day, he was also clean shaven, not like the many who sported the same facial hair as the Tsar (or pictures that I had seen of the Tsar) and his voice was always warm and friendly. I don't think that I had ever heard him raise his voice, either to me or anyone else. It was with Gregor that I spent many happy hours in his company learning all about life and the world and, of course, my lessons. He always made my lessons interesting. When he felt that I had learnt more than enough required for a young woman of my station, he would let me read the newspapers with him and we would discuss politics and the current news. Very often Mama joined in with us and frequently we would have a three-way debate where there was much laughter and joviality. I often thought that there was a mutual attraction between my mother and my tutor but due to their positions, Mama's marriage and Gregor's position as my tutor, nothing could ever come of it.

Sometimes, when I had free time from my lessons, I crept away from the house to spend playing with some of the children from our village. I had learnt to skate with them one winter on the frozen lake, just outside of the village. My skates had been supplied by the local doctor's son, who had outgrown them.

In the summer we would play hide and seek in the meadows and forests that surrounded our village. I was told, emphatically, that I could not join them when they went swimming, as it was a most un-ladylike pastime, splashing around in my underwear, Mama had said and heaven knows what sort of germs or bugs I might pick up.

I must be honest, I went against my mother's wishes on this and secretly went down to the lake with the other children, paddling and splashing and eventually learning to swim. Peter Urvanski was one of the local village boys. He was older than me by a couple of years, tall and good looking. Already he was the tallest boy in our village and had a mass of blond hair, which he kept neat and tidy, unlike the other boys in the village. He was the son of the local doctor, so his company with me was slightly more acceptable. It would not have been so though, if Mama found out about the swimming. Anya caught me one day returning from swimming in the lake with my hair and underclothes still wet. She tutted and immediately went to arrange a bath for me and wash my hair before Mama could see me. Strangely enough, Anya never told Mama about my misdemeanours. It was one of our little secrets, amongst many. Being a young lady of breeding, even though Peter was the doctor's son, he still wasn't really considered of good enough breeding for me, but our friendship wasn't quite frowned on by Mama. Anything further than friendship, such as romance, would have been frowned upon. Mama and my grand mama wanted a much better match for me.

Often, Peter and I would sit on the banks of the river and have a picnic, with food that I had stolen from our kitchens or we would read some books that had taken our mutual interest. I enjoyed Peter's company. We could converse on most subjects and I wanted to impress Peter. I suppose he was my first romance, although we never kissed or held each other but it was Peter that I had my girlish dreams about.

Peter wanted to follow in his father's footsteps and become a doctor.

When he was old enough, he left Smolensk and went to Moscow to study medicine. I missed his company for a while but in the following years my education left me little time to mourn his leaving, as Gregor was, with Mama's assistance, teaching me to dance, another accomplishment that any young lady of good breeding needed to know. Sometimes Gregor would dance with Mama to show me the correct hold while dancing and also the dance steps to a variety of dances. I think Mama enjoyed these moments being held in a man's arms and there seemed to be a lot of smiling and laughing during these lessons. I think, secretly, Mama was fond of my tall, slim, bespectacled tutor, with his quiet, gentle ways.

I was brought out of my daydreaming again as Mama touched my hand. "Lia darling, we are just pulling into the station, now. Put your book away and put your hat and scarf on, it's freezing outside. You don't want to get a chill, even before you can be presented."

By the time the train had pulled into the station at St Petersburg, the snow had already started falling again, covering everywhere with another layer of fine white powder. Throughout the journey, my heart had been beating in my chest like a frightened bird beating its wings against its cage. Now that we had actually arrived in St Petersburg and the meeting with my grandmother was imminent, the beating of my heart seemed to beat even faster and harder, as if my whole body shook with its rhythm, my mouth was as dry as the bottom of that bird's cage and I was scared that when I actually came face to face with my grandmother, my tongue would stick to the roof of my mouth and I would be unable to speak. I looked across at my mother who seemed to be eager to see her mother again after nearly seventeen years, which was understandable. She had a certain glow to her skin and her eyes a certain sparkle as if being in St Petersburg was bringing her back to life again.

The railway station was packed with people either just starting their journey or finishing their journey, like us. No matter whether they were rich, poor, old or young, with some it was hard to distinguish as we were all wrapped up against the bitter cold. Hats, scarves, gloves; the only thing you could see were people's eyes. Because of their clothing and their face coverings, it was hard to distinguish between men and women.

Anya was the first to alight from the train. She quickly found a porter, who took our cases from the train, placed them on a trolley and followed us along the busy platform. From out of the crowds a tall distinguished, elderly gentleman, broke through and moved towards us. Standing head and shoulders above the majority of the people on the platform, he was dressed very smartly in an immaculate long dark wool coat and traditional black lamb's wool Cossack hat, highlighting his thick, wavy, silver grey hair. Mama threw up her hands and, forgetting us for a moment, she ran towards him, crying.

"Oh Peter! Peter Abramovich. How good it is to see you."

A smile came on the man's face, as Mama flung her arms around him. "Mistress Bab… Baroness Bobrov," he said, correcting himself, remembering his manners and Mama's position. "It has been such a long time. Welcome home." Although he was behaving as was expected of one of his position, it showed on his kindly face how pleased he was to see Mama. With this new breath of life in her, even Mama's stance became more upright and positive, which for as long as I could remember she was stooped and cowering, as if in a permanent state of apology for being in the same house as my father. Mama linked her arm through Peter Abramovich's, as they made their way through the crowds. Mama turned to us all.

"Keep up," she cried. I could tell by the waver in her voice, tears of joy were not far away. She was as pleased at being back in St Petersburg as Peter Abramovich was at her being there.

A large, shiny black motor car was waiting for us as we walked away from the Station platform. I had heard of them and seen pictures of them, but they had never been seen in Smolensk, which on reflection, now, seemed to be in the middle of nowhere. Although there were still only a few motor cars around, in St Petersburg but in Smolensk everyone still travelled by horse, horse and cart or by horse drawn carriage. Just being in St Petersburg for only a few minutes I realised that Smolensk seemed to have been left behind in the middle-ages. Travelling by motor car was another whole new experience for me and I felt a little apprehensive as I climbed in the back seat with Mama, while Anya sat in the front seat. Peter Abramovich was instructing the porter to store our cases in the boot of the car. When our small amount of luggage was safely stored, Peter closed the boot and came around to sit in the front of the car and drove us away from the busy train station. Mama took my hand in hers and smiled reassuringly at me. I tried not to show my fear, as I weakly smiled back at her. I was finally going to meet the grandmother that I had heard so much about but never seen. What would she think of me? What would I think of her? I know that although I had Mama's brown eyes fanned by long, dark lashes, I had my father's hair colouring. Would that be held against me? Was I pretty enough or would all of the fancy clothes be wasted, after all you can't make a silk purse out of a sow's ear. If my father didn't like me, why should I expect any other man to? How could I make a suitable match? What sort of man would be interested in a girl from the middle of nowhere? How would Mama and Grand Mama persuade my father to pay for my clothes for my season? Now that we were on the last leg of our journey, my confidence was beginning to wane, and I was beginning to wish myself back in the safe confines of my bedroom back in Smolensk.

Grand Mama Lilia, as I had been taught to call her, had always been held up as a shining example to me, as the epitome of Russian aristocracy and perfect court manners. I had seen photographs of her, which Mama had brought with her when she came to Smolensk as a young bride. Grand Mama looked very much the matriarch of the family, sitting very stiffly and correctly in a high-backed arm chair with head held high, her hands crossed in her lap and just a hint of her crossed ankles under her long gown, with its high neck and long sleeves. From her ears hung long, beautiful earrings. Around her neck, she wore a five-row pearl choker, with the clasp to the front. The clasp was made of some large magnificent gemstone. Matching the five rows of pearls around her throat, she also wore a matching bracelet of pearls, around her wrist and an array of rings on her fingers. She did not smile into the camera but gazed into the lens in a cool, disinterested way. She looked to be a very formidable person, who, I was worried, would find fault with everything that I did, having only been brought up in the country. Would she look at me and think that I was the 'Country mouse' and sadly lacking in the finer accomplishments?

I was more curious than scared as the car travelled, quickly along, beautiful, wide, tree-lined, avenues, where the trees stood like tall snow-covered sentinels. The snow on the pavements had already been swept aside, giving a safe passage, for any St Petersburg pedestrians who dared to venture outside in such inclement weather. There were a few people walking the streets. I supposed that most were indoors, huddled around a roaring fire, trying to keep warm.

We turned right onto a wide road running alongside, what Mama told me was the River Neve, passing a massive building on the opposite side. Mama explained to me that this was the Winter Palace where I would be presented into Russian society. The palace was absolutely enormous. It could fit nearly the whole of our village under the one roof. A high, wrought iron fencing surrounded the palace. At various intervals, were high double gates, underneath arches carrying golden painted images of triple-headed, spread-winged eagles. This was the Romanov coat of arms. Apart from its impressive size, from the outside the palace looked to be anything but spectacular. (I suppose I expected it to look more palatial and ornate than it did on the outside.) I presumed inside the Winter Palace which would be opulent and breath-taking as I imagined the Palace of the Tsar of Russia would be. On the opposite side of the road, the river had frozen solid enough for people to skate upon. On its banks, small colourful stalls had been erected, for stall holders to sell hot drinks, hot food, I even noticed that one was putting ice skates on people's feet (those that had not brought any skates with them or did not own any). I promised myself, there and then, that while I was in St Petersburg, I would go ice skating on the frozen river.

# Chapter 2
## St Petersburg

By the time the car pulled into the large courtyard of Grand Mama's mansion, the snow was falling in large flakes, quickly covering any tracks. We drove through a tall-gated entrance to a sweeping driveway. I could imagine that in the spring and summer months, the edges of the driveway would be a riot of colour from plants on either side. In the middle of courtyard stood a large fountain, even taller than me, now frozen over but I could imagine the play of water that squirted from a couple of jumping, dolphin's mouths.

The car stopped just in front of a run of five, wide marble steps leading up to a large, portico entrance, housing a massive, heavy wooden door. The door opened immediately when Peter Abramovich had stopped the car and opened the rear door to help Mama and me alight. Even from the road, my grandmother's home had looked very elegant and impressive as it sat well back from the road. All the mansions along the same street looked impressive but Grand Mama's stood out amongst them. Was it because my grandmother was a Countess or was it because she was the younger sister to the Dowager Empress? I had never really given much thought about it before but on reflection, I was beginning to realise what being related to the Tsar of Russia meant and I was related to the most impressive man in all of Russia.

Mama took my hand in hers and squeezed it, trying to give me some comfort. She must have realised how nervous I was to be finally meeting my grandmother. We walked up the steps and entered the largest tiled hallway that I had ever seen. The floor tiles were black and white marble and in alcoves along the walls, opposite the front windows, stood tall, life size, statues on marble plinths, interspersed with delicate ornamented tables, on which stood large crystal vases filled with beautiful, fragrant, hothouse flowers. An enormous crystal chandelier hung from the ceiling, two stories above, lighting the massive entrance. From the hallway ran a large sweeping stairway to the first floor. The carpet on the stair treads looked thick and luxurious and designed in a rich red and gold pattern. Everywhere I looked showed understated opulence.

A maid, who was waiting for us, just inside the front door, gave a brief curtsy and helped us off with our hats and coats, to hang them on an ornate coat stand.

"The Countess will be waiting in the lounge for you, Baroness and Mistress Thalia. Do you remember the way?" Peter Abramovich said as he handed his coat and hat to the maid.

Mama smiled at him. "How could I ever forget, Peter?"

I felt like I was a scared child wanting to hide behind her mother's skirts going to see my grandmother.

Mama walked purposefully towards one of the many large doors leading off the majestic hallway, while I followed slowly behind, trying to take everything in but also delaying the moment when I should finally meet Grand Mama Lilia. I was so worried that she would find fault with me. My mouth went dry with fear as I followed my mother into the lounge.

On entering the lounge, the first thing that caught my eye was the huge marble fireplace housing a massive roaring fire, which managed to heat the whole of yet another enormous room. Over the fireplace hung a large, gold-framed mirror. The walls were covered in delicate cream and gold flocked wallpaper. Golden velvet-covered chairs and sofas were arranged around the fireplace, with some a little further way. I presumed, to allow people to speak in confidence, without being overheard. Another golden crystal chandelier hung in the centre of the room with matching wall lights to illuminate the space. I looked about the room, trying to find my grandmother, who, from the photograph that Mama had showed me over the years, looked as if she would be a tall, statuesque, unbending, critical woman, emanating an air of authority. I felt sure that I would be intimidated by her and braced myself for her appraisal.

"Oh, thank heavens you have finally arrived, my Babushka," said a small, petite woman, who, gracefully, rose from one of the armchairs. This small woman turned out to be my grandmother. She was so totally different to what I had imagined. She rose from one of the gold, velvet-covered, winged chairs facing the fire and came to Mama with her arms open in a warm, loving, welcome. Her perfume, as she moved closer to us, smelt of roses and lavender. She held my mother in her arms and placed a kiss on either cheek, then she turned to me and her warm smile widened as she saw me. "And this must be Thalia. Oh

I am so glad to finally meet you, my darling. I was sure that I would be dead before your father would allow you both to come home to St Petersburg." Again, she took me in her arms and kissed me on both cheeks, then held me at arm's length, so that she could take in every detail of me. Although my grandmother was small, she still held a certain look of authority. She smiled warmly at me but I was worried that if I didn't meet her expectations, she would certainly let me know.

I was trying to get over the shock of finding that this woman was the same matriarch who appeared in the photograph that Mama had shown me, so many times over the years. She was no more than five foot tall, (the same height as me), with her dark hair interspersed with flecks of grey, piled elegantly on top of her head in, what I presumed to be the latest fashion. As in the photograph, her dainty little fingers carried many rings of all kinds of gems and settings; rubies, diamonds, emeralds and sapphires. She had dark brown eyes, fringed with long dark lashes, the same as Mama's and my eyes. Even now she was still a very beautiful woman but, in her youth, I could believe that she would have been absolutely stunning. Mama, although very much like her mother, in looks was at least four inches taller than both Grand Mama Lilia and me.

After what seemed ages of being scrutinised by my grandmother, she turned to Mama. "Oh Babushka, she has your eyes and yet his hair, which is very unusual and yet a very attractive combination, plus she takes after me for height. Such a petite little flower! She is beautiful, my darling." She finally exclaimed. I could feel myself blush at her inspection and her glowing description of me. I had never thought of myself as beautiful or even attractive, (I suppose that was because of my father's treatment of me,) and I was shocked and pleasantly surprised. I began to relax a little now that I knew I had passed my grandmother's inspection with flying colours.

Grandmother took Mama's and my hand in hers and kissed them in turn. "Oh, it is so good to have you both here, at last and we shall have such great fun, together, preparing you both for Russian society. You will both have brand new wardrobes and we shall visit Faberge for some suitable jewellery for Thalia, as befitting a young lady about to be presented to the Tsar and Tsarina and of course my sister, the Dowager Empress." My grandmother looked at me to see if I had registered the fact the I was related to the Dowager Empress of Russia and therefore the Tsar of Russia. "I presume that your mother has told you that you are related to the Tsar of all Russia?" she said proudly.

How could I forget such a monumental connection to royalty? "Yes, ma'am," I replied. I was unsure how to address my grandmother.

"Oh, my darling, please call me Grand Mama. I want us all to be close, good friends, just as your mama and I were when we lived together and I gather, as you and your mama are also."

We all walked away from the heat of the lounge to the slightly cooler hallway. "Now I must let you go to your rooms to rest after such a long journey. Babushka, you are in your old suite and Thalia, you are in the one next door to your mama. I have taken the liberty of having one of the maids act as your own personal maid, Thalia. Of course, Anya will still act for you, Babushka." Once again, she kissed us both on our cheeks. "Now go to your rooms and rest. We shall have an informal dinner in the small dining room at seven o'clock, where we can catch up on all of our news and discuss our plans for the next few days." Grand Mama clasped her tiny, bejewelled hands together in childish delight. "Oh, my darling girls, what a wonderful time and what fun we shall have. I am so looking forward to our time together." Again, she kissed us both and left us, so that we could go up to our rooms on the first floor.

Mama first showed me her suite, all done in pale pink velvet with another large marble fireplace dominating the room. As in the lounge, a roaring fire, radiated heat to the room. Mama's eyes filled with tears. "It's as if I had never left here." She moved over to the ornate dressing table, where a large jewellery box sat. "Your father wouldn't allow me to take my jewels with me when we moved to Smolensk," she told me, touching the lid of the box lovingly. "He said he would shower me with new jewels as befitting a Baroness."

"Did he, Mama?" I asked; she never talked much about my father's courtship of her, so I pushed her on. "Did he shower you with jewels?"

She shook her head and sadly replied, "No, Lia, somehow he never got around to it and after he was told that I could not give him another baby, the son he had always wanted, the subject of jewels was forgotten completely." She lovingly touched the jewellery box again but didn't open it as I expected she would. Suddenly, her sad look changed and she was smiling once more. "Come, let us go and see your suite, Lia."

My bedroom, next door to Mama's was a mirror image, right down to the roaring fire in the marble place but where Mama's room was dressed in delicate pinks, mine was all done in pale peach-coloured velvets. A young girl, not much older than me was standing by the fireplace. She was a couple of inches taller than me, with mousey brown hair and an open, smiling face. She had soft grey eyes that sparkled when she looked at me. I thought that maybe in time we could become good friends like Mama and Anya were. She was dressed in a plain black cotton dress with long sleeves and white cuffs and collar. On her head she wore a little white frilled cap, similar to the one Anya always wore. She curtseyed when we entered the room. "Mistress Thalia," she announced. "I am to be your personal maid. My name is Tanya. I have already unpacked your suitcase and hung your clothes in the wardrobe. Is there anything more that I can do for you at the moment?"

I looked around my beautiful room, not being able to think much, other than how beautiful it was. I had liked my bedroom at Smolensk, it was cosy but it was nowhere near as beautiful and lavishly decorated as this one. One of the large windows, in the summer, would open and overlooked the rear gardens, which contained more fountains that fed three ponds which were frozen over at this time of the year. Ducks waddled about the gardens and on the frozen ponds, quacking away noisily to each other. A maze was in the gardens, not a true one with walls so high that you couldn't see where you were going or the way out but the walls were kept carefully manicured to about waist height. Dotted about the garden were more marble statues and benches to sit on and enjoy the sunshine in the summer. I could imagine that in the spring and summer, the gardens would be a beautiful riot of colour.

"Could I, perhaps, draw you a bath, Mistress Thalia? It will help you to relax after such a long journey?" Tanya asked me. I had been so busy looking out of the window at the garden now covered with snow, that for a brief moment, I had quite forgotten Tanya and also Mama. Mama came and stood behind me as I looked onto the garden.

I nodded my head. "That would be lovely, Tanya. Thank you."

Mama kissed my cheek. "It looks beautiful in the summer, with the fountains running and the ducks swimming on the ponds," she commented, as if reading my thoughts. "I will leave you now my darling. After your bath, I would suggest you try to sleep for a while. I will knock on your door to take you down to dinner at seven o'clock. Have a good rest."

She left the room, closing the door quietly behind her, leaving me alone with my own personal maid, Tanya. We had servants back in Smolensk and Mama had Anya as her own personal maid but if needed, Anya would also help me. Having my own personal maid was something completely new to me. I wasn't sure how I should treat her. I told myself that it was early days still and wondered if she would come back to Smolensk with me when we returned.

Tanya went into another room leading off my bedroom and I heard water running. I followed the sound and found that I had my own bathroom. I never imagined that I would be living in such luxury as to have my own bathroom, which was decorated in the same colour scheme as in my bedroom. Whenever I wanted a bath at home, a tin one would be brought into my bedroom, placed by the fire and endless jugs of hot water would be poured into it. By the time the last jug had been poured, the bath water had already lost some of its heat; so rather than a hot bath, I soaked in a warm one.

Having a nice deep bath with lots of hot, running water, with beautiful smelling oils poured into it was pure heaven. I lay back, letting the water sooth away all the tension that I had been holding within me, with the apprehension of meeting my grandmother, the fear of my father catching us and taking us back home and the experience of travelling first on the train and second in a motor car. Tanya washed my hair, commenting on it being such an unusual colour, beautifully thick and long, it almost reached down to my waist. I know Anya and Mama used to say how beautiful my hair was. It was 'my crowning glory' but I always thought that they were just biased. When Tanya had finished, I stepped from the bath into a large, thick, fluffy bath towel that she held out for me. This had been warming on the radiator that heated the bathroom. I wrapped the towel around me, then went and sat by the fire, while Tanya brushed and dried my hair by the heat of the fire. I had expected her to tug out any tangles that might have occurred in washing, but she was gentle, and I didn't feel a thing. Then it was time to get into the large double bed, with its peach velvet counterpane, matching the heavy, peach velvet curtains. I put on one of the night gowns, which I had brought from home and climbed into bed. I noticed that Tanya had run a warming pan over the sheets, making it toasty warm and inviting. She went and closed the curtains for me. "I will come and wake you at six thirty, Mistress Thalia, so that I can dress you and do your hair. Sleep well." She closed my bedroom door leaving me in the darkness of my new bedroom.

I know that over the years Mama confided a great deal to Anya and I sincerely hoped that Tanya and I could become good friends, the same, as well as mistress and servant. I had never really had a girlfriend that I could really talk to and confide in. I only had Peter Urvanski, but we never really became confidants, just friends who saw each other occasionally.

27

I thought that I would be too excited to sleep. I wanted to think about all the new experiences of the last few days, in my mind but the bed was so soft, warm and inviting, that I could not help closing my eyes and drifted off into a dreamless sleep.

# Chapter 3

## So It Begins

I was woken by a gentle tapping on my bedroom door. For a moment, I could not remember where I was, then after looking around me at my beautiful bedroom remembered that I was finally at my grandmother's house in St Petersburg. I sat up, stretched out my arm, switched on the bedside table lamp and called, "Come in."

Tanya came in and curtseyed to me. "Did you manage to sleep, at all, Mistress Thalia?"

I stretched in the bed like a well-fed cat. "I didn't expect to but I did. I didn't realise just how tired I was."

"Well, it was a very long journey, miss." She stated as she helped me into my old, thick dressing gown, which had been made to keep the draughts of my old home, away.

"I have never left St Petersburg," she told me.

"I had never left Smolensk until I started on my journey here." I said, sitting down in front of my dressing table and allowed Tanya to brush my hair.

I wanted to create a good impression to my grandmother, so asked Tanya if she could put my hair up for me. "Oh, Mistress Thalia, begging your pardon but a young lady of quality doesn't put her hair up until the evening of her debut. Once she has been presented, then she may wear her hair up every day, if she wants to," she explained to me. "Could I perhaps tie it back into a bow?" she asked me.

Was this the beginning of the rules of the Russian aristocracy? "I think you will have to instruct me on the dos and don'ts of Russian aristocracy, Tanya. Where I come from, we never had such restrictions."

"Did you have your hair put up where you used to live then?" Tanya asked as she brushed and brushed my hair till it shone like silver.

"No, I didn't but I thought I would try and make a good impression on my grandmother."

Tanya laughed. "There will be plenty of time for that, Miss Thalia. I will enjoy being able to try different hair styles on you, when that time comes."

I asked Tanya how she had learnt to do the different hairstyles that were in fashion. "Oh, my mother, your grandmother's own personal maid, shows me how to do them and lets me practice them on her."

"So you were training to become a personal maid before I arrived here?"

"Yes, miss. I think if you hadn't arrived, then I would have had to work in another household."

She brought out one of the two dresses that I had brought with me from Smolensk from the massive wardrobe that looked practically bare. Mama had told me that I should not pack too much as I would have a whole new wardrobe once we were in St Petersburg, so I had chosen my two best dresses, plus I had the thick woollen dress that I had been travelling in. Anya had told me that I would need to wrap up warm for the journey.

Tanya finished my hair off with a large bow of green velvet to match my gown.

As the grandfather clock in the hallway chimed seven, I heard Mama's tap on my door. Before I left my bedroom, I thanked Tanya, who curtseyed to me, then I opened the door.

At once, Mama inspected me and smiled her approval. Arm in arm, we went down the marble staircase and entered the small dining room, which was as large as our dining room at Smolensk. The table, which was large enough to seat six people was laid with a brilliant white table cloth and matching napkins. In the centre stood a crystal bowl full of, carefully arranged, yellow roses. Three places were laid, with an array of crystal glasses and knives and forks in front of each place. I looked across to Mama, who smiled, at me, knowing that I had never seen a table laid so lavishly, with such an array of glass wear and cutlery. When Mama was instructing me about table etiquette, she just told me, regarding the cutlery, to just work from the outside inwards. Seeing it all laid out so beautifully I looked at her in panic.

"Just watch what I do, darling. You will soon pick it up," she whispered to me.

Grand Mama sedately entered the room on the arm of Peter Abramovich, who saw her to her seat, pulled the chair out for her, then when he was satisfied that she was comfortably seated, bowed and left us.

Once my grandmother was seated, Mama and I took a seat either side of her.

"You both look so much better now you have rested. Did you manage to get some sleep?"

Mama nodded and I said that I didn't think I would sleep but I managed to and felt so much better.

"I am glad of that, Lia, because the next few days will be rather chaotic for you both. I have arranged for the court dressmaker to call tomorrow morning, so they can start on your wardrobes. I intend for you both to have completely new wardrobes, of clothes, undergarments, nightwear, everything."

That was all well and good but where would we put them all when we returned to Smolensk, I thought.

We didn't have massive wardrobes at home and when and where would I ever wear ball gowns in Smolensk? I felt sure that we would be returning to Smolensk at the end of 'the season' without me securing a suitable marriage proposal.

The meal went by with me matching Mama's moves regarding which cutlery to use and which glass to use. The meal itself was wonderful, with flavours such as I had never tasted before but I found them to be delectable to my pallet. Our cook in Smolensk provided very nourishing but plain food, compared to this. Grand Mama said that her chef treated every meal, each course, as a work of art, stating that the plate was the canvas on which he would create. The food wasn't just very tasty but beautifully, artistically presented.

When the meal was over, we retired to the lounge again, where Grand Mama explained to me more about what would be happening over the next few days. We would go shopping in the large, exclusive stores, frequented by St Petersburg aristocracy and also, we would visit Karl Faberge to choose some jewellery for me. I had heard of Faberge. I think that I had read about some of his commissions for the royal family, in the newspapers. I was told that it would be Madame Auguste Brisac and her workshop of dressmakers who would be making our gowns. Madame August was the dressmaker to the Royal family, so we were highly privileged to have her attending us, so Grand Mama told me.

Once Grand Mama had finished talking about what was to happen over the next few days, she then turned to the subject of my father, asking Mama, how she had managed to get my father to allow us to travel to St Petersburg? Mama blushed bright red.

"I am afraid he was still against us coming, so we left the house while he was away, Mama. This is an important time in Lia's life, and I was determined not to let him spoil it."

Grand Mama flung her hands in the air and began laughing with glee. "Good for you, my darlings! Did he think he could keep you imprisoned in the back of beyond forever?"

Grand Mama sighed and her face took on a serious look. "Babushka, you should divorce that man."

There was a sharp intake of breath from my mother. "I can't, Mama, you know that the church is against divorce."

"But, my darling, you have mitigating circumstances. You don't sleep together…"

Mama put up her hand in shock at Grand Mama's directness. "Mama, stop. Not in front of Lia, please."

"Darling, I am sure that Lia is old enough to know what goes on, aren't you, Lia?"

I looked over to Mama and sadly nodded.

"There, you see, Babushka. Now let us speak openly about this sham of a marriage. As you are no longer sharing the same bedroom and he is taking other women to his bed and has done so for the last seventeen years, since Lia was born. I have spoken to my solicitor and he says that with the adultery and his beating of you…"

"Mama, no more, I beg you. I made sure that Lia didn't know about that," Mama said, horrified and looked across at me.

Grand Mama, once she had started was like a dog with a bone. She would not let it go. "Well, now she does," Grand Mama said to finally stop Mama's protesting. "So, let's not pussy foot over the matter any longer. The man was an animal. A beast. I forbid you to go back to Smolensk, Babushka. I know you haven't told me all, but Anya has also kept me informed over all the years, as I asked her to, so don't go telling Anya off, she was just following my instructions and I know everything. I say, divorce the man, Babushka."

"Mama, I need to think about this," Mama said.

"Babushka, what on earth is there to think about? You have more than enough reasons to divorce him, so my solicitor has told me. He can have the papers drawn up in just a few days. By this time next year, you could be a free woman," Grand Mama persisted.

"And where would I live as a free woman, Mama?" I could hear her voice shaking with unshed tears.

"Why, here, of course, Babushka. This was always your home and it always will be; yours and Thalia's."

I thought to myself that this is where Grand Mama shows herself as the true matriarch and I would be scared to death to cross her. She might be small, but she certainly ruled in this household, as she intended to rule Mama and me with a steel hand in a silk glove as Anya would have said.

I thought that, maybe, it was time to excuse myself to go up to bed. I had already been smothering yawns for the last half hour, so I kissed them both on the cheek, bid them both a good night and retired, once more, to my beautiful bedroom, which if Grand Mama had her way, would be my bedroom from now until I married or Mama remarried.

Tanya was there, waiting for me when I opened my bedroom door. She helped me undress and get into my night gown. When I climbed into bed, I found that she had warmed it for me again. It was lovely and warm.

"Is there anything else that I can do for you, Mistress Thalia?" she asked as she stoked the fire in the fireplace, adding more logs, so that it wouldn't go out in the middle of the night and, heaven forbid, that I would get cold.

I noticed that the book I had been attempting to read on the train had been placed on my bedside table, so I told Tanya that she could leave me. She curtseyed to me, then, closed the door, quietly, behind her as she left the room.

I stretched in the luxury of my warm comfortable bed and secretly hoped that we would never return to Smolensk, not just for my sake, as much as for Mama's. How could my father beat her? She never did anything wrong, apart from us stealing away from home to come to St Petersburg. No matter how he treated her, she still remained a good and faithful wife. He was the one in the wrong; always drinking and taking other women to his bed. My hands balled up into fists under the bedclothes. I hated him. I could beat him for what he had done to my gentle, loving mother.

If she did divorce my father, Mama was still young enough, (only in her mid-thirties still), to find happiness and get married again to a decent man who wouldn't mind that she couldn't have any more children. I was sure that there were men out there that felt the same way.

Although I had decided to read for a while, in the warmth of my comfortable bed, again, I could hardly keep my eyes open. I found it so difficult to fight against sleep when my bed was so soft and warm. I decided to put my book down, turn off the bedside table light and go to sleep.

# Chapter 4
## The Transformation Begins

True to her words, the next day was as hectic, as Grand Mama had predicted.

Tanya woke me at nine o'clock in the morning with my breakfast tray. (This was a lot later than I slept in Smolensk, village life started a lot earlier there.) After she had placed the tray on my lap, in bed, she opened my bedroom curtains and let a weak, watery winter daylight filter in. Although it looked freezing cold outside of my window and snow covered the rear gardens, which my bedroom overlooked, inside in my bedroom it was lovely and warm. The fire in my hearth had already been stoked; more wood had been added and the fire was blazing by the time I had finished my breakfast and got dressed. Grand Mama had told us that Madam Brisac would be arriving at ten o'clock, so once dressed, I sat in one of the comfortable chairs by the fire and took up my book. Again, I tried to read but once more, I was far too excited, thinking about the beautiful gowns that I would be having made. I couldn't wait. I sighed and put down my book, finally giving up, for the time being and devoted all my attention and imagination to what my new clothes would look like. I had no idea what fashions were 'in vogue' only by the black and white photographs containing women that were newsworthy.

Mama knocked on my door at ten o'clock. "Lia, Madam Brisac is here. May we come in?"

At last, my transformation would begin. My heart was beating rapidly with anticipation as Mama came in with Grand Mama, followed by Madam Brisac, leading her entourage of staff. I never expected so many people to do what I thought was a relatively simple task of measuring me, suggesting suitable materials and styles. I just expected Madam Brisac. I did not know that someone who dealt with royalty, would not demean herself with such basic things as taking measurements or displaying patterns or materials.

Grand Mama was in charge again. "Auguste, this is my grand-daughter, Thalia, who you will also be creating a whole new wardrobe for. She is to be presented to the Tsar and Tsarina on Christmas Eve at the Grand Ball."

Madam Brisac took my hand and smiled warmly at me. "Oh, I am sure that we can do something very special for Miss Thalia." She eyed me up and down, then commented, "Such unusual hair colouring and so petite, just like her grandmother." August Brisac said, "First, we will take measurements, then we can discuss what clothing you will need. After that, we will look at some designs and finally materials."

One of Madam Brisac's girls brought the little footstool over, from by the side of the fireplace and Madam Brisac politely asked me if I would stand on it. Then the measuring began; such a simple task but one of Madam's girls did the measuring, with a flourish, first measuring me and then giving my measurements to another girl who wrote them down in a book. Madame Brisac commented on my tiny waist and said it would be pleasure, to make a wardrobe of clothes for someone so petite and beautiful. I blushed at her words. I had never thought myself to be petite and beautiful and wasn't used to such compliments.

"We keep all of these things recorded, measurements, dress designs and materials," Auguste Brisac explained to me, "so that we do not duplicate them, with any others we might be making for other young ladies or in years to come, for you, Miss Thalia."

I never realised just how much was involved. When we lived in Smolensk, there was a lady in the village that used to come and measure us for new dresses, but they were always one of about half a dozen styles and she did everything herself. She had saved her money and finally bought herself a sewing machine which cut down the time she spent sewing clothes right down, so that they were ready much sooner than when she had to hand-stitch everything herself.

Once my measurements had been taken, I could step down from the stool, to look at thick, catalogues of styles of dresses, coats, blouses and skirts. Grand Mama said that initially I would need five skirts and blouses, six-day dresses, seven evening gowns and five ball gowns, plus three coats, two jackets and four capes. I was shocked and amazed at how many clothes I would need. I had never had that many clothes in all my life. I was informed by Grand Mama that that was just the start of my wardrobe, which would be added to as time went by. My large bed was strewn with bolts of materials; rainbows of silks, satins, velvets and woollen materials all suitable for the young relative of the Tsar.

Two and a half hours later, Madam Brisac left with her retinue of seamstresses. I just flopped down on my bed exhausted. My head was spinning with all of the designs and materials. Never had I seen such an array of materials of beautiful colours, textures and fabrics. While discussing my requirements, for evening gowns and ball gowns, Madame Brisac showed us materials so delicate that I was concerned they might rip if handled too roughly, these were again laid in a rainbow of colours; materials beyond my imagination were ordered. There would be no throwing them over the back of a chair, as I had done at home. Tanya would look after them and put them away, carefully in my wardrobes, which would soon fill up with all my new clothes.

Madam Brisac had been told by Grand Mama that I needed a couple of skirts and blouses and one evening gown as soon as possible. Madam Brisac told Grand Mama that a skirt and blouse would be ready the next day and an evening gown, the following day. The rest would be delivered to us as soon as they were ready. I was looking forward so much to receiving all of the 'finished articles', but the one that I was really looking forward to was my ball gown for my debut, where I would be presented to the Royal Family. Never had I seen or even imagined to own anything so beautiful. It had a train (as was required for my 'coming out') and the bodice would fit me like a glove, cut low over my breasts and shoulders. Its colour was not white as most of the girls who were to be presented would wear, (Madam Brisac said that I would look like a ghost all in white with my pale hair) and so a 'Champagne' colour was chosen in silk. When it moved in the light, tiny shots of all the colours of the rainbow shimmered in the material. She assured Grand Mama that no one else would ever have a gown made from that particular material as it had just been exported from China. It would be exclusively for me. I felt like a child on Christmas morning, seeing my Christmas presents but not being able to open them. It was wonderful to me, to see so many beautiful materials and stunning styles. Some of the bodices of the evening gowns I thought were most daring, barely covering my breasts, such was my gown for my debut. I was told that this was very fashionable when I tried to protest. It was hard for me to believe that I would be wearing such beautiful creations. Never in my wildest dreams, back in Smolensk, could I imagine all that had happened and was going to happen to me. All of my evening and ball gowns, would be of pastel colours until after my wedding, when they would become darker and more vibrant. Such strange rules I thought, but when in St.

Petersburg…My heart was full to overflowing with happiness at the prospect of wearing such beautiful clothes. I could not stop smiling to myself.

After Madame Brisac and her girls had finished with me, they went next door to Mama's suite to discuss her requirements.

After Madam Brisac finally left, we sat down to lunch in the small dining room again. My wardrobe of clothes was discussed, and Grand Mama told us that we would go 'shopping' after lunch.

*What more could I need?* I wondered. I had a whole new wardrobe, (or I would have, when it was all finished). Grand Mama laughed. "Oh my darling Lia, there is so much more that a young lady in your position will need; underwear, nightwear, shoes, boots, gloves, handbags, hats and of course we will visit the Faberge store, for your jewellery. It is Faberge that designs and makes all the crown jewels for the Tsar and Tsarina and of course my sister but also for most of the nobility of Russia." I flushed with pride at the thought of being classed as part of Russian nobility.

I had heard of Faberge from Mama and I had also read about his design and creation of the famous Faberge eggs that the Tsar gave the Tsarina for special occasions. I would love to see them but doubted I would ever have the opportunity to.

After lunch we all climbed into Grand Mama's motor car. Peter Abramovich ensured that we were all comfortable in the rear seats, then sat in the driver's seat and we went shopping. The sky had cleared a little from the morning and although still bitterly cold, the sun had finally broken through. The shops we visited were large and lavishly decorated. Firstly, we went to get underclothes. I felt embarrassed to be discussing such intimate things with a complete stranger, but the underwear they showed us was so delicate and beautifully made that to me it seemed a shame they would never be seen. In the same department we chose nightdresses and matching negligees and then a thicker dressing gown made of soft peach velvet to match the colour scheme of my bedroom. Gone were the thick nightdresses that I had to wear in Smolensk to keep me warm in bed, my new nightdresses were very soft and delicate, really too beautiful to be worn in bed. Once we had finished purchasing these, Grand Mama took, from her little bag, her calling card, where the bill was to be sent and handed it to the shop assistant. All my purchases were carefully folded and placed in beautiful boxes, then tied with a pink ribbon and taken out to Peter Abramovich, who stood patiently waiting by the car. He stored them away in the boot of the car and waited for more.

We moved on to shoes and handbags next. No more the stout walking boots such as the ones we had bought from the local cobbler in Smolensk but boots made of the softest leather, which felt like slippers, when I tried them on. One pair of brown boots and one of black were purchased. A pair of cream leather, fur-lined slippers (mules, these were called, because they had no back to them. How I was to keep then on, I didn't know). Next came shoes made in soft kid leather, with tiny heels. Grand Mama bought me seven pairs of these, all in a variety of styles and colours to match my outfits. Again, Grand Mama had handed her calling card. These were also all boxed and dispatched to Peter.

Next, we bought gloves, no longer fur-lined mitts, to keep my hands warm but again soft leather, in brown, black, grey and cream and long silk gloves, in cream and white for evening wear.

After the gloves were beautiful fur muffs to put my cold, leather-clad hands in to keep them warm. These were all boxed up again. I could imagine the back of the car, by now was filled up to overflowing.

Finally, we moved on to hats. Grand Mama and Mama were in raptures over these concoctions made of straw, fur, velvet, beribboned, be-flowered, with tulle, silk, velvet ribbons, all in a rainbow of colours. We left there, after buying not only hats for me but also Mama and Grand Mama as well.

Oh we had such a wonderful time, the three of us, laughing and giggling like school girls. Even Grand Mama, who had started out on the outing as the staid matriarch, changed after Mama and I had tried on some hideous creations of hats and was laughing with the two of us. Obviously Grand Mama was well known and well respected wherever we went. No matter what was bought, money was never exchanged but the bills would be sent to Peter Abramovich to pay on Grand Mama's behalf, at the end of the month. It was decided that because of the size of all of the hat boxes, these would be delivered directly to Grand Mama's. Although it was wonderfully enjoyable, it was also very tiring. Grand Mama began to tire, as did Mama and myself.

"We will go for a cup of hot chocolate and a pastry in one of the restaurants and then on to Faberge," said Grand Mama, who led us over to a coffee shop, not far from the large stores.

We all nearly collapsed in our seats, pleased to take the weight off our feet. Once we had sat down and taken off our gloves, a young waitress came over, wearing a black dress, white apron and cap, who took our order for hot chocolate, then came over with a trolley full of delicious cakes. We all chose a slice and they were placed on delicate china plates in front of us along with a pastry fork. The restaurant was very busy with the 'well to do' people of St Petersburg, drinking tea, coffee, hot chocolate and eating the delicious pastries and cakes, displayed in the window.

People, who Grand Mama was acquainted with, came over and spoke to her. Proudly she introduced both Mama and me and after we had all shook hands and they handed us their calling cards the ladies had left. Amidst all of this, small, poorly dressed children looked, longingly, through the steamed-up restaurant windows where imitations of cakes and pastries were on show. Those poor children looked half-starved and inadequately dressed for the bitterly cold weather and by the looks on their faces at seeing the cake trolley laden with such wonderful cakes and pastries, their mouths were watering. I felt so sorry for them and wanted to give them cakes to eat but I could imagine my grandmother scowling at me in disapproval. Worse than the hunger, the poor little things looked frozen to their core. It was heart-breaking.

After we had finished, we all felt refreshed and ready to move on to Peter Karl Faberge's premises. These were not situated with the other shops but a little further away on Bolshaia Morskaia. We all got into the car again and Peter drove us the short distance to Faberge's shop.

The premises of Faberge were imposing; not just a simple shop but a large, four-story building. I had just expected a lavishly decorated shop and nothing more but, as I later found out, the premises housed a variety of workshops, with dozens of artisans making all sorts of things, not just the famous Faberge eggs but miniature hardstone carvings of people and animals, flowers from semi-precious gems and gilded with beautiful enamels and precious metals. Faberge also produced jewellery boxes, cigarette cases, little visiting card cases and of course wonderful jewellery, necklaces, rings, earrings, crowns, tiara's, cuff links, tie pins; even ornate buttons. A bell tinkled as we opened the door to his 'shop' and immediately Peter Karl Faberge, himself, came out to greet us, with a smile.

"Countess Popov, what a pleasure it is to see you again. It has been such a long time since you have graced us with your presence," he said taking Grand Mama's hand and kissing it. He was so courteous and when my grandmother introduced both Mama and myself, he again kissed our hands as we extended them to him. He escorted Grand Mama to a chair and had another two chairs brought out for Mama and me.

Peter Karl Faberge was in his mid to late fifties, with greying hair, piercing dark eyes, behind spectacles and wore a little goatee beard and moustache. There was nothing spectacular about his looks, as I had expected. To me he just looked like any man that you might pass by in the street but his reputation as an artisan was well known, practically worldwide. It was the famous Faberge eggs that he was best known for.

Although there were other well-known jewellers, such as Cartier and Tiffany, Grand Mama said that she preferred Faberge.

Grand Mama explained our situation and asked for us to be shown a range of earrings, necklaces and bracelets, to which Mr Faberge clapped his hands, for an assistant; and told him to bring several trays of jewellery. While his assistant went away to get the jewels, Karl Faberge clapped his hands again; another assistant came and he instructed them to bring three glasses of Champagne. Before long, both assistants arrived, one carrying several wooden, black velvet lined, trays of jewellery and the other carrying a small silver tray, on which stood three glasses of Champagne in beautiful crystal glasses.

I thanked the assistant as he handed me my glass and I took my first sip of Champagne. The bubbles tickled my nose as I sipped the crisp, clear, liquid.

Grand Mama began inspecting the trays of jewellery, first the single rows of pearls, picking them up one at a time and holding them to the light. When she found a row that met with her satisfaction, she put it to one side, then, began inspecting the multiple rows of pearls, going through the same process of holding them up to the light and tilting them one way and then the other. Again, once she was satisfied, she put that to one side. After Grand Mama had inspected the necklaces, she inspected the bracelets and earrings.

Mr Faberge complimented Grand Mama on her taste, "You always could pick out the quality items Countess. They are the best quality pearls that I have."

My opinion had not even been asked, regarding the jewellery, so I kept sipping my champagne until I had finished it, then thought that maybe, I should not have finished it so fast. I was beginning to become light headed and had an overwhelming urge to giggle. With great difficulty, I held myself in check. Our purchases were placed in beautiful padded boxes and wrapped. We walked from the shop, after thanking Mr Faberge for his help.

Grand Mama had finally chosen, for me, a choker of three rows of pearls with a diamond clasp, matching bracelet and matching dangling earrings. (These she told me were to wear in the evenings.) During the day she had chosen a single row of pearls and pearl stud earrings. On top of these beautiful jewels, she had bought me a cameo broach and again matching earrings.

Without making a fuss, I linked my arms through Mama's, to steady me, as we walked back to the car, as I felt very light headed. I hoped that today would not be the last time that I visited Faberge's, which to me seemed to be a veritable, Aladdin's cave.

One thing that struck me above anything else, about the day was that the aristocracy of St Petersburg never carried money with them but handed out calling cards, for the bills and goods to be sent to their specified home address, to be paid at a specified time.

By the time we arrived back at Grand Mama's, all of our previous purchases had been delivered and taken straight to my room. Igor, the footman, carried the parcels from the boot of the car and upstairs to my bedroom. He had to make three trips to bring all of my purchases in.

I was pleased that Tanya had left all of the boxes on my bed, unopened, as I was looking forward to opening them all myself. I could hardly see my bed as all the boxes were strewn across it; some even had to be placed on the floor because there was no room for all of them. It was like all my birthdays and Christmases, rolled into one. I undid box after box and held the enclosed contents up for Tanya to see.

"Oh, Mistress Thalia, they are wonderful. They are so pretty and delicate," she said as I showed her my nightgowns. Tanya kept exclaiming at each item as I unpacked them. I admit I felt a little impatient now, as I wanted all of my new clothes to be delivered, so that I could try them all on, with my new shoes and handbags, gloves and muffs.

I knew that I would have to wait and be patient and I did have all of my other purchases. I wanted time to pass quickly so that I could go to bed wearing one of my new nightgowns. I didn't know what would happen to my old clothes, as they were replaced by my new wardrobe of clothes.

I wore the same dress that I had worn the evening before as I went down to dinner that night, but I was wearing a pair of my new shoes, so that I could get used to wearing the little heels.

Mama and Grand Mama were already in the little dining room and stopped talking when I entered so I imagined that they had been discussing Mama's divorce from my father again. Throughout the evening meal, we discussed the day and my purchases and Grand Mama started talking about places to go to so that we would be seen. She had decided that my first social engagement would be when I was presented to her sister, the Dowager Empress Maria. Once it was known that I had been presented to the Dowager Empress, invitations would come pouring in for me. Grand Mama made a note that Mama and I should have our own calling cards printed, which was another thing to remember about being with the Russian aristocracy. Whenever you went to call on someone, you always left or handed your 'calling card'. This was yet another purchase, to come from Grand Mama's purse. I was told by Mama, before travelling to St Petersburg, that talking about money was considered 'vulgar', so I never mentioned such a 'vulgar' thing to either of them but I knew that I must be costing my Grand Mama an awful lot of money. On top of what Grand Mama had spent on me, she had also spent a lot of money on Mama as well, as all of Mama's clothes, like mine, had been from Smolensk and were very basic and provincial, compared to the creations Madam Brisac had been commissioned to make for us both.

When I went to bed that night, I put on one of my new nightgowns. As it slipped down over my body, it felt like my body was being stroked all over by feathers. I put on my new slippers and peach-coloured velvet dressing gown and sat in one of the arm chairs by the fire to read the book that I had been trying to read for the past few days since we had started on our journey to St Petersburg. Finally, I managed to lose myself in the pages of my book, until I felt my eyelids begin to close. I put my book on the bedside table, took off my dressing gown and slippers, put them on the small chair by the side of my bed and slipped between the sheets that Tanya had already warmed for me. Tanya came in to put my clothes away and asked what she should do with my old nightdress and woollen dressing gown. I didn't know. I told her that I would have to think about it.

"Whatever we do, they will need washing, then, maybe, some woman might like them," I said, then a thought came to me. "Would you like them, Tanya?"

Tanya said she would like them very much if I did not mind. I felt that it was the least I could do for her, so I let her have them willingly. Armed with my old nightclothes, she curtseyed to me, thanked me and then left me alone.

I had had such a wonderful day with Auguste Brisac, then shopping in the large department stores and finally Faberge's. What more could I want? This would be the first exciting day of many, I hoped. With thoughts of the day's activities running around in my head, I closed my eyes and finally slept. It had been a day, I could never, in my wildest dreams, have imagined or would ever forget. I felt like a princess in a fairy tale or Cinderella.

# Chapter 5
## My First Day of Freedom

At nine o'clock the following morning, Tanya came in with my breakfast on a tray and after placing it on my lap, opened my bedroom curtains to let the beautiful winter sunlight pour into my room.

"It's a lovely day outside, Mistress Thalia. Some of your new clothes have already arrived from Madam Brisac's. They are downstairs. Shall I bring them up for you?"

I nodded my approval. I think Tanya was as excited about my new clothes as I was. When I had finished my breakfast, I got out of bed and dressed in my new underclothes, (I didn't want to wear them until I could wear them under some of my new clothes, which seemed rather silly and childish, when I think back). Madame Brisac and her seamstresses had already made two skirts and two new blouses. It amazed me how quickly they had been sewn together. I imagined that she must have had women working on them through the night, to make sure they were ready, as Grand Mama had requested.

"I won't be requiring any of my old clothes now Tanya. Would you like them, as well, if they fit you?" I asked as I twirled around in front of the full-length mirror on the wardrobe, admiring my new grey woollen skirt and pale pink blouse with tiny ruffles all down the front and on the cuffs of the long sleeves. I had put on my new black boots and Tanya had brushed my hair and put it into a single loose plait then tied it back with a pink ribbon to match my blouse. To make a change from just tying my hair back, Tanya had left two pieces of hair, either side of my face curled into ringlets. I was so pleased with what Tanya had done, that I was, more than happy, to give her my other clothes. I thought that I might have sounded patronising offering Tanya my 'cast-offs' but she seemed happy to have them. They weren't exactly in the height of fashion, coming from Smolensk but they were of good quality material and hardly worn, as Mama had

had them made, unbeknown to my father, for us, just before we started out on our journey.

Tanya was pleased with her new clothes. She told me that she would wear them on her time off. She excused herself briefly and ran to put them upstairs in her bedroom. The servant's quarters were situated on the third floor of the house in the massive attic that was separated into bedrooms, bathrooms and a communal lounge, so Tanya told me one day when I asked her about her living accommodation. All of the servants ate downstairs in their own dining room next to the kitchen, and Tanya slept in a room with two other female members of staff.

I went and knocked on Mama's bedroom door to show her my new clothes. Still dressed in her nightdress and dressing gown, she bid me enter and twirl around, so that she could get the full effect of my new clothes.

"Oh, my darling Lia, you should have been dressed like this all of your life, not stuck in that backwater. The young girl that left Smolensk just a few days ago is already a lovely young woman but with your new clothes, you look so beautiful!" Her words brought a lump to my throat.

I leant over to kiss her and saw there were tears in her eyes. I hoped that they were tears of happiness.

I thought now might be the right time to ask about the divorce, so I skirted around the subject, not mentioning the dreaded 'D' word.

"Will we ever go back to Smolensk, Mama?"

"No darling," she said sadly. "Your grand mama and I had a long talk yesterday and I know she is right. Your father doesn't love me, nor I him. The only good thing to come from our marriage was you, my darling. I would go through it all again just for you. Grand Mama's solicitor is coming over this morning with the divorce papers for me to sign. Why don't you go out and explore this morning? You have a beautiful day but wrap up warm. Regardless of the sunshine it is still freezing cold out there. Ask Tanya to go with you. I am sure she would enjoy it and it would give you a companion. I am sure she knows St Petersburg well enough to show you around."

Speaking of Tanya, I told Mama that I had given my old clothes to her and asked if it was acceptable? Mama told me that she was glad I had done so. "I hope you and Tanya will become good friends as well, just like Anya and me."

I had no intentions of exploring, as Mama had suggested. I knew exactly what I was going to do on my first day of freedom in St Petersburg.

I went in search of Tanya, who quickly agreed to the prospect of getting out of the house for a while and away from her chores. We both wrapped up warm, with thick scarves around our necks, gloves on our hands and hats on our heads. I had to wear the same coat that I had arrived in, as Madam Brisac was still making my winter coats but I did put on my new grey leather gloves, grey lambswool, Cossack style hat and matching muff.

Tanya and I linked arms, once we had closed the front door behind us. It was so cold outside, as we walked our breath formed tiny clouds of moisture in front of us. Although there had been another heavy snow fall during the night, the pavements had already been cleared and the snow stacked in piles at the side of the road, so that the pedestrians of St Petersburg may walk in safety, without fear of slipping over. The trees along the way were still heavy with snow, occasionally dropping some of their weight on unsuspecting passers-by. Tanya and I saw it happen to one unsuspecting gentleman, who jumped and tried to wriggle from the snow that had dropped down his neck. Luckily, he was too far away to hear us giggling at his expense. Further along we saw some children were sliding on some ice that had been left on the pavements. They were sliding along and squealing with delight, even the ones that had slipped over were laughing.

Grand Mama's house was just two roads back from the Winter Palace. The road that she lived on had other large, impressive mansions, I noted but on closer inspection none were as grand as Grand Mama's.

Because I stepped out purposefully on our way to the river, Tanya thought that I had been to St Petersburg before. When I assured her that I had never set a foot outside of Smolensk until the day we journeyed to St Petersburg. She asked me how I knew where we were going. I told her that I had seen the frozen river and the people skating on it, when we drove past it on our way from the station, the day of my arrival.

A look of pure panic showed on her face. "Oh, Mistress Thalia, surely you don't mean to skate on there? It could be dangerous! The ice could crack and you might go under it and drown or you might fall and break your neck! Oh Miss Thalia, please don't go on the ice. I beg of you." She was nearly crying as she stopped and faced me.

I could see genuine concern on her face and assured her that I had ice skated many times before on frozen lakes and rivers of my old home and never hurt myself before. I felt very proud of that fact, after all of Tanya's worries of doom. We carried on walking as I tried to re-assure her that it would be safe.

"Tanya, please don't be so scared for me. It has snowed and frozen over again, so it will be even safer than it was the day before yesterday. There were people skating on it then and I presume they were skating on it yesterday as well. Surely you aren't going to stand on the banks and just watch? I could teach you to skate, it's not hard. It is more a matter of balance." I told her trying to persuade her to join me.

"I have never skated before in my life, Miss Thalia and, if you don't mind, I will feel safer standing on the bank and watching you, if you insist on skating on it." I was a little disappointed by this, as we walked along, I could imagine all of the fun we would have together. Being an only child and being restricted with friends from my home, I craved a friend that we could do things together; go places together. It didn't matter to me that I was the mistress and she was the servant. New rules applied in St Petersburg and we were allowed to go out together.

When we arrived at the river, I didn't really mind Tanya not skating with me, as long as she didn't stop me skating.

We found a bench on the bank, near to one of the brightly covered stalls I had also seen on the day of my arrival. Tanya sat down, while I quickly opened my coat to bring out my ice skates. (I had secretly packed them, hurriedly, before we left Smolensk) and I had them hidden under my coat, before we left Grand Mama's house. My skating boots were old and well-worn but I still wanted them with me, bringing me happy memories of Peter Urvanski teaching me to skate. I wondered what he would think if he saw me now. I hoped that someday we would meet again and I could show him that the moth that he had left in Smolensk had finally turned into a butterfly but I doubted that our paths would ever cross again, as we would more than likely be moving in completely different circles.

I handed Tanya my new boots before I bent down to tie the laces on my ice skating boots, then before she could say anything else, I stood up and made my way on to the frozen river. On such a beautiful crisp sunny morning and everything that had happened to me during the last couple of days, it felt good to be alive. The sky was a beautiful blue with tiny white fluffy clouds skittering along. My heart was soaring with happiness. Never in all my seventeen years in Smolensk did I ever think that I would be here in the capital, being clothed in such beautiful finery, as I was wearing and would be wearing from now on.

I skated for the beauty and excitement of my life, passing other young girls, giggling, who were also enjoying this feeling of freedom as they skated too.

There were a few couples on the ice as well, with their arms linked and their hands clasped together, skating around and around. How many of these single girls, were wishing that they would be escorted around on the ice by a handsome young man? I know that I did too but that handsome young man that I dreamt of was Peter Urvanski. He was really the only boy that I had ever formed a friendship with in all my young life.

I skated around and around, widening my circle all the time, until I was skating under over-hanging branches of trees, laughing with the pure pleasure of being alive and in St Petersburg, on such a beautiful morning. I waved to Tanya each time I passed her by and she waved back to me. I thought that we could probably sneak back into Grand Mama's and hide my ice skates without Mama or Grand Mama ever knowing, otherwise there would be long difficult conversations as to where I had got my skates from and from whom had I learnt to skate.

I tilted my head back and looked at the beautiful blue sky, feeling the crisp winter sun on my face making my cheeks pink with the cold and I could see my breath escaping from between my lips. I felt like I was flying like the birds. Suddenly my foot caught on something and rather than skating, I was flying through the air, landing heavily, in a lump, on the ice. I felt so foolish and embarrassed, just sitting there dazed, until I heard Tanya shouting to me from the bank. I looked about me to see if anyone had seen my fall from grace but it seemed that the other skaters were too busy enjoying themselves to notice me. I tried to get up until I felt two strong arms behind me helping me sit up. I stared into two twinkling grey eyes, framed by dark lashes. "No don't try to stand yet," my rescuer said, "until I have assessed whether you have broken anything." His hand rotated both of my ankles and I gritted my teeth so as not to make a noise and look even more stupid than I felt at that very moment. I don't know where my rescuer had come from. I didn't recall seeing anyone on the ice or the river bank dressed as he was. He was by my side so quickly, I thought that he must have been watching me and as soon as he saw me fly into the air, came to my rescue.

"No, there doesn't seem to be anything broken," he said then he bent down and put his arm around my waist and gently lifted me from my ungainly sitting position. "Is anything hurting, miss?" he asked, still holding me around my waist.

I tried to make light of it and not to blush as I laughingly said, "Only my pride, sir." I tried to shake off his hands but he held me in a grip of iron, as he assisted me to the bank, trying to take most of my weight. Tanya was nearly beside herself with worry.

I could hear her muttering to herself, "Oh, Miss Thalia, oh I should never have let you go onto the ice. I feared something would happen and now it has. Oh, what will happen to us?"

The man helped me to the bench, where I sat down, thankfully. I was so embarrassed and in pain, that I couldn't look at him. I just wanted to be left alone with my pain and humiliation.

"Thank you, Mr…?" I managed to say.

"Ivanov, Nicholas Ivanov and you are…?"

"Thalia Bobrov," I replied, bending down to unlace my skates to put on my boots. I could feel pain searing through my ankle as I pulled off my right skate. I gritted my teeth and kept my face lowered so that they couldn't see the pain I was in. I never made a sound as I pulled on my boot, then bent down to undo my other skate and pull on my other boot. I stood up, trying not to wince with the pain in my right ankle and smiled at my rescuer, who towered above me.

"Thank you again, Mr Ivanov, for your kind assistance," I said politely, hoping that my voice wasn't shaking with the terrible pain that I was experiencing.

As he was all wrapped up against the winter chill, with a hat, scarf and gloves, there was little I could see of him apart from his twinkling grey eyes. His scarf was pulled over his mouth and nose. He looked over at me. His eyes were full of concern. "Could I give you a lift anywhere? I have my motor car just up on the road. It is at your disposal, Miss Bobrov."

Grateful as I was for his assistance and tempted as I was to take him up on his offer I just wished that he would just leave, so that I could sit down and recover. I noticed that my hair had come lose from my pink ribbon, which hung limply, clinging to a loose strand of my hair. My hat had been knocked lopsided on my head. I must have looked a terrible sight, before this stranger. What on earth would my grand mama think?

"Thank you, Mr Ivanov. You have already been too kind. We will be perfectly all right but thank you for your kind offer." I still could not look him straight in the eye. I just wanted him to disappear and for the ground to open and swallow me. Mentally I was giving myself a good scolding for being over confident and brash on the ice. Well Thalia Bobrov, pride certainly does go before a fall, I thought.

"Very well then, if there is nothing more I can do to help you, I will wish you a good day, Miss Bobrov." He gave me a brief bow, turned and left us on the pathway in front of the Winter Palace. Once I had watched him get into his motor car and drive away, I was able to raise my eyes fully and look at his car leaving. I pulled my scarf over my nose and mouth so that Tanya could not see how much pain I was in and linked arms with her again as we slowly walked back home. I was too proud to say it, but every step was absolute agony. The pain from my ankle seemed to go right through my body like a knife. I gritted my teeth and carried on, leaving Tanya to chatter away about the handsome Mr Ivanov (not that I had a chance to look at his face).

"Oh, Miss Thalia, oh wasn't he handsome? He had a look of the Tsar about him, don't you think?" she mused. "And he was so kind. Why didn't you accept his offer of a ride home? I could have walked."

"Can you imagine what my grandmother would say with me turning up on her doorstep, in the motor car of a complete stranger? As for his looks, I was too embarrassed to look at him and most of his face was covered by a scarf anyway. I don't know how you could see his face. I could only see his eyes," I said gritting my teeth with the pain. We had only walked as far as the Winter Palace, when Tanya stopped and looked at me, to see my eyes creased with pain. I was thankful that she couldn't see my mouth as well as I was gritting my teeth. I was sure that the pain was etched all over my face.

"Oh, Miss Thalia, you are hurt!" she cried. "Why didn't you say something?" She stopped and looked around us. "You sit here on this wall and I will run to the house to get help! I knew we should never have gone skating!"

"We didn't, Tanya. I did and I will not sit on the wall," I said firmly. "We are nearly home now. Let's carry on. It's not that bad," I lied.

She muttered something, then put her arm around my waist on the right-hand side to help take some of the weight off my ankle.

I couldn't listen to what Tanya was saying. I was in too much pain. I gave a great sigh of relief as we finally reached the bottom of the steps leading up to Grand Mama's front door, but I couldn't get up the steps without crying with pain. At some stage trying to walk up the steps, I would have to put some weight on my injured ankle and finally I realised that I had to give in. I asked Tanya to go up the steps and get Grand Mama's footman, Igor, to come and pick me up and carry me inside. I was angry at myself for giving in, for going skating and not looking where I was going, for falling over and looking a complete idiot in front of a total stranger.

Igor came and picked me up and carried me into the hallway. There seemed to be such a commotion around me that I hadn't realised Grand Mama had come out from the lounge.

"What on earth is happening here?" she asked. (One did not shout if one was a lady.)

Tanya went over to her, nearly in tears, apologising profusely for letting anything happen to me while in her company.

Finally, she explained to Grand Mama's satisfaction what had happened. Grand Mama then took charge of the situation.

"Igor, carry Mistress Thalia up to her room, then go and call for the doctor. Tanya, go and put your coat away, then go and see to your mistress's needs," she said quite sharply. I felt so sorry for Tanya. It was not her fault that I had fallen and hurt myself. The blame for it was purely placed on my own shoulders. It was excitement about being able to escape from the house and go and skate and my own stupid pride that I wouldn't ask for help, I tried to explain to Grand Mama.

Mama never came into the hall through all of this which I was surprised about, then I remembered Grand Mama's solicitor was coming that morning to discuss Mama's divorce from my father. She was probably still with him.

Grand Mama followed Igor, as he carried me carefully up the staircase, into my bedroom, then, carried me over to my bed where he gently placed me down on the mattress. I think Tanya must have run up the stairs as if the devil was at her heels to the third floor and dispose of her coat, because she was beside me as soon as Igor had left the room.

Grand Mama told Tanya that my boot would have to be taken off and to go and get some heavy scissors to cut my boot off.

Not my new boots!!! I couldn't have my new boots ruined. "No Tanya," I said firmly, "don't cut my new boots. Just pull it off. I will be all right," I told her bravely.

"But it will hurt, Mistress Thalia. Your ankle is very swollen already."

"I can manage the pain, Tanya. Just do it," I told her, then gripped the side of my bed and gritted my teeth, so that I would not cry out, as she managed to gently ease the boot from my swollen ankle. When she had removed the boot from my right foot, she then removed my left boot with no problem or pain. Finally, she removed my stockings, with hardly any discomfort.

Grand Mama turned to her asking her sternly what had happened.

Before Tanya could say anything, I butted in, telling my grandmother that it was all my own fault, as Tanya had practically begged me not to go skating on the ice and I suppose I had been showing off.

"Please, Grand Mama, don't blame Tanya, it was my fault, completely," I begged her.

I did not think she would let the matter go so easily but she nodded, telling Tanya to go and fetch a bowl of hot water from the bathroom.

"It really was my fault, Grand Mama, don't be angry with Tanya. She just followed my instructions."

"Thalia, this sort of thing must stop immediately. If you don't think of yourself, then at least think of the repercussions on your staff. When you are a young lady of the aristocracy, you must always consider your actions and how they will reflect on your staff. There is not just yourself to consider from now on," my grandmother scolded me. She might only be the same height as me, but she certainly knew how to make her displeasure known and demand respect.

I knew she was right, so I apologised profusely yet again.

"I had thought that we would go out this evening to the theatre, so that you could wear one of your new evening gowns and your new jewellery but I think that is out of the question now," Grand Mama said making me feel even more guilty.

Feeling bad enough about Tanya getting into her bad books, I told Grand Mama that she and Mama must go out this evening. "I will be perfectly all right here, Grand Mama. Please go out, I don't want to spoil things for you and Mama."

Grand Mama sniffed. "We will see what the doctor says."

The doctor, a cheery, bespectacled little man, about my mother's age, examined my foot and ankle, which had now swollen to twice their normal size, asking me to wiggle my toes and rotated my ankle the same as Mr Ivanov had done and pronounced that the ankle was not broken but badly sprained and said that it must be rested and elevated for a period, to allow the swelling to subside. In the meantime, he bandaged it up and told me to stay in bed for three days.

"You were very lucky, my dear child, that it was nothing more serious. The bone could have been broken and you would be spending not just a few days in bed but weeks. Then again, you were a very brave young lady to walk all the way back home, when it is obvious to me that you must have been in a great deal of pain. I know many a young lady would have had a fit of the vapours being in your condition. Having said that, my dear, please be more careful in future. I do not want to have to call on you again," he said, I think this was a form of reprimand, even from the good doctor. I lowered my eyes humbly and said that I would be more careful in future. "The next time that I call on you, I hope, will be when you are a married woman and about to have your first child." He smiled and winked at me then looked across at Grand Mama. "Ah youth, Countess, they know no danger. Good day, Miss Bobrov."

Grand Mama thanked him, and Tanya saw him downstairs to the front door. When Grand Mama and I were left alone, I pleaded with her, "Will you now please go out this evening with Mama, now you know it is nothing more serious than a sprain? I am sure Mama could do with a diversion from all of this."

Grand Mama grudgingly agreed to go out with Mama. Her parting remark was that she would arrange a special treat for us all when I was fully recovered. Tanya came back after seeing the doctor out. She came back with an extra pillow to elevate my swollen ankle, which the doctor had told her would reduce the swelling.

When we were on our own, I asked Tanya more about my rescuer. "How did you know what he looked like? He was wrapped up with a hat and a scarf. I could only see his eyes."

"He had been watching you since you stepped onto the ice and at first, he had undone his scarf. He must have done his scarf up again sometime before you fell," she explained as she plumped up the pillows behind my back.

For the next three days, I took all my meals, on a tray, in my room, which really was no hardship, resting in such luxurious surroundings. Grand Mama and Mama came to visit me every day. Anya, Mama's personal maid and confidant, came to visit me two or three times a day, to make sure that Tanya was looking after me well. Anya often told me that I was the child she never had.

For three days I lay upstairs in my bed and finally read my book, as I had been trying to do since we started our journey to Grand Mama's.

While I was on bed rest, Madam Brisac sent more of my completed clothes, including a new winter coat in a dark green that would go well with either of my skirts or day gowns.

Every time a new package for me came from Madam Brisac, Tanya hurriedly carried it to my room and unpacked it with as much enthusiasm as if it were hers. To the two of us, it felt like Christmas. Tanya now had all of my 'old' clothes, which she was delighted with and like me was looking for an opportunity to be able to wear them .

When my three days of internment were over, I was allowed downstairs, for my lunch and evening meals, for which Igor carried me gently down the stairs and returning me back upstairs to my room. I was still being treated like a precious china doll.

On the final evening of my recovery, Grand Mama announced that she had heard that her sister would be attending the ballet, of Tchaikovsky's Swan Lake, so she had asked Peter Abramovich to book a box for us to the same performance, in order that we could be presented to the Dowager Empress.

"Once you have been presented to my sister, invitations to other functions will come flooding in. The grapevine of the Russian aristocracy is extremely quick, efficient and accurate," Grand Mama explained.

Mama turned to me in excitement and said, "You will be able to wear one of your new gowns for that, Lia. Won't that be wonderful?"

I must admit that I was impatient to wear my beautiful gowns. What young girl of seventeen would not be?

# Chapter 6
## Swan Lake

The day of our visit to the ballet dawned. Once more the doctor was called back to check on me and give me a clean bill of health and said that I could resume my life as normal once more. Grand Mama insisted that we go to a perfumery that morning to have some perfume, specially blended for me, so that I could wear it firstly for our meeting with the Dowager Empress, that evening but also one for day wear as well.

Peter Abramovich drove us to a street not far from Faberge's premises; but our experience at the Perfumery was so very different. Upon walking into the premises, beautiful aromas, assaulted our noses as soon as the door was opened. A gentleman came up to us and bowed low over Grand Mama's and Mama's hands. "Ladies, Countess, I am highly honoured that you would visit my establishment," he said humbly. He pulled three gilded chairs over to the counter for us to sit. On top of the counter was an array of beautiful glass perfume bottles of various shapes, sizes and colours. Behind Mr Tominsky, the shop owner, were shelves stacked with larger bottles filled with various liquid fragrances. Mr Tominsky was a very tall, skinny, Jewish gentleman, dressed in a black suit and a black skull cap on his head, called a kippah, so my Grand Mama told me later on. The hair on either side of his face looked like corkscrews as they hung down to his chin. His beard was dark and full, unlike the beards worn by many men of the day, in the manor of the Tsar, which was short and carefully trimmed.

Once seated, Grand Mama explained to me that, humble as Mr Tominsky was, his perfumery was well known to the ladies of St Petersburg, as a master at his craft of blending individual perfumes for each of his clients. Grand Mama said he had a very unique way of prescribing certain perfumes, to certain ladies.

Again, Mr Tominsky bowed, humbling himself in our presence. "Countess Popov, you flatter me."

"Rubbish man, you know very well that you are sought after, throughout the city, for your skills. Now I want you to make perfumes for my grand-daughter."

Again, the tall man bobbed to us. "Of course, Countess. For the young lady. Of course."

He looked at me over his half-moon spectacles. "What unusual colouring, might I say, miss…"

"Bobrov," I answered him, "thank you for your compliment."

"May I ask, when would you be wearing this perfume, Miss Bobrov?"

"My grand-daughter requires a perfume for daytime and one for evening, Mr Tominsky," Grand Mama interrupted.

"Day and evening," he reiterated, stroking his bushy beard with his long slim fingers. He cleared his throat before asking me a series of questions. "And may I ask, what is your favourite colour, Miss Bobrov?"

I thought that it was a strange question to ask me regarding perfumes, but I told him that my favourite colour was green. He then asked me which fragrance I favoured, fruit or flowers? This question seemed more relevant to perfume.

I told him that I loved the smell of flowers.

He nodded his head, then he asked me what was my favourite flower or flowers? I told him that I loved the smells of Lilly of the valley and Freesia's, again this seemed relevant to perfume.

He repeated what I had told him and then turned to run his fingers slowly along the rows of bottles, muttering to himself, as he hesitated over each bottle, finally reaching down four bottles, then using a clean pipette for each, measured a few drops of each into one of the two perfume bottles I had chosen. He put the stopper into the bottle and shook it, then removed the stopper and sniffed. "Yes…" he said with satisfaction. "I think you will like that; a very light and young fragrance, I think you will agree?"

He passed the perfume bottle to me to smell. "Is that to your liking, Miss Bobrov? It is very fresh, young and light."

I sniffed at the bottle and could smell a delicate perfume of Lilly of the Valley and something else but the Lilly of the Valley fragrance over-rode the others coming from the un-stoppered bottle. He then passed the opened bottle to Grand Mama for her approval and then to Mama.

Both nodded their heads. "May I suggest, Miss Bobrov, that you wear this perfume during the day time?" Once we had all given him our approval, he emptied the contents into the atomiser which I had chosen from those displayed on his shop counter.

He then ran his fingers along the row of bottles again, repeating the fact that Freesia's were another of my favourite flowers.

This time he took out half a dozen bottles, un-stoppered each one, sniffed it, then added to the other of my chosen perfume bottles. This he did with all the bottles, using a clean pipette, each time, to measure each fragrance accurately. Again, he stoppered my perfume bottle, shook it, un-stoppered it again and sniffed. A smile of satisfaction spread across his face.

He handed the bottle to me to smell. I sniffed and had the fragrance of Freesia's, musk, lavender and other perfumes assaulted my senses. Overall was the scent of the Freesia's but something else as well. It smelt beautiful.

When I passed the bottle to Grand Mama and Mama again and received their nod of approval, I handed it back to Mr Tominsky.

"This perfume is oil based, so that as your body warms it, the intensity of the fragrance will increase. I thought this would be best as you had chosen a bottle with a dropper for your evening perfume and for your day perfume, it is a spray. Just a few squirts or drops behind the ears, on the" – he cleared his throat, as if slightly embarrassed – "on the décolletage; also on your wrists. Now before I forget, I must write this all down for you, Miss Bobrov, so that when you want to replenish your stock of either of the perfumes, I will be able to get exactly the same mix." He pulled a little notebook from under the counter, wrote down my name on a fresh page and the fact that I was the grand-daughter of Countess Popov and daughter of Baroness Bobrov, then he wrote down carefully each of the measures of which fragrance that contributed to my perfumes. When he had finished, he put the notebook back under the counter, found two boxes to house the two beautiful, now full, perfume bottles, then handed them to me. Grand Mama thanked him, handed him her card and told him to send the bill to her for payment.

We all returned home with my new purchases. Grand Mama suggested that I relax for the rest of the day, until it was time for me to have my bath and to prepare for the evening ahead.

Excitedly, I placed my two bottles of perfume on my dressing table. Tanya gazed at them taking in their beauty. My day perfume was in a clear crystal bottle with a peach-coloured atomiser, which matched my bedroom colour scheme. The other bottle was heavy and square, made of crystal, which reflected a rainbow of colours as you moved it. It had an unusually heavy square stopper attached to a glass rod, with which you applied the oil-based perfume. Although they were both beautiful, I thought the latter was my favourite. It was solid and I loved the play of colours of the square bottle.

By now both my dressing table and wardrobe were filling up. Madame Brisac had had two more of my evening gowns delivered as well as a cream velvet cape edged with cream fur on the openings and around the hood. I was in a state of excitement waiting to be able to wear my beautiful dresses. I had three evening dresses now, one of a pale peach velvet edge with cream lace, another was pale green silk, again with cream lace and finally a pale lilac satin with white lace, all in different styles. I was finding it hard to decide which gown to wear for my evening at the ballet and my introduction to my great aunt, the Dowager Empress of Russia.

I rested in the afternoon. Tanya had closed my bedroom curtains and I lay on top of my bed. I dozed, not fully asleep but not fully awake. At four o'clock Tanya came in with my tray of a light meal and tea. Once I had eaten my fill, she ran my bath, added some fragrant oils and then, let me lay in if for some time, allowing the lovely smelling bath water, to enter every pore of my body. She came in later with a jug full of fresh water to wash my hair. Eventually I stepped out of my bath and into a big peach fluffy towel, which she held out for me. I dried myself off and put on clean underclothes, soft as down and light as a feather, then my peach dressing gown and sat in front of the fire while Tanya dried my hair.

We had decided that I should wear my pale green silk evening gown with cream lace on the neck, sleeves and short train. This was laid out on my bed, just waiting for me to step into it. Once Tanya had finished drying my hair, she helped me step into the gown and then buttoned all the tiny pearl buttons up the back. Dressed in my gown, Tanya arranged my hair in a single loose plait entwined with green silk ribbon. I had two corkscrew curls, frame either side of my face, then the rest of my hair pulled back and tied low on my neck, with another matching pale green silk bow, then pulled the long plait over my right shoulder.

I picked up my heavy glass, evening perfume bottle and touched the glass stick with the oil-based perfume to all of the areas that Mr Tominsky had instructed. Tanya placed my, three-row, pearl choker around my neck, then the accompanying earrings.

I couldn't believe the vision that looked back at me from my dressing table mirror. I was unrecognisable from the young girl that had stepped from the train in St Petersburg just two weeks ago. I stepped into my cream kid leather evening shoes, pulled on the long cream silk evening gloves, fastening the matching bracelet to the pearl choker, over the gloves. Finally, I stood in front of the full-length mirror on my wardrobe door, hardly able to believe my eyes. The little girl who thought that she was never beautiful had been transformed, from a caterpillar to a butterfly. Tanya handed me my cream velvet cloak and cream lace fan, then opened my bedroom door for me to go down stairs. For the first time in my life, I did not have to think about my posture, shoulders back, head up. It came naturally once I had put on the gown. Tanya whispered to me at the top of the stairs, "You look beautiful, Miss Thalia," she said.

I couldn't help myself, I turned and kissed her cheek. "All thanks to you, Tanya," I whispered back.

Mama and Grand Mama came in to the hall, from the lounge, both dressed in their evening finery, to stand at the bottom of the stairs, looking up at me as I descended.

Mama hugged me once I reached the bottom of the stairs "Oh, my darling, Lia, you look so beautiful."

"You do indeed, darling," Grand Mama said behind her.

Igor helped Grand Mama and Mama into their long evening cloaks, while Tanya draped my cloak around my shoulders. We were finally ready to go and be presented to the Dowager Empress of Russia.

Peter Abramovich drove us to the ballet and helped each of us from the motor car. He took Grand Mama's arm and escorted her into the theatre, to the box that had been reserved for us. I looked all around me at the golden opulence of the theatre. The foyer was lit by a massive crystal chandelier, larger, even than the one in Grand Mama's hallway. It hung from the roof three stories above us and with the smaller crystal lamps on the walls all around, helped illuminate the rest of the theatre foyer. As soon as we stepped over the threshold of the theatre, our feet sunk into a luxurious, deep piled carpet of a majestic deep blue. Peter helped us remove our cloaks, then bowed and left us, closing the door to our box, quietly behind him. While we were waiting for the curtain to rise on the ballet of Swan Lake, the noise in the auditorium was deafening. Everywhere I looked, in the boxes, in the stalls and up on the balconies, everyone was chattering away excitedly, dressed in their finery. I had never been to a ballet before and sat forward in my seat to drink in the whole scene before me.

I looked from our box, down at the people in the stalls. The men were all dressed in evening suits with white bow ties or uniform of the Russian army, whereas the women wore beautiful evening gowns of various colours, like many exotic butterflies. The house lights in the auditorium touched their gems, giving them life as they twinkled a myriad of colours on the women. The fragrance of hundreds of different perfumes around me drifted up from the women in the stalls.

Down in the orchestra pit, in front of the stage, we heard the roll of a drum and the sound of a single trumpet signalling the start of the Russian anthem and the entrance of the Dowager Empress, who was representing the Royal family that evening. The whole of the auditorium rose as one, at the sound of the national anthem and there was silence until, the anthem ended and the audience clapped for her. The Dowager Empress waved her hand, regally, to the audience, then sat down. Just hearing the national anthem, made me shiver with excitement. I was actually in the presence of the Dowager Empress of Russia. A footman bowed over her as he made sure that the important guest was comfortably seated in the Royal Box, hung with garlands of flowers. This was opposite our box.

As soon as she was seated, the rest of the audience sat down. The house lights dimmed and the curtain rose on a woodland scene. The music was wonderful; lifting you up and transporting you to that woodland scene. The dancers seemed to float across the stage, as if on wings but above the sound of the music was a thump, thump, thump, like a loud heartbeat. I leaned across and asked Mama what the noise was, only to be told that it was the 'pointes', on which the ballerinas danced. I could hardly believe that these beautiful, dainty, elegant dancers that practically floated across the stage could make such a noise. I tried very hard to ignore the thump, thump and listen to the beautiful music, composed by Tchaikovsky, which rose and made you want to join in with the dancers on stage; but it was difficult to ignore the background thumping of their 'pointes'. I tried to concentrate on the story unfolding below me on the stage.

At the interval, Grand Mama handed one of the ushers her calling card to give to the Dowager Empress. Shortly after the usher departed our box, he returned to say that the Dowager Empress would receive us in the Royal box.

This was one of the moments I had been waiting for. My heart was thumping wildly in my chest and I was shaking with nerves.

Grand Mama left our box first, followed by Mama and finally myself.

I expected the Dowager Empress to be an older version of Grand Mama. I also expected that when the two sisters met, they would immediately embrace. I was wrong. We entered the Royal box and the Dowager Empress rose from her chair. She looked nothing like Grand Mama. She was taller and of a slightly heavier build. Dowager Empress Maria was covered in jewels, around her throat, in her ears, in her hair, on her dress and on her fingers. As she rose, Grand Mama immediately curtsied, followed by Mama and myself. It was only as we rose, that she embraced Grand Mama.

"Oh my dear Ludmilla, it is so good to see you," she said, "I keep thinking that we should spend more time with each other, then something happens and all thoughts of our meeting are pushed from my mind. Please accept my apology."

"Your Majesty, I understand that being in your position, your time is very precious. May I introduce my daughter, Marguerite Babushka Baroness Bobrov and my grand-daughter, Thalia Marguerite Titania Bobrov."

Again, Mama and I curtsied to Mama's aunt and my great aunt, the Dowager Empress of all Russia.

"I am sure that I have heard the name of Thalia Bobrov before," came a deep male voice behind us. I thought that I recognised the voice but couldn't think where I had heard it before. I had not really met anyone from St Petersburg, in my short time here, especially a man. He stepped forward from the shadows and stood between Mama and me, to hand the Dowager Empress a glass of champagne, then he turned and looked directly at me with twinkling grey eyes, framed with dark lashes. This time his face wasn't covered by a scarf or a hat covering his head.

In front of me stood my rescuer from the frozen river. It was true what Tanya had said about him, he did look like a younger version of the Tsar, whom, as yet, I had only seen in pictures but the man before me looked very muscular, with broad shoulders and a narrow waist with a devilish twinkle in his eyes and a cheeky grin on his face. My heart began to beat even faster in my breast and my mouth suddenly went dry.

"Nicky, don't tease," the Dowager Empress gently scolded him. "You are embarrassing Thalia. Ludmilla I am not sure that you have met our nephew, Prince Nicholas Frederick Dimitri Ivanov; our dear, late sister's only child. Nicky, this is your Aunt Lilia, cousin Marguerite and your second cousin Thalia."

He kissed the hands of Grand Mama and Mama, then as he raised my hand to his lips he stared straight into my eyes. My stomach flipped. "It is so nice to finally meet you, cousin. I trust your pride has recovered from your fall?" he teased, still holding my hand near his lips.

Why did my breath catch in my throat and my heartbeat increase while this man was holding my hand? I was unable to speak.

"How do you know Thalia, Nicky? You never mentioned it to me?" asked his aunt, the Dowager Empress.

"I came to Miss Bobrov's rescue when she fell over on the ice a few weeks ago." Still he was holding my hand. "I trust you suffered no ill effects from your fall?"

"Thalia had badly sprained her ankle, your Highness," Mama explained.

"Then how did you manage to get home with a sprained ankle?" he asked, looking deep into my eyes. My stomach did another summersault.

"She walked," Mama said.

Did I sense a touch of reproach in her voice as she replied?

"The Prince did offer to drive me home, but I refused," I told her, before she began blaming the Prince.

"Why on earth didn't you accept the lift, child?" Grand Mama asked me.

"Because he was a total stranger to me, Grand Mama. What would you have thought if I arrived at your door in the car of a stranger?" I replied.

The Dowager Empress broke in, "Nicky, darling, where are your manners? A glass of champagne each for the ladies, if you please."

The Prince bowed low to his aunt. "As your Highness commands."

Already Grand Mama, Mama and the Dowager Empress were talking, leaving me to look about me.

The Royal Box was similarly laid out to ours but the chairs were gilded in gold leaf and looked a lot more comfortable with thicker padding than those in our box, (not that our chairs were uncomfortable). There were vases and garlands of fresh hothouse flowers all around the Royal Box.

Behind the two chairs at the front of the box, another three were placed. In the corner was a small gilded table, on which stood a silver tray, carrying a silver ice bucket, with a bottle of champagne in and also a further three glasses. They must have been brought in by usher, just in case they were required.

The Prince went over to Grand Mama and Mama to hand them their glasses of champagne, leaving mine till last.

He handed me my glass of champagne, allowing our fingers to touch just a fraction longer than necessary, then he sat down beside me to talk.

"Is this your first visit to the ballet, Miss Bobrov?"

I took a sip of my champagne before replying, "Yes, Your Highness."

"And what do you think of it?"

"I love the music," I told him.

"Tchaikovsky," he told me.

"I know," I replied.

"And the dancing. What do you think of the dancing?"

"Beautiful… So elegant and evocative…" I said enthusiastically and then hesitated.

"I sense a 'but' coming. Am I right?" he said, enticing me to elaborate on my statement.

I nodded.

"Let me guess; the thumping of their pointes?" he asked with a cheeky grin. His eyes twinkled in merriment.

"They all look so graceful and elegant as they dance across the stage…"

"But the thumping spoils the illusion?" he interrupted.

"Yes, I am afraid it does. I hoped that the wonderful music would drown it out but…"

"You can still hear the thump, thump, thumping?" he said, smiling at me. "I totally agree. It does spoil the beauty of the dance. They look like dainty fairies flitting across the stage but sound like a herd of calf elephants. You do enjoy the music, though?" he prompted me.

"Oh yes, Your Highness, very much so. The music is wonderful. It conjures up all sorts of wonderful images and transports you to wonderful places in your imagination." I blushed then, realising that I had said 'wonderful' three times in one sentence.

"I agree," he said and then changed the subject to me. "Your name is rather unusual. I don't ever recall having heard it before, apart from when you fell over that day."

"Mama had been reading about the Greek Gods and demi-Gods when she was expecting me," I explained, "I believe that Thalia was the daughter of Zeus and a human woman. She liked the name so much that when I was born, she could think of no other name at the time."

The Dowager Empress, Grand Mama and Mama by this time were engrossed in their own conversation, leaving the Prince and myself to continue ours, now that we had been formally introduced.

"It is a very unusual name, Thalia but it suits you. With your colouring who could but think that you were not born of the Gods." I could feel myself blushing to the roots of my hair, now that he was talking of more personal things other than the ballet. To spare me further blushes he changed the subject. "If you enjoy the music of Tchaikovsky, there is a concert the day after tomorrow, if you would like to go with me?"

The opportunity to be able to spend more time with the handsome Prince was very enticing. He was very good looking; a younger, more muscular, version of the Tsar. There definitely was a similarity. I presumed that it must be a family trait but there was something different in the Prince. He was funny. I thought that any photographs I had seen of the Tsar, he always looked so stern, whereas the Prince had a devilish gleam in his eyes. He looked as if he did not take anything in life too seriously. Knowing that the Prince was cousin to the Tsar, I realised what elevated circles of acquaintances I would be moving in. This would be the very pinnacle of Russian aristocracy.

Prince Nicholas took my silence as refusal but pushed the appointment. "Of course, I will ask your mother and grand-mother's permission for you to join me."

I knew that if I had permission from my elders, I would, gladly, agree to go with him. On this, only our second meeting, his presence and his scrutiny of every aspect of me, had me blushing and my mouth dried out so that I could hardly speak without my tongue sticking to the roof of my mouth. Before speaking I had to take a sip of champagne to loosen my tongue.

"Your Highness," he said addressing the Dowager Empress, "may I ask permission of Miss Bobrov's mother and grandmother to give their consent for her to join me for the Tchaikovsky concert the day after tomorrow? After all, we are cousins?"

"Nicky, you are second cousins," the Dowager Empress pointed out.

"Very well, Aunt, second cousins. May I have your permission, Aunt Lilia; cousin Marguerite?" he asked, easily breaking protocol of calling Mama and Grand Mama by their Christian names without being told to. His eyes twinkled with devilment. I thought that he would be able to get away with anything, with the opposite sex. He really was very handsome and oozed charm.

Both nodded their agreement and the Prince gave me a gleaming smile that set my heart fluttering again. "Then it is settled. I will come and collect you about seven o'clock, the day after tomorrow, Miss Bobrov. Maybe we could go for a meal at Minsky's before the concert?"

I was about to agree, when Grand Mama interrupted, "Your Highness, Thalia has not been presented to the Tsar yet. She has not come out. I think the concert will be sufficient for now."

The Prince nodded, "Very well, just the concert. Would you or the Baroness like to chaperone Miss Bobrov, Aunt Lilia, Cousin Marguerite?" he asked cheekily.

"I don't think that will be necessary, Your Highness, as you are related," Grand Mama replied.

The bell to signal the beginning of the second half of the ballet was sounded.

Grand Mama stood and said that we should return to our box. We all curtsied to their Royal Highnesses. The Prince quickly took my hand again and pressed it to his lips. His lips felt so warm and soft and he let his moustache and beard tickle the back of my hand. I felt myself blushing again.

He looked up into my eyes, his own eyes twinkling with mischief, "Until the day after tomorrow, second cousin Thalia."

I snatched my hand away, scared by the feelings his touch invoked in me.

"Thank you," I whispered.

We returned to our box and sat down to await the start of the second half of the ballet. As soon as the orchestra started up, the curtain rose again. The dancers came back on stage and began dancing remembering the Prince's remarks about the thumping of the ballet dancers' pointes, I struggled not to giggle, covering the bottom half of my face with my fan, until I felt the episode had passed.

I briefly took a look over to the royal box, with my theatre glasses to see the Prince from a distance and found that he was looking across, directly at me with his theatre glasses. I felt myself blush with embarrassment and my heartbeat quicken when I knew that he was looking at me as well. Quickly, I turned my gaze away from him, to the stage, hoping that he didn't catch me watching him.

I was longing to get home to tell Tanya that I had met my rescuer again and he was a Prince and a cousin to the Tsar.

The evening ended with the dancers bowing to the theatre and then the royal box, after which the two, leading ballerina's and the male lead, receiving massive bouquets of flowers and once again bowed to the audience. Finally, the curtain came down. Overall, I had, greatly enjoyed my first visit to the ballet, even more than I had expected.

As if by magic, Peter Abramovich entered our box and helped Grand Mama on with her cloak, while Mama and I put our own around our shoulders. From the snowflakes on Peter's coat, I could tell that it was snowing again outside, so I put up my hood before leaving the theatre and pushed my gloved hands into my cream fur muff.

Just outside the theatre, the Prince strode up to us and handed me his calling card. I slipped it into my muff without looking at it, knowing that I would examine every inch of it, once alone in my bedroom. He also handed Grand Mama another card, which, I found out later, came from the Dowager Empress, inviting us all to tea with her, the following afternoon at three o'clock. Prince Nicholas, once he had delivered the cards, smiled specifically at me then disappeared into the crowds as they exited from the theatre.

Peter drove us back home through the heavy snow. How he could navigate in such dreadful conditions, when you could hardly see more than a few yards in front of you, I didn't know. Thankfully it was not too far to Grand Mama's home, just across the city but because of the snow, our homeward journey was so much slower, than our outward journey to the theatre.

Both Grand Mama and Mama asked me if I had enjoyed the ballet and I could honestly say that I did. The ballet dancers were beautiful as they moved across the stage and of course the music was wonderful, besides that, I had met the Prince and enjoyed what little time we had spent together. Already I was looking forward to going to the Tchaikovsky concert with the Prince.

I was relieved when the motor car pulled up outside the front steps leading up to the front door, as once or twice I felt the back wheels of the car begin to slide on the road. Someone had swept the snow away from the steps, at some time during our absence but the snow was beginning to lay on the steps again. As soon as Igor heard the motor car pull up outside, he opened the front door, letting the light from massive chandelier in the hall illuminate our way. We only had a couple of feet to walk to the bottom of the steps and already they were covered in snow again.

Once inside Ava, Grand Mama's personal maid helped Grand Mama off with her cloak. Anya helped Mama and Tanya helped me.

Grand Mama led us into the lounge, where the fire was roaring away in the hearth, giving us a warm welcome home.

Peter, once he had shed his outer clothes, followed us into the lounge and went over to the drinks table to open the bottle of champagne that had been chilling in the ice bucket, waiting for our return. In the large hallway, I heard the grandfather clock strike midnight. I had never stayed up so late. Ten o'clock was our usual bedtime in the country, sometimes earlier if it was very cold and we would seek the warmth of our beds and snuggle under the bedclothes.

Peter handed us all a glass of champagne then left the room. Grand Mama sat in her usual chair by the fire, satisfied that our first meeting with the Russian royalty had been such a success. "You, my darling Lia, certainly made an impression on my sister and the Prince. Well done, my darling." She congratulated me. "You looked particularly beautiful the way Tanya had done your hair. Very fetching."

I thanked her as I stifled a yawn. "And now my dear," Mama said caressing my cheek, "I think it is time for bed for you."

I finished my drink, bid them both 'Good night' and left.

Tanya was waiting for me in my bedroom, to help prepare me for bed. I was bursting with excitement to tell her all about the evening, especially the Prince.

"You would never believe who my rescuer from the other day on the river was Tanya?" I said as she began unbuttoning my gown. "None other than the cousin of the Tsar," I told her.

"I said that he had a look of the Tsar, about him, Miss Thalia."

"I don't know how you could tell that he looked like the Tsar when all but his eyes were covered. It is obviously a family resemblance," I commented as I sat down in front of my dressing mirror, so that Tanya could brush my hair before I went to bed. Tanya's eyes met mine in the dressing table mirror, "I did tell you, Miss Thalia, he hadn't got his face covered when he was watching you skating on the ice. He put the scarf around his face when he was running to help you."

My heart began beating faster knowing that he was already watching me on that fateful day.

I told Tanya more about my meeting with the Dowager Empress and her nephew, Prince Nicholas Ivanov. I told her that, the Prince had invited me to go to a concert of music by Tchaikovsky the evening after tomorrow and we had all been invited to tea with the Dowager Empress, the next afternoon. I also said that Grand Mama had complimented me on how Tanya had done my hair and described it as "Very fetching."

I never mentioned about the Prince giving me his card. I would look at that once I was alone. When Tanya had finished putting my jewellery away in my top drawer and hung my clothes away, she finally left me alone in my bed.

As soon as she shut the door behind her, I got out of bed and went over to my wardrobe where she had stored my muff and took it back to bed with me. I opened the small pocket inside the muff and pulled out his card, then returned my muff back to where it belonged in my wardrobe. I went back to my bed and looked at his card. It was edged in gold leaf, with the family coat of arms above his name; Prince Nicholas Frederick Dimitri Ivanov. Still with his card in my hand, I lay back among my pillows, closing my eyes and trying to bring a picture of him to my mind.

He was very handsome with dark brown hair, a moustache and beard, carefully clipped, in the same style as worn by the Tsar. His hands, as he held mine, were so soft, strong and warm. My stomach did another summersault when I recalled his kiss on my hand. Then told myself not to be so stupid. I opened my eyes again and turned his card over to see that he had written on the back, "I am glad that we have met again." It read. He signed it with a flourish of his signature. Dare I hope that he might really be interested in me or was he just being kind to his second cousin from the country? For a brief moment, I allowed myself to believe that he was interested and fell asleep with his calling card clutched in my hand and his handsome face in my mind.

# Chapter 7
## Afternoon Tea

The next morning, I was allowed to sleep late after the previous evening. Tanya didn't knock on my bedroom door, until ten o'clock, with my breakfast tray, by which time I had had my sleep out and stretched as she opened my bedroom curtains. A pale, wintry light entered my bedroom, telling me that we would probably get more snow before the day was out. I slipped, the Prince's calling card under my pillow, then began my breakfast.

Tanya took one of my skirts from the wardrobe, with one of my blouses. "I can't wear those today Tanya. We are taking tea with the Dowager Empress this afternoon," I explained.

"Miss Thalia, you can come back and change into one of your tea gowns before you leave. There is no problem with that."

Another mistake on my behalf. Once I had put on one lot of clothes in Smolensk, I wore them for the rest of the day. Now I was being told that I could change them to suit the occasion as often as needed. I had noticed that Grand Mama changed her clothes even for dining with just Mam and myself. I could understand changing to an evening gown when I went out in the evening but during the day seemed to be a bit too much to my poor country mind. Practically, I thought of all the washing that would need to be done with all these changes of clothes, then shrugged and resigned myself to the fact that in St Petersburg one changed as often as one needed during the day and that I need not concern myself with the chores of the staff.

I went down stairs after breakfast and went to the library, next to the lounge, to search for another book to read. I had never been in this room before, although I knew that it existed, from the stories my mother had told me about her childhood here. She told me that she had often come into the library as a child and sat on her father's lap, so that he could read to her. As with all of the rooms in the house in the winter, a fire was roaring in the hearth. By the fireside was a large, green leather, winged chair. I chose a book from the shelves, which covered floor to ceiling, around three of the walls of the library and sat down in the chair to begin reading. I was so engrossed in the story, that I forgot the time. Before I knew it, the gong had sounded for lunch in the small dining room.

When I sat down at the table with Mama and Grand Mama, they asked what I had been doing during the morning. When I told them that I had spent the morning in the library, Mama smiled and told me again how she had spent many happy hours in there.

"I remember you telling me, Mama, about climbing on Grandfather's lap for him to read you a story when you were little."

Grand Mama laughed at the memories, "If your mama ever went missing, I always knew where to find her: in the library, curled up on her father's lap, listening to him reading her a story or as she grew older, just curling up in her father's chair and reading to herself. She was a real book worm."

Mama reached across and took my hand, "I think that Lia has taken after me for my love of books."

The conversation moved from Mama's youth and our love of books, to the ballet from the night before. Grand Mama complimented me on my behaviour, when I was presented to the Dowager Empress. "You made a very good impression on my sister. She told me that she is looking forward to your debut on Christmas Eve. It is only three weeks away now, Thalia, which reminds me, I must employ a dance and deportment tutor, for you, also you must start practicing on how to manoeuvre your train."

Mama pointed out that I had practiced dancing with Gregor, my tutor in Smolensk, with Mama supervising. "Very well then, Thalia, I will trust that your Mama and Gregor suitably instructed you in dancing but for your presentation to the Royal Family, you must be trained in court etiquette. I don't want my grand-daughter making any mistakes when she is presented to the Tsar and the rest of the royal family."

Whatever Grand Mama said was done without question.

Before I started on my lessons, we still had the meeting to take tea with the Dowager Empress. I hoped that the Prince might be with his aunt again, so took particular care with my dress.

Peter Abramovich drove us to the Dowager Empress's private apartments within the Winter Palace. I thought that Grand Mama's home was lavishly decorated but the Dowager Empress's private quarters were even more so. All around, there was gold leaf on walls, chairs, tables, sofa's, pictures and mirrors. On entering the private apartments, my eye was immediately drawn to the large painting of the late Tsar, a tall, good looking, muscular man, dressed in all of his royal finery. A footman led the way to where the Dowager Empress was waiting for us. Once again, despite the family connection, royal protocol was observed as we all curtsied to our hostess. The tray of tea had arrived, with a variety of tiny sandwiches and cakes placed on silver stands. The maid carefully placed them on the occasional table, curtseyed and departed, leaving us all alone. When we were alone in the privacy of the Dowager Empress's apartments the atmosphere relaxed. Grand Mama and the Dowager Empress talked of their childhood together in Denmark. I was fascinated by the story of their youth. The Dowager Empress told us that she was originally called Maria Sophie Frederike Dagmar as a Princess in Denmark. She explained that she had been engaged once before she had been engaged to the Tsar but her fiancé had died a year after their meeting and before they could marry. It was when she married the late Tsar, that, she had to change her name to Marie Feodorovna. Not only did she have to change her name but also her religion, from Lutheran, which she had been born into, to adopt Orthodoxy which was the religion of the Russian royal household.

She laughed with Grand Mama over incidents they recalled from their youth. They talked of their other sister, Prince Nicholas's mother, Olga, who, with Nicky's father Frederick, had both died when Nicholas was fourteen. They had been shot in Novgorod.

After his parents' murder, Nicholas then went to live with his aunt and uncle, who, at the time, were the Tsar and Tsarina. Nicholas spent a lot of time with the young Tsarevich (now the Tsar) who was older than him. They spent a lot of their time together shooting, hunting and riding. I heard more about Nicky as she called him and his life after his parents' death.

Of course, on his father's death, the Prince inherited his father's title and estates but could not claim them until the age of twenty-one, which had been five years ago. "I know that he has a devilish streak in him, but he has taken his responsibilities of running all of his estates, very seriously. He works hard when he is with his staff. He is well liked and respected, by the people who work for him. He is a good and fair employer. I am proud of him, for how he has behaved. These days, apart from his own responsibilities, he also helps me out quite often with various things, like being my escort, as he did yesterday evening."

It was interesting hearing more about the Prince, who worked out was going on nine years older than me, but I was more than just a little disappointed that he wasn't with us that afternoon. If he had been, though, I doubt the Dowager Empress would have talked so openly about him.

What prestigious circles I was moving in now. I still had trouble believing that I was taking tea with the Dowager Empress of Russia, in the Winter Palace of the Tsar and the royal family.

When the ornate clock on the mantelpiece chimed five o'clock, Grand Mama rose saying that we would not intrude upon the Dowager Empress's time, any longer and, that we should leave. The Dowager Empress said how much she had enjoyed the afternoon and hoped that it wouldn't be the last.

"We must do this again, Ludmilla, I have enjoyed myself immensely, talking about our youth and without any of the court protocol. It has been fun."

Protocol did return and Grand Mama, Mama and I all curtsied again to the Dowager Empress. We were handed our coats, after we had left the royal presence and helped into them. Grand Mama led the way back out to where, it seemed that, Peter Abramovich had been waiting with the car for the last two hours.

Later, when I mentioned this to my mother, she assured me that he would not have been waiting out in that cold weather but would have gone home, to return again, just before five o'clock. She hugged me and told me that she was very pleased at how I had conducted myself again in the presence of the Dowager Empress. I wondered if she had ever doubted that I would fit into Russian society. I know that I had done so but I did wonder.

I went to my room, feeling very pleased with myself. The first thing Tanya asked me was, "Was he there? The Prince. Was he there Miss Thalia?"

I shook my head sadly. "But I will be seeing him again tomorrow evening."

"And he did say that he was glad that he had met you again," she said then blushed and apologised, as she handed me his calling card. "I am sorry, Miss Thalia, but I found this under your pillow as I made your bed. I didn't mean to read it. I am very sorry."

I told her that there was no need to apologise and asked her to put it in the drawer with my jewellery.

When I went to bed that evening, I was already planning on what to wear for the concert with the Prince, as Madam Brisac had had more of my new wardrobe delivered.

I fell asleep in my soft, warm bed, with a satisfied smile on my lips.

# Chapter 8

## The Unexpected Visitor

I spent most of the next day in my room preparing for my evening with the Prince. I wanted everything to be perfect and I wanted my appearance to please the Prince. I asked Tanya to run me a bath and soaked in its fragrant waters until the water began to cool. Tanya washed my hair again and I sat in front of the fire while she dried and brushed it. This time I had chosen a pale lilac evening gown which seemed to highlight the colour of my hair, bringing out more of the silver highlights than normal. I asked her to do my hair the same as she had when I went to the ballet, but asked her if she had a pale lilac ribbon to thread through my hair. Tanya grinned and produced some pale lilac silk flowers that she placed within the plait. Even Tanya complimented me on my appearance, telling me that the Prince would find me irresistible.

"Tanya, he is my cousin, I don't think there can be anything between us. He is probably just being considerate towards me knowing that I have spent all of my life in the country." I pointed out to her.

Half an hour before the Prince was due to pick me up, the front doorbell rang. I picked up my cape and gloves and hurried down to the lounge to await the Prince being shown in. Already Mama and Grand Mama were there in the two armchairs either side of the fireplace.

"You look particularly lovely this evening, Lia. Is that your Prince at the door?"

"If it is, Mama, then he is early," I said, sitting down in one of the other chairs.

Igor knocked on the lounge door and entered to announce Baron Bobrov.

Mama went deathly white. I just wanted to get out of the room but before anyone could move, my father had barged his way in, past Igor and stood in the lounge huffing and puffing, his face all red.

75

Grand Mama was the first to speak, taking total control of the situation, "What is the meaning of this intrusion? How dare you enter my presence without my permission?"

Without saying a word to his mother-in-law or me, he pulled some papers from inside his coat and began waving them, menacingly in front of Mama.

"And what is the meaning of this, madam? You sneak away without telling me. You are here only two weeks and I get a letter saying that you are divorcing me!"

He was towering menacingly over Mama. I thought that he was going to hit her.

Everything happened so fast after that that I don't really remember what happened next, only the consequences. The next thing I knew, I was lying on the floor, Peter Abramovich and Igor were both holding my father by his arms and Mama and Grand Mama were standing over me, crying and fussing over me as I lay on the floor dazed.

Mama then turned on him and although it was not lady-like to shout, she shouted at him, "Why would I want to remain married to a brute like you? Lia is the only good thing to come out of this marriage. Go back to your..." I don't know what Mama was going to say but Grand Mama stopped her.

Grand Mama's voice dropped to a threatening tone as she spoke, "Get out of my house and don't ever, ever come back again. My daughter will divorce you and I will be there to support both Babushka and Thalia. Peter, Igor, take him out," she told them, then spoke to my father again, "and if you ever come anywhere near either of my two girls again, I will have you imprisoned." Grandmother didn't shout but lowered her voice to a menacing whisper, which seemed to have more of an effect on my father than anything else.

I saw my father struggling in the grip of the two men as they man handled him from the room and from the house.

I tried to get up from the floor but my head was spinning. Apparently, according to Mama, I had stepped between her and my father and he had lashed out, knocking me to the floor.

Mama and Grand Mama helped me get up and onto one of the chairs by the fire. My head and face were throbbing and my face and right eye were on fire.

Peter Abramovich came back into the room after disposing of my father and shutting the heavy front door on him. Grand Mama told him to get the doctor.

Grand Mama gave me a glass of something very strong and told me to drink it but I was shaking too much to hold the glass, so she held the glass gently to my lips and made me drink. I could feel the liquid setting fire to my throat and burning as it went down into my stomach. I grimaced but Grand Mama insisted that I drink it all.

I did as I was told.

There was a knock on the front door. Igor went to answer it and came back saying that Prince Nicholas Ivanov had come to collect me.

With my father showing up unexpectedly and lashing out at me, I had forgotten about the Prince. I looked pleadingly at Mama, not to let him see me in such a state. She told Igor to tell the Prince that I was indisposed and, unfortunately, would not be able to keep our appointment. Igor nodded and went back out to the Prince.

"I think you may have a black eye, my darling," Grand Mama said, taking the empty glass from me and putting it on the table.

"I think maybe he has been dying to do that to me since the day I was born, Grand Mama," I said. I struggled to speak through swollen lips. I let my tongue move around my mouth, checking that he had not loosened any of my teeth. I was pleased to find out he hadn't but when he hit me, he must have split my lip and I must have bit my tongue, as I felt a trickle of blood from my lips and there was a metallic taste in my mouth.

Igor returned to the room with a note in his hand from the Prince. He handed it to me and from the look of shock on his face, I must have looked to be in a terrible state. More than anything, I wanted to see what the Prince had written but I wanted to read it in private, so slipped it into my bag and waited for the doctor to arrive.

I think that I had seen more of Dr Smirnov in the short time that I had been in St Petersburg than I ever had of Doctor Urvanski in Smolensk but then I had always, if possible, stayed out of the way of my father.

Once more I was carried up to my room, by Igor, where Tanya helped me out of my evening gown and into my night clothes, all the time crying, "Oh, Miss Thalia, Miss Thalia. Oh dear!"

I was thankful that no blood had got onto my new evening gown. I asked Tanya, through swollen lips, to check it.

The same doctor arrived, who had originally diagnosed my sprained ankle.

"Well, Miss Bobrov, we meet again," he said cheerfully. I was pleased that he never asked the circumstance leading up to my beating. After examining me, he was pleased to report that nothing was broken, just bruising and swelling and prescribed witch hazel and cold compresses to bring out the bruising, also more bed-rest for the shock.

My bedroom cleared of every one once the doctor had left. It was just Tanya and myself and I asked her if she would bring me my evening bag.

"Don't you go looking in the mirror, Miss Thalia, otherwise you will have another shock," she warned me.

I tried hard to smile but felt that my smile was lopsided. I promised her that I wouldn't look for now. I was more interested in reading the Prince's note.

Reading with only one eye open was extremely difficult; near impossible.

While my eye was swollen, I misjudged distances and knocked over the glass on my bedside table. Tanya was very kind and very patient and, in the end, I gave up trying to read the Prince's note and asked her to read it to me.

It read, *"My dear Miss Bobrov, I am so very sorry to hear of your indisposition. After your exuberance at the ballet, I am sure that you are as disappointed as I am that you could not attend the concert this evening. Be assured that eventually we will get to go to a Tchaikovsky concert together. In the meantime, please hurry up and get well.*
*Kind regards*
*Nicholas Ivanov."*

It gladdened my heart to hear his words and I began to feel that maybe my father had, eventually, done something to help me, painful though the consequences were.

Because I struggled to read, every day either Tanya, Anya, Mama or Grand Mama came and read to me. After five days, I was allowed to get up for a while. The first thing I did was to go over to my dressing table and look at my reflection. I had to sit down on my dressing stool, knowing that it had looked worse. Now the bruising wasn't quite as dark but it was still a terrible shock. My eye was still a little swollen as was my lip but I didn't think my injuries would leave me with any physical scarring. Mental scarring? No. Over the years I had resigned myself to the fact that my father would never change towards me, so I toughened my resolve against anything my father could do to hurt me. I treated him with the contempt he deserved. As I meant nothing to him, so he meant nothing to me.

The swelling on my eyelid, over time, receded slightly so that I was able to read a little better but I still would not dare be seen in public, especially by the Prince. All invitations, we had received since going to the ballet, had been cancelled, making me feel bad, that Mama and Grand Mama had cancelled because of me. Mama said that she didn't want to go out without me as this was all for my benefit; so three unattached ladies remained house bound. The time that I spent convalescing was not completely wasted, it gave me time to practice 'manoeuvring' a court length train and practising being presented to the Tsar. For this particularly special exercise, my grandmother became my tutor.

# Chapter 9
## My Debut

I received several notes, over the following days, from the Prince always asking after my health. Once the swelling had gone from my eye, I was able to read and write to him by return, to reassure him that I was on the road to recovery and, hopefully, would be able to attend the ball on Christmas Eve.

My isolation from St Petersburg was not all bad. I practised dancing with Mama in the lounge under Grand Mama's supervision. I practised my manoeuvring a long train with a table cloth tied around my waist. I must admit that I was a little disappointed that the Prince hadn't offered to take me out again, but my days became busy with preparation for my debut.

Tanya and I were trying different hairstyles for the big day, spending hours in front of my dressing table mirror. I kept looking in the wardrobe at my beautiful gown, wishing that the time would fly by so that it might become the day of the ball.

Soon enough the big day did arrive. I had rested most of the day, sitting by the fire in my room and reading. In the afternoon, I had a long soak in a hot scented bath and had my hair washed. While Tanya was drying my hair in front of the fire, Grand Mama knocked on my door and came in carrying a dark blue, leather box, about the size of a large book.

"Lia darling, I have brought you this to wear for this evening. I wore it at my debut and your mama wore it at hers, so now it is yours." She lifted the lid and nestled in the matching velvet interior were a diamond tiara, a matching three-row diamond choker, bracelet and earrings. I gazed in awe at them, unable to speak. Never had I seen such beautiful jewellery. As the nights had drawn in and we had to put the lights on early, when the lights hit the jewels in the box they twinkled and sparkled at the slightest movement.

"Now, darling, I will leave you. I have arranged for a photographer to come and take some photographs of you on your big day. He will be here at half past six. Now I will go and leave you to rest before getting dressed in your ball gown."

With my hair dried and Tanya brushing it until it shone like silver, she then began on the creation of my hair style, chattering all the time, making me promise to tell her when I returned home, all the details of my evening, leaving nothing out. Over the weeks that I had been in St Petersburg, Tanya and I had become close friends. She knew everything about me and of course when I was unable, she would read the messages from the Prince to me. I promised her several times, that I would tell her everything from my debut ball, knowing that she wished she could be there with me. She had put my hair up in masses of curls leaving some lose to brush my shoulders in ringlets. Mama had brought me some hair pins with diamond hearts attached from Faberge's and gave them to me as a gift, at my breakfast, that morning. Tanya had placed the six pins, carefully in my hair, amid the masses of curls. When she had finished, she put the diamond choker around my neck, while I put on the earrings, leaving the bracelet to be put about my wrist after I had put on the long cream evening gloves. Then came the time to put on my gown. I took off the peach velvet dressing gown that I had been wearing after my bath and stepped into the gown that Tanya was holding for me. She pulled the gown up and started doing up the masses of tiny crystal buttons at the back. The style was very simple but it was the beautiful material that created the real beauty. The bodice was low, the neckline seemed to follow the gentle curve of my breasts. There were no sleeves but a cream tulle that lay off the shoulders, covered in a myriad of different coloured sequins. The skirt was straight at the front, gathering at the back to form a three-foot-long court train. The final 'topping' was the diamond tiara. I held a cream lace and ivory fan and tiny reticule made of the same material as the dress. I turned and walked to the large mirror on my wardrobe door. I stared at the vision before me. Who was this vision of elegance and sophistication? Having my hair up and the low cut of the bodice of my dress, made my neck look longer.

I couldn't believe that it was me. Tanya stood looking at me exclaiming how beautiful I looked. Tears were in her eyes as she examined her creation, just like an artist examining his finished masterpiece. I felt beautiful. Who could not wearing such finery as this? I wished that Tanya could experience what I was experiencing but she seemed contented for me to enjoy everything and report back to her.

As I left my bedroom and made my way downstairs, the clock in the hallway chimed half past six. Already waiting for me in the hallway were Mama and Grand Mama dressed in their finery for this special occasion. Grand Mama wore a gown of black silk with pearl jewellery and a black feather in her hair which had been put into a chignon. Mama's dress was of a deep sapphire blue. Around her neck and in her ears, she wore sapphires. She had never looked more lovely. I had never seen my mother look so beautiful.

When they both saw me on the stairs, I could see Mama's eyes fill with tears. I don't think Grand Mama was far from tears either.

Tanya followed me down stairs, carrying my cream velvet cloak trimmed and lined with cream fur.

Once I reached the hallway, Mama came over and kissed me. "Darling, you look absolutely beautiful. I hope you are well rested, because I have a feeling that your dance card will be filled for the whole of the evening."

Grand Mama looked at me and told me, with a slight quiver in her voice, that I looked an absolute vison, then carefully hugged me, mindful that she did not want to spoil 'the finished product'.

The photographer took over then, asking if I would mind standing on the bottom step, resting my hand on the marble banister. I did as I was told and looked straight at him, with a slight smile on my lips. I could not stop myself smiling anyway. My father might have disliked me and all my life I was aware of that, thinking that if my own father did not like me, why should anyone else. That night I decided that whatever my father felt for me was totally irrelevant. By the looks on the photographers' face, as well as Tanya's, Mama's and Grand Mama's faces, I knew that on that night of my debut, I looked beautiful, thanks to Tanya and Auguste Brisac as well as her team of dressmakers.

The photographer took several more photographs of me in various rooms downstairs. Mama kept arranging my train to fan about my feet. Then I asked him if he would take a photograph of Mama, Grand Mama and me. The photographer asked for Grand Mama to stand in the middle, and as she had said more than once before, her girls on either side. Finally, it was over. The photographer bent over Grand Mama's hand, saying that he would have the photographs ready after Christmas and would get them delivered as soon as they were ready.

Peter had bought the motor car to the front door. Outside it had begun to snow hard again. Tanya helped me into my cape and handed me my, long cream evening gloves, to put on again, followed by putting on the matching bracelet to the diamond jewellery that Grand Mama had given me, then she handed me my fan and reticule. Before I left the hallway, she held up my train and the bottom of my gown up, so that it didn't get dirty with the snow. Once I had sat in the back of the car, she arranged my train about me and whispered, "Good luck," to me.

Peter assisted Mama and Grand Mama into the back of the motor car, on either side of me. Once he was satisfied that we were all comfortable, he closed the rear door, got into the driver's seat and drove us the short drive to the Winter Palace.

We slowed down near the main gates leading to the Winter Palace grounds. They had been closed against the masses of people who had angrily congregated in front of them. Members of the Royal guards were standing to attention and keeping the masses back from our motor car. Peter got out to go over to talk to the officer in charge. I saw him gesturing to Peter but could not hear what was being said over the noise of the angry crowd. It was so bitterly cold outside that I thought they would have done better staying at home in front of their own hearths rather than protesting outside.

Peter came back to the car and said that he had been re-directed to the East Gate. No one mentioned the crowds. No one wanted to ruin the magic of the evening for me with talk of anything as unsavoury as the protesters. It was the first time that I had come up against any of the real ugliness and anger of St Petersburg. It was rather unsettling, but I would not let anything spoil my special evening. Not this evening. However, I did make a mental note to myself that I would start reading the newspapers to inform myself about what was going on in my adopted home of St Petersburg. I would no longer be ignorant about what was happening around me.

We drove through the opened East Gate to the Winter Palace. It looked like every window was shining with light from inside the palace. I was relieved to find that there were no angry crowds outside this gate. Peter drove slowly through the large courtyard of the palace to where double doors stood open under a large covered entrance. Leading from this entrance ran a wide red carpet, for us to walk upon, to save ruining our shoes or our gowns. Maids came to take our cloaks from us. Peter showed them our invitations, so that when it came time for us to claim our cloaks back, the maids would know which cloaks or coats belonged to whom. Peter left us then I presume to go back home and wait for the appointed time to return and collect us again.

A footman, who had collected our invitations from the maids, led the way into the grand ballroom. On a table by his side were dozens of dance cards edged in gold with a tiny pencil attached to give to the ladies to record which gentlemen were dancing which dance with them. At the door leading to the enormous ballroom, he handed the invitation to another doorman holding a large gilded staff, which he banged on the floor three times, then announced us. I followed Grand Mama and Mama around the ballroom where they stopped occasionally to chat to various people and to introduce me. I smiled politely and curtsied to them, then we moved on to the next. There were so many names and faces to remember and with the excitement of being presented, my mind just would not retain that amount of information.

I had seen an example of the lavish beauty of the Winter Palace when we had gone to tea with the Dowager Empress but that paled in comparison to the massive ballroom with over a dozen enormous, brilliantly lit chandeliers, hanging from the ornately decorated ceiling. They sparkled and twinkled like a million stars. Along the wall opposite the windows were gilded, floor to ceiling mirrors reflecting the dancers on the floor as the danced past. Already the ballroom was filled with happy, chattering, beautifully dressed, guests. I was so nervous about being presented to the royal family that I couldn't think of anything else. In my mind, I kept going over what I had to do to be presented; stand up straight and wait in line, wait for my name to be called, walk to the steps of the dais, curtsey low, straighten up, then take my train from the footman who held it, place the loop over my wrist, curtsey again, take three steps backwards and then I could turn to return to Mama and Grand Mama.

The music, which had been playing while people assembled in the ballroom stopped as a lone trumpeter began to play the Russian anthem announcing the arrival of the Royal family. The rest of the orchestra joined in and the crowd moved to either side of the ballroom, to await the passage of the royal family to the thrones placed on a dais at the far end of the room. The royal procession was led by the Tsar and my great aunt, the Dowager Empress Maria. As they passed by us, we all bowed or curtsied low, until they had moved on. The Dowager Empress stopped by me and lifted my chin to look directly into my eyes. "You look exquisite, my dear." She smiled at me. "Enjoy your evening." I thanked her quietly, then again, lowered my eyes to the floor, until they had all gone by.

Following them came the Tsarina Alexandre, who was the granddaughter of Queen Victoria of England and the young Tsarevich Alexi. After them followed the four young Grand Duchesses, Olga, Titania, Maria and Anastasia. Olga and Titania looked to be more or less the same age as myself. Maria and Anastasia were younger than me, as was the young Tsarevich.

Once the royal family were seated, there was another banging on the floor. This was the signal for all of the debutants to line up to be presented to the Tsar and Tsarina. With the floor cleared, we all had space to walk up to the royal dais. I could see that the young Grand Duchesses and the young Tsarevich were sitting beside their parents and grandmother. To the right of the Tsar sat the Dowager Empress and, on the left, sat the Tsarina. I expected to see the Prince among the royal family but could not see him anywhere. Maybe he had decided not to come. In what little conversations or correspondence we had had, he had never mentioned that he would be there on that particular night.

I heard two girls behind me whispering, then one of them tapped me on my shoulder, "Excuse me but are you an Alberto?"

I looked at her trying to work out what she meant. "Your pale hair," she explained. "Are you an Alberto?"

I couldn't help but smile, "I think you mean albino. If I was, I would have pale eyebrows and lashes and have pink eyes."

The girl blushed having been corrected. "Well, excuse me. We can't all be scholars," she said and turned back to her friend and they began giggling like children.

The girl in front of me smiled. "Take no notice of her, she might have looks but lacks in schooling. I am Katrina, by the way. Are you nervous? I am."

It was good to find someone who wanted to be friends with me. I smiled at her.

"I am Thalia. I am terrified that I will either lose my balance when I have to curtsey or fall over my train as I step back."

Again, she smiled. "We should be all right with the train part as a footman will hand us our train, but I can't stop shaking."

"It seems strange that a small moment of our lives should give us such trepidation," I replied. At least I was not alone in my nerves.

At the bottom of the steps leading up to the royal dais stood a very tall, skinny man, dressed in white traditional Russian dress. He had a long straggling beard and long, dark greasy hair interspersed with grey, which looked like it had not been washed for months. Around his neck he wore a simple wooden crucifix. I wondered how they could allow such a scruffy looking man in to the presence of the royal family. I didn't understand. I certainly didn't like the look of him or the way he stared at each of us debutants as we made our way up to curtsey to the Tsar. He looked as if he was undressing us all with his dark eyes. As I waited for my name to be called, I tried to ignore him, but I could smell his unwashed body and alcohol.

Katrina's name was called and nervously she made her way to the dais. She curtseyed and received her train from the footman, stepped backwards and then moved back to her family.

"Miss Thalia Marguerite Titania Bobrov." I heard my name called and remembering my tutoring, I made my way to the bottom of the dais and curtseyed low.

"Miss Bobrov, you are most welcome," the Tsar said.

I stood up and was about to take my leave when the Dowager Empress leaned over to him and whispered something in his ear. He nodded and looked at me again. "I understand that you are the granddaughter of my aunt, the Countess Popov?"

I whispered, "That is correct, Your Majesty." I was so shocked that the Tsar of all of Russia had spoken to me!

"Then I am sure that we will be seeing more of you at court. Thank you, Miss Bobrov. Enjoy your evening."

I knew, then, that I had been dismissed. A footman came up behind me, gathered my train and handed it to me by the loop, which I put around my wrist. I curtsied again, took three steps back and turned to return to the safety of Mama and Grand Mama.

"You have been very honoured to have the Tsar speak to you," Mama whispered.

I nodded. "I know," I replied in a whisper.

Another five girls were presented to the Tsar, including the one that had asked me if I was an Alberto. She gave a rather wobbly curtsey I noted with a satisfied grin. When the last one had turned around and walked away, the Tsar stood up and welcomed everyone, saying that the new year would be the tercentenary of the Romanovs, saying there would be a great many celebrations throughout the coming year. People cheered and clapped their hands. When the cheering abated, the Tsar held up his hands and told everyone to enjoy the evening. People began chattering among themselves. Mama leaned towards me and said that she saw me talking with some of the other debutants. "The one that gave the wobbly curtsey asked me if I was an Alberto Mama." Mama looked at me in question.

"An Alberto, what is one of them?" she asked.

"I think she meant an albino because of my hair colour." I told her.

"And you were worried that you might not be as well educated as some of the debutants!" she laughed. The music started and a stream of eligible young men came over and asked if I could reserve a dance for them on my dance card. I felt very shy, under the scrutiny of so many men. I had never been the centre of attraction for so many people. I could also see that Katrina had several men wanting her to save a dance for them.

I danced two dances, after I was returned to Mama and Grand Mama, then someone came behind me and whispered in my ear. "I have asked the orchestra to play a Tchaikovsky waltz, so this is my dance I believe." Whoever was next on my dance card had to stand aside as Prince Nicholas Ivanov led me onto the dance floor. He put one arm firmly around my waist and whisked me around. For a while he didn't speak. I just enjoyed being held by him. We were so close that I could smell his cologne, feel the warmth of his body and his breath on my face. How could my evening get any better? I wished that I could halt everything so that I could just savour the moment being held by the prince. I felt that no one else existed for those few moments in his arms on the busy dance-floor.

"You do realise that you are the most beautiful woman in the whole ballroom, cousin? Every eligible bachelor in this room is looking at us and is envious of me right now," he whispered to me.

I didn't know what to say, "You flatter me, Your Highness."

"I only tell the truth and please will you start calling me Nicky. Everyone does. We are related after all and I feel that we will be seeing a lot more of each other. And I will call you Thalia."

"My family call me Lia and I will call you Your Highness," I replied.

"That is absurd of you to insist in calling me by that ridiculous title." We danced in silence for a while, then he whispered in my ear, "But I will call you Lia, nevertheless. I like that name, although Thalia is a beautiful name. I looked up the original Thalia in the library. You were right, she was the daughter of Zeus and a mortal woman. The original Thalia was beautiful too but I cannot believe that she could have been more beautiful than you are tonight." I could feel myself blushing to the roots of my hair. "Have you completely recovered from your indisposition now?" he asked, changing the subject and sparing my blushes.

"Yes, thank you, Your Highness," I replied.

"You must have been very ill to have been out of circulation for so long."

I couldn't tell him what really happened so changed the conversation. "Thank you for sending me notes wishing me a speedy recovery," I said as we whisked past the dais.

"Thank you for replying to me when you were able. I am sure that we will be able to finally get to a Tchaikovsky concert in the near future. I insist that the next time, we will go to it, come hell or high water."

I laughed at that then saw the scruffy man looking over at us. I asked Nicky who he was.

His normal cheerful grin faded as he briefly looked across to the man. "Father Gregory Rasputin, confidant and advisor to the Tsarina. A very un-savoury man in my opinion but there again my opinion doesn't count for much in the royal family, only with the Dowager Empress."

The music ended and the Prince retained his arm around my waist as he took me back to where Grand Mama was sitting. Mama was on the dance floor with some tall stranger and for the first time in a very long time I could see her laughing and enjoying herself. I realised that with her upcoming divorce from my father, she deserved some happiness. I truly wanted Mama to find someone that she could love and would love her in return.

"Aunt Lilia, will you please tell Miss Lia that she may call me by my given name, instead of 'Your Highness' all of the time."

"I am afraid that I cannot make Thalia do something that she does not want, Nicholas, although she has my permission to call you by your given name if she wishes."

Knowing that my addressing him by his title was irritating him, I continued to do so. "Thank you for returning me to my grand mama, Your Highness," I said with a cheeky grin.

"Later, Miss Lia. I will claim you for another dance and sooner or later, I will have you calling me Nicky."

"Come hell or high water, Your Highness?" I replied, re-iterating what he had said to me earlier.

"Bah!" he exclaimed. "Women." Then he winked at me to let me know that he was not really angry with me and he enjoyed the banter. He bowed and left us.

Grand Mama scolded me, "Darling, why do you insist on calling him by his title?"

"Because it irritates him," I replied.

"You have a lot to learn, darling, about courting a gentleman. Don't you think that that is a little childish, darling?"

"Maybe, Grand Mama, but it is fun." I couldn't help but grin.

Grand Mama smiled as she came to realise that in my own way, I was flirting with the Prince in the only way that I knew.

"Then you have your fun, my darling." She tenderly patted my cheek.

I was claimed by one man dressed in the uniform of the higher ranking, cavalry guards for the next dance. He was very tall and, in his way, good looking. He flattered and charmed me, as we danced around the floor. I found out that he was Count Sergei Suvorin. We danced past Prince Ivanov, who was dancing with the Grand Duchess, Olga or I thought it was Olga but couldn't be sure, as all the Grand Duchesses were wearing the same gowns and all looked very similar.

After that dance was over, I was then claimed by Captain Olaf Kapinski. He was very handsome; clean shaven, unlike many of the men but not very talkative. The Prince whisked by us, dancing with another of the Grand Duchesses. I presumed that he would work his way through all four, before the evening was out.

Throughout the ball footmen were milling around the guests with silver trays bearing glasses of champagne. I think in total through the evening, I must have had only had three glasses, as I was so busy dancing. I was claimed by gentlemen old and young, short and tall, fat and thin. Many of their names eluded me but I was thoroughly enjoying myself. I enjoyed dancing with the Prince, most of all. He set my pulse racing whenever he spoke my name or smiled at me or held me and danced with me. I wondered then if my mother had felt like this when she first met my father.

An elderly gentleman had come over to me to ask if he could have the next dance. Once again, the orchestra played another Tchaikovsky and before the old gentleman could put his arm around my waist, I heard someone whisper in my ear, "Ah, another Tchaikovsky. Our dance I believe. Please excuse us."

An arm was placed possessively around my waist and once more I was swept onto the ballroom floor amongst the dancers, leaving the poor gentleman staring at us as we waltzed around the room.

"Are you always this difficult, Miss Bobrov?" the Prince asked.

"Oh, much, much more, Your Highness," I replied. "Are you always so rude as to dance with another man's partner?" I retaliated "Do you have any interests, Your Highness, other than taking over another partner's dance with me?"

"By any, what do you mean, Miss Bobrov?"

"Well, as well as Tchaikovsky," I replied.

"I have gold mines in the Americas," he told me. "I own diamond and emerald mines in South Africa and I have just purchased a share in a couple of opal mines in Australia. I do work for my living, cousin. I supply Faberge, Cartier and Tiffany with jewels from my mines, but mainly Faberge." He looked down at me and smiled. "Did you know that for each month of the calendar, there is a specific gem that is your birthstone?"

I shook my head.

"Ah well, there is," he said knowledgably. "What month were you born in, cousin?" he asked me.

"October, Your Highness."

"Ah, October, a very unusual stone; the opal, I believe. Have you ever seen an opal, Lia?"

Again, I shook my head.

He looked down at my gown. "It is very much like the colouring of your gown, only some are more colourful than others, that's opals I am talking about not dresses." I laughed. "Some opals are very pale, these are usually poorer quality, like all gem stones, having superior quality and inferior ones. Take the diamonds you are wearing, I can tell that they are of excellent quality, by the colour, the clarity and the cut."

He moved his head closer to me as he whispered in my ear, "Did I tell you how beautiful you look this evening, Lia?"

"Yes, Your Highness, in our last dance together." I whispered back.

"In fear of repeating myself, Miss Bobrov, you look exquisite." He grinned down at me, causing my heart to race with his compliments. "Having danced with a few young ladies this evening, I can say there is no young lady whose beauty compares to yours." He danced us around the ballroom, past Father

Rasputin, who glared at me with his cold fish eyes. I felt myself shudder under the man's gaze.

"Are you cold? I felt you shiver," the Prince asked and looked down at me. I could see the genuine concern in his eyes.

"Father Rasputin was looking at me in such a strange way," I replied.

I could feel the Prince's grip on my waist tighten, protectively. "Thalia, if you do nothing else that I ask you, please do this, for your own safety. Stay well away from Gregory Rasputin. He has a very, very bad reputation."

"Then why does the Tsarina entertain him?" I asked.

"I honestly do not know, Lia, but what I do know is that he is a dangerous man. No woman's virtue is safe around Rasputin. Will you promise me?"

I didn't have to promise him. Rasputin made my skin crawl with his skeleton like features, crooked teeth, straggly beard and hair After that, the Prince made sure that we did not dance anywhere near the dreadful man.

All too soon the dance ended and Prince Nicholas took my arm and walked me back to where Grand Mama and Mama were.

"Cousin Marguerite, I return your stubborn daughter. Can you please ensure that you never allow Father Rasputin near her? He has been looking at her in a most unsavoury way."

Both Mama and Grand Mama nodded in agreement.

"I enjoyed our talk about birth stones, Your Highness," I said trying to draw the conversation away from the unsavoury subject of Father Rasputin and keep the prince with me a little longer.

I hadn't noticed but although he had returned me to Mama and Grand Mama, he still had not let go of my arm.

"Perhaps, one day, I may be allowed to take you to Karl Faberge's premises, then he can show you some samples of your birthstone." he said.

"I would enjoy that very much, Your Highness," I replied.

The evening was coming to a close, much to my relief. I had danced nearly every dance and my dance card had been practically full the whole evening. My feet were throbbing and I was beginning to tire. I had begun to feel weary. I didn't know what time it was but I was sure that it must have been very late. People were slowly beginning to drift away from the ballroom, leaving only a few on the dance floor.

Before we turned to leave, several of my dance partners from the evening, came over to us and presented their calling cards to me, asking if they may call on me. Grand Mama nodded her permission.

The last to come over to us was the Prince, who bowed low over my hand and kissed it. I glowed to feel his warm, soft lips on my hand.

"Aunt Lilia, now that we are all better acquainted, may I have permission to call on you all?"

"My door will always be open to you nephew," she told him graciously.

"I look forward to that," he said looking at me, as he said it, then pressed his calling card into my hand.

I curtsied to him, after I had placed his card with the others in my reticule, without looking at it.

Grand Mama led us from the ballroom, along the warren of hallways back to where our cloaks were kept. Already Peter Abramovich was waiting for us. He held out our cloaks and helped Grand Mama with hers, while Mama and I put our own on.

The car drove us home through the main gates, where the crowds had finally dispersed at such a late hour. I noticed it but I am not sure that anyone else did. The unsavoury subject was never mentioned.

When we reached Grand Mama's and stood in the hallway while our cloaks and gloves were taken from us, the hall clock chimed one o'clock in the morning on Christmas day. I excused myself and slowly went upstairs to my bedroom, where Tanya was waiting, excited to hear all of my news. I was much too tired to talk and told her that I would tell her everything in the morning.

Tanya helped me undress and put on my nightgown.

"Did you enjoy yourself, Miss Thalia?" she asked as she picked up my beautiful ball gown. I nodded, smothering a yawn.

"It was wonderful," I said while she took all the pins out of my hair and all of my jewellery, placing them carefully in the leather box Grand Mama had given me earlier.

"Was the Prince there?"

I smiled and nodded. "He danced with me twice," I said as I crawled into my warm, soft bed. Shortly after Tanya bid me goodnight, I fell into a, deep, fitful sleep with a picture of Prince Nicholas in my mind once again and a smile touched my lips.

# Chapter 10
## Christmas Day 1912

I slept until Tanya came to my bedroom to wake me at ten o'clock on Christmas morning. She hadn't brought me my usual breakfast tray, just a hot drink. We would go to morning Mass, then come home for Christmas lunch. I told her that I would tell her about the ball later on.

When I went downstairs fully dressed and ready to go to Mass, I finally noticed that a large impressive Christmas tree had been put up in the hallway. I realised that I must have been extremely tired the night of my debut, not to notice that there was a large ten-foot-high Christmas tree at the centre of the large hallway. On its branches were tiny candles in holders and a beautiful array of tree ornaments. It looked so festive. I don't think I would ever forget the beauty of that Christmas tree on my first Christmas in St Petersburg. To add to the excitement of Christmas day it had begun to snow again.

Peter drove us to the Cathedral, where we were to hear Mass. Outside it was freezing cold but inside the magnificent Cathedral, amongst all of the worshippers, it was warmer. Grand Mama led us to our family pew, where we knelt to pray.

While we sat waiting for the service to begin, I looked all about me at the frescoes on the walls and on the ceilings. The Altar was made of gold leaf, with jewels and golden icons of all the saints. It was breathtakingly beautiful. I sat looking at it all while I was waiting for the service to start.

The priest entered and the congregation rose. I noticed that in the front pews sat the royal family consisting of the Tsar, Tsarina, Tsarevich and Grand Duchesses. Behind them sat the Dowager Empress, the Prince and another man, a lot older than the Tsar. I asked Grand Mama who he was and was told that he was Duke Cyril Vladimirovich Romanov, the Tsar's uncle. I realised that he was one of Mama's dance companions from the evening before.

Our family pew was on the opposite side of the aisle, to the Royal family and one row back, from the pew shared by the Dowager Empress and the Prince. I saw the Prince turn to look at me several times and gave me a cheeky grin. I knew then that he would not let the festive morning pass without speaking to me.

Before I dressed that morning, I had emptied the contents of my reticule, from the evening before. My eyes briefly skimmed over the various calling cards of possible suitors to the one of the Prince. This time I turned his over and looked at the back, hoping that he had put some little message for me. I was not disappointed. "I enjoy our little banter." It read and then signed with a flourish. I grinned to myself.

Secretly, I hoped that he might be interested in becoming a suitor for me. He had not asked me if he may call but he had asked my Grand Mama. How would I know his true feelings? Then his words of flattery from the night before came to mind and I flushed remembering them, or did he say those same words to every young girl that he danced with?

Now as he was sitting across the aisle from me, occasionally grinning back at me, I sincerely hoped that he was interested. I wondered, *Could it be as easy as this to attract a suitor?* Was he the one? I had once thought that Peter Urvanski, the village doctor's son, had been the one but I was only fourteen at the time and then he had disappeared to Moscow to train to be a doctor like his father and I had never heard any more from him.

I never heard a word of Mass, I was too busy in my daydreams of the Prince.

The Royal family were the first to leave, then the rest of the congregation followed.

It was still snowing when we finally left the Cathedral. I pulled up the hood of my cloak and pulled on my gloves, then put my cold hands inside my muff. First Count Suvorin came up to us and bowed low, before handing me a posy of winter roses.

"Miss Bobrov, may I wish a happy Christmas to you and all of your family?" I took the posy and thanked him, returning his good wishes. He asked if he could call on me in the New Year, as his duties would keep him busy before then. I nodded and he turned and left us.

An older gentleman whom I had also danced with came over and bowed.

"I trust you are not overtired from last night, Miss Bobrov?" I thanked him and told him that I had had a restful sleep. He also asked if he might call on me, within the next few days. Grand Mama interrupted, saying that we were at home on Wednesdays. He bowed and left us.

I was asking Grand Mama, how to control the 'flow' of suitors, especially those that I was not interested in. She was just about to answer me when the Prince came and planted a kiss on Mama's and her cheeks.

"Merry Christmas, Aunt Lilia, Cousin Marguerite," he said, then bent over my hand and kissed it, very formally. "Merry Christmas, Miss Bobrov." He was playing me at my own game!

I curtsied and remained silent. I smelled the bouquet of winter roses that Count Suvorin had given me. I think that I was trying to make the Prince jealous, thinking that if he was interested in me, he might have given me a small token for Christmas, as the Count had done. I saw the Prince looking at me.

I walked over to the motor car and got inside, waiting for Mama and Grand Mama to follow.

We all drove home to Christmas dinner, which I ate with relish. Because we were going to mass, on Christmas morning, we fasted before going, just having a hot drink. By the time we returned home, I was really hungry.

While we were out, someone had lit the candles on the tree and beneath it were presents, not just for us but for the staff as well.

After all of the Christmas food had been cleared away, all of Grand Mama's staff lined up in the hall, beside the Christmas tree. Besides Peter Abramovich, Anya, Tanya, Igor and Grand Mama's maid Ava, who we saw little of but I found out that Ava and Peter were Tanya's parents. (I had not realised that Peter was even married). In total there were, including the cook, kitchen maids, general maids and gardeners, fifteen. All the female staff were given material for new dresses and the men were given new hats, scarves and gloves. I had also bought a box of cigars for Peter, new boots for Tanya, (because my boots had been too small for her) and a new shawl for Anya. It was then time for us to receive our presents from under the tree. Mama had bought me a jewellery box for my increasing number of jewels. Apparently now that I had 'come out', the diamond jewellery that I had worn on the evening of my debut became mine, until my daughter, if I ever had one, would be given them on her debut. It was an old family tradition, so Grand Mama had told me. Mama also gave me a silver card case from Faberge with Lilly of the valley and Freesias done in enamel and engraved with my initials. I had a beautiful pair of white booted ice skates from Grand Mama, then there was another small present for me under the tree. Grand

Mama handed it to me, and I thought that it was another present from her. "Oh, Grand Mama, you have already given me so much," I exclaimed.

"It's not from me, my darling. It was left on the doorstep this morning, by whom, I have no idea. You had better open it and find out."

All sorts of ideas ran through my head as I took the small present. One silly thought was that it might have been from my father as an apology for hitting me. I went and sat down beside the fire in the lounge, feeling that I needed to be sitting down for this. The outside wrapping gave nothing away of its sender but it was beautifully wrapped. I carefully took off the wrapping paper and found a box inside, bearing the name of Faberge. I took off the lid and found a miniature painting in a gilt frame with semi-precious jewels. The miniature was of the Prince. My heart flipped as I looked at his handsome face. Underneath the miniature painting was a note.

*"My dear Lia, I have to go away for a while. How long, I am not sure. I thought this might remind you of me, so that you won't forget me and of our friendly banter, which I enjoy enormously. Merry Christmas. Nicholas Ivanov."*

I felt guilty now after being so cold towards him outside the Cathedral. I showed the miniature to Mama and Grand Mama but not the note, which I kept in my hand. Nothing was said, apart from how beautiful the frame was. I handed Mama my Christmas present to her, which was a book on the Greek Gods and for Grand Mama I had bought a beautiful cream cashmere shawl.

After the presents had all been handed out, I decided to put the Prince's miniature on my bedside table, so that it would be the last thing I looked at, at night and the first thing I would look at in the morning. I tried not to let anyone know how I felt but I don't think I was fooling anyone. The Prince had never given me any real reason to think that he had any feelings for me, except what he said to me at the ball, while we were dancing but I decided that he had probably said the same thing to all of the young debutantes and the Grand Duchesses that he had danced with. I thought that I was just a young second cousin to him and that he had decided to take me under his wing.

When I went upstairs to my room after lunch, Tanya was waiting for me, firstly to thank me for her boots, she asked me to tell her more about the ball. I told her about all of the suitors who had asked me to dance but her main question was, "You said that you danced with the Prince twice. Did you dance with anyone else twice?"

I told Tanya that I had danced with many other men but none twice. I could not remember all the names of my dance partners. I told her that the prince gave me his card with a brief note on at the ball.

"Oh, Miss Thalia, he is really interested in you, otherwise, why would he write you a note?"

I also told her that he had given me the miniature of himself as a Christmas present, along with another note saying that he had to go away for a while. Once again Tanya reinforced the fact that she thought that Nicky was interested in me. I told her that I did not understand the workings of men's minds. Secretly, I hoped that he might be interested in becoming a suitor for me. He had not asked me if he may call but he had asked my Grand Mama. How would I know his true feelings? I was very ignorant in the matter of men and romance. Then his words of flattery from the night before came to mind and I flushed remembering them. Other men had flattered me while we were dancing but no one's words had such a profound effect on me as the Prince's.

Before doing anything else, I wrote him a brief note and had it sent over to his home address, hoping that he hadn't left already. I thanked him for my beautiful Christmas present and wished him, Merry Christmas and a safe journey. I didn't know what else to say to him to let him know that I was interested in him. I asked Tanya if she had a man friend. She told me that she didn't, "I don't really go anywhere to meet young men, Miss Thalia."

So, Tanya was not the person to speak to about romance and men. I supposed that I could ask Mama or Grand Mama, but I did not want them to know that I was interested in the Prince. They might laugh or tell me that because we were related that we could not enter a relationship. I might be seventeen, but I was so immature regarding relationships. Maybe if the Prince continued to show an interest in me, then I might ask Mama what she thought were his intentions.

# Chapter 11

## Count Suvorin

Once the Christmas festivities were over, life settled down to a routine. We had several invitations to dinner, to dances, to the theatre, the ballet and ice skating.

Between Christmas and New Year, Count Suvorin came and asked me if I would like to go ice skating with him. The weather was still bitterly cold, so the river was still frozen. According to the Count, it had been a number of years since the river had been frozen for this long. Before the two of us left home, Mama told me to be careful this time. The Count assured her that he would take great care of me, which he did. We drove in his motor car to the river, where he parked. Once again, the stalls were set up on the bank. The Count linked my arm through his as we made our way down the bank to one of the benches by the river. He used his handkerchief to brush any dirt and snow from the bench before allowing me to sit down, then when I put my new skates on, he bent down and laced them up for me. He really was extremely attentive towards me and he was very handsome with his sandy blond hair and moustache. Once he had laced up my boots, he did his own, then offered me his arm again as we went down onto the ice. There were plenty of people on the ice, many couples but also many unattached young girls, who stared, longingly, at the Count as we skated past them. I was very flattered that he only had eyes for me. He put his arm protectively around my waist and held my hand, as we skated around, avoiding any areas where tree roots might be. It started out as a bright sunny day but after a short while the sky clouded over with great bulbous clouds threatening more snow. We made our way back to the bench where he removed my skates and helped me on with my boots, then changed his own and drove me home. I enjoyed his company, but he was so intense, he never seemed to really smile. His lips smiled but that smile never touched his eyes. He seemed so serious most of the time.

Hardly a day went by that I did not receive something from him, either flowers, chocolates, a book of poetry, an invitation to the opera.

New Year's Eve he came to collect me and took me to another ball, this time it was just the two of us; no Mama or Grand Mama to chaperone us as Grand Mama had come down with a cold and had been ordered, by the doctor, to stay in bed for a few days. Mama insisted on taking care of her, so I was left alone in the Count's company.

I danced nearly every dance with the Count. He was there at my side when we went into dinner. When the clocks struck midnight, he bent over and gently kissed my lips.

1913 was the year of the Tercentennial celebrations of three hundred years of Romanov rule, which would be marked by various activities to which the Royal family would attend. Just after midnight, Count Suvorin and I left the ball for him to take me back home. The Count told me that once the celebrations started, his time would be taken up, providing an escort to the Tsar and his family to various events but he hoped that when he did have any spare time, he could call on me.

We stopped outside Grand Mama's front door, where again he leaned over and kissed me, briefly before coming around to open my door and help me alight from the motor car. Why did I feel nothing? I thought that maybe in time, my feelings for Sergei would change, after all, no one could want for a more caring, attentive and attractive escort.

When Igor opened the front door to me, I went inside and turned to wave goodbye to Sergei. Mama was waiting for me in the lounge in one of the winged chairs by the fire. I could tell by her red eyes that she had been crying. With Grand Mama not being well, I immediately feared the worst. When I asked her if Grand Mama's health had deteriorated, Mama shook her head.

"No, darling, your grandmother is on the way to recovery."

I was greatly relieved. I had only really known my grandmother for a few months now but during that short time I had grown to love and respect her. To her, Mama and I were everything.

"Why are you crying then, Mama?" I asked her, sinking down by her side in front of the fire. She showed me the contents of a letter that had arrived for her that morning. It was about the divorce from my father. The marriage had finally been dissolved, due to my father's actions.

"He must have signed the papers the same day as he came here. Maybe what he did to you made him feel guilty enough to sign them," she explained.

"Then something good came from it," I said, knowing that all of my pain and suffering had not been in vain. "But why are you crying, Mama? Surely this is a good thing?"

"My life is over, Lia," she said tearfully.

"What on earth do you mean Mama?" I asked taking her hands in mine.

She told me that although she had been married to a brute, she was still the Baroness Bobrov of Smolensk but now with the divorce having gone through, she was nothing.

"Does that really matter, Mama? You are still the daughter of Countess Popov and you can marry again. You are still young and very beautiful." I told her, confident that she would get many suitors.

"What man will want a woman that can't give him any children?"

I gently squeezed her hands and looked into her eyes, "A man that has already got children. There are plenty out there."

"How do I know that he wouldn't turn out to be just like your father?"

I told her that she could take her time in choosing, this time and she was more mature now and knew what sort of men to avoid and what to show interest in. There was no rush. I stifled a yawn. Mama kissed my forehead and asked how my evening had been. I explained that it might be the last time for a while, before I saw Sergei again, as the duties would take him away from St Petersburg, to escort the royal family for the celebrations.

I went to bed shortly after I had re-assured Mama that she still could have a wonderful life ahead of her. As usual, Tanya was waiting for me in my bedroom ready to help me undress and get into bed. She asked me if I had enjoyed myself; after telling her that I had, she left me to go to sleep. I reached over to my bedside table and picked up the Prince's miniature. I had not seen or heard from him since Christmas morning. I wished that I had been friendlier towards him now. Maybe then he might have stayed? Who could tell?

I slept poorly that night, wondering what had happened to the Prince. Had I put him off me with my stupid, immature games?

As I had promised myself after my debut ball, I had been reading the newspapers daily after I had eaten my breakfast. My interest surprised both Mama and Grand Mama, but they never stopped me. In fact, I was the only one to read them from cover to cover and what I read was not good news. One minute the Duma, the Russian Parliament, had control over the country, then they did something that the Tsar disliked and he would dissolve it. The Okrana, which was the secret police, would then be in control of the country, along with the Tsar. Then something happened and the Duma was reinstated. There was an awful lot of unrest in Russia, which I found very disturbing. There were riots, killings, breaking into bakeries, stealing food, the sort of things that should be kept from a young woman such as myself. The worst and most disturbing was that the monk Rasputin was mentioned in some reports and not in a good way either. His relationship with the Tsarina and the young Grand Duchesses was mentioned in none too favourable terms. I skimmed over this propaganda, feeling sure that it was pure speculation and none of it was true.

Contrary to the bad news, I read that the whole country was getting excited about the celebrations but reports of killings still seemed to mar the excitement that I should have felt.

It was a Sunday morning. The church bells all over the city were ringing loudly. I had told Tanya that Sergei was to be on guard duty outside the Winter Palace that day. I thought that it would be nice for me to see him carrying out his duties. It was beginning to snow again but it had turned a little milder than it had been. Although not completely thawed, the river was beginning to flow, sluggishly again, still with large pieces of ice floating on it. The snow was settling on the ground. In places it was turning to slush. Once, Tanya and I were wrapped up, warm, against the weather, we strolled arm in arm to the palace railings. I saw Sergei sitting astride a massive black horse, in front of his regiment. The horse's coat shone like black silk, where, I presumed Sergei or some groom had brushed it till it shone. I tried to wave to him but he was looking straight ahead, to where there was a terrible noise coming towards the palace. At first I thought it was a crowd of people starting the celebrations of the Tercentenary early but as the crowd came nearer, I realised that they weren't celebrating at all. They had stern faces which reminded me of the people that had stood by the gates of the palace, the night of my debut. Their eyes were sunk into their skulls and even underneath the rags, that they wore, they looked thin and starving. They looked frozen to the core as their clothes were totally unsuited for the bitterly cold weather. The crowd was headed by a priest carrying a paper in his hand. I could hear what he was shouting, that he wanted to hand the paper to the Tsar. They obviously didn't realise that the Royal family were at the Alexandra Palace in Tsarskoye Selo. As they neared the guards, the crowd and

101

the priest began to chant that they wanted to see the Tsar. I heard Sergei shout to them to turn around but amongst all the shouting and the noise of the church bells, the angry mass kept moving forward obviously not hearing Sergei. Again, I heard Sergei shout to them but still they didn't hear him. I don't know whether it was my imagination but it seemed that the noise from the church bells was getting louder and louder. Sergei then shouted to his men to prepare. Still the crowd moved forward. Sergei lifted his sword, then lowered it. Immediately, there was a barrage of gunfire. I saw the front rows of the crowd crumple to the ground, smothered in their own blood, then Sergei and his regiment were charging forward, swords at the ready and began slashing away at the standing remains of the crowd. Arms, legs, heads were cut off and I stood, transfixed, not able to move forwards or backwards. I heard Tanya sobbing beside me and vomiting at the bloody sight, before us. Rivers of blood ran, staining the snow. Finally, I took her hand and we ran all of the way home. I ran up the steps of the Grand Mama's house and hammered, persistently on the front door until Igor opened it. I stepped inside and collapsed. Somewhere I heard someone screaming not realising that it was me doing the screaming. Tanya was in floods of tears, trying to tell Peter what had happened. In the end Ava was summoned and took Tanya up to her room and put to bed with a couple of drops of Laudanum. Anya, Mama's maid, took me by my shoulders and steered me up the staircase to my bedroom, got me undressed as if I were a child again, into my nightgown and into bed. I was also given some Laudanum.

While all of this was going on, Grand Mama had come into the hall to see what all of the ruckus was. When she saw the state of Tanya and me, she sent Peter to find out what had happened. It was known where we were going. I had told Mama, so Peter knew exactly where to go.

Shortly after Peter returned, looking grey and ill, shaking his head, saying just one word: "Carnage."

Both Tanya and I lay in our respective beds, for two days, while Ava and Anya looked after us. Sergei called to see me several times but I refused to see him. I returned his gifts and notes, untouched and unread. Grand Mama finally instructed Peter to tell him not to return again. She never asked me what had happened that morning for fear that it would bring back memories of the horrifying scene.

In the ensuing days I read reports in the newspaper, calling it a massacre at the Winter Palace. I read that several hundred people had died and several more were seriously injured. It never mentioned Sergei but Tanya and I knew that he was the one to blame for the massacre. Although the crowd was angry, they were unarmed. They had no way of defending themselves against Sergei's regimental onslaught.

# Chapter 12

## The Tercentennial Celebrations Begin

On the morning of 21 February, I was awoken by the sound of terrible bangs. I sat bolt upright in bed, my mind returning to that terrible day of the massacre. I was awake even before Tanya had brought me my breakfast tray. The bangs continued, as I finally realised that it was the thirty-one-gun salute from the Peter and Paul Fortress, signifying the beginning of the Tercentennial celebrations, as had been mentioned in all of the newspapers. It was as if the beautiful sunshine had been ordered specifically for this special day. When Tanya came to my room with my breakfast, after placing the tray on my lap, she opened the curtains letting the sunlight to flood into my bedroom. Through my window I could see the sky, a lovely blue, heralding a beautiful morning, with hardly a cloud in the sky.

The thirty-one-gun salute was to be followed by a special Mass at Kazan Cathedral, which, of course, we attended, along with hundreds of other people. Many waited outside the Cathedral, to catch a glimpse of the Royal family. Once again, we sat in the family pew, just across and back from the Royal pews, the same as we had on Christmas morning. I looked across to see if I could see the Prince but his seat was empty. I felt my heart plummet like a great stone in my chest. I hadn't seen or heard anything from him for nearly two months. I had no idea where he was or when he would return, if he did return.

I had decided to try hard and put him from my mind. I was crying after the moon. Why should a Prince be interested in a nobody like me? Besides, we were cousins. I didn't even know if cousins could marry one another. There was no point in even entertaining such an idea, so why waste time on finding out about something that will never happen?

Tanya said, rumours were, that he might be in line to marry one of the Grand Duchesses, possibly Titania, as Olga might have to marry a king or prince from another country to forge foreign alliances. My hopes and dreams were dashed but I still had his miniature. Every time I looked at it my heart seemed to skip a beat. As time passed by, I moved it from on top of my bedside table to inside my bedside table drawer. I didn't look at it as often as I had at first, once Tanya had given me that information.

I never heard any of the service at the Cathedral, I was so wrapped up in my dreams and memories of the prince. Thoughts that he might get married to one of the daughters of the Tsar left me with a heavy feeling in my heart. I really was not doing myself any favours by dwelling on thoughts of Nicky but I couldn't deny the feelings I had when he had held me in his arms to dance. Even just thinking about it again started my heart beating rapidly in my breast like a captured bird.

At mid-day, Tanya and I walked along to the Winter Palace, trying to put images of the terrible day of the massacre behind us. Tanya had desperately wanted to watch the royal family leave Palace Square in three open carriages and I thought that seeing the Winter Palace under happier circumstances might drive away the ghosts from that awful scene. Inside, my body was still shaking at the memories of our last outing we had together. I don't know if Tanya felt the same but neither of us really relaxed and enjoyed the spectacle as much as we would have done if we had never gone to see Sergei that fateful day.

The royal family drove out in open, horse drawn carriages. In the first carriage rode the Tsar and the young Tsarevich, both dressed in uniforms of the Russian army. Tanya had never seen the Royals in the flesh, only photographs in the newspapers and was in raptures at how handsome the Tsar and the young Tsarevich were. In the second carriage rode the Tsarina and the Dowager Empress and finally in the third carriage rode the four young Grand Duchesses all dressed in matching outfits. Tanya commented on every one of the Royal family, how beautiful they looked. As I had seen the young Tsarevich before, I thought he looked very pale and ill. I knew that he hadn't attended the mass at the Kazan Cathedral, so I presumed that was the reason why.

All the way back home Tanya was chattering away about the royal family, telling me that it was the best day of her life (seemingly all thoughts of the 'massacre' had been forgotten, although during the night our fears returned in the form of nightmares. I had awoken a few times, shouting and crying out, since that fateful day, to find Anya at my bedside, stroking my forehead and whispering words of comfort).

Later on, the night the sky was lit by masses of fireworks, exploding in multitudes of colours. I had never seen fireworks before and couldn't stop myself from going, "Ooooooooh," as they exploded. All around the city were crowds of people out to see the spectacular display.

The following evening, Grand Mama, Mama and I attended the theatre. The Marinsky Theatre held a Gala performance of an opera by, Mikhail Glinka called 'A life for the Tsar'. Although Glinka had been dead for many years now, he was thought to be the 'Fountainhead' of all Russian music.

The Tsar and the Grand Duchesses sat in the royal box, which was dead opposite the stage, so they had a very good view but there was no sign of the Tsarina and the young Tsarevich. We sat in a box near to the royal box. Occasionally I looked across to see whether the Grand Duchesses and their father were enjoying the opera, (which they seemed to be). The auditorium and all the boxes were full. People wanted to see the Tsar and the royal family but of course they wanted to see the opera by the well-known composer. As the opera ended and the curtains closed, down in the auditorium a terrible commotion erupted. As people were already trying to leave the auditorium, no one seemed to notice anything unusual, until someone at the front, near the stage, shouted out, "He has been shot!" Then everything happened all at once. I looked across to the royal box, thinking that someone had shot the Tsar but the Tsar and Grand Duchesses were all huddled together towards the rear of the royal box. I think the Tsar was trying to protect his daughters from the terrible sight of a man shot down. Some members of the royal guards caught the man before he could leave with the other members of the audience and make a getaway. Eventually everyone left the theatre. Nothing more was said. It had all been passed over very quickly as if nothing had happened at all to spoil the celebrations.

It was not until the following morning that the incident at the theatre was reported in the newspapers which were on sale at the railway station. Five men had been captured in association with the shooting. They had all been hung, without even a trial.

We all travelled by train to Moscow for the dinner and ball at the Nobleman's Assembly. Anyone who was connected to the Royal family had been invited to the dinner and ball. As we were related to the Romanovs', we were to be dressed in our finery, to attend. Once again, I travelled by train only this time from St Petersburg. All our maids travelled on the train but in a different carriage. We stayed in one of the large hotels in the city. Because of the Tercentenary celebrations, every hotel was filled with Russian Aristocrats in preparation for the ball. Our suite of rooms seemed filled with boxes containing our ball gowns and a change of clothes to travel back to St Petersburg in. Our maids were unpacking and hanging up our gowns, so that any creases caused during the journey would drop out in time for the ball.

We travelled to the gala dinner by horse-drawn carriage. At the assembly rooms our carriage joined several others waiting to deposit their passengers at the entrance. Once we had handed our cloaks to maids, we made our way to the massive dining room and were shown to our table. Our places were denoted with name cards. In front of each place was a menu detailing all the courses, written in beautiful copperplate and edged in gold leaf. When everyone was seated at their allocated table, we waited for the royal family to take their places at the top table. Once they were seated, waiters came out carrying the first course. The whole meal was carried out with military precision, course followed course and between us being given our meal to the time when our plates were cleared away, the waiters, stood to one side until they were needed again.

The meal was absolutely delicious and decoratively laid out on our plates like a work of art. (Although Grand Mama had a chef to prepare her meals, they paled in comparison to the menu at the gala dinner.) The Nobleman's Assembly was attractively decorated but I thought that it paled into insignificance compared to the Winter Palace. The chandeliers were not as large or brilliant, there was less gold leaf in evidence but it was still a beautiful building.

Once the meal was over, we all adjourned to the ballroom. At the far end of the ballroom, the orchestra, which had been setting up, began playing as soon as the first of the guests began to slowly trickle in. The Tsar and his mother the Dowager Empress led the ball with a waltz. Slowly others joined in. The room became mass of brightly coloured ladies, flying like butterflies, around the floor in a rainbow of colour. Their gentlemen were dressed either in black and white evening dress or in their military uniform. I saw Sergei, who looked, briefly, across to me, then turned away and began talking to one of the other girls that had debuted with me. Just seeing him in the distance still made me shudder and brought back memories of the bloody scene from only a relatively short time ago. Relieved, I thought, that he would be one less partner for me to dance with. I was glad that he didn't speak to me.

I saw Katrina Tomorovsky who had stood in front of me at our debut ball. We waved to each other and then we were whisked onto the dance floor. I hoped that at some time during the evening we would be able to talk to each other. I had one dance with Captain Olaf Kapinski, who said very little, as usual. As soon as he had returned me to Grand Mama, I felt an arm go around my waist and I was whisked onto the floor again before I had chance to register who my partner was.

"A Tchaikovsky Waltz. My dance I presume?"

I couldn't believe my ears. I had to look up. I saw a cheeky grin and smiling, grey eyes looking down at me. Suddenly my lips began to tremble, and I was struggling to fight back the tears that threatened to spill down my cheeks. I don't know whether it was relief at seeing Prince Nicholas again after so long an absence or the sight of Sergei bringing back memories of that terrible day of the massacre, which still gave me occasional nightmares but whatever it was, I struggled to hold back the tears.

I was quickly steered to one of the doors opening out on to the gardens. There, under one of the arbours, I rested my head on the Prince's chest and cried. "Oh, Nicky, I am so glad that you are back. It's been absolutely terrible without you," I sobbed, not really knowing what I was saying. I think it was all the things that I had wanted to say and his absence for so long seemed to spur me into saying how I really felt, regardless that some might class me as 'forward'. I couldn't let any more time pass by, without letting him know how I felt.

His finger tilted my face up to his and he dabbed away my tears with his handkerchief. "If this is the welcome back that I get after being away and for you to start calling me by my name, then it was well worth it."

I was shocked. Did he not realise all that had happened to me since he had left?

"No, don't say that, Nicky. All those poor people were massacred in front of the Winter Palace and yesterday someone was shot in the theatre. I don't know who it was. I don't even know if they are dead or alive."

He looked at me puzzled, not knowing what I was talking about. We sat down on the bench and I told him all about what Sergei had done.

His arms went around me protectively as I rested my head on his chest. I could hear that Nicky's heartbeat was matching mine, as he held me closely.

"Oh my darling, darling Lia, what terrible things you have had to witness while I have been away. You say that Suvorin started it, the massacre?"

I nodded.

"There has been too much of this going on around the country. It ought to be stopped." He held me close in his arms, kissing the top of my head and I realised this was where I always wanted to be. I also realised that I had been in love with Nicky all of this time, probably since we met at the ballet of Swan Lake, and didn't even know it. I dabbed my eyes dry with his handkerchief again, then asked him when he had arrived home?

"Just a matter of a few hours ago, I was supposed to go to the theatre but there wasn't enough time for me. I knew that you would be here and wanted to see you again as soon as possible, so I made this my priority. You say there was someone shot at the Marinsky Theatre? Was it the Tsarevich or the Tsarina, I notice that they are not here this evening?"

I shook my head. "No, neither of them were at the theatre, just the Tsar and the Grand Duchesses and when the Tsar heard that someone had been shot… I saw them all huddled in the corner of the Royal Box. So, it wasn't them. I think it was someone in the auditorium. After the man was arrested, I think the Tsar went to find out who had been shot and who shot them. They had caught five people that were involved in the shooting and they were all executed without, even, a trial."

When Nicky knew that the royal family was safe, he gave all his attention to me.

"My darling love." He held me away from him and made me look deep into his blue-grey eyes, so that I would know that he really meant what he said. My heart began racing in my breast and I found it difficult to breath, as if I had been running a distance.

"As long as you are safe, that is all that matters to me at this moment in time. I couldn't wait to see you again, Thalia. Not a moment has gone by when I have not been thinking of you, my dear, darling Lia. These past weeks I have held a picture of you in my mind. In fact, you have never been far from my mind since I left St Petersburg. I instructed the conductor to play some Tchaikovsky waltzes, just so that I could take you in my arms and dance with you again. The conductor wasn't very happy about me changing his play list." I laughed then felt his lips on mine. He kissed me and held me against his chest. For a while I just stayed held against him, enjoying his closeness. All of my dreams from the last few months had come true in this moment. We were silent for a while. I could hear his heart beat with a steady thumping in his chest. The heat of his body warmed me as he held me so close. I didn't want to move away. After another brief kiss, he held me away from him as he reached inside his jacket pocket.

"Do you remember me telling you about your birthstone?" he asked eventually.

I nodded, unable to speak.

He reached inside his jacket and showed me a small box. He lifted the lid and there, inside was a gem the size of his thumb nail, on a heavy gold chain. "I found this in Australia. It came from one of the mines that I have shares in. When I saw it polished up, I knew that I had to have it for you."

I fell in love with my birthstone from that moment: the opal. I held the stone, so that I could look at it and watch the play of blues and greens, pinks, mauves and golds, change as I moved it from side to side.

"Do you like it, Lia?"

"Oh, Nicky, it is absolutely beautiful. I love it. It's true what you said about the play of colours being like the material of my debut gown. Thank you."

He took the opal pendant from the box and fastened the golden chain around my neck. I thanked him again. Instead of kissing my hand, I felt his lips gently, briefly, brush mine again causing my heart to do a summersault. Inside the gift box was a note but I wanted to wait and read that in the privacy of my bedroom. I put the box with the note into my reticule. I would look at them later.

Nicky said that we had been outside long enough. People would start to talk, if we didn't return soon. I stood up for us to go back into the ballroom.

His arm slipped around my waist, to stop me leaving. "There is something else that I want to ask you, Lia." He took my hand and kissed it. "I know that we have not known each other very long and we have only met each other a couple of times but you have had such an effect on me already. My darling Lia, I want you to marry me. Not a day went by, in these last months, that I didn't think of you. Lia, darling Lia, will you consent to be my wife?"

Too amazed for words, I just stared at him, scared that I would start crying again and hardly believing what he had just said. I was never an emotional person but since arriving in St Petersburg, all that had changed. This was what I had dreamed of since he held me in his arms and danced with me at my debut. I had kept giving myself reasons why he would not want me but had I convinced myself? No.

"It was meant to be us from the moment I picked you up from the ice to us meeting again at the ballet. Do you believe in fate, my darling?"

I had never thought about it but on reflection it seemed very strange both of our initial meetings.

110

"I know that I will have to ask permission from your grandmother but I thought that I needed to know from you, how you felt about it first… After all I know that we hardly know each other and I am sure that your grandmother and mother will point that out but I don't want to risk anyone else sweeping you off your feet."

I reminded him that he had already said that.

"In fact, we have had only a few meetings," he continued.

I told him that he had said that before as well. He took my hands and kissed my fingers. I could feel him trembling nearly as much as I was.

"When I am with you, I become a jabbering wreck but those few meetings were enough for me to know how I felt about you. That is why I gave you that miniature of me for Christmas, so that you wouldn't forget me, with all of your line of suitors."

I asked him about the Grand Duchess Olga. I explained that some people thought that a marriage had been agreed between them.

He laughed. "How on earth could I be interested in Olga once I had met you? Besides Olga is destined for someone better than me. I think all the girls will be married off to some ruler or other, of another country, to forge alliances. As soon as I saw you sitting on the ice with your hat nearly off your head and your beautiful hair coming loose from your ribbon, I knew that I wanted to spend the rest of my life with you. It must have been fate that we met again. Even if you had been a 'nobody', as I originally thought, it would not have mattered. I know that I will be marrying a very attractive and brave young lady. No woman I know, would have struggled to walk back home with a sprained ankle. They would have had a fit of the vapours if they broke a finger nail. I was smitten with you on that very first meeting. So, will you marry me, my darling Lia?"

"Yes, Nicky," I whispered as if in a dream, "I would love to be married to you." The time would come when I would tell him that I had looked at his miniature painting practically every night and every morning since he had left.

Arm in arm we walked back into the ballroom and Nicky lead us straight over to Grand Mama. Once again Mama was dancing with someone. I think it was Arch Duke Cyril Romanov, the Tsar's uncle. I hoped that she was beginning to realise that her life was not over after all.

"Good evening, Nicholas. We haven't seen you for quite a while?" Grand Mama said, looking at the two of us, grinning like idiots.

"I have been away on business, Aunt Lilia." Was all he said on the subject? As if he had been practicing what he was going to say to her, he took a deep breath, pulled his shoulders back and spoke. "Aunt Lilia, I would like to formally ask for your permission… to have… your granddaughter… Lia's hand in marriage?"

Grand Mama was quiet for a moment considering her reply. "Nicky, I can tell by the look on both of your faces that you are very much in love with each other and I am pleased about that but…"

Before she could say any more, Nicholas butted in, "I know, that we have not spent much time together but not a day has gone past that I haven't thought of Lia."

"Nicky, Lia is still very young…"

"But so was Mama when she married my father," I pointed out; not that that was a very good example.

"Look how that ended, Lia!" Grand Mama reminded me. "You hardly know each other. You need to spend more time together, before you can know if you are both doing the right thing."

She could see the look of disappointment on our faces; my face.

"If and I do say if I did agree," she paused and sighed, "It would have to be a long engagement. I must insist on that and of course you must get Lia's mother's blessing as well." She paused to see the effect on our faces, "At least a two-year engagement."

Mama came back to us on the arm of Arch Duke Cyril, who bowed to her and left us, after briefly nodding to Nicky.

"Nicholas," was all his uncle said.

"Uncle," Nicky replied.

Mama saw our serious faces, "Is anything wrong?" she asked.

Nicky was the first to speak. "I have just asked Lia to marry me, cousin Marguerite. Aunt Lilia …"

"They hardly know each other, Babushka," Grand Mama interrupted. "I have said that they must have time to get to know one another."

"Does that mean, that if we agree to a long engagement, we can announce our engagement tonight?" I asked, my voice, all but pleading, with her.

Grand Mama sighed, "Very well, Nicky, Lia, but I would like to see you tomorrow morning, Nicholas, so that we can discuss this further. You might be my nephew but like Lia, I hardly know anything about you; your prospects…"

Nicky planted a kiss on Grand Mama's cheek, "Cousin Marguerite, do I have your permission?" he asked. Mama nodded.

"Thank you." He kissed Mama's cheek. "I must speak to my cousin the Tsar, to see if he will announce our engagement, this evening, before anyone else whisks my fiancée away."

Nicky took my arm and squeezed it, like an excited child, then lead me over to the dais, where the royal family sat.

The Dowager Empress was the first to speak to us, "Thalia, my dear, you look radiant."

I curtsied to her and the Tsar. Nicky held my hand as he spoke to his cousin, the Tsar. "Nicholas, Your Highness, I have just asked Lia to marry me and she has agreed. Would you do us the great honour of announcing our engagement this evening?"

The Tsar took Nicky's hand and shook it vigorously. "It would be my pleasure, Nicky; Miss Bobrov. Congratulations." He leaned over and placed a kiss on my forehead.

I had been kissed by the Tsar of all of Russia!

When the music stopped, the Tsar took Nicky and me by the hand and announced our engagement to all of those congregated before us. When the applause stopped, Nicky took my hand and we began a waltz around the ballroom floor, with others joining in. I never wanted this evening to end. I wished that I could bottle this evening, this moment, like the perfumes Mr Tominsky had bottled for me.

"I knew Tchaikovsky would come in useful," Nicky whispered in my ear. "Whenever you hear one of his waltzes from now onwards, you will always remember the evening when I asked you to marry me." He placed a gentle kiss on my forehead, setting my pulse racing.

"Of course, we will have to make a visit to my good friend Karl, tomorrow," he said.

For the moment I could not think who Karl might be. "Darling, my good friend Karl Faberge. I shall commission him to pick the finest diamond or diamonds to make into an engagement ring for you. I want the world to know that you have promised to be my wife, especially as it will be a long engagement."

We were both acting like children, laughing as we danced around the floor.

"Are you happy, darling?" he asked me, holding me closer to him, if that was possible.

"Ecstatic, Nicky," was all I could say.

My whole body was quivering with happiness and anticipation that this man, my fiancé, evoked in me. I felt as if I might burst with happiness and pride. Everyone who danced past us, congratulated us.

I still felt that I had to tease him. It was one of the things that had attracted me to him, his sense of fun. "I never realised just how romantic you could be, Your Highness," I whispered.

His arm tightened around me, again, bringing me even closer to his body. I could feel his body heat through the thinness of my gown. "My dear, darling Miss Bobrov, you have no idea just how romantic I can be."

After the announcement of our engagement, we danced every dance together. Now that people knew that we were engaged, no other man came forward to claim a dance with me. I didn't want anyone but Nicky.

Katrina Tomorovsky walked over towards me grinning from ear to ear. "Congratulations, Thalia, Prince Nicholas. I wish you both every happiness." She leaned over and kissed my cheek, "I think that you have put a couple of people's noses out of joint," she whispered to me. "Do you remember those two girls that stood behind you when we were about to be presented?"

I nodded. How could I forget them?

"Well, they are fuming, saying that you had tricked the Prince into proposing to you."

I had never been a subject of jealousy and didn't know what to say or how to deal with it.

Katrina turned to Nicky saying that his announcement was breaking a young girl's heart and pointed to the girl across from us. I could tell just looking at her that she was not happy.

"Do you know her, Nicky?" I asked.

He shrugged his shoulders, "I might have danced with her a couple of times but I have not said more than a dozen words to her. Why?"

"She is claiming that Thalia tricked you into proposing to her."

Nicky laughed loudly and the girl looked over at him. "I don't even know her name."

"It's Nadia Putin," Katrina said.

"They called her name at the ball on Christmas eve," she added.

Nicky turned to go and speak to her but I held his hand and pulled him back to me. "No, Nicky. I know it is just sour grapes. Let's not spoil our special evening," I said as he stood by my side, with his arm possessively around my waist.

He turned and placed another kiss on my forehead, then turned to Katrina. "Thank you for telling us that, Katrina."

Feeling uncomfortable after being the bearer of bad tidings, Katrina again repeated her good wishes then left us.

"Lia, I have never given her any reason to think that I was interested in her. I think the night of the ball I danced with all of the debutants."

I squeezed his hand, "Nicky I believe you. She asked me if I was an 'Alberto'."

I grinned remembering that the poor girl didn't even know that it was the wrong word.

"What on earth is an Alberto?" he asked me.

"She meant an albino because of my hair colour. I told her that if I was, I would have pale eyebrows and lashes and have pink eyes."

He grinned at me. "That is another reason why I love you, Thalia Bobrov. You are intelligent." Again, he kissed my forehead.

Finally, the evening ended. I didn't return to the hotel with Mama and Grand Mama but we followed behind them in Nicky's motor car. We finally came to the hotel where we were staying. Nicky got out and came around to my side of the motor car to help me out. He took me in his arms again. "Are you happy, my darling?" he asked.

"Oh, Nicky, you have no idea how happy I am." He kissed me briefly on the lips, "I looked at your portrait nearly every night and every morning while you were away." I finally admitted to him.

"Only, nearly?" he asked raising his eyebrows quizzically.

"Well, I was told that you might be marrying the Grand Duchess Olga."

"Never. I love my cousins very much but marry one of them after I had met you? Impossible." He laughed and then bent down to brush my lips with his own. Strange feelings, unknown to me, began exploding in my body, leaving me breathless and my heart hammering in my breast.

He kissed me again holding me safe and secure in the shelter of his arms, then saw me inside the hotel, telling me to tell Grand Mama he would be there promptly, at eleven o'clock in the morning.

He waited until the porter had closed the door behind me, before he climbed into his motor car and drove away.

Grand Mama and Mama were both sitting in the lounge of our suite. Grand Mama looked carefully at my face. "I can tell by the way your eyes are sparkling right now that you are very much in love with Nicky, that is why your Mama and I gave our permission for you to get engaged. But I must insist that you have a long engagement for both of your sakes."

Mama nodded in agreement with what Grand Mama had said, "Really, darling, you know nothing of each other but I remember how I felt when your grandfather asked me to marry him. I know how you are feeling right now and I would never want you to lose the magic of this evening."

I tried to smother a yawn but Grand Mama saw. She smiled at me, "Now, my darling, you must go to bed, it is very late and your mother and I need our beauty sleep. Good night, my darling." She kissed my forehead, then I went to Mama.

"I am so happy for you my darling," she said, "I wish you both all the happiness in the world," Mama kissed my cheek. "Good night, my darling."

I couldn't wait to tell Tanya my wonderful news. She clasped her hands together in joy when I did tell her. "My mistress will be a princess soon." She cried, "Oh, Miss Thalia, I am so very happy for you. Who would have thought that morning on the ice would turn out like this?"

Personally, I think that I fell in love with Nicky at the ballet as soon as he kissed my hand and it did seem that the fates did have a role in our relationship.

Once in bed and on my own, I took Nicky's miniature portrait that I had brought with me from my bedroom at Grand Mama's, from the bedside table draw, in my bedroom and placed on the top, where I promised myself it would stay. I looked at his note that he had put in the box with my opal necklace, *To the light of my life. Love Nicky.*

I lit up inside at his words.

# Chapter 13

## The Prince and I

Next morning, although I had had a late night, I was awake before Tanya came in with my breakfast tray at nine o'clock. She opened the bedroom curtains to let the sunshine stream in. I felt that it was the prefect beginning to my first morning of being engaged to my prince. Knowing that Nicky was coming to speak to Grand Mama, I asked Tanya to pick out my most becoming morning gown that I had packed. She took extra special care with my hair. I had some golden hoop earrings and of course I wore my opal pendant from Nicky.

Precisely on the stroke of eleven o'clock, I heard Nicky knocking at the suite door. Impatiently I waited in my room until Grand Mama, summoned me to the lounge. It seemed like ages before I heard the knock on my bedroom door. I hurried out to see Nicky again.

"Thalia, darling, come on in," Grand Mama said as I reached the doorway. I noticed that Mama was there also and Nicky sitting opposite them on one of the sofas. I sat down next to him, where he immediately took my hand and pressed it to his lips.

"Thalia, Nicky and I have been talking. I gave you both permission last night to get engaged but I also stand by what I said that it will be a long engagement. Your mama and I have explained to Nicky about your Mama's hasty marriage to your father and I will not have that happening again, in our family. They didn't know each other well enough before they married."

"But Grand Mama," I tried to interrupt but my grandmother held up her hand to silence me.

"No, Thalia, I will have my say. I can't ever imagine Nicky being anything like your father but I insist that you spend more time with each other. I am sure that you won't mind that." She said looking at us with a twinkle in her eye. "How many times have you actually met each other?"

117

"Five times, Grand Mama," I said quietly.

"Exactly. In five meetings you cannot know someone. Nicky understands this and has agreed to abide by my ruling. With him being a few years older than you, Lia, he is somewhat more sensible. He has told me of his prospects, which I admit are very good and he assures me that he will be able to keep you in a very good manner. I will say that we will review the situation in twelve months, time. In the mean time we will announce the engagement in the newspapers and you may wear Nicky's ring, which he tells me that he wants to take you, as soon as we arrive back in St Petersburg, to go to Monsieur Faberge's to choose a suitable ring. Now are you happy with what I have said? Will you abide by my ruling, Lia?"

I nodded, knowing that it would be no use arguing with my grandmother. She then turned to Nicky, "Nicky, you are more mature than Lia by eight years, I hope that I can trust you to abide by my words and also behave with Lia until your wedding night?"

I blushed to the roots of my hair. Nicky just nodded.

After Mama's marriage being such a disaster, I really did understand their reasoning but it still would not make the waiting any easier or the passage of time go by any faster.

"Then you and Nicky may travel back to St Petersburg together and go to choose your ring," Grand Mama said.

I went over and kissed Grand Mama and my silent Mama, who I presume was embarrassed, because Grand Mama had been openly discussing her disastrous marriage to my father, with Nicky.

Tanya helped me into my coat and hand in hand Nicky and I left the hotel suite. I knew that Tanya would pack my things, properly, before travelling back to St Petersburg on the train with Mama, Grand Mama, Peter, Ava and Anya.

Nicky helped me into his motor car, then slipped into the driver's seat and we headed to back to St Petersburg and Bolshaia Morskaia to the Faberge premises.

The journey back to St Petersburg was the longest time that we had spent together. He told me about his childhood and I told him about mine, also finally explaining why I could not attend the Tchaikovsky concert with him. He was horrified.

"How could he do such a thing?" he fumed; so I told him how things were between my father and me, also the fact that Mama was divorcing him and why.

He held my hand and pulled it to his lips, not taking his eyes off the road. "Darling, I am so sorry." He said, "I can understand why your mother looked so uncomfortable when your grandmother was talking about the divorce. Do you think that your father meant to hit you or your mother?"

"I think he meant to hit Mama but I jumped in the way."

He brought my fingers to his lips again and kissed them. "I have never met such a brave young woman as you, Lia, and I really mean that. Most aristocratic young women are cosseted and spoilt. They rely on their looks to get a husband rather than intelligence. They have never known any form of hardship in their precious little lives. I never wanted a wife that would swoon at the slightest problem or go running back to Mama and Papa. Needless to say, that I never thought I would marry, that is until you fell into my life and I have never been the same since." He kissed my hand again.

It seemed to me that the journey from Moscow to St Petersburg seemed faster travelling by motor car than it did by train or could it be that because of the company the miles just melted away?

When we reached the outskirts of St Petersburg, Nicky drove the car straight to the Faberge premises. He seemed to think that the purchase and wearing of his ring cemented our betrothal.

As soon as the bell over the front door tinkled, Karl Faberge came out with his usual smile on his face.

"Ah, Nicky, what a pleasant surprise and Miss Bobrov." The top buttons of my coat were undone. The winter was nearly over and the temperature was slowly beginning to climb. (It wasn't cold enough for winter clothes but not warm enough for summer clothes.)

"Ah, I see you are wearing your birthstone. What do you think of the opal, Miss Bobrov?" Karl asked, noticing my pendant around my neck.

I told him that I thought it was beautiful.

"Do you know, Miss Bobrov, that no two opals are exactly the same? Similar but never, exactly, the same. Would you like to see some more?" I could tell by his enthusiasm, which was similar to Nicky's, when talking about gems, that he loved working with all of the beautiful stones he used on his premises.

I nodded and he clapped his hands to summon one of his employees. He told him to bring down the trays of opals. Once they were laid out on the counter top on black velvet, he picked them up individually and moved them around in the light to exhibit their rainbow of colours. I was speechless at their beauty as it was displayed in front of me. He explained enthusiastically of the superstitious rumours about opals being unlucky, which he told me was because of their make-up, they tended to shrink and if one was not careful, they could shrink and fall out of their setting. "That is why they are called unlucky, Miss Bobrov. If you want to know more about opals, I would suggest that you ask the Prince, as he owns mines in Australia, where these came from. He probably knows more than I, in fact."

Nicky laughed, "You flatter me, Karl, but enough of opals for now. We have come for something much more important. Miss Bobrov agreed to marry me last night, Karl. My cousin the Tsar made the announcement at the ball in Moscow. I was thinking maybe a diamond solitaire would be best as no other stones can take away the simple beauty of the solitaire, Karl." Nicky looked across at me, "But, of course, Lia, it will be your choice." I nodded and agreed with Nicky on something simple but elegant.

Monsieur Faberge asked if Nicky wanted to choose the stone to be made into a ring or a ring already made? Nicky explained that we wanted to choose the stone.

"Well, Your Highness," Karl teased Nicky, "you have as good knowledge of gems, to match my own, so I will bring you only the very best. Please be seated, both of you and I think this also calls for champagne." Again, he clapped his hands and three members of his staff came. One to take the opals back to the safe, another to bring the glasses of champagne and another to bring the tray of the highest quality, unset, flawless diamonds.

When the champagne arrived, on a silver tray with three crystal glasses, Karl Faberge toasted us, wishing us a long life and happiness together.

Nicky took my hand and squeezed it gently.

Nicky examined all the diamonds which were brought to him, by using Karl Faberge's eye glass. He picked out three stones, all of the same weight of one and a half carats. (He told Karl that he thought anything bigger on my tiny fingers would look garish.) The three diamonds were different shapes, one square, one round and one oval. Nicky asked me to choose one. I had seen square cut diamonds and round ones but rarely seen oval diamonds, so I chose the oval one.

Monsieur Faberge, looked across at Nicky, smiling. "Your future wife seems to have your eye for gems, Nicky. That would have been the one that I would have chosen."

Nicky looked at me proudly. "Yes, Karl, I would have chosen that one as well."

We chose a simple gold setting for my ring, one that would highlight the beauty of the stone, then Karl took my ring size, commenting on how small my fingers were, "Almost the same size as a child's," Karl commented.

When everything was finalised, Karl said that he would get his best man onto the job and that he would telephone Nicky when my ring was ready for collection.

"Er before you go, Nicky, would you like to see the egg that I have designed for your cousin, the Tsar for the Tsarina, for the tercentennial celebrations?" I looked pleadingly at Nicholas and he nodded. Karl took us through the shop towards the back of the building and up to one of his workrooms on the first floor.

The 'Tercentennial egg' as Karl called it was being worked on by Henrik Wigstrom, the work master at Faberge's. The egg was about seven and a half inches high covered in artwork in gold, with miniatures of all eighteen of the Romanov rulers, painted on ivory by another artist, Zuiev. Each miniature was framed by rose cut diamonds. The egg rested on a pedestal, in the form of the three headed Imperial eagle. The whole thing was an exquisite work of art.

"I am sure the Tsar and Tsarina will be impressed by it," I told Karl and Henrik.

"I sincerely hope so," replied Henrik.

I told Karl that I had seen photographs of other eggs that he had been commissioned to do but I never thought that I would be so fortunate to see one in real life.

Finally, Nicky told Karl that we had taken up enough of his and his employees, valuable time and he looked forward to Karl's telephone call to say that my ring was ready for collection. I hoped that it would not take long. I wanted the world to know that I was promised to Nicky.

We left the Faberge premises and Nicky drove us to a restaurant for lunch. We were shown to a secluded little table away from the rest of the diners. We sat holding hands away from the distant gaze of on-lookers. Already word had got out in Russian society of our engagement.

"Did you read my note, the one that I put in with your necklace, Lia?"

"You called me the 'light of your life', why that, Nicky?" I asked him.

"Ah, well, that fateful day when you fell over on the ice and your hat was nearly knocked off. Your beautiful hair came loose from your ribbon; your hair was like a beautiful light in the greyness of that day. That is how I saw you, like a light coming into my life, Lia."

I laughed at his explanation. "I must have looked a frightful sight then."

He held my hand across the table, "Never. I knew there and then that I wanted to see more of you and even marry you."

"But I might just have been only a …"

He interrupted me. "Lia, I have told you that it wouldn't have mattered to me whether you were a Princess or a scullery maid. Unlike, the majority of Russian aristocracy, titles and positions mean nothing to me." His face changed suddenly. "Why didn't you tell me before that you stayed at home because your father had hit you, Lia?" he asked, changing the subject.

"Because I was too embarrassed. I looked a terrible mess."

"Yes, darling, and after your parents' unhappy marriage, I can understand your mother and grandmother's trepidation, although, I want you to know that what your father did to your mother was despicable, in my opinion. I also think that you are the bravest young woman I know, what with walking back home with your sprained ankle, the incident outside the Winter Palace and also your father hitting you. You have never made a fuss, no matter what has happened to you. I think that is one of the reasons that I love you, Thalia Marguerite Titania Bobrov." He kissed my hand. "I am looking forward to seeing that ring on your finger to tell everyone that you have agreed to be my wife.

"But, darling, your grandmother is right, we do hardly know each other and I want to know all about you and you should also want to know more about me, Lia."

I assured him that I did want to know more about him but for the moment I was just happy to bask in his love.

Nicky looked around to see if there was anyone within hearing distance. Once satisfied that we were outside of anyone's hearing, he began whispering.

"There are certain things, Lia, that I cannot tell you about at the moment but I can tell you that besides buying jewels for Karl, I also work for the Dowager Empress."

I told him that I already knew about it. "Not this you don't, darling. I help the Dowager Empress as an…" he hesitated, trying to think of the right word without giving too much away, "I work as an… Ambassador for her."

This confused me a little, surely if he was an ambassador, he would be working for the Tsar. I asked him why he wasn't employed by the Tsar.

"The Tsar has other things on his mind at the moment like the celebrations." He replied simply.

"Does the Tsar know about what you are doing, Nicky?"

"No, darling, and he must never know, well not for the time being. You know that there is a lot of unrest in our country. My cousin knows about it but cannot believe that he is the main reason for this. Don't get me wrong, I love and respect my cousin but … I have already said too much, my darling. You must forget this conversation, Lia. You can tell no one about this. Not even your grand mama and mama. Do I have your word on this?"

I nodded solemnly. "Can I ask just one thing, Nicky?" He nodded. "Were you away on business for yourself or the Dowager Empress after Christmas?"

"Nothing would have kept me away from you otherwise," he said rather diplomatically.

"When you gave me my opal pendant, I thought you had been to Australia to one of your mines and saw it."

"Karl had it in his stock, which I had brought from Australia some time ago. Before I left, just after Christmas, I asked him to make it into a pendant for you."

As we sat in that restaurant, with all the people watching, we talked of many things, one of them being another Tchaikovsky concert the following week. We decided that we would attend it. "Come hell or high water," we said in unison and laughed.

Two days later, Nicky came to Grand Mama's house unexpectedly. I was still upstairs in my room reading by the fire. Igor knocked on my door, which Tanya answered. He whispered something to Tanya, then left. Tanya came over to me and handed me Nicky's calling card. Just seeing that started my heart thumping wildly in my breast. I took a brief look in my dressing table mirror before going downstairs and into the library, where I was told he was waiting for me. I entered the library to see him standing by the fireplace looking up at a portrait of my grandfather. I ran to his arms and he kissed me on my lips. I loved the feel of his soft lips on mine. I asked him what he was doing there, as he was not expected until that evening.

"I have been on a little shopping trip and I wanted to show you my purchases." He took me over to the winged fireside chair and asked me to sit. Then he went down onto one knee and produced from his inside pocket a box with the Faberge name printed in gold on the lid. Nicky opened the box and inside, nestled amongst black velvet was a Faberge egg. I looked at the beautiful creation of Karl's with Lilly of the Valley done in pearls and enamels. Next to the egg was the stand in gold. It truly was a beautiful work of art.

I just stared at the egg in awe. I had heard about Faberge eggs and I had, seen one in the making but I never thought that I would own one.

I told Nicky that it was beautiful, "How did you know that Lilly of the Valley was one of my favourite flowers?"

A cheeky grin came to his lips. "Oh, I asked here and there. Are you going to open it up?" he asked.

I carefully took the egg from the box and opened it up. Inside on a tiny dark blue velvet cushion was my oval, diamond engagement ring.

"I wanted to do this right, as when I asked you to marry me, it was all a little rushed and muddled, so…" He took the ring from the tiny cushion, "Thalia Bobrov, will you consent to be my wife, when your grandmother thinks it is time for us to name a date for our marriage?"

I nodded. This was the sort of proposal all girls dreamt about. Nicky placed the ring on my finger and holding my hand in his, kissed me. "You have a child's hands and on reflection I wondered whether the stone might look too big on you but it looks perfect. Anyone can see it on your finger and will know that you have agreed to be my wife. I don't care how long it takes, we will be married, Lia." He promised me. He held me within his arms and kissed me, setting fireworks exploding in my body again.

I just wanted to stay within the circle of his arms, enjoying his closeness, smelling his familiar cologne of sandalwood.

I was beginning to know him better and as I saw more of him, I knew that he did bear some resemblance to the Tsar but Nicky's chin was stronger and his eyes were bluer but there was something else about him that was so totally different from the Tsar and I couldn't quite put my finger on it. I gave a mental shrug. It didn't matter, not for the time being.

As the weather was becoming warmer we often walked arm in arm through Grand Mama's gardens. Nicky spoke of his life with the Dowager Empress who was the Tsarina at the time and his time he spent with the Tsarevich (now Tsar) and the things they used to do together in their youth. It seemed that although Nicky had lost his parents he was happy in his time spent with the 'Royals' as he called them Nicky told me of his home in St Petersburg called Chesminsky

Palace, but I could tell from the change in his voice that it was his home in Tallin that he loved the most. His face came alive as he spoke of it, telling me that when we were eventually married, he would like us to move to Tallin to live, keeping his home in St Petersburg for the times when we would spend in the capital. We would walk arm in arm through local parks where he wanted to 'show me off to the residents'.

When I was not with Nicky I would walk in the gardens of Grand Mama's. I often looked up at the tall marble statues and wondered if they represented anyone in particular like Zeus or any other Greek gods or maybe famous people in Russian history. My favourite pastime, when I was alone, was taking some bread from Grand Mama's kitchens, (The staff there were beginning to know me by now), and feed the ducks. I loved to watch them as they waddled along the paths or swimming in the many ponds with their fountains peacefully tinkling. Sometimes the ducks would use the fountains to bathe in shaking their feathers when they had finished. They were such funny little creatures and as time went by, whenever they saw me, they would waddle over to me because they knew I always brought them food.

Nicky and I saw each other every day leading up to the Tchaikovsky concert. I wore the original gown that I was going to wear, the first time that I was supposed to have gone to the Tchaikovsky concert.

Nicky collected me from Grand Mama's in his motor car and we drove to the hall. People dressed in evening attire, poured into the concert hall. I think that I was more excited than most. This would be the first time for me in a concert hall and although the orchestra at the ballet had been excellent, it had been spoilt by the noise of the dancers. This time it was, purely, just the music and also, I was wearing Nicky's ring. We were now officially a couple as Grand Mama had had our engagement announced in all of the Russian newspapers the following day after the ball. I briefly wondered whether my father might have seen it in Smolensk, then tossed the thought to one side as totally irrelevant.

We sat in our seats and waited for the lights to go down. Nicky took hold of my hand in his and held it throughout the concert, sometimes fiddling with the ring he had given me. Once the concert began, I closed my eyes and let my mind drift away with the music. Once or twice, I felt Nicky looking at me and I opened my eyes to find him smiling. During the interval he commented. "You are really enjoying this aren't you my Lia?"

I told him that I found the music wonderful and inspiring. Magical. I could imagine the ballet dancers gliding across the stage, without the sound of their pointe's, to spoil the pleasure. It made me want to dance or maybe ice skate to such beautiful music.

"My darling, you are an incurable romantic. That is another one of the many reasons I love you," he said. I asked him, what the other reasons were. "You are brave, you are beautiful, you are kind and you love life. I think one of the main reasons is you have a great enthusiasm about everything."

"I suppose being a country girl for the first seventeen years of my life then being brought into the glittering circles of Russian society, I would have a great enthusiasm for everything that was happening to me."

We went back into the hall for the second half of the performance and once again I was transfixed by the music. I was sad when the concert came to an end. I could have listened to Tchaikovsky's music for hours. Nicky told me that he would play for me one day.

I hadn't known that Nicky played a musical instrument. That was something else that he hadn't told me but we were trying to cram all our lives into a matter of days.

He told me that he had learnt to play piano as a boy and when his parents had died, the Dowager Empress, who was the Tsarina at that time, had insisted that he continued with his piano tuition.

"At my home, the Kadriorg Palace at Tallin, I have a music room, where I have a grand piano, which I play whenever I can. Once all of this is over and the Royal family have gone to their Palace at Lavardia for the summer, I shall invite you and your family to Tallin. It's on the coast. It is a beautiful home, which I hope you will come to love as much as I do."

When, we were in the car, driving home, Nicky told me more of the history of Kadriorg Palace. It had been built originally for Catherine the first, by Peter the Great and had been designed by an Italian architect from Rome. Nicky told me that the style of the Palace was Roman Baroque but he said that the grounds and fountains were modelled after the palace at Versailles. "It's an ideal place to spend the summer months swimming in the sea and lazing around on the beach." I told Nicky that I had never seen the sea and it sounded like heaven. I was looking forward to seeing it. Coming from the centre of the country I had only swum in lakes and rivers near my home in Smolensk.

"The royal family used to use it as their summer retreat, several years ago, then, they found Lavardia and decided to use that as their summer retreat. Now Kadriorg Palace is mine; or should I say, it will be ours when we get married. It really is a beautiful place." He told me enthusiastically.

I grinned at him, "Well if it was good enough for the royal family, then I am sure that it will be acceptable to us."

Nicky took my hand and brought it to his lips, "I can't wait for you to see it; to see what you think of it."

Being the fiancée of Prince Nicholas Ivanov, we were never short of invitations, either Nicky and myself or Mama and Grand Mama. Everyone wanted to be associated with the family of the Tsar, however tenuous.

The main part of the tercentennial celebrations was that the Royal family undertook a tour of, old, Russian towns, following in the footsteps of the first Romanov, three hundred years before. During the tour they travelled to Nizhniy Novgorod, where Nicky's parents had been shot when Nicky was just 14 years old. From Nizhniy Novgorod the royal family boarded a steamer to travel down the river Volga. Throughout the tour the royal family were met by cheering crowds. The celebrations were always well received by the Russians, who, for a short time, seemed to forget all that had happened before; the riots, the mass murders, poor living conditions, poor wages. From sailing down the Volga, the royal family transferred to a train that led to the final celebrations in Moscow, on 24 May 1913.

By the time the royal train had reached Moscow, we too had all travelled to the city for the final celebrations. Grand Mama, her maid Ava, Mama and Anya, Tanya and myself, all travelled to Moscow a few days before the arrival of the royal family, Peter Abramovich had taken care of all of the travel arrangements, making sure that we had sufficient food and drink on the journey and comfortable rooms at our journey's end. Nicky was travelling with his aunt, the Dowager Empress, promising me that he would meet me at the Grande Ball.

Taking advantage of our free time, before the arrival of the Tsar's entourage, Tanya and I went sightseeing. Although, thoughts of the bloodshed outside the Winter Palace had subsided, being amongst the crowds in Moscow, Tanya and I held tightly, on to each other, scared that we might get separated, as we toured the sights of the great city. St Petersburg in my eyes was understated elegance, whereas Moscow was colourful and vibrant, from the brightly coloured onion shaped domes of St Basils Cathedral, to the Red Square, a massive paved open space in front of the Kremlin Palace. Another day, we went on a tour around the Assumption Cathedral, with its gold topped domes and beautiful paintings on the walls and the pillars inside the building. Tanya had never seen so much gold and we both stood and looked in awe at the wonderful art work. To make our day out special, I took Tanya to a little coffee house before we went back to our rooms to prepare for the evening festivities. The little coffee house was busy with the well-to-do of Moscow, at first Tanya was a little apprehensive to be seen in such a place, that would normally only be frequented by 'her betters' as she put it. When one of the waitresses walked up to our table with a sweet trolley filled with beautiful cakes and pastries, all thoughts of class were forgotten as she picked a cake to eat.

It was the perfect end of our day of sightseeing together and as we travelled back to our rooms, Tanya told me that it had been the best day of her life and for once our outing together hadn't ended in some disaster or other.

I found it hard, now, to think that my fall when I was skating was a disaster. If I hadn't gone skating that day and fallen over, then I might never have met Nicky, I thought, then reminded myself that I would still have met him when we went to the ballet. The fall had just hastened the inevitable meeting.

We returned to our rooms by mid-afternoon in time for me to rest before the ball that evening and also to take time for bathing and Tanya to create another new hairstyle for me. Considering she had never been a ladies' maid before, Tanya's hair styles had always been very creative. Tanya told me that because of my unusual hair colouring, it cried out to have unusual styles as well. Even the Dowager Empress and the Tsarina had complimented me on my hairstyles, when we had the occasion to meet. Being Nicky's fiancée, I was almost part of the royal family now, which I wasn't sure would be a good thing or a bad thing in the long run.

A few weeks before we had travelled to Moscow, Grand Mama had called on the services of Madam Brisac and her team of seamstresses to provide us all with new gowns for the grand state ball at the Kremlin Palace in Moscow. Every time Madam made a new gown for me, I was impatient for the time to come, so that I could wear it.

I had had a gown of pale silver-grey silk made for me and again I wore my diamonds. The Kremlin Palace was a magnificent building. I think it was even more magnificent than the Winter Palace in St Petersburg. It had gold leaf on the pillars, ceilings, beautiful marble floors and myriads of crystal chandeliers lighting all of the rooms. Outside the Palace, crowds of people were trying to catch a glimpse of the royal family in all of their finery, as well as their guests.

Nicky was waiting inside for us. I could tell by the look on his face that he approved of how I looked and felt a warm glow radiate from my stomach. He immediately took my arm and we walked behind Mama and Grand Mama into the ballroom.

"My cousins want to meet you, Lia, once the royal family has entered and settled down, I am to take you to greet the Grand Duchesses and the Tsarevich."

My heart began to thump rapidly in my chest. I was to be under scrutiny once again, from members the royal family, not just the Tsar and Tsarina this time but their children. Would I be good enough for their cousin, in their eyes? I know that I had the Dowager Empresses approval but now that it was known that I was engaged to Prince Nicholas Ivanov, the Tsar's cousin, I would be stared at and scrutinised by everyone who was anyone in the higher realms of the Russian Aristocracy. I had to be on my very best behaviour to give a good impression to all concerned. I wondered what they would think of me. In the months that I had been in St Petersburg under Mama's and Grand Mama's instruction, no longer was I the scared little country mouse. I walked around with my head high, with more confidence and poise than that little country mouse in Smolensk would ever have.

Twin doors at the far end of the ballroom opened and the royal family entered. First came the Tsar and Tsarina, followed by the young Tsarevich who still looked very pale but he walked proud and alone behind his parents, followed by the four Grand Duchesses, Olga, the oldest first, followed by Tatiana, then Maria and finally, Anastasia, the youngest of the girls.

The Tsar stood and gave a speech about the three hundred years of the reign of Romanov, to which everyone applauded. Once the speech was over the Royal family took their seats and the music began for dancing. Nicky took my arm and we walked up to the dais. All of the time, as we walked toward them, I could feel the eyes of the Grand Duchesses looking at me, scrutinising my every move and assessing whether I would be suitable to marry into the family. We reached the bottom of the dais and stopped. I did my best curtsey to them all, as Nicky introduced me to his cousins. I don't think they liked me, on sight. They all looked down on me as if they thought that I was not good enough for their cousin. I was relieved when my hand was taken and I looked up to find the Tsar looking at me. The Father of Russia was actually holding my hand.

"Miss Bobrov, welcome to our family." Again, I curtseyed low and thanked him. "Have you set a date for your wedding?" he asked.

"Aunt Lilia insists that we have a long engagement to enable us to get to know one another better," Nicky said.

The Tsar threw back his head and laughed, "A very sensible proposal, I must say. Well, Thalia, if I may call you that? I have four young ladies that would love to be asked to be your bridesmaids, that is, when you and my cousin decide on a date."

I told the Tsar that I would be honoured to have the Grand Duchesses as my bridesmaids. From the way they were looking at me, I didn't think that they would be hammering at my door to become my bridesmaids. I think that they looked at me like the country mouse. I did not mind, it was true. Until six months previous, I had never even left Smolensk, travelled by train or motor car, stayed in hotel and never drank champagne. I suppose, to them, I was a country mouse. I had only ever read about such a life style before this.

Nicky introduced me to his cousins, firstly the Tsarevich Alexei. I curtsied to him, then Olga, who I curtsied to, next came Titania, Maria and finally Anastasia. I curtsied to them all but knew that they would never become close friends with me, even if I did have them as my bridesmaids. If they had any real feelings of friendship for me, I would have expected them to be excited and asking to see my engagement ring and would want to discuss the gowns for the wedding but they didn't.

Nicky bowed to the royal family and again I curtsied, then he swept me onto the ballroom floor. Nicky asked me what I thought of 'our cousins'. I told him that I didn't think they approved of me.

"My darling Lia, they are such a close-knit family, the girls have no friends, except for each other and I don't care whether they approve of you or not, I am still going to marry you." He lowered his voice and whispered in my ear, "Even if the Tsar himself didn't approve of you, I would still marry you."

"But he does approve of me, doesn't he?" I asked, wondering that if the Tsar did oppose our marriage, what would happen?

"Yes, he does and so does the Dowager Empress and they are all that really matters," he said. We walked back to Mama and Grand Mama and stood talking about my introduction to the Grand Duchesses and the Tsarevich. Grand Mama asked what they had said to me but I tried avoiding the answer. I didn't want to spoil the evening with negative thoughts or feelings.

It wasn't until the following morning, after I had had breakfast, dressed and gone to see Mama and Grand Mama that I told them about my meeting with the Grand Duchesses. I told them that I felt like an insect under a magnifying glass, they didn't like or approve of me.

Grand Mama said the same as Nicky, that the family was very secular and allowed very few people to enter into their close family circle. Apparently if Nicky hadn't been orphaned and had the then, Empress of Russia, take him under her wing and bring him up along with her own son. It was doubted that Nicky would be so close to the royal family.

"The thing is, my darling," said my grandmother, "they never go anywhere to meet people of their own age, so for years the girls have had to rely on each other for friendship."

I said that if that was the case then I would have expected them to want to get to know someone new.

"One would expect that but I believe that the Tsarina keeps a tight rein on her daughters and son. I don't think that she wants her daughters to have friends. They are never allowed outside of the palace or if they are they are with either their tutor or a member of the palace staff and of course Father Rasputin."

"But that man is vile. He is revolting with his lecherous looks. I cannot understand the hold that he seems to have over the royal family," I said remembering the way he looked at me at my debut. It made my skin crawl.

"Neither does anyone else, even my sister but the Tsarina will not have him banished from court."

I remembered items that I had read about him in the papers and seen on flyers circulating around the country, speculating some tie between Rasputin and the Tsarina and the Grand Duchesses; surely, they couldn't be true?

"Whatever the reasons, I doubt that the Grand Duchesses will ever be hammering on your door to become your bridesmaids or friends, Lia. You must accept that and move on with your life. I am sure that their attitude to you is nothing personal, darling."

# Chapter 14

## The Summer of 1913

After the ball at the Kremlin Palace, the royal family retreated to their summer palace at Livadiya and for a few short months the Russian aristocracy was disbanded to go their own way until the middle of September. Nicky had invited us all to Tallin, on the coast and to Kadriorg Palace, Nicky's home away from St Petersburg. Grand Mama and Mama were driven by Peter Abramovich, following behind Nicky and me in Nicky's motor car. The rest of our staff, our personal maids, travelled behind us in another car driven by Nicky's man Rudolph.

Nicky had inherited Kadriorg Palace five years earlier when he reached his majority. I could tell by the way Nicky spoke about Kadriorg Palace that he loved his home and was very proud of it. It was over two hundred miles from St Petersburg and took us over five hours to get there but the journey was worth it. As far as the eye could see were green meadows and summer flowers. The sky was a beautiful blue with tiny clouds gently moving in the summer breeze. About half an hour before we drove through the large, wrought iron gates leading to Kadriorg Palace, we could see the sun glittering on the sea. My heart was fit to burst with joy at seeing the sea. I had never been to the coast before. The only water I had seen were rivers and lakes but nothing as breath-taking as the sea. It was a beautiful summer's day and the sun was still high in the sky when we drove into the Palace grounds. To either sides of the long drive way were beautifully manicured gardens with fountains playing musically in the quiet of the summer afternoon. At the end of the drive was a beautiful three-story building painted in russet, cream and white.

Nicky looked across at me as he pulled the car to a halt in front of the building, "Welcome to my home, Lia. Does it meet with your approval? While your mother and grandmother rest after the journey, could I take you on a tour of the palace and grounds?"

I told him that I would love to. I felt as impatient to see all the house and grounds, just as I was always impatient whenever Auguste Brisac was commissioned to make me a new gown, I was impatient to wear it.

"Once we are married, I would like us to spend most of our time here, away from the troubles of St Petersburg," he told me as we walked arm in arm to the front door that had been opened, by a footman, as soon as we stepped from the car. I could imagine our children running around the grounds in the summer. Nicky told me that at the back of the building were more formal gardens, a lake and a walk down to the beach.

The main entrance hall was massive; two-stories high, with two huge tiled fire places on opposing walls, I imagined that these kept the impressive hallway warm when the cold weather took over, welcoming any visitors in from the cold. I could also imagine spending Christmas here with a massive Christmas tree in the centre decorated with tiny candles, garlands and beautiful ornaments and on opposing walls the fires in the large fireplaces would be lit. The hallway was painted in dove grey and white with touches of gold leaf. I looked up at the ceiling above us. It was magnificent with a beautiful Florentine-like painting in its centre. Although there was a lot of stucco, decorative plasterwork, on the fireplaces and ceiling, it had the feeling of understated elegance.

Rudolph showed Grand Mama and Mama to their rooms with their maids following behind, to unpack, the trunks, for the holiday. Nicky said that he would take me on a tour of the palace and then he would show me to my room. Tanya was already shown to my room, by Rudolph so that she could unpack my things. We hadn't brought massive trunks of evening gowns with us, although we were to stay for a month, we had packed understated clothes, this was meant to be a holiday and a well-earned rest after the hectic lifestyle of St Petersburg season.

Arm in arm Nicky took me through the downstairs rooms, seeking my approval for what would eventually be our home together; we walked through the library, then the drawing room and into the music room, which housed his beautiful grand piano. I asked Nicky if he would play for me but he was eager to show me the rest of his home, first, saying that he would probably play for us that evening, after dinner. Once we had seen all the downstairs rooms, we went out of some floor to ceiling glass double doors from the beautiful elegant lounge that opened on to the rear of the palace and a full-length terrace. We walked, from the terrace, down some steps to the rear gardens, through a small wood, towards the lake where there was an island, housing a brilliant white gazebo. From there we walked down the pathways and shortly after, came to the beach. I thought, what a wonderful home it would be for us and our children. I couldn't imagine me ever wanting to return to St Petersburg after living at Kadriorg Palace.

We stood together on the beach, looking out to sea, when Nicky turned and took me in his arms, kissing me deeply and longingly, melting my insides so that I quivered with his touch. "Do you think you could love this place as much as I do, Lia?" he asked holding me tightly.

He awoke feelings in me that I had never known existed; a feeling of wanting more but what 'more' was there?

"Oh, Nicky, Kadriorg is just perfect," I replied. He stopped kissing me and left me leaning, breathlessly, against his chest. My legs were quivering so much that I nearly collapsed there on the sand, if it hadn't been for Nicky holding me, tightly, against him.

"Darling Lia, do you realise what you are doing to me?" he whispered into my hair. I wanted him to kiss me again and lifted my lips to his but he held me away from him. "No, darling, I can't kiss you again otherwise it will be my undoing. Let me just hold you like this for a while, while I try to compose myself enough for us to walk back home."

I didn't understand what he meant by his 'undoing' but I know that I liked the way he made me feel with his kisses. I wanted to ask him what he meant but thought maybe it would not be a suitable question for a young unmarried woman.

After he had planted a playful kiss on the end of my nose, he pulled my arm through his and we made our way back to the building. He took me up the beautiful winding marble staircase to the second floor where I saw portraits of Nick's family. Nicky looked a lot like his father, but I could see some features of his mother who bore a resemblance to the Dowager Empress and Grand Mama. Nicky told me that she was tall like the Dowager Empress and had a very loving, caring nature. Nicky told me that his mother took after the Dowager Empress in height. From the portraits Nicky took my arm again and showed me my bedroom, which had floor to ceiling windows that opened out onto an upper terrace overlooking the rear gardens where there were more waterfalls playing. My room was done in golds and creams with golden curtains to the windows and hanging from the massive four-poster bed. The walls were done in a cream with gold flocking. On the wall opposite the windows was a massive cream marble fireplace laid with logs but not lit as the weather was so warm.

I told him that my bedroom was beautiful, then asked him where his room was, "Darling, as far from you as possible, otherwise I wouldn't be held responsible for my actions." He laughed, "I am not sure how I am going to behave like a gentleman when I know that you are so near me."

He had said the words that I had felt in that moment in his arms, on the beach. "Oh, Nicky, I wish we didn't have to wait to be married," I said.

"I know, darling, but we must abide by Aunt Lilia's ruling. The waiting will make it all the more worthwhile when we finally do get married. We must be patient however difficult that may be."

Over the weeks there were several occasions where we would kiss until we were both breathless, and Nicky told me that he needed to 'compose' himself before returning to my family.

Our month in Tallin and Kadriorg Palace was wonderful. Tallin was a beautiful, medieval, walled city, dominated by red tiled rooves. It's quaint cobbled streets and Gothic buildings looked like something out of ancient paintings. The main square had shops and restaurants and twice a week housed a farmer's market. The struggles of the rest of Russia seemed so very far away. It hadn't been tainted by the Russian politics of Moscow and St Petersburg. Nicky proved to be good with his people and wherever he went he took time to stop and speak to them. I thought that when Nicky and I moved to Tallin, I would want to make it a permanent home away from St Petersburg and away from the riots. Although we hadn't been affected much by the troubles of our country, I was always on edge whenever I saw crowds of people as it brought back memories of the massacre outside the Winter Palace that Tanya and I had seen.

Mama spent a lot of her time writing letters and reading books from Nicky's vast library. Grand Mama spent her time reading and playing card games on her own. Even the servants were more relaxed at Tallin and I noticed that Tanya and Nicky's man Rudolph spent quite a lot of time together when not in attendance on Nicky or me. One day I caught Tanya laughing at something Rudolph had said, then when she saw me watching, she blushed to the roots of her hair. Peter Abramovich and his wife, Ava, Grand Mama's personal maid, spent more time together. It was a wonderful and relaxed time which I enjoyed I think more than most. There were not the restrictions of St Petersburg society. Nicky and I used to walk around the large park attached to Kadriorg Palace, holding hands or arm in arm. We also went horse riding covering more of the grounds surrounding the palace. Nicky didn't have vast stables and he told me that he didn't get much chance to exercise the horses that he had, spending so much more of his time in St Petersburg, than in Tallin. He complimented me on my horsemanship as we often took two of his four horses out for exercise. The following time we went out riding we would take the other two horses. I told Nicky about the time when I saw my father in the distance, who I thought was watching me, while out riding on my own at home. I jumped a high fence to try and impress him but when I looked, again he was nowhere to be found. I told Nicky that at the time I still hoped that my father would accept me. As our horses were so close, he stretched across and took my hand, kissing it. "His loss was my gain, Lia. I can't see why he should be so against you because you are female, it wouldn't really matter to me. All children deserve love and kindness whatever their sex." he told me.

"I wasn't the son he expected to inherit his lands and title when my father died," I explained.

"It still wouldn't matter to me, any more than titles and positions bother me."

We turned the horses to the beach and galloped along the water line as the beautiful summer sunshine set the sea sparkling before us.

We read the newspapers every morning, that told us more of what was happening in Russia and St Petersburg and discussed what was happening. Although there had been a feeling of goodwill during the Tercentennial celebrations, now they were over, the riots had begun again but not in the magnitudes before the celebrations. Nicky had said that he was concerned for the state of our country and that there were murmurings of war but there was nothing concrete, as yet, so we ignored them, not wanting to spoil the peace and harmony of our first holiday together. Once or twice Nicky had meetings with his grounds staff but he kept those meetings brief, wanting to be back with me as soon as possible.

When we wanted a moment alone, Nicky would take the little whitewashed rowing boat and row us across the lake to the island with the gazebo, away from prying eyes, where he kissed me until we were both breathless and wanting 'more'. We would sit down, on one of the benches and talk for a while about our hopes for the future, not just for us but for our country. I told Nicky that I hoped Mama would find someone to love her and take care of her. We discussed Mama's divorced state and talked of ways for her to maybe meet someone that would love her and treat her right. Finally, we would get back in the boat again and he would row us back to the shore. We went swimming, in the sea, then lying on large fluffy towels on the sand to dry off in the sun. During this time Nicky told me more about his mines in South Africa and Australia. He told me stories of how the miners in Australia lived in rooms underground to keep them cool from the heat of the Australian day and promised me that he would take me there one day to see the mines, where my birthstone came from. He told me that it was Karl Faberge, whose real name was Peter Karl Faberge, that taught him all about jewels and gemstones, how to pick stones; which were of good quality and excellent quality and inferior quality; how to look for flaws or occlusions in the stones. In the evenings after dinner, we would play cards or Nicky would play to us on his grand piano. I was impressed at how accomplished he was; even Grand Mama said so. He also had a gramophone which he played records on and we would dance, sometimes he would ask Mama or Grand Mama to partner him. There was a lot of laughter, when we would play cards or chess and a lot of childish cheating. It was a wonderful month and I was hoping that Grand Mama might change her mind and say that we could marry sooner but the day before we were to return to St Petersburg, Nicky had a message from the Dowager Empress and he told us that he would have to go away again for a while, once we had returned to St Petersburg. I didn't like to ask him anything, as I knew that it must have been the message from the Dowager Empress, which had courted such an action.

The time came for us to pack up and return home. I felt a lump in my throat as I took my final look at what would eventually be my new home. In the month that we had been staying at Tallin, I had fallen in love with the palace nearly as much as I had fallen in love with Nicky. Several times we had walked into the town itself, which was only a short distance from the Palace. People had spoken to Nicky with respect but with a friendliness that must have been built up over the last six years of his ownership. This kind of mutual respect was never seen by anyone in St Petersburg, then I remembered what the Dowager Empress had said, about how respected Nicky was by his staff and the towns people. Everywhere we went, he introduced me as his fiancé. I had smiled and said hello to them all, interested in who they were and what they did. Soon these would be my people, I reminded myself. Being Nicky's fiancée, I felt that I was well received and because of the interest I took in 'Nicky's people', I think they liked me as well. I hoped that they did.

We travelled back to St Petersburg in the three cars, the same as we did on our outbound journey to Tallin but the atmosphere in Nicky's car was very different. For the major part of the journey, he still held my hand but neither of us spoke much, both caught up in our own thoughts. Finally, I had to ask Nicky what was on my mind, "When do you have to leave, Nicky?"

"More or less, as soon as I have taken you home."

"Do you know where you are going or how long you will be away?"

As we were behind the other two cars, Nicky pulled the car to a halt. "Darling I don't know when I will be back, this time." I tried to stifle the sob that rose in my throat.

"Lia, there is a lot more going on in Russia than is reported in the newspapers. There is a lot of disgusting things written about Rasputin; you remember him from your debut?" I nodded. How could I ever forget those cold fish-like eyes raking over my body?

"The Tsarina is not well loved by her people and there has been disgusting flyers circulated depicting her and Rasputin and also the young Grand Duchesses. I won't say any more but in certain quarters some people think that she is a spy."

"Oh, Nicky, never!" I cried. "I know that I don't really know her or the Grand Duchesses but I still can't imagine that." His thumb stroked the back of my hand sending shivers throughout my body.

"No, darling, neither can I but our opinions don't matter one jot. People say that the Tsar should divorce her but I can see, even after all these years of marriage, that they are still very much in love with each other. I can't say too much, my darling, but the Dowager Empress wants me to try and get support for the Tsar from other countries if we go to war, which seems imminent."

"Can't the war be stopped, I mean it hasn't started yet, surely someone can do something?"

"No, my darling," he said kissing my fingers, "because the one person that could stop it won't listen to any reason from me or the Duma, his ministers or even the Dowager Empress, his mother."

"Are you talking about the Tsar?"

"Yes, and if anyone knew of this conversation, I could be hung or put to the firing squad for treason. You must never repeat a word of this to anyone, do you understand, my darling?"

I nodded.

"I know you must be upset and scared, Lia, but you are a brave person. The bravest and strongest person I have ever known and you are going to have to be brave now, braver than ever before. I don't know how long I will be away and it will be difficult for me to send you any letters but, darling, know that wherever I am or whatever I do, I will always hold you here in my heart." He held my hand against his beating chest. His heart was pounding strongly against his ribs, matching mine. I felt that he was as scared for me, as I was for him.

"I wish we could get married now, Nicky, so that we could have just one night together."

"So do I, my darling, but one night with you would never be enough for me." He kissed me as he had that first day on the beach at Tallin. I responded with as much passion as him, until we were both breathless. Tears were choking me, my throat ached like a great lump of stone had lodged in it and wouldn't move, only with the release of my tears and I just had to let them flow. I snuggled up close to him, sobbing against his chest. He let me cry for a while, until my sobs subsided a little, then he dried my eyes. "You are the light of my life, Lia Bobrov, and you are a brave and courageous woman, I want you to look at that miniature of me every night and every morning and know that I will be thinking of you wherever I am."

We travelled the rest of the journey talking about our dreams for our life together as man and wife. His dreams were my dreams and it seemed that my dreams were his. I didn't ask him whether his life was in danger, although I thought it and I doubted very much that he would be honest with me anyway.

Finally, he drew his motor car up outside Grand Mama's. He gave me one final kiss and told me to be brave and he would write to me when he could.

I told him to wait before he drove off. I ran into Grand Mama's and up to my bedroom, where I picked out one of the photographs from my debut and took it down to him waiting patiently in the car.

"Keep this with you, Nicky, and look at it every night and every morning, just as I will be looking at your miniature."

He looked at the photograph and smiled. "I will, my darling, knowing that you will be doing the same."

He told me that he had to leave to see the Dowager Empress. He blew me a kiss and mouthed, "I love you."

I cried after him to 'stay safe', as he drove away.

I ran straight upstairs, flung myself down on my bed and cried, until I could cry no more. How could life be so cruel as to give us a whole month together, then part us for, God knows how long. I felt that life was grossly unfair.

# Chapter 15
## Biding My Time

When Mama knocked on my door to tell me that dinner would be served shortly, I told her that I was not hungry and had a headache.

Over the next few days, I seemed to wander around the house aimlessly. I tried reading but couldn't concentrate. Tanya and I took to walking around St Petersburg, trying to enjoy the lovely sunny weather but whenever we saw groups of people standing around, it brought back memories of the massacre at the Winter Palace and we turned around immediately to go back to the security of Grand Mama's and for me, the peace and quiet of the library.

Days turned into weeks and I had heard nothing from Nicky. His miniature held pride of place on my bedside table. I often looked at it and wondered where Nicky might be and prayed that he was safe.

Apart from Grand Mama, Mama, Tanya and I all seemed to be pre-occupied with our own thoughts. Because I was so worried about Nicky, I spent more time with Tanya, than Mama and didn't really notice Mama's pre-occupation, which on reflection was unlike me. Until I met Nicky, I seemed to be aware of all of Mama's moods.

I slept poorly at nights, tossing and turning and when I did finally sleep my dreams were troubled. I kept thinking of everything that Nicky had told me. I tossed and turned wondering if there was anything that I could do help Nicky. The long, lonely nights stretched before me. I refused invitations to balls or dinners or even going to the theatre. Katrina had invited me to visit her but I made some excuse not to go.

I finally decided that the only way to pass the time, would be to keep busy. I racked my brain as to what I could do, to keep myself occupied, then in the early hours of the morning, an idea hit me. Nicky's interest and business were in jewels and Karl Faberge had taught Nicky all that he knew about them. I wondered if

Karl would teach me, also. Hopefully by the time Nicky returned home, I would be as knowledgeable or nearly as knowledgeable as my fiancé.

Finally, with that resolved and spending hours tossing and turning, I eventually fell asleep, dreaming of Nicky holding me in his arms and kissing me the way that he had, the first day on the beach of Kadriorg Palace.

Tanya woke me as usual with my breakfast tray and opened the curtains to my bedroom, letting in the beautiful sunlight. She looked as if she had been crying too and I asked her what was wrong; never thinking that she was so emotionally involved with Nicky's man Rudolph. She didn't want to bother me with her burdens but I insisted that she told me. When she told me, I then realised that where Nicky went, Rudolph would go, also. We were both deserted by our men and, although, I knew more than she did, I couldn't tell her. I wasn't sure whether she would have been able to keep it as a secret and thought it unfair to burden her with what little I knew, anyway. Besides I had given my solemn promise to Nicky to discuss it with absolutely no one.

After I had dressed in one of my summer dresses, I went down stairs to find Grand Mama to ask if Peter Abramovich could drive me to Faberge's. She asked why I wanted to go to Faberge and I told her as much of the truth as I could; that while Nicky was away, I thought I might try and learn as much as I could about the gems business as he had and the only person I could think of to teach me was Karl Faberge.

Grand Mama commended me for my enthusiasm but, as if I was as child, told me not to get in the way.

Peter dropped me off at Faberge's and I told him that I would make my own way back. He insisted that I rang him on the telephone, when I was ready to come home. Secretly, I felt relieved that he would come and collect me again as I would feel very nervous walking the streets of St Petersburg alone. I think reading the newspapers daily made me more than aware of the dangers of walking, alone, in St Petersburg, especially a woman of means would attract. After living in St Petersburg for some time now, I felt that the brave young woman that had stepped off that train many months ago and had also hobbled back home with a sprained ankle barely making any fuss, I felt that I was becoming softer, like any of the young female aristocrats.

There was one redeeming feature about Smolensk there was no underlying element of fear, of danger, only that of my father.

I agreed with Peter Abramovich and went into the shop. The little bell above the door tinkled as I opened it to go in. As if by magic, Monsieur Faberge came to the counter.

"Ah, Miss Bobrov, what a pleasant surprise. I have not seen you since you came with Nicky to choose your engagement ring. I hope that everything is all right with it?"

I assured him that it was then went on to put my idea to him. "What a beautiful idea, my dear, to take an interest in your fiancé's business. It would be an honour to teach you, Miss Bobrov."

"I won't be in your way at all Monsieur Faberge?" I asked.

Karl Faberge shook his head. "Not at all my dear," he said smiling at me. When he looked at me, I thought he looked as a doting father would at a treasured child.

I was relieved that at least I had something to keep me occupied while Nicky was away. I thanked Monsieur Faberge and asked him when I could start my tuition.

"Firstly, you must call me Karl, as Nicky does," he told me.

"Then you must call me Thalia, Karl." He took my hand and planted a kiss on the back of it.

"Very well then, Thalia, would you like to start now?"

I nodded and he took me to the back of the shop where the safe was. It was quite a large room, holding a safe the size of a small room, within it. "Every evening when we all finish work, we put all of our work away in this safe, as well as keeping a stock of gems in it at all times, thanks to Nicky," he explained. He took me to the various rooms where his artisans were working on different commissions, explaining what they were doing and asked them to explain how they were doing it. For five hours I was totally immersed in the world of Faberge and jewels. At four o'clock I used the telephone in Karl's office to ring for Peter to come and collect me.

When I reached home, there was a bouquet of salmon pink roses waiting for me on the hall table. In amongst the roses was a small card, saying, *"Forever my love, Nicky."* I picked up the bouquet and buried my nose in the blooms, savouring their perfume.

I took them up to my bedroom and asked Tanya to find a vase for them. They sat on my bedside table next to Nicky's photograph.

Every day I went to Karl's premises for more tutoring on gemstones and also watching what the rest of his artisans were doing. To me, it was like entering Aladdin's cave every day. For a while I was able to forget what was going on in Russia and also being without Nicky. Karl talked to me about the colour of the stones, how emeralds of good quality had an almost deep blue tinge in colour. The occlusions in diamonds were of carbon. The blue of good quality sapphires was so dark as to be nearly black. Good quality rubies were as dark as blood and of course my beautiful opal, which I was so keen to know more of were of so many colours from blues and greens, gold and pinks, mauves and ambers; no two stones were exactly the same and to get deeper colours from paler stone they were overlaid with more opal either double or triple layers, which became doublet or, triplet opals. Karl told me what or how the gemstones were made over hundreds and, thousands of years in the ground.

My final test was going through his trays of gemstones and picking out the best of each, which I was pleased to say that I passed with flying colours. Karl also taught me about the various cuts of stones to bring out the beauty of each stone. It was all so very interesting to me. What woman wouldn't enjoy being surrounded by beautiful jewels?

Over the next few months, I had a couple of letters from Nicky, telling me how much he loved me but not telling me where he was or what he was doing. Tanya heard even less from Rudolph and was convinced that he had been toying with her affections. I tried to keep her spirits up but two months ran into three months, then October came and my birthday with no word from Nicky. In the meantime, Mama was being very secretive, disappearing from the house and not saying where she was going or where she had been, which began to worry me. I tried asking her where she had been and she just replied that she had been out, 'taking the air'. Never had I known my mother taking in the air and coming home with a twinkle in her eye. I thought that she might have found herself someone that she could be happy with and spend the rest of her life with, but if that was the case why hadn't she introduced him to Grand Mama and me?

The evening of my birthday arrived and Grand Mama held a reception for me, at Minsky's, with a meal and an orchestra for dancing to, rather than holding it at home and getting extra staff to help with the catering. She told me that I could invite anyone I wanted. I asked her if I could invite Karl Faberge and his wife, Augusta. We were to be a party of twelve, friends and acquaintances of Mama, Grand Mama and mine, although I hadn't really made any friends in St

Petersburg, apart from Tanya, my maid and Karl and his wife, who used to come and spent some time with me when I used to go to Karl's premises. Although she was somewhat older than myself, we had one thing in common: jewels. Of course, Augusta knew Nicky as well, so we also talked often about him and she told me stories of when he first came to Karl's to learn his business. I would have invited Katrina but after turning down all her invitations she had stopped trying and I would have felt uncomfortable if she asked me where my fiancé was.

Peter Abramovich drove the three of us to Minsky's and parked the car outside. If I had had my way, I would have invited some of the staff from Grand Mama's as I thought more of them as friends than anyone else, especially Tanya and some of Grand Mama staff such as Igor the footman, Peter Abramovich and also his wife Ava, but I knew that Grand Mama and Mama wouldn't approve of I had seen some of the girls that had been presented to the Tsar the same time as myself at various events that I attended but we never said more than a few words in passing. They had their sights set on making a good marriage and some had already made good marriages. Although I wasn't married to Nicky yet, there was some jealousy between the other debutants that had not yet got suitors and there were some nasty remarks on my 'spectacular catch', with Nicky being a prince, a close relative to the Tsar and also handsome and moneyed. I had been told that some of the unfortunates had said that I had 'tricked' Nicky into proposing. I think Nicky had hoped that the Grand Duchesses would have been friendlier towards me but since being introduced to them at the ball at the Kremlin Palace, they had not made any move to contact me, regarding my wedding and because it was protocol, for the royals to make the first move, I had not contacted them.

Minsky's had been someone's home at some time or other and was in one of the beautiful tree lined avenues, not too far from Grand Mama's. The history of how Minsky's moved from a private house into a smart restaurant, I hadn't been told but whoever's home it had been, it was very beautiful and lavishly decorated now, probably at little garish with all of the gold leaf, crystal and mirrors but it was still very beautiful. Before we all sat down to dinner, Mama disappeared briefly and I saw her walk towards the front door, where she met a very smartly dressed man wearing a Cossack styled hat. She reached up and kissed him, briefly on the cheek, then one of the restaurant's staff took his hat and coat from him. Although I couldn't see clearly what was happening, I could not really see the man's face, as he had his back to me, until Mama walked arm in arm with him, over to our table. I stood up when I saw them approach and could not believe

145

my eyes. It was my tutor from Smolensk, Gregor Gregorovich. I was so pleased to see him, that regardless of protocol, I flung my arms around him and kissed him on the cheek. Gregor had always looked a typical tutor in my eyes. He was tall, slim with soft, wavy, brown hair, slightly greying at the temple and sides and glasses. I remembered, sometimes he would look at me over the top of his glasses when he put a question to me and awaited my answer. He was a very clever man and could talk to me, very knowledgeably on any subject. In all of the years that he had been my tutor, he had never said a harsh or unkind word to me. In fact, over the years, he had become my confidant, along with Anya, Mama's maid.

Mama stood by smiling. I looked across to Mama for an explanation and she shook her head as if to say, "I'll tell you later."

Gregor sat down in the empty seat at our table, next to Mama. I wasn't sure but I thought, at times, during the meal he and Mama held hands under the table. I looked at Gregor to see if he would shed any light on the matter but like Mama, he just smiled at me. The meal was wonderful, starting off with caviar on tiny pieces of toast, followed by salmon in a hollandaise sauce, after which came the main course, of chicken stuffed with truffles, followed by a chocolate and brandy mousse and of course we drank champagne throughout the meal. It wasn't the same without Nicky being there but after dinner Karl handed me one of the Faberge boxes. I thanked him, feeling guilty that he had even brought me a present and told him that he need not have bothered, then he told me to open the box. Inside was a beautiful opal bracelet and earrings. Under the lid I saw a little note. I took the note and opened it.

It was in Nicky's handwriting, *"My darling Lia. Happy Birthday. I am sorry I couldn't be there for your birthday but know that I love you with all of my heart and that I think of you every minute of the day. Forever, Your Nicky xx."*

He hadn't forgotten my birthday. I longed for him to be with me, so much that I felt a physical pain, like my heart was a lead weight banging in my chest.

Karl leaned across and whispered, "I am sorry that I can't take credit for it, Thalia. Nicky commissioned it before he left, choosing the most colourful opals that I had in stock." I knew how much Nicky must love me to have thought so far ahead to my birthday, especially when he had so many other pressing matters on his mind.

Mama and Gregor came and stood behind me, to look at Nicky's present.

146

I looked over to Mama and taking up the attitude that she had done to me over the years, said, "Well, Mama, I think you have some explaining to do," I said with a cheeky grin on my face. Gregor, over the years, had become more of friend than a tutor, especially when he said that he had taught me more than any young lady in my situation would ever require. We had begun to read the newspapers and discuss politics and current affairs. Mama used to join in with these conversations with us and although Mama was married to my father, I had often thought that she would be more suited to Gregor but of course she was married and baronesses could not marry tutors. Even though Mama and my father were divorced and she was no longer a baroness, I still could not see how they could be together but from the way Mama had her arm possessively through Gregor's and the way they kept looking at each other, something must have changed but what? I was dying to know.

"Lia darling, can I introduce you to Count Gregor Pinegin," she said with a flourish of her arms. The music began and Gregor asked me to dance with him. I looked at Mama, who nodded her permission. Gregor put his arm around my waist and whisked me on to the dance floor. I noticed that some of the other couples on our table had got up and were dancing, including Karl and Augusta. The floor was very busy with couples twirling to the music and the temperature in the room rose.

"This reminds me of our dance lessons, Thalia. Do you not think so?" Gregor asked me.

"When we were dancing before, I was just dancing with my tutor, now it seems that I am dancing with a count. How did that happen, Gregor?" I asked him.

"My uncle who was the original Count, died without issue, children and I, being his younger brother's only child, inherited his title and his estates."

I told Gregor that I was so pleased for his good fortune. "I have a house here in St Petersburg and a hunting Lodge in Tula but I have not managed to get out there yet. I intend to go there before too long but with winter coming, I am not sure when that will be. I still have a lot of things to sort out with the solicitors but I have already moved in to my house in St Petersburg."

I was genuinely pleased for his good fortune. Then I asked him about Mama. It was as I suspected. While tutoring me, Gregor and Mama had become good friends but of course, while he was just a 'lowly tutor' and Mama was still married to my father, nothing could happen. He had heard of Mama's divorce. In fact, Mama had written and told him. Then when he found out that he was the new Count Pinegin, he contacted Mama to tell her of his good fortune. They had met up a few times and then when we were in Tallin, kept in touch by mail. Eventually they told each other how they had felt and Gregor wanted my permission to ask Mama to marry him.

My heart was bursting with happiness for both Mama and Gregor. I knew that the fact that Mama could not have any children would not bother him. I was sure that they would be so very happy together. I told him that I gave him my permission wholeheartedly, then asked him about Grand Mama, if he had asked for her permission yet.

"I wanted your permission first. After all, I will be your step-father," he said with a smile on his face.

I knew that my step-father would be so much kinder to me than my real father ever had been. I felt so happy for Mama and Gregor, that I felt tears of sheer happiness welling up in my eyes. "If I could have ever chosen someone to be my step-father or my father, even, you would have been the first person I would have thought of Gregor or would you rather that I called you Father?" I asked him.

"I have quite gotten used to you calling me Gregor. I know that your father was a very difficult man but his blood still runs through your veins, Thalia. I could not take that away from him. So, Gregor I am happy with but I thank you for the compliment of asking me." He planted a brief kiss on my forehead.

My eighteenth birthday was turning out to be such a happy occasion as I watched Gregor dancing with Mama and the pair of them laughing together. Mama looked like a young girl in the first flushes of romance. I hoped that they would have a wonderful life together in the coming years.

It was gone midnight when we all left the restaurant. Everyone at our table had come to me and, again, wished me a happy birthday, then departed for their own homes. Karl and Augusta thanked me for inviting them. I told them that it had been my pleasure and I really meant it. If I could have done, I would have invited Tanya, Anya and Peter Abramovich as well as Grand Mama's maid, Ava but knew that it would be frowned on.

Grand Mama and I got into the motor car with Peter Abramovich, while Mama and Gregor followed behind in his new motor car.

"Your mama and Gregor seem very happy together," Grand Mama said. "It seems that, maybe my plans for them both are coming to fruition."

I looked at my grandmother in the darkness of the car and she laughed, "My darling Lia, did you think that I would send just anybody to tutor you. I did a lot of research on Gregor Gregorovich before I employed him to go to Smolensk and tutor you. I knew that he was a good, kind man and hoped that he might befriend your mother. From Anya's reports to me, knowing what an absolute beast your father was, I knew that if I could manage to get you and your mama here, I could finally persuade your Mama to divorce your father. I knew Gregor's background and that he was due to become a Count on the death of his uncle. I was right."

I couldn't believe that my kind and loving grandmother could be so devious but the proof was staring me in the face.

"So, you know that Gregor has already asked my permission to marry Mama?"

"Of course, my dear girl, and when we get back home, he will ask my permission, also and I will give it."

I couldn't help but laugh at her intricate scheming. "Grand Mama. I would never have thought it of you."

Grand Mama laughed with me. "My darling, you don't know me very well," she said patting my cheek gently.

I grinned to myself and wondered if I ever would.

The lights of the house were blazing when we got home. Ava and Tanya came to take our capes from Grand Mama's and my shoulders. I thanked Tanya as she took my cape.

Grand Mama led the way into the lounge and asked Peter to bring a bottle of champagne.

Not long after, Mama and Gregor arrived and hand in hand, came into the lounge.

"Gregor, Thalia has been telling me of your good fortune. May I congratulate you, Count Pinegin?"

Peter handed him a glass of champagne. "Thank you, Countess, for your kind words. However, I have a favour to ask."

Grand Mama nodded for him to continue. "I would like to formally ask for your permission to marry your daughter, Marguerite?"

My grandmother should have been on the stage, the way she feigned surprise at his request. "My dear Gregor, I had no idea," she said. She hesitated and looked across to Mama, who looked pleadingly at her. "Of course, I could not have given my consent while you were a tutor, Gregor, but now with your fortunate change of circumstances…" again she hesitated.

She sat down on one of the chairs by the fire and stared into the flames for a short while, then, she sighed and turned to Gregor and Mama, with a smile, "Very well, I can see that you are obviously very much in love with each other. Love is not just for the young, you see, Thalia. You have my permission." She stood up and kissed them both on the cheek, then announced that she was going to bed.

*Oh bravo Grand Mama*, I thought as she walked regally from the room. *A brilliant performance.*

I kissed Mama and Gregor goodnight and followed Grand Mama upstairs. I saw her just before she went into her bedroom. She was grinning like a Cheshire cat.

# Chapter 16
## Christmas 1913

Christmas brought an end to the peace and the celebrations of the Tercentennial year. Once again we were at the Winter Palace for the Christmas ball. I had a brief note from Nicky who still professed his undying love for me. Every night and every morning religiously I would kiss his picture but as time went by, I felt that part of me was dying. Tanya had given up, totally, of expecting to hear anything from Rudolph, so she told me. I couldn't speak for Rudolph but I knew that somewhere in the world was the man that I loved. It didn't matter how long it was before I saw him again, I knew that I could never love anyone else.

I danced with other men, who asked if they could call on me and several times I had to remind them that I was engaged to Prince Nicholas Ivanov. Some asked where he was and, I admit it, I lied to them and told them he was in Australia working. I don't think that I had ever felt as lonely as I did that night at the ball. I remembered the previous year's ball, when I was presented to the Tsar and wanted to cry but somehow, I managed to keep the smile fixed on my face. I was so relieved, though, when it was time for us to leave.

I went to bed, sad and disillusioned and when Tanya had left me, I looked at Nicky's picture and burst into tears, crying into my pillow to stifle the sound of my sobbing. It had been six months since Nicky had left. I had tried to understand when he first went away but as time went by, I found it becoming harder and harder to understand. The Dowager Empress had been present at the ball as had the rest of the royal family, including that terrible man Rasputin, all smiling and enjoying themselves, while my Nicky was God knew where. It sounded very childish but it just didn't seem fair. I had been so upset that I didn't even notice the huge Christmas tree standing in the marble hallway. Christmas morning arrived. Tanya woke me with my cup of tea and opened my curtains. I could see, from my bed, it was snowing heavily. My heart felt as heavy as the snow clouds outside.

Tanya seemed happy as she wished me a merry Christmas. Had she found someone to replace Rudolph? I had heard that Grand Mama had hired a new footman, Illia. Maybe he was the new love of her life?

I knew that we would all be going to Kazan Cathedral for Mass. The thought of sitting through the long service did not appeal to me and I felt very tempted to plead a headache. The only problem was, I had never suffered with headaches, only when I was running a fever. I sighed and resigned myself to sitting in a cold, albeit, beautiful cathedral and take Mass.

Tanya picked out one of my more elaborate day gowns for me to wear and I told her that I would prefer one of the plainer ones from my wardrobe.

"But Miss Thalia, it is Christmas day, surely you want something a little more elaborate than your plainer dresses. See, if you wore your opal jewellery, they would go beautifully with this green gown." She pleaded with me.

In the end I gave in and wore my green velvet gown with my opal jewellery. I asked her to just tie my hair back but she said that I needed it up, to show off my opal collection. I knew that Tanya got pleasure of dressing me to look my best, so eventually I gave in. Dressed in my best, I went downstairs to the lounge to find Mama and Grand Mama still hadn't come down, so decided to move to one of the large winged chairs in front of the fire. I jumped and cried out when I realised that someone was already sitting in the chair.

"You are the future Princess Ivanov?" I was asked. The voice I thought that I recognised but couldn't be sure that it was who I thought.

The man who rose from the chair was clean shaven but from the cheeky glint in his eyes, I knew that it could be no one else.

"Nicky," I cried, I tried to say more but the tears that I had welling up since my birthday began to flow unchecked down my face.

He picked me up in his arms and covered my face with kisses.

"When did you get back, Nicky?"

He told me that he had arrived back in St Petersburg at midnight. "I would have come to the ball but I was so tired after all of my travelling, so I thought that I would go to sleep and be here when you woke. Your grandmother, mother and a Count Pinegin have already left for the Cathedral. They said that they would meet you back here after Mass. I have been invited to dine here."

He held me tight and pulled me down onto the chair beside him, which was rather unconventional but it felt wonderful to feel him so close beside me.

I lay my head on his shoulder, where I could smell his cologne, "Will you have to go away again Nicky?"

He kissed me again, "Not if I can help it, Lia. You don't know how much I have missed you, all of these months, not hearing your voice or seeing your face and after a whole month spent together at Tallin, it was sheer torture."

"There were so many times that I wanted to write to you but never knew how to get in touch."

I told him that I had looked at his picture every morning when I woke and every evening before I went to sleep and numerous times in between. He told me that he had done the same with my photograph and wondered if I was doing the same. I reassured him that I had.

When I entered my room, I heard Tanya singing as she tidied up my clothes. "You knew," I said to her. She just grinned and nodded, "You have seen Rudolph?" I asked and she nodded again. Now it all made sense to me.

My maid, friend was becoming more devious like my Grand Mama. I picked up Nicky's photograph from my bedside table, kissed Tanya on the cheek and ran back downstairs, to my fiancé.

We had so much to say to each other, so much to catch up on. I told him about Mama and Gregor and, of course, my grandmother's scheming, which made him laugh. He told me that the Dowager Empress and his mother were schemers like their younger sister. He asked me what I had been up to while he had been away and I told him about my time with Karl. Nicky said that he thought it was admirable.

"You still haven't mentioned this," he said, indicating his clean-shaven face. "I needed to go incognito, so thought this was the best way. People have always commented that I looked too much like my cousin, so I shaved it off. Do you approve? I can always grow it again if you want me to."

I thought the new clean-shaven look made him look younger and more my Nicky, rather than like the Tsar.

"In that case, my darling, I will make the laborious effort and shave every morning."

# Chapter 17
## In the Beginning

Christmas day was the last day of peace amongst the Russians. The newspapers were full of stories of student riots and unrest. More and more flyers were seen of indecent images of Rasputin and the Tsarina, which meant that the Okrana were doing their own rioting of breaking into premises where they suspected the offending printing presses were and the perpetrators were either shot or hung, without a trial. If they had a printing press on their premises, then they were guilty, no matter what they printed.

Of course, this was also reported in the newspapers, although the subject-matter of the offending flyers was not divulged, not in the papers. It wasn't needed. There was enough of the flyers in circulation. One day while out with Tanya, walking, someone thrust one of the offending papers in my hand. I didn't look at it, at the time, but when I returned home, I took it from my pocket. I was disgusted with what I saw and threw it immediately onto the fire. I couldn't understand how anyone could imagine the Tsarina would even want anything to do with the ugly man or what sort of a hold he had over her but why would the man still be in the company of the Royal family? I asked myself.

Up to June the newspapers were filled with news of 'minor skirmishes' but on 29 June the headlines shouted out the assassination of Archduke Franz Ferdinand of Austria, by Gravilo Princip of a Bosnian separatist group, Young Bosnia.

This had happened a few days after Mama and Gregor's wedding.

Their wedding was expected to be a big affair but as Mama had been married before, she wanted something a lot smaller and I think Gregor was happy with that. Grand Mama wanted something more extravagant but for once Mama had her own way. The ceremony was not in a Cathedral, as Grand Mama had wanted but the smaller, intimate little church of St Catherine of Alexandria, which was a beautiful church of understated elegance. Mama wore a gown of silver grey. I gave her back the tiara, necklace and earrings that she had given me for my debut but she insisted that they were just on loan and would be returned to me before they left on their honeymoon. Nicky had offered them the use of Kadriorg Palace for the month. Mama just glowed with happiness as Gregor placed the wedding ring on her finger. I could feel tears welling up in my eyes, so pleased for hers and Gregor's happiness. Although older than most brides, she looked the epitome of the blushing bride. Nicky who stood with Grand Mama and myself on the front row squeezed my hand, which he had been holding, as if to say that sooner or later that will be us getting married. Grand Mama still had not told us when we could name the day but the way we looked at it, the more Nicky and I saw of each other, the nearer we came to Grand Mama telling us that we could name the day.

With Mama's marriage to Gregor, that left just Grand Mama and me in the house, along with the servants, of course. It felt very strange just the two of us. I saw Nicky every day and every day we did something together, either boating on a lake or just walking through the park arm in arm or go visiting, as a couple, to friends and acquaintances. We found that 'Table tipping' was something new in St Petersburg. It was all about contacting the dead through a séance. Some people believed in it, others not. Nicky and I went to one such event once, but decided it was a ruse as most of the people around the table's history was known. They even told me that I would marry a Prince. That was obvious as our engagement announcement had been in all of the newspapers so we laughed it off as an 'experience' that we wouldn't be repeating. Of course, the first question we were always asked at any meeting we were invited to was had we named a day? Nicky kept saying that because of his busy work schedule, we were having trouble, to find time to sit down and discuss it. This seemed to be accepted by most. For those that didn't accept this, we agreed that that was all we would say, regardless. Of course, some of the girls that had their debut at the same time as me were already married or engaged and had a date for their wedding. I must admit that I was envious of them.

In the meantime, Mama and Gregor returned to St Petersburg after their honeymoon at Tallin, a month later and were installed into Gregor's town house. At their first opportunity we were all invited to dinner. Although the house was not as big as Grand Mama's, (but there again Grand Mama didn't have a hunting lodge as well), already Mama was beginning to put her stamp on the household.

They had a staff of ten servants, most of them had served Gregor's Uncle, until his death, then stayed on ready to serve their new master. It was, after all, better than being homeless and on the streets. They still had a roof over their heads and the solicitors, in charge of the estate, were still paying their wages, until the new master arrived. Gregor, as I expected was a good master and it seemed that he was well-liked by his staff. Of course, Mama had staff before, so soon got them working the way she liked.

On the whole, life in our family was quiet and harmonious, which was more than could be said for the rest of the country.

On 23 July 1914 Austria-Hungary issued an ultimatum to Serbia, demanding the right to investigate the assassination of Archduke Franz Ferdinand. Serbia refused.

The papers were full of the news and speculation that war was on the horizon. Nicky asked for a meeting with Grand Mama, Mama and Gregor and me. I had never seen him look so serious and it scared me. We all met at Grand Mama's house.

Nicky waited until Peter Abramovich had served us all champagne and left the room, closing the door behind him.

"Thank you for allowing me to speak to you all," Nicky said. He seemed to be struggling to find the right words. "I am sure you have all seen the newspapers. Believe me I am pretty sure that war is imminent."

"What can we do about it, Nicky?" Gregor asked.

"I think the time might come when we will have to consider leaving Russia. The country is waiting to see what will happen but whatever way it goes, there is a terrible unrest in this country. Let me just say it is between the 'Haves and have nots. We are the Haves along with the rest of the Russian aristocracy and the Have nots are the rest of the country. The Tsar thought that the Tercentenary celebrations might diffuse the situation. In fact it has made things worse, by demonstrating to the Have nots that the amount of money spent on the celebrations, would be enough to feed and clothe practically the whole country. Many of our people can't read or write, we need schools for them to learn in and hospitals for the sick, no matter who they are. I am afraid that there will be a revolution. More and more people are voicing their protests. If we go to war, they will have no say in the matter. They will be conscripted, whether they like it or not." The silence in the room was palpable.

"If you have any money, valuables, art, jewellery then I suggest that you move it out of the country now, probably to the Americas. I have already moved a lot of mine there and I will give you the name of a good shipping company that you can trust. Some of the aristocrats are already leaving the country. I suggest that you start preparing to do the same."

Silence followed, for quite some time, as we were all trying to digest what he had said.

"What about the Tsar, Nicky? What will he do?" Grand Mama asked.

"The Tsar will do what he always does, says he knows what is best for his country and bury his head in the sand. The Dowager Empress has already moved a lot of her things into storage ready to be shipped away when the time is right. It is what I have been helping her with, the times that I have been away. I have also been gauging the atmosphere over in Europe and it is not good. Because the Dowager Empress is beloved, of the majority of the country, she has been able to move around quite freely without question but even so, it is getting harder. Now she is getting ready for flight from the country. I am sorry to say that although, she loves her son, as would any mother, The Dowager Empress has already spoken to her son, several times but she knows that he is influenced by the Tsarina and the Tsarina is influenced by Rasputin." Nicky stopped and looked at us all. "What I have said to you all must stop within this room otherwise we could all be held for treason and that would mean the firing squad."

I heard Grand Mama gasp loudly, "Nicky, what have you brought to us?"

"I don't mean to scare you, Aunt Lilia. I am trying to warn you: To prepare you. So that, when I think the time is right, we will all go to Tallin and from there I will have a boat standing by to transport us all to America. You will have to leave many things here, friends, staff, as well as furniture but I am afraid that it will have to be done if we want to stay alive."

"If we go to war, Nicky, will you have to join the forces?" I asked, thinking of us being parted once again but this time knowing very well that he could die.

Nicky squeezed my hand comfortingly. "No darling. I am the last of my line, so the Tsar would not send me off to become cannon fodder."

Mama looked with fear to Gregor. Nicky tried to put her mind at rest, "Gregor is the last of his line as well."

Grand Mama sighed, "Well, if we have to leave Russia, I would like to see my grand-daughter married in her native country."

157

I couldn't believe my ears. Was Grand Mama telling us that we could finally name our wedding date?

It was as if she could read my thoughts. "I thought maybe next July would be a good time for the wedding. What do you think, Babushka?"

I looked at Nicky. He also wore a look of disbelief.

"I think you two have proved your love for each other through your separations and now with this, you have stayed true to each other," Mama said. "Yes, I think we should name the date for your wedding. It has been long enough and if Nicky is right, which I don't doubt that he is, then yes, I would like you both to be married here in St Petersburg."

On 30 July a few days after the Austrian/Hungarian issue with Serbia, Russia mobilised its troops to defend Serbia and two days later Germany declared war on Russia in defence of Austria-Hungary. The numbers of Russian troops increased to thousands. All the male lower classes thought that they would have a better life in the Russian army, than at home, with warm winter clothes and plenty of food and money to send back to their families. Quite a few of the 'Have not's' were willing to join up. The Tsar and Tsarina went to one of the train stations, where the troops were departing, to bless them and give words of comfort and cheer. Spirits were high. The rumours were encouraging, saying that the war would be over within a couple of months.

Meanwhile, in St Petersburg we were busy, finally, with wedding preparations; ordering invitations, booking rooms for the reception, (as Grand Mama's would not be large enough), booking Kazan Cathedral or delivering flowers. A year seemed a long time but preparing for our wedding, the time seemed to be flying past. Now that we had finally named a date for our wedding, people stopped asking Nicky and me about it, thankfully.

Surprisingly, in November we had an invitation to the Winter Palace to tea with the Dowager Empress, the Tsarina, the Tsarevich and the Grand Duchesses. I thought it was about the Grand Duchesses wanting to be my bridesmaids but it was something completely different.

Nicky came with us thankfully, as he knew that I always felt uncomfortable in the presence of the Grand Duchesses. Their mother and grandmother were friendly enough towards me but I always felt that the Grand Duchesses still looked on me as 'The country mouse' even though I had now been in St Petersburg for two years.

It was the Dowager Empress who seemed to break the ice. "I am so glad you could all come. I am sorry that it is not a more frequent occasion but as you can imagine we are living in perilous times but still here we all are. How are your wedding plans going, Thalia?"

"Very well thank you, Your Highness," I replied shyly.

"Of course with this war with Germany, there will be a lot of changes. We are opening up Tsarskoye Selo to be a hospital for our wounded soldiers," the Tsarina told us. "As a matter of fact, Olga, Tatiana and myself are going to train to be nurses there. We feel that it is the least we can do for our brave men."

"That is truly an admirable vocation, Your Highness," I said, then without consulting Mama or Grand Mama or Nicky, I continued, "One that I would like to do. Could I ask if I might join you, Your Highness?"

The silence in the room was uncomfortable, until Mama spoke up. "But, Lia darling, think about this first before making such a drastic decision. What about what you and Tanya saw…"

I knew what Mama was going to say and within our present company, I could not let her make the mistake of bringing the slaughter outside the Winter Place up in the presence of the royal ladies.

"Mama, I am sure that if the Tsarina and the Grand Duchesses can do it, then so can I. I want to be useful during the war to help our poor, brave soldiers."

Mama knew best not to start an argument in front of our present company and just smiled shyly.

Nicky joked trying to break the uncomfortable silence, "Oh I do love a young woman in a uniform. Pray Olga, tell me what does the uniform of a nurse look like? I have been so lucky that I have never had the need for these ministering angels."

For the first time I saw the two oldest Grand Duchesses smile. The smile transformed their faces. Maybe they were just shy, I began to wonder.

"It is a grey serge dress with white collar and cuffs, white apron with a large red cross on the bodice and a beautiful white headdress, rather like a nun's." Titania, the younger of the two older royal daughters told him.

"With black, 'sensible' flat shoes," added Olga, pulling a face, "very attractive!"

"I am sure that if you are standing all of the time, you will be appreciative of your 'sensible' shoes, Olga," Nicky said, teasing her. Obviously, the Grand Duchesses were used to Nicky's teasing.

Eventually it was agreed with the Tsarina that I would travel to Tsarskoye Selo for the fitting for my uniform the following week.

"Tsarskoye Selo has so many public rooms that could be used for wards. Already, we are having them stripped of their contents and prepared. We are having, a fleet of lorries delivering beds, linen and medical equipment all this week and next. So, once they are delivered and in situ, we will be able to start receiving patients," the Tsarina told us. Then she took a breath. It seemed that what she was to say next was difficult for her. "But with the war, it would not be right for us to be seen in public, enjoying ourselves, so I am afraid that we will, sadly, have to decline your kind invitation to your wedding, Thalia. I am so terribly sorry," she finished.

I don't know whether I was pleased or disappointed. Not having the royal family at the wedding of their cousin could be seen as a slight against Nicky but, for me, not being under the scrutiny of all of the Grand Duchesses was a relief, even though I would be working with the two oldest Grand Duchesses and the Tsarina. The palace at Tsarskoye Selo was a massive place, so maybe I would not see that much of them, I thought.

With Nicky agreeing to drive me to Alexandra Palace at Tsarskoye Selo the next week for my uniform fitting, we finally took our leave.

Peter Abramovich drove Mama and Grand Mama back to Mama's home, while Nicky and I followed behind.

"Are you disappointed not to have the Grand Duchesses as your bridesmaids, Lia?" he asked.

"No. I can understand what the Tsarina meant. It would not seem right for them, to be seen, enjoying their selves, whatever the occasion."

"The Dowager Empress has told me that she will still come to the wedding to represent the Royal family."

"Oh, Nicky, I am so pleased about that. I thought that with no one from the Royal family attending our wedding, it might make it look, as though they disapproved of our marriage."

Nicky reassured me that if we had married before the war, they would all be there in their finery. This made me laugh.

"I don't think your mama and grand mama were very happy about you volunteering to become a nurse. You might have a bit of a battle there."

I told Nicky that if the Tsarina and Grand Duchesses Olga and Titania could do it, then I certainly could. In fact, I wanted to show them that I might be a country mouse in their eyes but I could work just as hard, if not harder than the royals; also, Grand Mama and Mama would not be seen to change their minds to the royal family.

Nicky didn't say anything but I knew that he knew that in my own way I was drawing up my own battle plan against the royals and Mama and Grand Mama. It wasn't so much a battle plan but I did want to prove that I was as good as they were regarding nursing.

Nicky was right, when we arrived back at Mama's, both Mama and Grand Mama fired questions at me, also reminding me of my reaction the day of the Winter Palace massacre.

"It was something that I wasn't expecting, then, that was all," I replied, "I was caught unawares. I will be ready for what nursing has to show me."

"But, Lia darling, you are a naive young woman and you will be nursing men," Mama cried.

"So are the Grand Duchesses, Mama."

Grand Mama looked at Nicky, hoping to get his support. "And you, Nicky, how do you feel about your future wife, seeing strange men's bodies?"

"Aunt Lilia, I understand you and Marguerite's concerns but Lia is a headstrong and brave young woman and I think that once she has made her mind up, nothing will change her. The fact that she will be seeing other men's bodies, does not concern me, as long as she is faithful to me, which is more important. She has tolerated us being separated for months on end and still stayed faithful to me even through everything."

"Are you sure that you have not spoken in haste, Lia?" Grand Mama asked, "If you regret offering your services, you can always say that your marriage preparations are taking up too much of your time."

I assured Grand Mama and Mama that it was something that I really wanted to do. The more I thought about it, the more that I wanted to do it. I wanted to do something for the men who were fighting for our country. I wanted to feel useful. I was not the sort of person to just sit around prettily, reading or embroidering, which was one of the reasons I went to Karl Faberge's, to keep myself occupied. That was not in my nature. In fact, I was pleased to have something to keep me occupied.

Eventually, very reluctantly, they all agreed that I could go and train to be a nurse, along with the Tsarina and the Grand Duchesses. I am sure they expected me to either fail or give up.

# Chapter 18
## Nurse Bobrov

On the appointed date, Nicky picked me up from Grand Mama's house to drive me the twenty-four miles to Alexandria Palace, which was another massive building. Already there were lorries parked outside the front entrance and soldiers moving in and out of the palace itself, carrying boxes, beds, all things to transform the palace into a hospital. Inside, the palace was a hive of activity. Still members of the royal household continued their duties, as a footman walked up to Nicky and me. "Prince Ivanov, Miss Bobrov, the Tsarina is expecting you. If you would follow me, please?"

All of the activity seemed to be on the ground floor at that time and the footman led us up the elegant, sweeping, marble staircase to, where, I presumed were the royal apartments. As Nicky and I were walking down the hallway, following the footman, we saw the figure, of who could only be, Rasputin, walking away from the royal apartments. I guessed that it was him from his tall, skinny body and his un-kept appearance. I gave an involuntary shudder. Nicky looked down at me and smiled comfortingly.

We stopped outside a set of heavily embellished, double doors leading to the royal apartments. The footman knocked on the door and entered to announce us.

"Prince Ivanov and Miss Bobrov, your serene highness."

The Tsarina came over and welcomed us, kissing Nicky on the cheek and offering me her hand, which I held very tentatively and curtseyed. "I think as we will be working together Thalia, we should dispense with the courtly gestures. We would never get any work done if you were bobbing up and down every time you saw me or my daughters. Regarding names, I will call you Thalia. You must call my daughters by their given names of Olga and Tatiana and me by my given name of Alexandria."

The thought of calling the Grand Duchesses by their given name, gave me no real problem, (I thought that it put us all on the same footing) but to call the Tsarina of all Russia, by her given name was too much for me. I shook my head. "I am sorry, Your Highness, but I couldn't call you by your given name, it is too informal for your status."

The Tsarina laughed, "My dear girl, when we are working together, we are all of the same status." She could tell that I still felt uncomfortable. "What if you just called me 'Ma'am' instead? I understand that in England, they used to call my grandmother Victoria 'Ma'am'. Would you feel more comfortable with that, Thalia?"

I nodded, "Yes, Mam, I would feel more comfortable with that."

The Tsarina smiled at me.

With that sorted, we got down to the work of getting me measured for my uniform. Olga and Tatiana told me that they had already been measured. "We have to wear thick black stockings as well Thalia," said Tatiana. "I am sure they will be terribly itchy."

"I suppose that they will at least keep us warm in the winter," I replied.

It was one of the nurses, who came and measured me, not a seamstress. I thought that our uniforms were to be made but apparently, we were to wear the same uniforms as the rest of the nurses, which would be taken from stock. The nurse who measured me was supervised by a senior nurse called Sister Procopy. She was a tall, stern-looking woman, who's dark hair was scrapped back under her cap, who I thought might be against having royalty nursing, which was distasteful to her. She looked to be roughly the same age as the Tsarina, but obviously having a harder life than the Tsarina, time had taken its toll on her looks. I think that she felt as uncomfortable as me working with 'the Royals', as I began to call them, collectively.

Once I had been measured, the younger nurse left us, I presume to go in search of our uniforms.

Sister Procopy cleared her voice and pulled back her shoulders, taking on an air of authority. I thought that maybe she had prepared her speech to the 'Royals'.

"Ladies, firstly thank you for volunteering to be trained to be nurses, we do need as many as we can get." I thought that she must be desperate to be recruiting us but kept quiet.

"When the other nurse comes back with your full uniforms, I will explain a few things about wearing it." I couldn't believe that we would be instructed in wearing clothes.

While we were waiting for our uniforms, Sister Procopy talked to us about our first chore, which would be making up the beds for the influx of patients.

Nicky realising that this was really nothing to do with him, begged to be excused and left, saying that he would return in an hour.

Sister Procopy told us that before we began to make the beds, they would all have to be disinfected, so that no germs could live on any of the surfaces and cause infections. "Our patients will have enough to cope with, without the fear of additional infection."

She told us that this must be done every time a bed was, 'vacated', I think the Royals thought that 'vacated' meant that they would be well enough to go home or back to the front. My thoughts went more along the lines of patients dying.

She told us that after touching any patient, before moving on to the next, we should always wash our hands in carbolic soap, to stop the spread of infection. "By the end of each day, your hands will be red raw with all of the handwashing; such are the pitfalls of our profession. Firstly, then ladies you will wash down each mattress, thoroughly, that is top, bottom and sides. After that I will demonstrate how to make a bed. That will be your first duty until all of the beds are made. Of course, there will be other nurses in other wards doing exactly the same as you. I will then teach you how to change a bed with a patient in it; you will be able to practice this on each other, before we actually get patients."

She told us that once we had mastered the 'art' of making a bed with a patient in it, we would then go on to learning how to take temperatures and blood pressures and mark them down on a chart. This would help the doctors on their rounds to assess their patients. When we had learnt this, we would then go onto bandaging but before that there would be hundreds of bandages for us all to roll, ready for applying to the patients.

The more Sister Procopy talked about our duties, the more I realised that we wouldn't have much spare time, if any, while we were on duty.

"I am sorry to say, ladies, you will feel bone weary at the end of each of your shifts, until you get used to it," she said finally.

The other nurse came back in the room after collecting our uniforms from stores. They were all piled onto a hospital trolley. She handed a pile to the Tsarina first, then Olga, Titania and finally myself, explaining that our uniforms must be washed daily and we should not go out in them unless it was in the grounds with a patient. We would wear a cape, which again, we could not wear to go home in. We had two grey serge dresses each, three aprons, one nurse's cap, which looked more like something a nun would wear.

Nicky returned just in time to see our piles of new cloths and looked sorry that we were not wearing them.

Before we left, the Tsarina told me that a small room had been set to one side off the main hallway for me to change out of my daily clothes into my uniform and vice versa. If for any reason, I could not get home at the end of my shift, then a room next to that of the Grand Duchesses, would be set aside for me.

I thanked the Tsarina and Sister Procopy, said goodbye to Olga and Titania and was reminded that I would be expected at seven o'clock the next morning to start my shift.

Nicky pulled my arm through his as we walked out to his car. He helped me in and then got in the driver's seat. Once we were settled and on our way back to St Petersburg he turned to me. "Seven o'clock in the morning. You will have to be up very early for us to get you there on time darling. Are you sure that this is what you want?"

I expected that sort of question from Mama and Grand Mama but was surprised at Nicky. From the expression on my face, he knew that I was surprised at him.

"Oh, don't get me wrong, darling, I am so very proud of you; that you want to do this but you are a lady, you are not used to getting up so early or working."

"Nicky, if the Tsarina and the Grand Duchesses can do it…"

"I know, darling," he interrupted, "then you can do it. It sounds to me like you are setting to prove yourself against the Tsarina and Grand Duchesses. If you couldn't cope with the hours, it would not matter to me or them, that you couldn't do it."

"Nicky, that is one thing that I don't do," I told him. "I never have and I never will give up."

He stopped the car for just a moment to kiss me. Then he gave me a cheeky grin. "A stubborn little madam, aren't you? One might even say wilful, Miss Bobrov, but really not unexpected, knowing you."

I told him that I thought he liked me for being stubborn and brave, then he kissed me deeply, setting my body on fire with wanting more than just kisses from him. I wound my arms around his neck, holding him against me, savouring our closeness. I could feel his heart banging hard against mine.

"At least with me nursing, the time will pass so much quicker to our wedding day," I said against his cheek.

"For you, maybe but what about me?" he replied, not moving from our close, comfortable position.

"Do what I did; go and work with Karl or you can take over my place organising our wedding or make our city home more suitable to a married couple and not just a bachelor, also if you think that we will have to leave the country, maybe you should help Grand Mama, Mama and Gregor to prepare."

He laughed, "Typical woman, already finding me plenty to keep me occupied while she is doing other things."

I knew that he was really joking and didn't mind helping. By working with my family, it was allowing them to get to know my future husband better and for him to get to know them better.

I had seen his town house in St Petersburg or should I say just on the outskirts of St Petersburg. It was very spacious but very masculine in its décor. I liked pale, muted colours, whereas Nicky's colour schemes were bolder and darker. He knew that I had fallen in love with Kadriorg Palace, as he had. Chesmenskiy Palace paled into insignificance to our future home by the sea.

We had talked about this after my first visit to Chesmenskiy Palace, which was on the road to Tsarskoye Selo. This would mean that I would be nearer the hospital, once Nicky and I married. In the meantime, it would be a six o'clock breakfast before Nicky collected me to take me to the hospital. I had asked Nicky if he minded getting up so early to take me, otherwise I could ask Peter Abramovich to drive me there. Nicky had insisted that he did not mind one little bit, that it gave us extra precious moments together.

I must admit that I didn't like Chesmenskiy Palace as much as Kadriorg Palace. I couldn't see our children running through the rooms or around the gardens as I had immediately, the moment I saw Nicky's home in Tallin. Nicky had said that once we were married, we would spend, most of our time in Tallin, anyway, so I was glad. I sounded very spoilt, if I voiced my feelings about Chesmenskiy Palace, because whatever else it might be, it was still larger and more lavishly decorated that my old home in Smolensk and one thousand times better that the pitiful homes of the majority of Russian people. Much as I disliked it, there were the "Haves" and "Have not's" and it was the latter that I felt so sorry for. At least while I was nursing, I could contribute to the poor people of my homeland in some small way.

Once I arrived back at Grand Mama's I was greeted by a barrage of questions from my grandmother. When I told her that I had to be back at Alexandria Palace by seven o'clock the next morning, she was horrified. I told her that I would need my breakfast by six o'clock and Nicky was going to pick me up half an hour later. I spoke to Mama on the telephone to tell her how my time with the royals went. Like Grand Mama, she was horrified but accepted that if it was something I wanted to do, I would have to take the rough with the smooth, not that I expected there to be any 'smooth' in nursing wounded soldiers.

It must have been the thought of the hard work awaiting me on the wards or the fact that I hadn't slept well the night before, wondering what my meeting again with the 'royals' would be like but I felt exhausted after Nicky had dropped me off at Grand Mama's. Before he left me, he kissed me firmly on the lips, holding my body close to his. "I am very proud of you Lia. You know that, don't you?"

I nodded, returning his kiss. "I want to make a success of this, Nicky, not just to show the 'royals' but never in my life have I been tested and stepped up to the mark. Now is my chance. I want to be a good nurse." I wished him goodnight and made my way to Grand Mama's front door, then turned to him and waved.

Grand Mama and I had an informal evening meal in the small dining room, that evening and shortly after, I went upstairs to bed, after kissing Grand Mama on her forehead. She grasped my hand, "Lia, I am very proud of you, for what you are doing, darling." I kissed her again on her forehead and went upstairs to my room. Wearily I climbed up the elegant staircase, struggling to carry myself from one stair up to the next. I sat down in front of my dressing table and let Tanya tend to me, then undress me and help me into the bath that she had drawn for me, waiting for me to come upstairs to bed. Thankfully I closed my eyes and relaxed in the fragrantly steaming water as it covered my body. I must have drifted off to sleep in the bath as when Tanya touched my arm, I jumped awake. She helped to dry me then helped me into bed, where I fell into an exhausted sleep.

I jumped the next morning when Tanya brought up my breakfast tray. She looked as tired as I felt but still had a smile for me. I suppose being a servant Tanya was used to getting up earlier than me, anyway but not quite this early. No longer was I able to take a leisurely, breakfast but ate it hastily, then dressed and was downstairs just as Nicky's car pulled up outside the front door. Grand Mama was still in bed asleep, when I closed the front door behind me.

Nicky kissed me when I got inside the car, then he drove us both to Tsarskoye Selo. I think we were both tired but neither of us complained. Although I was tired, I was also excited. Nicky said that he would wait until I had changed into my uniform.

"I am sure that you will be the most beautiful nurse there," he told me.

"Even with dark circles under my eyes?" I asked him.

"Dark circles, bags under your eyes, fallen arches through all of your standing and a hunched back from all of the bending." He teased me.

Even at seven o'clock in the morning, the downstairs of the palace was already a hive of activity. I went to the room where I was told I could change, to find my uniform waiting for me. I quickly changed, inspecting myself in the mirror, which had been placed on the wall for me to check that my nurse's cap was on straight.

When I went back to where Nicky was waiting for me, I could tell by the look on his face that he liked what he saw. "I told you that it wouldn't matter whether you were a scullery maid or now even a nurse, I would still love you." He leaned forward to kiss me just as Sister Procopy came into the hallway.

"Nurse Bobrov, it is good to see you here on time." She looked at my engagement ring on my hand. "I am afraid that you won't be able to wear your ring on your hand. I would suggest that you put it on a necklace around your neck, under your uniform. Are you wearing any other jewellery?" I told her that my ring was the only jewellery. As I didn't even wear a necklace, I handed my ring to Nicky for safe keeping. "You may collect your fiancée at seven o'clock this evening sir," she told Nicky as a form of dismissal. Nicky winked at me then turned and left.

I followed Sister Procopy into what used to be the ballroom on the ground floor. It was a massive space with some huge floor to ceiling doors. This wasn't the only 'ward' in the palace she told me that there were another five wards, plus some private rooms for senior officers. As well as the wards, there were three operating rooms, x-ray rooms, plenty of washrooms and toilets as well as store rooms and a plaster room. The whole ground floor of the palace had been transformed into the hospital.

The ballroom had been stripped right back so that only the beautiful paintings on the ceilings remained. It had fifty beds along the front wall, with windows opening onto the gardens and another fifty beds along the back wall. The beds had all been assembled with rubber mattresses on top but, as yet, unmade.

Sister Procopy told me that my first job was to wash down all of the mattresses with carbolic. Once they had dried, she would show 'us' how to make the beds. I presumed the 'us' also related to the royals, who had, as yet, not shown themselves.

Sister Procopy showed me the sluice, where I could find a bucket, water and carbolic, as well as cleaning cloths. She told me to roll up my sleeves so that I didn't get them wet.

I had already washed ten mattresses front and back, top and bottom, before the Tsarina and the Grand Duchesses arrived. Sister Procopy briefly showed herself, telling them that I would tell them what I was doing and they should follow. I told them where to find the buckets, water, carbolic and cloths, then told them that I had been told to clean the mattresses top, bottom and sides. I didn't think that the royals would like being told to do anything, so I tried to make it more of a request, rather than an order. As soon as they saw that I had rolled up my sleeves, they did the same then they went to get the buckets. I just carried on with what I was doing. I was well ahead of the royals when I finished one side of the ward and they were still ten beds away from finishing.

Sister Procopy came back once all of the beds had been disinfected (I didn't know whether it just occurred to me or the royals as well but Sister Procopy always seemed to arrive just as we were finishing one job, ready to instruct us on our next chore). She then began showing us how to make up the beds. All of the bed linen was stored in another room, with shelf after shelf of sheets, blankets and pillow cases and pillows. She told us that each bed was made up with one of each, then, told us to put the required bed linen on each bed, before making them up. I took a pile of bed linen and placed them on each of the beds, while the royals were taking enough bedclothes for one bed at a time, which in my eyes meant more walking. I didn't say anything but noticed that after a short time, they followed my lead.

Miraculously Sister Procopy appeared again, when each bed had the required bed linen on it. She then showed us how to make the bed. When she had finished, she asked if we had any questions. No one said anything, so she said that she would leave us to it.

I started on the first bed, firstly putting on the bottom sheet, making sure that it was free of any wrinkles, (we had been told that these could cause bedsores,) then put the pillowcase on the pillow. Once I had placed the pillow on the top of the bed, I set to putting on the top sheet and then the blanket. Once these were all in place, I folded the corners at the bottom and top, then folded the top sheet and blanket back in line with the bottom of the pillow and tucked it in. I felt a great sense of satisfaction seeing the bed, all crisp and tidy, just waiting for a patient.

"Oh bother! Mama, I can't get it right," Olga said after making the third attempt on her first bed.

Titania and the Tsarina looked just as confused as well.

"Thalia, yours looks perfect. Could you show us how to do it, again, please or tell us where we went wrong?" asked the Tsarina.

I didn't want to contradict them, so I showed them again how to make the bed again, only slower than Sister Procopy had shown us.

"Ah now I know where we went wrong, we folded each sheet under separately. How did you learn to do it so quickly, Thalia?" asked the Tsarina again.

I told her that I had also watched Tanya, my maid, make my bed before now and she made it the same way.

"Our beds were always made when we were out of the room," added Titania.

The Tsarina thanked me for showing them and we continued with our bed making until between the four of us, we had made one hundred beds in our ward. Sister Procopy came back in, glanced around at the rows of made beds and complimented us. "Well done, ladies. I think that is enough heavy labour for one day. I will go and get some bandages, which you can all spend the rest of the afternoon rolling them. If you would all sit down at the big table in the middle of the room, I will go and get some bandages, then show you the quickest way to roll them. Slowly we all made our way to the large table, glad to sit down and rest our aching feet and backs. I think hard labour brought us all together on an even keel and we began chattering about many things." Olga admitted that she had never felt so worn out and wondered if she would ever get used to it. Her mother asked if she was thinking of giving up. The Grand Duchess hesitated as if the thought had entered her head. "Olga, you can't just give up after one day," said her mother.

"But, Mama, I feel fit to drop," she protested.

"I don't think we will be making up a hundred beds every day, Olga. This is probably just a baptism of fire. Give it a few days at least," said her mother.

I think we were all shattered but I was enjoying myself and I felt sure that the next day would be better and the following day, so that eventually I would be able to take it all in my stride.

By the end of the day, there was a mountain of rolled up bandages in the middle of the table. Sister Procopy, came in and told us that we could finish. The royals stood up and wearily made their way to their private apartments, while I went to the changing room to change back into my day clothes. I didn't realise that I was being followed.

"Nurse Bobrov, just a minute if you please," said Sister Procopy once I had changed from my uniform to my normal clothes.

I stopped in my tracks and hoped that she wouldn't keep me long. I was exhausted.

"You did very well today, under very difficult circumstances. I noticed how the royals turned to you for help and advice." she smiled at me and that smile transformed her face from the hard regimented ward sister to someone that I thought I would like to get to know better. "I don't know if they will make the grade but I have a strong feeling that you will. If I was you, I would go home, have a nice soak in a good hot bath and then straight to bed."

I smiled at her. "Is that your professional opinion, Sister?" I asked her.

"It certainly is. I remember my first week of nursing. I felt so tired that I could hardly move. Rest assured it passes," she said with another smile. "I see your fiancé is waiting to take you home. Have a good night, Nurse Bobrov. I will see you tomorrow morning," she said and left.

Nicky came over to me and took my arm. "You look absolutely exhausted darling."

I admitted that I was.

"You look like you are in need of a hot bath and bed, Lia"

I smiled at him, "Just what Sister Procopy prescribed."

"She seems a right old harridan, that woman," he commented.

"Actually, I think that is just an act to have authority over the other nurses." I told Nicky about the day, how the royals had to ask me to show them how to do things and Sister Procopy had noticed and commented on it, just before I left. "She thinks that I might make the grade as a nurse."

Nicky asked me if that was what I wanted. It didn't take much time for me to think of my answer.

"Yes, Nicky, it is. Do you mind?" I asked him wearily.

Nicky hesitated then. "You had to wait all of those months for me to return to Russia, not knowing where I was or what I was doing. I suppose I can wait for you."

"When I am not working, we can spend all of our time together. I won't always be this tired, Nicky, but today, between us we prepared a hundred beds ready for when the wounded arrive."

Nicky asked if the royals pulled their weight. "Once I had shown them how to make a bed again, they did but I had already washed ten beds before they even showed up."

Nicky asked me what Sister Procopy had said at their being late.

"Darling, what could she say? You can't discipline the royals."

He laughed.

When we arrived at Grand Mama's, Nicky said he wouldn't come in. He would let me get an early night and would see me in the morning, then he stopped. "I completely forgot, I have your engagement ring and I have brought you a gold chain so that you can wear it underneath you uniform. I went to Karl's especially for it today." He handed me a Faberge box. In it lay my engagement ring on a beautiful golden chain. I leaned over in the car and kissed him. His lips felt so warm and soft beneath mine, that I just wanted them to remain there, with him holding me and his lips upon mine. I stifled a yawn, not wanting him to see but my Nicky seemed to know everything about me and told me to go inside and get to bed. Again, I kissed him goodnight, then got out of the car and went inside. Tanya was waiting for me inside the hallway, to take my coat. She commented how tired I looked. I told her that I would have a light meal in my room, then a bath and bed.

I popped my head around the door of the lounge to say hello and good night to Grand Mama. She asked me how my day had been. I just said that it had been tiring but enjoyable. I then told her that I was going up to my room.

"What about food, Lia?"

I told Grand Mama that Tanya was going to bring me something on a tray.

"You must eat properly, darling, if nothing else but to keep up your strength," she said to me.

I said that I would and wished her a goodnight. Slowly, wearily, I made my way up the staircase to my bedroom. I was thankful that Tanya had already got a tray of food for me and something to drink. I sat down and ate my fill, while she prepared a hot bath for me.

Like a child she helped to undress me in the bathroom then left me to soak away all of my aches and pains. I must have dozed off, because the next thing I knew was the noise of the water running down the plug hole. Tanya was waiting for me with a thick fluffy towel to wrap around me. I dried myself off, then put on my nightdress. Tanya took down my hair and brushed it, then realised that I was nearly falling asleep again. "Let me open your bed for you Miss Thalia," she said and steered me to my bed, where I sank gratefully into the softness. As soon as she turned off my bedroom light and wished me a good night, I fell fast asleep.

The next day at the hospital, Sister Procopy taught us how to take temperatures and record them on a chart, then how to take blood pressures and chart them, then to take a pulse. For this she gave us all a watch with a second hand on it, which we pinned on our aprons, to help us take the pulse. Explaining that we took the pulse for thirty seconds on our watches, then double the pulse rate which would give us the final reading. Once we had mastered that, we had a bit of light relief while we were shown how to change a bed with a patient in it. The Tsarina volunteered to be the patient first of all and we all took turns making the bed as Sister Procopy had shown us, also taking turns being the patient. There was a lot of laughter going on, as we, gently, rolled the patient, first one way, then the other. I heard Titania tell her mother to lay still and to stop trying to help her. Olga said that maybe if Titania asked nicely the patient would get up off the bed and let them make it that way, which caused Titania and the Tsarina to burst into fits of the giggles. I laughed as well. Obviously, the more we practised, the better we got. Sister Procopy came and tested us on what we had learned that day, then we spent more time rolling bandages. Looking back, I was surprised how many bandages one ward would get through in a day. It was phenomenal. Titania asked the sister why we had to roll so many bandages. Sister Procopy told us that in some cases dressings were changed three or four times a day, so one ward could get through hundreds in a day. It was nearly time for us to finish for the day. We were told that over the next couple of days we would learn all about bandaging various limbs.

Nicky came to fetch me again and briefly, spoke to the Grand Duchesses Olga, Tatiana and the Tsarina. They all said that they were thoroughly enjoying themselves, although very tired.

We did have fun over the next few days practising the various skills taught to us by Sister Procopy but nothing would prepare us for the reality of dealing with patients.

After five days working in the hospital, I had two days off so had a chance to catch up on my sleep and with our wedding preparations. I saw Nicky during my time off. We made sure that we spent as much time together as we could. The weather had turned bitterly cold and we had the first snow of the season, which lay thick on the ground. Nicky came to collect me from Grand Mama's and took me on a Troika ride out into the countryside. The war, which everyone was talking about, seemed so very far away at that moment, while we sat snuggled under piles of furs, bundled up against the cold. It was still snowing as Nicky turned the sleigh towards the outskirts of town. Motor cars were all very well but, in the snow, the Troika was still the best form of transport. What vibrant colour there had been in St Petersburg in the summer months, had now been covered by a blanket of white. It reminded me of a scene from fairy tales that I had read as a child. (Probably the Snow Queen.) I wondered how the land could look so beautiful when so many men were being killed or maimed. Although we had not been introduced yet to the ravages of war at the hospital, thoughts of it, now, were never far from my thoughts. What if I could not stand the sight of blood, mutilation or death? I did ask myself if I thought that I could do what was expected of me. Up until now, Alexandria Palace still had not received its first patient, we were all just preparing for the onslaught, which was due to happen while I was away.

I noticed after a while that the Tsarina was becoming more bowed over. I asked her if she was all right. She told me that she suffered with back problems which with all the bending over was irritating her back. I told her that I was sorry that she was suffering.

The Tsarina said that she would try to continue but wasn't sure how long she could continue.

Nicky touched my face after we had been driving for a while.

"Where are you, darling? You are so quiet, immersed in your thoughts. What are you thinking about, Lia?"

I voiced my fears to him and told him about the Tsarina and he smiled tenderly at me. "Do you think that you are the only one having these thoughts, darling. I am sure that the royals are feeling the same and they have led a very privileged life, very sheltered, if anyone will fail at the nursing, I am sure that it won't be you, Lia, you are made of stronger stuff. I am sure that anything you set your mind to, you will succeed at." He kissed me gently. "I have faith in you,

Lia. Now to change the subject, how are the wedding plans coming along? Is there anything that still needs to be done?"

Only Nicky could read me so well and do the right thing to take me away from my thoughts of war.

"We still need to go and order our wedding rings," I told him, returning to happier thoughts. "I want Gregor to give me away. I don't think my father would attend the wedding even if we did invite him. After our last meeting, anyway, I wouldn't want him at my wedding. Gregor, over the years has been more like a father to me than he ever was."

Nicky said that he thought Gregor would be perfect. "I am sure he would be flattered as well. Would you like to go to Karl's today and discuss your wedding band?"

I nodded.

I was sorry that I let thoughts of the hospital spoil our time together and tried to forget it. Nicky said that he had booked a table at Minsky's for the evening, where we would eat and drink and dance away my thoughts.

Karl was always happy to see us. We didn't just discuss my requirements but many other things as well. He took us up to his workshops to see more items which were being made there. I always took an interest in this. What woman wouldn't? I suppose if I had wanted to work, Karl would have employed me but I wasn't artistic enough and as he told us, many commissions for his work had fallen off since start of the war.

"But women will always want jewels and men will still want their cigarette cases and cuff links, so all is not lost." He said cheerfully.

After our visit to Karl's workshop, Nicky took me back to Grand Mama's to rest, bathe and change for the evening ahead.

Minsky's, as usual, was very busy. Nicky and I were escorted to our table in a quiet corner, to enable us to talk and if we wanted, later, to dance. Our meal, as always, was superb. Between courses Nicky held my hand and kissed my fingers, telling me how impatient he was for us to be married. When we were alone like this, my body ached to be held closer to him. I was still a virgin and knew nothing about marriage or the marriage bed but my body was telling me that there was more than just kissing, holding hands and cuddling and I longed to know more, feel more but like all good young ladies, I would be expected to wait until my wedding night to find out.

After our meal, Nicky took my hand and led me onto the dance floor. This was a lot smaller space than any of the ballrooms we had danced in before and due to the number of other dancers, he held me so much closer. My heartbeat increased, my breathing came faster and shallower and I could feel my temperature rise. Nicky whispered in my ear, "I think you are looking forward to our wedding night as much as I am, Lia. Time seems to be passing by so slowly for me and I am getting impatient."

I looked at him and could see that his feelings were matching my own. "Don't worry, darling," he said, "I will be patient but I just wanted you to know."

I told him that I knew little about love and marriage and Nicky told me that it was expected of a young woman. "I think once you start nursing patients, you will learn a little more about the male body and I must admit that I am not sure how I feel about that."

I didn't know what to say to him but to re-assure him of my love. I told him that I was marking the days off on a calendar to our wedding day. "Do you realise that it is only two hundred and twenty-one days now till our wedding day?"

He laughed, "Only two hundred and twenty-one days. It seems like a lifetime but I will be patient. I have waited for you for this long and another two hundred and twenty-one days will soon fly by." He kissed me again. "Miss Bobrov, have I told you how much I love you?"

"Not in so many words, Your Highness." The moment of unfulfilled passion had passed and we were back on an even footing again.

The temperature seemed to have risen slightly from our ride in the troika and the snow was beginning to melt into a dirty grey slush.

When we left Minsky's just before midnight, I was surprised to see so many people in the street. Nicky put his arm protectively around my shoulder as we made our way to his motor car.

"Hey comrade, do you realise that the amount of money you have just paid out on that meal would feed a family for nearly a year. Those jewels you are wearing would feed and clothe a dozen families for a year."

Nicky told me to keep on walking to the car and say nothing. He let me into the passenger seat and told me to lock my door. Immediately, he went to the driver's side and got in, locking his door behind him. My heart was racing again but this time not in passion. I gave a great sigh of relief once we were driving away from Minsky's back to Grand Mama's.

Igor opened the front door when he heard the car pull up. Nicky came and opened my door for me and kissed me, then he told Igor to lock the gates behind him, explaining about the angry crowds that we had bumped into and he told me that he would see me the next afternoon. He had told me while we were eating that he would leave me to sleep, for as long as I could, tomorrow, so that I would feel refreshed.

I stood at the top of the steps to watch his car drive off and Igor ran to shut the tall gates behind him.

"Miss Thalia, what is going on?" Igor asked when he came back to the house.

I told him about the crowds outside Minsky's. "I think it is just a precaution, Igor, nothing more." I wished him goodnight and went upstairs to bed. Grand Mama had already retired for the evening, rather than wait up for me.

Tanya helped me undress and then turned out the light, once I was in bed. I lay there thinking about what the man outside Minsky's had said. If what he said was true, no wonder there was so much unrest in the country. I tried to stay awake, thinking what I could do to help the situation. When it came down to it, I could do no more than I was doing, for the time being.

Nicky paid his people a more than fair wage. They had above average working conditions and seemed to be contented. I was going to be nursing our fallen soldiers. What more could two people do? Nicky had told me some time ago that the Tsar, our cousin, buried his head in the sand when it came to what his people wanted. Anyone who went against him would be shot or hung. That was how Nicholas III ruled Russia.

I fell asleep and slept till late the next morning, knowing that it would be the last time I would be able to sleep late for another five days.

August Brisac called with her entourage of seamstresses the next morning to discuss my wedding dress. I wanted something that would stun Nicky, the moment he saw me. We discussed styles and patterns and then moved on to materials. It seemed, just as it had been, when I first arrived in St Petersburg, with bolts of material for my wedding dress strewn across my bed. So many things had changed, mainly the beautiful city that I had fallen in love with, now had a nasty, cruel side to it and there wasn't any easy solution to it.

Nicky came in the afternoon and we went through the acceptances for our wedding. We discussed our honeymoon, which we decided we wanted to spend at Kadriorg Palace. The weather would be good, so we could swim in the sea and lie on the sand in the sun to dry off. He left early so that I could get another good night's sleep, ready for the early start the next morning.

# Chapter 19

## The Ravages of War

Nicky arrived earlier the next morning as it had snowed again during the night and the snow was still on the ground. The trip to the hospital was particularly treacherous and I told Nicky that I would stay at the hospital overnight, to save him the journey in such bad weather. It didn't seem fair for him to keep getting up so early to take me to work and with the roads as bad as they were, I was worried that he might have an accident. The time we had already spent apart was excruciating to us both. I couldn't imagine my life without Nicky now. I don't think I would want to carry on living if anything happened to him.

If I thought the Palace was a hive of activity before the arrival of the patients, it was even more so now, after Nicky deposited me at the main entrance. Nurses were moving around like busy bees. The atmosphere had changed dramatically from one of light-heartedness to one of serious business. I went to the room to change into my uniform and went to the ballroom, where I had been working the previous week. I stood at the entrance shocked. Every bed was occupied. Other nurses, who I had not seen before, were already working there, then I saw Sister Procopy come towards me.

"Welcome back, Nurse Bobrov, I hope you are rested after your time off. I think you will notice a big change from last week. I want you to start on the temperatures and blood pressures. You remember how to do them?" she asked.

I nodded. She told me to start at the far end of the ward and told me that she would check on the first two patients, after I had done their observations.

I looked at the row of faces as I passed down the ward. Some smiled at me, those that seemed to be on the road to recovery; the more serious patients were nearer the large table in the middle of the ward, so that an eye could be kept on them.

I approached the patient in the furthest bed, looked at his name on the chart and called him by his name, then told him that I needed to take his temperature and blood pressure. I remembered everything I had been taught and although I was shaking inside, I tried to maintain a calm exterior. Once I had done one patient, it got easier as I went along the row of beds. Sister Procopy checked the first few and nodded her approval, "Carry on, Nurse Bobrov," she told me.

I didn't see the royals at all that day. I wondered if I would still be allowed to stay overnight due to the weather. It had been snowing constantly while I had been at the palace and the driveway alone was blocked by snow. It would be impossible for Nicky to get to me tonight. When I had a break, I took the stairs up to the second floor to see if I could see the Tsarina or someone to just make sure that it would be acceptable for me to stay the night. I found a maid, who seemed to be attached to the royal household. I told her who I was and what I was doing at the palace. She seemed to know who I was. She said the Tsarina had told her to make up a room for me. She showed me to a room, which wasn't as lavish as my bedroom at Grand Mama's but it was clean and comfortable. The maid told me that she would bring me a tray of food to my room at the end of my shift. She asked me if there was anything else she could do for me. I said that I couldn't think of anything. She curtseyed to me and said to just ask if there was anything they could do. I went back to the ward and was told that I needed to help change some dressings. Sister Procopy looked at me, "Do you think you feel up to it, Nurse Bobrov?"

I nodded and followed her to the first bed. She told me that the patient had had his left leg shot off below the knee and we needed to change his dressing. I looked at the patient, he was about the same age as me. I tried not to think about it but smiled and asked him if he would mind me changing his dressing.

"No, nurse, I don't mind, as long as you don't mind me looking at you while you are doing it." He smiled cheekily at me.

Sister Procopy observed my every move. She instructed me on preparing a trolley with everything I needed to change the dressing.

I tried not to shudder when I saw his mutilated limb. "Not a pretty sight, is it, nurse? I can't see any young woman wanting me now."

I smiled at him, "I shouldn't think any woman would bother about it when your silver tongue could charm the birds from the trees."

I cleaned the wound then placed a pad over it and bandaged.

"What do they call you?" he asked me.

"Nurse Bobrov."

I finished his dressing then pulled his sheets back over him.

"Well done, Nurse Bobrov," Sister Procopy said. She asked me if I felt up to doing more then gave me a list of beds in which the patients needed their dressings changed. I did the first three, trying to keep a cheerful smile on my face. On the fourth patient I noticed his face was slightly flushed. His eyes were glazed. When I lifted the sheets, I could smell the wound. Something seemed wrong. I started to undo the dressing then noticed that his leg was turning black. I put the dressing loosely over the wound again then quickly pulled his bedclothes back over him before going to find Sister Procopy. I explained the situation to her and she followed me back to the bed. She told me to pull the screens around him then began to remove his dressing.

"Well observed, Nurse Bobrov. I need to call the doctor to have a look but it looks like gangrene has set it. Wait here with the patient while I go and fetch the doctor."

The poor man was moaning. I wasn't sure what to do but thought that maybe a cool cloth on his forehead might help. By the time Sister came back with the doctor, the patient had stopped moaning and lay quite still. The doctor checked his pulse, which he said was weak, then checked the wound. "We will have to remove the whole leg if we are to save him." Then he asked Sister Procopy, who had brought her attention to the matter. Sister explained that it was me and said that I was one of the new nurses. The doctor turned to me, "Well spotted, nurse." I was dismissed and left Sister Procopy and the doctor behind the screens. I continued with my duties until Sister Procopy came up to me.

"Nurse Bobrov, the patient we have just seen, it is gangrene. I thought that they might operate to remove the rest of the leg to save him but the doctor has examined the patient and his opinion is that the gangrene has gone too far. I am afraid there is nothing more we can do. He is dying."

It was a shock to me. Foolishly, naively, I thought that I would be able to save everyone I helped. Now the realities of nursing were thrust in front of me.

"We can't always save them, Nurse Bobrov, as you now know but we can help to ease their passing and make sure that they don't die alone. I know that I am asking a lot of you as you are still very new to all of this but I was wondering if you would sit with him till the end. You can keep a check on his breathing. It will slow dramatically, until it stops altogether." I hadn't said a word through all of this. "You can do it, Thalia," she said giving me a smile of encouragement. "I know I have already given you a baptism by fire, only because I thought that you could handle it. Just hold his hand and talk to him, to let him know that there is someone there. The hearing is the last sense to go. Come and find me when it is all over and I will show you what to do next. I have faith in you, Thalia." She patted my shoulder reassuringly and left me.

I returned to the poor soldier and pulled up one of the chairs from the central table. One of the other nurses, whose name was Katya Patenko, gave me a sympathetic smile.

"Your first?" she asked. I nodded, "It will get easier," she assured me.

I sat down and took the soldier's hand. His chart said that his name was Pavlov Gagarin.

"Pavlov, my name is Thalia Bobrov. I hope you don't mind if I sit with you for a while." His eyes fluttered as if he was trying to open them. What did I say to a dying man? I had no idea. I took a deep breath and looked over to the large window opposite his bed. "It's still snowing outside. At least it is nice and warm in here. I came from St Petersburg this morning. The roads were treacherous. They must be worse now. The snow has not let up all day. Mind you the snow would be perfect for building a snowman or snowball fights, (I used to love playing in the snow when I was little.)"

I was just speaking my thoughts out loud. His eyes flickered open briefly and he tried to speak but his voice came out in a whisper, so that I had to lean closer to hear what he said.

"Are you an angel?" he asked.

I smiled at him, "No, Pavlov, just a nurse. Can I get you anything?"

He shook his head and closed his eyes again, as if keeping them open took too much energy. I watched his chest move up and down as he struggled to breathe.

I stroked his hand. "I can remember as a child having snowball fights with the other children in my village. We used to be so cold but having fun was more important than going home and getting warm." I watched, the time between each of his breaths was getting longer. I continued talking. "When we got tired of the snowball fights, we would then build a snow man. We had teams; one team would roll the ball for the lower body, another team would build the top body and another team would roll a smaller snowball for the head." He took one more breath and breathed out. I waited for him to take another breath in but it never came. His hand was already turning as cold as marble when I finally let it go. I felt a lump come to my throat with unshed tears.

I went to find Sister Procopy. I found it hard to stop the tears from flowing. I didn't even know the man, yet I could shed tears at his passing. Sister Procopy could see the state that I was in and steered me to one of the store rooms.

"Now you can let your tears flow." She handed me a handkerchief. "We all cry after our first death, Thalia. The secret is not to let the patients see. Always come away from the patients before you let the tears flow, they are suffering enough, without letting them see a woman cry."

I asked her if she had cried. She told me that she still did, even now. I dried my eyes and thanked her. "Are you ready to go back and perform your final duty for him?" I nodded and followed her back out to the ward and to the bed with the screens still pulled around it. She told me that I should wash him all over, while she went to get a porter to come and collect him. I collected a bowl of hot water, a cloth and towel. Katya Patenko popped her head around the screen.

"Sister sent me to help you. This is a two-nurse job."

We stripped the body of his pyjamas. It was the first time I had seen a naked man. I was embarrassed and tried not to look.

"It's a day of firsts for you, Thalia isn't it?" Katya asked. I nodded, unable to speak. "Once you have seen one, then you have seen them all," she said cheerfully. We finished washing Pavlov just in time for the porter to arrive with the trolley to take him away. When the porter left with his body, I was told to wash down the bed with carbolic and remake it.

The bed was soon filled again.

By the end of the day, I was both, physically and emotionally exhausted. I handed over to another nurse, giving my report on the patients I had dealt with during the day, then left the ward. Sister Procopy came and spoke to me. "I hope that I haven't scared you away Thalia. I know that it has been a hard first day for you but I had faith in you. You have not let me down. You will make a very fine nurse, Thalia. Well done for today."

She asked me if Nicky was collecting me. I told her that because of the snow, I was staying at the Palace. She told me that all of the nurses had rooms in another wing of the Palace and asked me if I wanted to join them, rather than stay with the royals. I told her that I would go and visit there but would go back to my allotted room, for the time being, so as not to offend them. Sister Procopy told me that she was just finishing her shift and would show me the nurse's rooms.

The nurse's quarters were on the second floor in the opposite wing to the royals. It was a good job, I thought, as the nurse's quarters were noisy with women's chatter and laughter.

"They tend to let out all of the pressure and strains of the day, in laughter." She explained. "I think you could do with the same." As a senior nurse, Sister Procopy had a room all to herself, whereas the nurses shared a dormitory or should I say dormitories. There was well over a hundred staff for the hospital. The minor staff had dormitories and the senior staff had their own rooms. It was the dormitories where all of the noise was coming from.

She opened a door from the hallway and switched on the light. "This is my room, be it ever so humble. Would you like a cup of tea?" She filled a kettle and put it on the single ring.

"Can I ask you where the royals were today? I thought they would be working along with me?"

Sister Procopy told me that the Tsarina was suffering with a bad back that her put her in bed but she had assigned the Grand Duchesses to another ward, where the patients weren't so demanding. She didn't think that the Grand Duchesses could do it on their own without their mother encouraging them. She told me that she didn't think it right for the Tsarina or Grand Duchesses of Russia to be soiling their hands with seriously ill patients. "I have had them put on the ward where the patients are recovering and getting ready to be discharged.

"I am sorry that I dropped you in at the deep end today but we need good nurses and I knew, by how quickly you picked things up and my instinct and experience of years of nursing, told me that you would make a good nurse."

I told her that I was pleased that she had such faith in me. "I hope that I don't let you down, Sister Procopy."

She told me that her name was Olga when we weren't working. We talked about all sorts of things; how long she had been nursing. She told me that she had worked in a field hospital for years and that her quarters in the field hospital were very makeshift compared to what she had here, then she had had a breakdown and they had eventually moved her to the Palace to run a ward. She said that it was the biggest ward she had ever, been in charge of. One hundred beds all in one room was much larger than a normal ward, which she said usually held about twenty to thirty beds. She asked about my childhood, which I told her something of but not everything and we talked of Nicky and our forthcoming marriage. I told her the date of the wedding and asked if they would allow me a month off for our honeymoon. She seemed surprised that I wanted to return after my marriage.

I told Olga that I wanted to be useful and I felt that I was doing something for my country, by nursing and I worried that without nursing, however difficult it might be, made me feel that I was contributing, to Russia. Olga asked me what Nicky thought about me wanting to carry on after I was married? I had not even thought about whether Nicky would approve or not. That would be something that we would have to discuss before too long.

At that moment I missed him more than ever. I wanted to talk to him, to be with him and tell him all about my day.

We were snowed in for three more days. Tsarskoye Selo was cut off for the whole of the time. It was only on the fifth day that lorries managed to get through with more patients and medical supplies. The wards were extremely busy. Another twenty beds were put on the ward I was on, making a total of a hundred and twenty, which made our workload even heavier. There were eight nurses on the ward at the same time as me. Some were fully qualified nurses, some were like me a, trainee nurse. Each evening after my shift, I spent some time in the nurse's quarters making friends with some of the other nurses. The atmosphere there was so much more relaxed than in St Petersburg. I enjoyed it. I had never had any girlfriends near my own age before and the past few days had been fun. Olga Procopy and I spent quite a lot of time together, as well and she had leant me some of her nursing manuals, from her training. During the nights that I had to spend at the Palace because of the snow, I sat reading those books.

Nicky came to pick me up, as soon as the road from Tsarskoye Selo was cleared. It coincided with my two days off, which I was relieved about. When I was staying at the Palace, I didn't have to get up quite so early. When Nicky came and collected me, I was nowhere near as tired as I had been after my first week.

When I saw his face, all of the incidents from the week faded away. We waited until the car had left the Palace grounds before Nicky stopped the car and kissed me, telling me what hell it had been, not seeing me for four days. How long we remained locked together in the car, I didn't know but it was like water in a desert to me. When he held me, I felt whole again; replenished. He started the car again and we were on our way back to St Petersburg. Nicky began asking me about the royals. I told him that the Grand Duchesses we were on different wards now and the Tsarina was suffering with her back and had not been on the wards for some time. He told me that the Tsarina suffered considerably with back pain that sometimes had her bed bound or wheelchair bound. I asked him that if that was the case, why had she volunteered for nursing? He shrugged his shoulders. "I don't know the workings of her mind but I know that she had heard the rumours, so maybe she did it to try and prove that she was not a spy."

I asked Nicky whether she knew about the flyers being circulated about her and Rasputin or the Grand Duchesses and Rasputin.

Again, Nicky shrugged and said he sincerely hope not.

I told Nicky about my first day and my first death and he looked horrified. I told him that I had to wash and prepare the body and he asked me what that entailed.

When I told him, that we had to strip the body, then wash it all over, he went quiet for a while, mulling over, in his mind, what it meant.

His reply, when it came, completely took me by surprise, "Well by the time we get married, your bathing skills will be honed to perfection. I look forward to sampling them." I had expected him to get angry or something but he seemed to take it all in his stride and make a joke about it, as he always did.

"You don't mind that I have seen another man's body?"

"Well, he was dead, darling... I'm sorry," he apologised, "that sounded very callous. I didn't mean it to be. I would have been very naive to think that you would never see a naked man, dead or alive, doing what you are doing. At least you won't go to our marriage bed, completely ignorant, unlike many other young women."

I asked him if that was a bad thing.

"It will make it... interesting, darling."

I asked Nicky what he had been doing while I was away. He told me that he had kept busy. "I have been helping your grand mama and Gregor and Marguerite organising the moving of some of their things."

"Do you still think we will have to leave Russia?"

He told me that the newspapers were full of details of riots and break ins. Every day and night the gates to both Grand Mama and Gregor and Mama's had been closed and locked. He had to honk the horn on the car, so that they would be opened and let him in.

St Petersburg had had heavy snows as well and most people had stayed inside in the warm, apart from the students who seemed to be continually rioting, miners seemed to be continually striking and Russia was sending more and more men to the front.

The streets of St Petersburg had mounds of snow piled up on the sides but there was still snow, which had turned to slush on the roads. Even now, there were very few people around. It was dark when Nicky stopped outside the gates to Grand Mama's. He honked the horn and Igor came out to unlock the gates and let us in.

When I walked into the hall, I was surprised to see Grand Mama waiting for me. She came and put her arms around me, telling me how much she missed me and how worried she had been for me. She invited Nicky to stay for dinner and told us that Mama and Gregor would be coming to dinner as well.

It felt good to be able to see everyone again under the same roof. I told Grand Mama that I was longing for a nice long soak in a hot bath and wear something more glamorous than the rough grey serge dress of a nurse.

They both told me to go and enjoy the luxury of a deep, hot bath. Nicky said that he would keep Grand Mama, company, while I did so.

It was good to see Tanya waiting for me in my bedroom. She began running my bath and then came to help me undress. Much as I enjoyed my time at the hospital, I realised how much I missed the luxury of my own bedroom, maid and a good soak in a hot perfumed bath. Tanya was full of questions about my time at the hospital, when I told her what I had been doing, she was shocked, telling me that she couldn't do anything like that. She let me soak for a while before she came and washed my hair. I felt so much better as I stepped from my scented bath into the warm, soft towel which she wrapped around me. This was so much better than the roughness of serge and the smell of carbolic. It felt good to be pampered again.

After Tanya had dried my hair in front of the roaring fire in my bedroom, I asked her to pick out one of my evening gowns. She dressed my hair up in a simple chignon, which she said always suited me, emphasising the length of my neck. I put on my engagement ring, which had been hanging around my neck on a gold necklace, under my uniform and wore my choker of pearls and pearl drop earrings, with the matching bracelet. It felt wonderful to be dressed elegantly again and I knew that I would be happy to spend the week in my uniform, if I could come back for a couple of days of complete pampering, which was more than any of the other nurses had. I had become friends with some of the other nurses at the hospital and was spending more time in the nurse's quarters.

When I eventually went downstairs, I found that Mama and Gregor had already arrived. They both hugged me and Nicky made some comment about me being the vision of loveliness and hugged me again, breathing in my perfume. "So much more appealing than carbolic, darling," he said cheekily.

I was bombarded by questions about what I had been doing and how I was getting on with the Tsarina and the Grand Duchesses. I explained that I hadn't seen them all week and we weren't working on the same ward now.

We all sat down to dinner in the large dining room and Grand Mama's chef had outdone himself. The food at the hospital was good and wholesome but very basic compared to the food from Grand Mama's house chef. When we had finished, we all retired back to the lounge and Grand Mama asked Peter Abramovich bring up a bottle of champagne from the cellar.

When we had all been served, Mama said that she and Gregor had an announcement to make. We all stopped talking to hear their announcement.

"We are expecting a baby," Mama said.

Grand Mama cried out and pressed a hand to her mouth. "Oh no, Babushka, didn't you tell Gregor what the doctor said after Lia was born?"

"Mama, that was nearly twenty years ago. Things have changed. Great advances have been made in medicine since then," she said and looked at me, pleading for support. "They have, haven't they, Lia?"

I agreed with her but there was still a small knot of fear in the pit of my stomach.

I would have to speak to Olga Procopy when I returned to Tsarskoye Selo, to see what she knew, if anything, about child birth.

Gregor told us that they had spoken to a specialist doctor in St Petersburg about things and he had assured them that he would keep a special eye on Mama and ensured her of a safe delivery.

I said that I would do all that I could to read up on childbirth, which Grand Mama looked at me horrified. "Lia, you are an unmarried young woman!"

Nicky looked at me and winked as if to say that she would be even more horrified if she knew all of what I had been doing while nursing.

I told them that I intended to carry on with my nursing and if it took me into midwifery, then so be it. I wanted to do everything I could, to help Mama through her pregnancy.

Mama and Gregor left early. I think Gregor wanted to make sure that Mama rested as much as possible. After they left, Grand Mama retired to bed, leaving Nicky and I alone and unchaperoned.

I thought now that we were alone was the right time to broach the subject of my continuing with my nursing training after we were married. I wasn't sure how he would react but I couldn't, not tell him about it.

"Why do you want to carry on after we are married?" he asked.

"That last time we were at Minsky's. The things those men were saying about what we had paid for the meal… It got me thinking, Nicky. However, much money we had, it would never be enough to help them all. Nursing our poor soldiers back to health or even just sitting with them holding their hand and talking with them until they take their last breath is the only thing that I can do and I have been told that I am good at it. Nicky, I can make a difference by doing what I am doing." I pleaded with him.

"I can understand how you feel, Lia, and I am proud of you and what you are doing, I really am. But will they allow you to carry on nursing after we are married and what about babies? What happens when you get pregnant?"

"If and when I get pregnant, then I will stop nursing, obviously. I don't even know if I will be able to carry on after we are married, Nicky. I will have to find out but if I am allowed to, will you support my decision?"

"I will but what about your mother and grandmother, what will they have to say about it?"

I told Nicky, that once we were married, it would be no one's business but ours. He told me that the first thing I should do is to see if I would be able to carry on nursing after our marriage.

Our time together was so precious, that when it came time for me to go back to work, I knew that I would miss him terribly. Once I was on the wards again, duty overtook anything else and my thoughts of Nicky were pushed to the back of my mind. We had new admissions on the ward, which is only to be expected after two days away, also there was another new nurse on the ward. I was surprised to see that it was the Tsarina.

She came and greeted me like an old friend. Obviously, it was known who she was and I could see the icy glares from the patients. I noticed when she had passed by some of the patients, I heard them talking about her behind her back. What they were saying was nasty and hateful. I couldn't help but feel sorry for her, remembering how we had all laughed, when we had been practicing how to make a bed with someone in it. I was told that the Tsarina could take temperatures and blood pressures but was unable to do any heavy work due to her back condition.

I know the Tsar was her husband but surely, she could not be held responsible for his actions and what was happening in our country.

# Chapter 20
## The Sword of Damocles

Over the following weeks, we didn't have much time to talk on the ward as we were always very busy. One week after returning from two days off, I noticed that Sister Procopy had asked the Tsarina to work on our ward again and to take the temperatures and blood pressures. I, on the other hand, had all of the more unsavoury tasks to do, like changing dressings.

I heard other conversations between the patients, about the war and the conditions they were in. Obviously, it was bitterly cold at the front, with snow, rain and mud. They had little or no food and nowhere warm and dry to sleep. It made me shiver just thinking of it. I took a certain amount of comfort that at least now they were warm, had a comfortable bed to sleep in and good nourishing food. I think because of my hair colour of white blonde, I heard some of the patients calling me 'Angel'. That brought a smile to my face. I thought that they must have liked me. When they spoke of the Tsarina behind her back, one of the names they called her was 'German Bitch', another was 'Rasputin's Whore'.

Before the day was out Sister Procopy moved the Tsarina from the ward. The atmosphere, while she was there was so palpable that you could nearly cut through it with a knife.

Sister sent her back to the other ward, which she had been on previously, thanking her for helping us out with our 'busy time'.

I was busy doing my rounds checking dressings. One of the patients that had been on the ward since we had first taken in patients and always called me 'Nurse Angel' to my face, looked very flushed when I got to him. His name was Igor Pavlova. He had asked me, more than once, if I could write a letter to his wife, just to let her know that he was safe. He had a little boy of three called Mikhail, who he thought the world of. He often talked to me of his wife, Maria, and Mikhail and showed me a photograph of them, while I changed his bandages. He had lost his left foot and was making good progress getting around on crutches, hobbling around talking to the patients that were bed bound.

When I reached Igor's bed, he was not in his usual position, sitting on the edge of his bed swinging his good leg but lying down with his eyes closed.

"Igor, you don't seem to be your usual cheery self today. Are you alright?" I asked him, automatically feeling his forehead, which was burning up.

"Do you have a headache?" I asked him.

He nodded listlessly. "My leg is aching as well. I told the other nurse but she just took my temperature and noted it down. She didn't say anything else."

I asked him what nurse he meant and he told me that it was the Tsarina. I double checked his temperature and blood pressure then pulled the sheets back and was about to undo the bandages. I didn't need to. The smell hit me as soon as I pulled the sheets back. I remembered the smell, covered him back over and went to find Sister Procopy. I didn't tell her about Igor complaining of a headache to the Tsarina I made out that I had just spoken to Igor and after checking his temperature and pulling the sheets back to change his dressing, I could smell something that I didn't think was right.

Sister Procopy marched down the ward with me following in her wake. Without being told, I pulled the screens around Igor's bed.

Sister looked at his chart, rested the back of her hand on his burning forehead, then she pulled back the bedclothes. Like me, she didn't need to remove the dressings. She turned on her heel and went in search of the doctor.

Igor looked at me, as if to ask the dreaded question, "What is wrong?"

I tried to smile comfortingly at him, "Your temperature is a little high, Igor. That's why you have a headache. We are just going to get the doctor to see what he recommends. I am just going to get a cold compress for your forehead in the meantime."

I hated to see the look of fear in his eyes and knew that there was little that I could do for him.

When I returned with the cold compress for his forehead, he looked at me, "Oh that feels so much better, Nurse Angel… Will I be all right? I am sure once this headache goes, I will be back to my old self, hobbling around the ward, causing more mischief."

I just nodded and smiled, my throat ached with unshed tears that had been building up since I first checked him.

I suppose I felt close to him because of the time that he had been on the ward and also him telling me about his family. Sister Procopy returned with the doctor, who removed the dressings and said that the gangrene had spread up the leg and we should prepare him immediately for theatre. He turned to Igor, "Gangrene has set in, we must amputate your leg, soldier."

All of the time the doctor was pronouncing this sentence on Igor, I could see the poor man's eyes fill with tears. To the doctor he was just one of the many; the 'cannon fodder'. I knew that we had to keep a calm exterior, whatever happened. I clasped his hot hand in mine. He started crying that they could not take off his leg. He could still work without his foot but not his leg."

I tried to calm him down, "Igor, it is better to lose your leg than to lose your life. What would Maria and Mikhail do without you? You must think of them, Igor, they need you."

He looked at Sister Procopy and asked her if I could be with him throughout the operation. Sister Procopy nodded and told me to get the trolley for his medication. Once we were out of his hearing, she told me that I could stay with him until he was under the anaesthetic, then I was to return straight back to the ward. I thanked her, fetched the trolley and asked a porter to wheel it to theatre. I held Igor's hand all the way to the theatre. He kept calling me his 'Guardian Angel' and saying he knew that I would look after him, through it all. We arrived at the anaesthetist's room where they gave him an injection and held a mask over his face. I held his hand, until his hand went limp in mine as he fell asleep under the anaesthetic. The theatre nurse told me that he was asleep and I could go back to the ward. They would bring him back to me when it was over. I smiled and thanked them.

All through that day I waited and waited, my eyes forever going to the entrance of the ward, in anticipation of Igor's return. Just before I finished my shift, Sister Procopy called me to one side and told me that Igor had died on the operating table. I was shattered. I couldn't speak. She told me that I could finish a few minutes early.

I went to the little room to change into my everyday clothes, ready for Nicky to collect me and take me home. As soon as I closed the door, I let my pent-up tears flow. *Poor, poor, Igor. Poor, poor Maria and Mikhail, what would they do now without Igor's wages supporting them?*

Nicky was waiting for me, when I left my changing room. He gave me one look and gently steered me to his car.

He sat down beside me and drove down the long driveway from the estate to the road. "I can tell by your face that you've had a bad day, Lia." I was expecting him to suggest that maybe it was getting too much for me but he didn't. "Do you want to talk about it, darling?"

I told him everything, from me writing to Igor's wife and son, to telling him the events of the day.

"Lia, you did everything you could for him. You stayed with him, held his hand. Darling, you are not God. Igor's life, all our lives, are in his hands. All you can do is what you are already doing. I am so very proud of you, my darling."

"You're not going to tell me that it is getting too much for me and I should stop?"

"Do you want me to, Lia? I now know what a determined woman I am marrying. The only time you would give it up is if you thought it was too much and even then, I don't think you would give in so easily. You are stronger than that."

I told him about what Igor had said that he had complained of a headache to the Tsarina, who hadn't reported it or his rise in temperature. He asked me if I had told anyone about it. I shook my head. She was the Tsarina.

"Would it have made any difference if the Tsarina had reported his temperature and headache Lia?"

I told Nicky, that I didn't know.

When I arrived at Grand Mama's, Nicky kissed me then told me that he would let me go in and get a good night's sleep. He would collect me in the morning.

I popped my head around the lounge door, where I knew that Grand Mama would be and told her that I had had a busy day and I was going to bed. Tanya brought me some food on a tray, up to my bedroom. I ate it, hardly tasting it. I had thoughts of all sorts, going around in my head. Was the Tsarina and the Grand Duchesses, just playing at being nurses? Would Igor be alive if the Tsarina had reported his condition? Did she hear the names that the patients were calling her and rebelled or had it just been a genuine mistake and she had forgotten it in all the urgency of our ward?

I slept badly that night, tossing and turning, wondering if I should report the Tsarina. When I did finally sleep, I dreamt of standing in front of a firing squad, accused of treason.

By the time Tanya came in with my breakfast tray in the morning I had made some decisions. Firstly, I would ask Sister Procopy if I could write to Igor's family and tell them what had happened. Secondly, when my next free days came around, I would go and see his wife and son and see what I could do to help them. Thirdly I would ask Sister Procopy if it would have made any difference, if Igor's condition had been reported earlier.

I told Nicky what I planned to do. He told me that I looked as if I had spent all night deciding on a plan of action. I told him that I had.

"Darling, I know that you want to help Igor's family but you can't help every family that is suffering."

"I know, Nicky, but I feel that I know his family from the time that he had been on my ward and through writing to them on Igor's behalf. What will happen to them, now that they don't have his money to support them?"

He sighed, "I suppose the same as many others; struggle."

I told him that I couldn't let that happen. Nicky told me that helping Igor's family was like a drop in the ocean. So many families were in the same position. The majority of Russians were struggling to survive. Nicky reluctantly agreed to drive me to Igor's home and meet his wife and son on my next free day.

When I got to Alexandria Palace and after I had changed into my uniform, I went in search of Sister Procopy. I asked her if I could write to Igor's family and tell them of his death. She told me that I could.

"Nurse Bobrov," she asked, "who took the temperatures yesterday?" She showed me Igor's chart. "Is that your signature?"

I told her that it wasn't. Mine was the signature underneath the one she pointed out to me. She nodded, "I thought not."

I then asked her if the delay in reporting Igor's condition had caused his death. Apparently, it would not have made any difference. It was only a matter of an hour's difference from one set of observations to mine, he was already dying before our eyes. "Even so I shall be having a word with the Tsarina. We cannot allow these mistakes to happen. These men that we are looking after and hopefully nursing them back to health, if not we are making their last moments easier by staying with them until the end, and letting them know that they are not alone, but they are placing their lives in our hands, trusting that we will do our very best for them."

I asked her if she knew what some of the patients were saying about the Tsarina.

"Yes Thalia I have heard them." I stood silent, "Are you asking me if I think it was done on purpose by not reporting Igor's health?" I remained silent, hopefully encouraging her to tell me what she thought. "If that is the case then they have no right to be around the wards. When they enter the wards, they are no longer the Tsarina and Grand Duchesses but nurses. I shall be having a word with Nurse Romanov as I am sure that that was her signature above yours. I shall also ask her if she wishes to continue nursing knowing the thoughts of some of the soldiers"

Inwardly I gave a great sigh. Thankfully the matter had been taken out of my hands. When I returned to the ward, I felt that a weight had been lifted from my shoulders. I carried on with my observations, talking to the patients and asking how they were feeling.

I didn't see the Tsarina again and for that I was relieved, for although I hadn't reported it, in a way I still felt guilty.

When I had a spare few minutes, which happened to be on my break, I wrote to Maria, Igor's wife, telling her how sorry I was to have to give her such grave news for her and Mikhail. I told her that, I felt that I knew her by the way Igor talked about her and Mikhail. I told her that I had stayed with Igor until he was asleep and I had to leave him, which was true and that his last thoughts were for his wife and son. I didn't tell her that I would come and visit, I don't know why, maybe I was afraid that she might not want to talk to me as I was looking after her husband and failed.

# Chapter 21
## Maria and Mikhail

Nicky was as good as his word. On my first free day after Igor's death, we drove to Nizhny Novgorod. I asked Nicky if he minded going there, as it was where both of his parents had been killed. He told me that he had been there several times since to visit their graves.

"It is such a long time ago since it happened and the time I have spent with the Dowager Empress and the Tsar, has really taken the reality and horror of what happened to them, away from me."

I asked him if he remembered much about his parents. Nicky told me that he had some vague memories but the nature of their death and the shock to him, had caused a form of amnesia. What things he did remember, were like remembering a dream. He said that when one of the servants found him hiding in a cupboard under some stairs. He remembered running there to hide after he had seen his parents shot and he remembered people searching for him shortly after.

"How long were you there for, Nicky?" I asked, shocked at what he told me. This was the first time he had talked about that terrible part of his life.

"I don't remember. A few days, I think. It was one of the servants who found me and contacted the Dowager Empress. By the time she came to collect me, I had been bathed and dressed in clean clothes. As there was no one else to take care of me, she took me in. I spent a lot of time with the present Tsar. He became like my older brother to me. I looked up to him. We used to go hunting together. I spent time with him and the royal family at Tsarskoye Selo, the Winter Palace and on the royal yacht, The Standard, as well as spending time with the Dowager Empress. In fact, as I got older, I seemed to spend more time with the Dowager Empress, than the Tsar, because once his father had died, his duties took up more and more of his time and our ideas began to differ, not that I told him but from the things that he said to me, some of them I thought were wrong and bad for the

197

country. His mother could say against him but I couldn't. I wasn't in so privileged a position. The Dowager Empress has grave reservations about the Tsarina and the Tsar's ability to rule." He reminded me that he was telling me this information but it must not be repeated.

I sat quietly in Nicky's car and let him carry on. He told me that he did get flashes of memory of his parents, mainly his mother. It was his mother who had taught him to play the piano. When he went to live with his aunt, the Dowager Empress, she hired a music teacher to help him improve.

I asked Nicky if he ever called the Dowager Empress by her name of Maria or Aunt Maria in his case. He laughed and shook his head saying that that was getting too informal. "I suppose that is why I took to calling your grandmother Aunt Lilia. I wished that I could have spent some time with her and your mother but somehow, the Dowager Empress had so many other things on her mind that it just never happened." He reached over and squeezed my hand, telling me that he was glad that it had happened now.

It was not hard to find Igor's wife and son. I looked at Mikhail and could see his father in his features. Maria, his wife, would have been beautiful, if she had had a better life but life had taken its toll on her features and her body. She looked old beyond her years. I just introduced myself as Nurse Bobrov and Nicky as my fiancé.

Maria knew who I was from my letter and thanked me for coming to see them. I asked her how she was coping and she replied that with her husband being away in the war she was used to it being just herself and Mikhail. She ruffled her son's hair. "He keeps me going. He gives me something to keep going for." Their home was little more than a shack. I thought the people of my home in Smolensk lived poorly but this was heart breaking.

Nicky asked her if she worked. She told us that she did what she could to keep them fed but times were hard. Without even talking to me about it, Nicky told her that he had a home not far from St Petersburg and he was looking for a woman to help with the cleaning in his home, a maid. "You could bring Mikhail with you. You would stay in the servants' quarters and be paid a regular wage. You would have regular meals and when Mikhail is old enough, you could send him to school."

She looked at us both, "Why are you doing this for us, Nurse Bobrov, Master Nicky?"

Nicky looked at me, smiled and just said, "Because we can."

Maria took mine and Nicky's hands and kissed them. "I don't know how we will ever repay you."

I told her to just make Igor proud. I gave her some money and Nicky said that we would pick them up the following week. In the meantime, to use what money I had given them for food, to see them through till we returned for them.

We left them standing at the doorway of their hovel of a home, waving us goodbye but for the first time since meeting Maria, a smile lit her face. She looked as if a great weight had been lifted from her shoulders.

When we were in the car again, heading back to St Petersburg, I asked Nicky why he offered Maria and Mikhail work and a home. He grinned at me, with that devilish twinkle in his eyes, which I loved. "Do you think you are the only one in this family who wants to do something for this country's poor people?"

"I love you so much, Nicholas Ivanov, that my heart is full of love for you," I told him and said what a fortunate day it was for me when he picked me up off the ice.

He took my hand in his and brought it to his lips to kiss. "No, Lia, I was the fortunate one. Never in my life have I met a woman so brave and courageous and as thoughtful as you, Thalia Marguerite Titania Bobrov, soon to be Princess Ivanov."

# Chapter 22

## Our Night Together

It was dark when we arrived back on the outskirts of St Petersburg. We were going to go out to Minsky's after we had had a chance to bathe and change. The nearer we got to the town, the busier the streets became with angry protesters, waving flaming torches and armed with anything they could get their hands on to use as missiles. Nicky reversed his car and headed the car down another road, to try and avoid them, only to find that at the far end was another crowd. I was beginning to panic that we would be caught up in the middle of it all. He cursed. "Karl's premises are in the next street. I could get us there," he said, as he quickly reversed the car back down the road.

We arrived in Bolshaia Morskaia. At the far end of the road, we could see yet another angry crowd making their way towards us. My heart was hammering in my breast and my mouth had suddenly gone so dry with fear that my tongue stuck to the roof of my mouth.

"Get into the shop, Lia. Tell Karl to lock the shop up and pull down the shutters, quickly. I'll take the car around to the back yard and lock the gates behind me. Tell him to come and let me in," he said, nearly pushing me from the car.

I looked both ways before I left the car, to make sure that I wouldn't get stopped trying to get into the shop. I dashed from the car, slamming the door behind me and ran into the shop, shutting the door and locking it.

Karl came out as soon as he heard the bell above the door tinkle. His face had its usual welcoming smile on it, until he saw my face.

"Thalia, what is wrong? Are you ill?"

I told him quickly that there was a mob heading his way and he was to close up the shutters and lock all of the doors.

"Is Nicky with you?"

I told Karl that Nicky was parking his car in their back yard and locking the gates behind him. He would be by the back door.

I had never heard Karl shout, his voice had always been gentle and welcoming but he shouted orders, "Peter, Ivan, close all of the shutters and lock all of the doors except the back one. Nicky will be coming in through that. When he is inside, lock that one as well and start bringing in all of the jewellery from the shop and workstations and store them in the safe, then tell the staff that they will have to stay here tonight. It is not safe for them to go home."

Karl put his arm around my shoulder and led me through the shop to the back room. Shortly after, we heard Nicky hammering on the back door, to gain entry to the premises. Then I saw him, his usual smile had left his face.

"Is everywhere safely shut up, Karl?" he asked as he came through the door. Karl nodded.

"How many people are out there do you think, Nicky?" Karl asked him.

Nicky guessed about fifty or more. "I didn't get a close look, I just saw them coming this way. We couldn't even get to Lia's grandmother's. It seems all of the roads in the city are blocked by protesters. Can we use your telephone to ring her and Lia's mother? Tell them to lock everywhere up."

Karl automatically said we could and showed us where his telephone was situated.

When I rang Grand Mama's, Peter Abramovich answered. I told him that we couldn't get home because of the mobs. I told him to tell Grand Mama what was going on and to make sure the gates and doors were securely locked, then I told him that we had found shelter at Karl's. Peter told me that he would relay my message, then the telephone went dead.

Next, I rang Mama and Gregor's and told their servant who answered the telephone the same as I has told Peter. He said he would tell them.

I put the telephone down and thanked Karl for its use.

He said that he would find us somewhere to stay for the night. He told us that it wouldn't be luxurious, as he had all of his staff to house as well.

In the end we stayed in the safe room which he said was the safest place to stay as it was in the middle of the building. Nicky, with his cheeky grin, told him that we wouldn't take anything.

Karl slapped him good naturedly on the back and said he would only be stealing his own stock anyway.

Auguste, Karl's wife, came down with a couple of pillows and some blankets, apologising profusely that it couldn't be more comfortable.

I told her not to worry, it was still safer and more comfortable than the motorcar.

Nicky laid a couple of blankets on the floor and put the two pillows on top of them. There was a wicked glint in his eye, "Tonight, Miss Bobrov, you are all mine!" he said twisting an imaginary moustache like some dastardly villain in a play

I think my face showed fear first, at what he might do, then my body took over and I knew that I wanted him.

He grinned at me. "Don't worry, my darling, I was just jesting. When I take you, it will be in our own home and in our own marriage bed."

My body was shaking with unsuppressed passion as I leaned against his warm body.

"We can do this, Lia." he said. "Our wedding night is not too far away now. It will be good just to hold your body close to me throughout the night and fall asleep in each other's arms."

Auguste brought a tray of hot food and some crusty bread for us, again apologising for the poor fayre, while Karl brought us a bottle of champagne and two glasses.

"Will you both be all right down here?" Karl asked again.

Nicky and I assured him that we would be. He excused himself then and said he had to make sure his staff were settled and wished us a good night.

We took off our coats and lay down on our makeshift bed. Nicky put his arm around me. He felt so warm and comforting.

We heard angry voices outside, not long after we had settled down which made me jump and snuggle closer to him, then the banging on the shutters began. I couldn't help letting out a cry of fear when the banging began incessantly on the shutters. Nicky assured me that they wouldn't be able to break through the metal shutters. He kissed me briefly and poured champagne into the two glasses. "To us, Miss Bobrov." He toasted us.

"To us, Your Highness." I sipped the champagne, still feeling on edge as the noise outside continued. Above us we heard glass break and I looked across at Nicky for assurance.

Someone screamed within the building, then silence.

Shortly after, Karl poked his head around the door. From the look on his face, I could tell that he was stressed but he smiled reassuringly and told us that there was nothing to worry about, someone outside had thrown a brick at one of the first-floor windows, which scared one of his staff.

"They can't get up there and they certainly can't get in here. We just need to sit it out," he said, then as an afterthought asked us, again, if we had everything we needed. Nicky assured him that we had. Once assured, Karl, again, wished us both a good night and closed the door behind him.

We sat in the middle of our 'bed' with the tray of food and the glasses of champagne. "If it wasn't for the noisy neighbours," Nicky said trying to make me laugh, "this would be a perfect picnic, mind you the scenery leaves a lot to be desired."

The noise continued through the night, until the early hours of the morning. It seemed that the mob enjoyed banging on Karl's shop's shutters to make as much noise as possible. What caused the rioters to stop we weren't sure?

We never heard the horse's hooves and screams, where we were safe and secure behind the shutters at Karl's.

After we had finished our 'picnic', we lay down; Nicky holding me tightly in his arms where I rested my head against his chest. I could hear the reassuring rhythm of his heartbeat and eventually fell asleep after the crowd outside had finally given up banging on Karl's shutters and moved on. It felt so natural to fall asleep with his arms around me and snuggled up to his warm body. Nicky was as good as his word. We kissed but it never moved further than that. If he had made a move at more intimacy, I don't think I would have protested. His will was obviously stronger than mine was.

Although we were sleeping on the floor, our 'bed' felt quite comfortable, if a little hard but when I slept, I was aware of Nicky holding me safely in his arms.

When I woke up, Nicky was still holding me. He was leaning on his elbow looking down at me, a night's dark stubble shadowing his cheeks and chin. I had never seen him so un-kept and I liked it.

"Good morning, my darling. Did you sleep well?" he said giving me a kiss on the tip of my nose.

I yawned and stretched. "I like sleeping curled up next you," I told him, unashamedly, then asked how he had slept.

"Knowing that you were with me, I slept wonderfully. I am now wishing the months leading up to our wedding would fly by just so we could be like this in our own home and our own bed, without the restraints of these," he said tugging at his clothes. Nicky said when I had stood up, that we should be going home and we both started to fold up the blankets.

Karl knocked on the door. Nicky told him to come in. After Karl entered asking the usual courtesies, he asked us if we would like to stay for breakfast. Both Nicky and I said that we had already taken up enough of Auguste's and his hospitality and as it sounded quiet outside Nicky said that we should be going back home. Karl told us that it was the least they could do under the circumstances. "Well," Nicky said holding out his hand to shake Karl's, "my friend, once again, thank you very much for your hospitality. I now have to face Lia's grandmother and assure her that …"

Karl interrupted Nicky, "Auguste and myself will say that you had separate rooms if that will make things easier for you both, Nicky?"

Nicky told him that it would certainly make things easier for us and save my reputation.

"Then that is what we will say," Karl replied. I gave him a kiss on the cheek.

"Thank you, Karl. I would appreciate that."

Nicky handed me my coat and said that we should go. Karl and Nicky shook hands again as Karl let us out of the rear door leading into the back yard, where Nicky had parked his car. He checked around the car, to make sure that no thrown missiles had damaged it, then opened the gates and looked around outside.

"All clear, Karl. Thank you again, my friend. I should close the gates behind us again, just in case," he said as he held my door open for me.

When we were driving through the streets back to Grand Mama's, Nicky told me that we should say what Karl had said; that we had slept in separate rooms, otherwise, people would always be speculating. I agreed, knowing that it was to save my reputation.

The previous night's riots had certainly left their marks on the streets. Houses had ground floor windows, broken. Bricks lay strewn all over the roads and in some cases, houses fronting onto the roads, had been torched and burnt to the ground leaving only charred remains. Nicky drove slowly, trying to avoid running over some of the missiles that lay in the way. Because we were in the car, I didn't take much notice of the dark stains in the road, I had seen them all before. I didn't realise that the cavalry had broken up the rioters and it was blood, from slaughtered crowds. Once again, the army dealt with the rioters the only way they knew, kill, kill, kill, just like they had done to the poor innocent souls, which they had slaughtered outside the Winter Palace, that Tanya and I had unfortunately witnessed. There must have been some other way to solve the problems of rioters and protesters other than killing?

We pulled up outside the gates to Grand Mama's and Nicky honked the car horn for Igor to come out and open them. Even Grand Mama's driveway was strewn with broken bricks and bottles, luckily her house was set quite a way back from the gates and any missiles thrown, had not reached their targets of her windows. Nicky asked me if I wanted him to come in and face Grand Mama. I told him to leave it to me and to go home and shave and change. He grinned, "I must look a terrible sight, darling."

I shook my head. "Not to me, you don't. I could quite happily get used to this but I can't speak for my grandmother. She might think that you look a rake and wouldn't believe anything you said." I grinned at him.

He ran his hands over his stubble, "Ah, good point. Well, I will leave you for now darling and come back for you this afternoon after lunch." He kissed me again and came to my door, to open it and let me out.

As soon as I entered the hall, Grand Mama came out from the lounge. She hurried over to me and hugged me. "Oh my dear child, are you all right? You are not hurt, are you? Where is Nicky? Is he all right?" I linked my arm through hers and we walked back into the lounge.

"I am fine Grand Mama. I am not hurt. Nicky is unhurt and has gone home to change, wash and have some breakfast."

Grand Mama was horrified that we had not had breakfast. I told her that we didn't want to impose on Karl and Auguste's hospitality, any more than we already had, although they did offer us breakfast. She kissed my cheek and said that I should go to my room and bathe and she would arrange for breakfast to be sent up to me. Although she hadn't asked about our sleeping arrangements, I had an idea that she might. I hated to lie to her but by lying to her, it would save an awful lot of speculation about what happened.

When I opened my bedroom door, Tanya came rushing over to me, her face full of concern. "Oh, Miss Thalia, I was so worried about you?"?"

I told her that I was fine but in much need of a lovely long soak in a hot bath. She went into my bathroom and immediately began running the bath water.

It felt wonderful to sink into the beautiful warm scented water. The warmth of the water made me sleepy and I began to yawn.

"I have brought you a breakfast tray up, Miss Thalia," Tanya said, as she held out the big warm bath towel for me.

I didn't realise how hungry I was. I ate everything in front of me. Generous as the Faberge's had been to us, in their hospitality, when I did wake up in Nicky's arms, I was already hungry but didn't think it was fair to take any more of their food. They had the rest of their staff to feed.

Tanya suggested that I go back to bed and catch up on my sleep. As it had been the early hours of the morning before it went quiet outside Faberge's, I felt that I did need more sleep and I would be getting up early the next morning ready for work. I curled up in my lovely soft bed, which Tanya had warmed while I was in the bath and fell asleep, instantly.

It was gone one o'clock in the afternoon when I woke again. Tanya told me that my mother and Gregor were downstairs and Nicky had also arrived.

I dressed hurriedly and went downstairs. Of course, all of the talk was about the previous night's riots. Nicky was telling them that some houses had been torched, while others had had all their windows, which overlooked the roads, broken. He told them that a lucky shot had broken one of Karl's upper windows but there was no other damage. "It was lucky that he had the shutters, which covered all of the downstairs windows, otherwise it could have been a lot worse."

It was Gregor who asked us where we had slept. I told him that I had slept on a bed in Karl and Auguste's spare room, while Nicky slept on the floor in a room downstairs."

"Karl provided me with pillows and blankets. It wasn't that bad really, apart from the noise outside but once the crowd had moved along, it was all quite quiet."

Gregor handed Nicky the morning paper, "It's in this morning's papers. The military broke up the riots, Nicky. It doesn't say how many were killed but it suggests that there were many fatalities."

I was shocked; horrified. "If I had known there were injured people, I could have helped them, Nicky," I cried.

He shook his head. "Darling, they wouldn't have let you help them. You would have been caught as well. They don't like witnesses to these things."

I started to cry. Life in Russia was so brutal to those who tried to point out the wrongs of it and rebelled against it. Why didn't someone do something, say something? It was all so very, very, wrong. Twice now I had been a witness to results of what happened to those who protested against authority. War wasn't just being waged against Germany, as so many of the patients at Tsarskoye Selo proved but also there on the streets of St Petersburg and as the papers reported, Moscow as well.

Mama came over and put her arms around me and I cried against her shoulder.

Gregor asked Nicky if it was time for us to leave Russia. Mama heard and cried, "No, not yet. I want our baby to be born in Russia and Lia and Nicky are getting married in Russia. The invitations have all gone out and you said that the best doctors were here in St Petersburg, Gregor. We can't leave yet."

Gregor went and put his arms around his wife, trying to calm her down for fear of an adverse effect on their baby. He led Mama over to one of the sofas and made her sit down, muttering soothing words for her ears alone. Grand Mama went and sat by her, taking her hand and stroking it soothingly. Nicky came and sat by me, holding my hand. "No, I don't think we should leave, not yet anyway. Optimistically, I am hoping that there is still a chance that it might right itself. With this war going on, it wouldn't be safe for us anyway. Everyone is so busy with the war and its outcome, that these, minor skirmishes, as some people will see it, will be overshadowed."

Gregor said, "We really need to stay in St Petersburg for Marguerites sake and the baby. I don't want to put their lives at risk by travelling at the moment. The doctors know Marguerite and the problems she had when having Thalia, so they are keeping a careful eye on this pregnancy." He smiled lovingly down at Mama, who lay her hand protectively over where their baby lay.

Grand Mama spoke then, "So we stay, at least until Babushka's baby is born and Thalia and Nicky are married. Is there anything we can do more in preparation, Nicky?" It seemed everyone was relying on Nicky for common sense and advice.

"If there are things that you can't do without but want to take to America with you, then I would suggest that you get it moved over to Kadriorg Palace. Please be careful that what you do, does not seem obvious. I am telling anyone who is interested that when Lia and I are married, we will be spending most of our time there, wanting to make it our main family home.

"Whenever we leave," Nicky said, "it will be from Tallin. In the meantime, just stay safe and be careful. Keep the gates to your homes closed and locked.

"Lia, darling, I hate to say this but if the atmosphere here is bad and I see rioters, I will telephone the hospital and leave a message for you to stay there overnight. Wherever we go, there could be protesters, like that night we went to Minsky's, Lia. I would suggest, that we stay in our homes at night, as much as possible. I think that a lot of the social life in St Petersburg has been curbed, since the war, anyway."

Grand Mama nodded in agreement, "Yes, the invitations have certainly dropped off. I don't think we will be missed." Then she made a great dramatic sigh, "Well, maybe I shall have to start knitting for my new grandchild to keep me occupied in the evenings."

That seemed to break the tension in the room and we all seemed to start talking at once. Nicky told everyone that he had gained a new cleaning maid and her son from Nizhny Novgorod. I told them that it was the wife and son of a patient that I lost. I told them of the dire circumstances of Maria and Mikhail and how Nicky offered them a home and work.

"I just hope that Lia doesn't find anymore waifs and strays, otherwise I will have more staff than I can cope with," he joked.

Mama told him that she would need a nanny at some time for the baby and as Maria had brought up one child, maybe she could help to bring up their new baby.

I told her I thought that would be an even better idea. Nicky teased, saying that we were stealing his staff from him and I playfully punched him on his arm.

After my two days off work, I went back to the hospital. The night that I had spent with Nicky at Karl's premises remained in my mind. Every night when I went to sleep, I imagined Nicky's arms around me, as they had been that night and fell asleep with a smile on my lips.

The following week, we went back to Nizhny Novgorod to pick up Maria and Mikhail and their possessions, however meagre they were. Once we had them in the car and were on our way back to St Petersburg, we told them that they weren't going to be a member of Nicky's household but that of my mother's and step-father's. At first Maria's face showed fear but when I explained that Mama was expecting a baby and would need someone to help with the baby. "And Mikhail, what about Mikhail?" she asked.

"You will be able to keep Mikhail with you and he will be like a companion for the baby as it grows older. This position will be so much better for you both. You will be under the supervision of Mama's maid, Anya, who helped bring me up."

"Oh, Nurse Angel," Maria cried, "I don't know how to thank you. Mikhail and I will be always in debt to you."

I told her that I needed no thanks.

On the way back to St Petersburg, with Maria and Mikhail in the back seat, Mikhail fell asleep on his mother's lap. I felt so sorry for the little boy, who would grow up without a father.

We drove straight to Mama's and Gregor's town house; taking Maria and Mikhail in and introducing them to Mama, Gregor and Anya. I could tell by the look on Anya's face that she instantly fell in love with little Mikhail and took to Maria. Anya loved children. We were the children that she never had. I also knew that Mama and Gregor would be kind and considerate employers. Anya took their small bag of possessions and Mikhail's hand and showed them to their quarters.

I asked Mama if she thought that they would be all right.

She nodded. "I am sure they will be. We will give them good food, new clothes and a lovely hot bath and I am sure they will settle in very well."

Gregor nodded in agreement. "It will be good to teach again, and Mikhail looks to be a sharp minded little boy. I think that he will learn very easily."

"I never realised that you missed teaching Gregor?" I said.

"After you and your mother left Smolensk, I didn't know what to do. I thought of teaching at a university, but the news of my uncle's death came along and before I could teach any more, I became a Count and any thoughts of going back to teaching were forgotten." Then he shrugged his shoulders, "So here I am and about to become a father." He took Mama's hand and kissed it.

# Chapter 23
## Christmas 1914

I returned to work at Tsarskoye Selo. The wards were busier than before. I sought out Sister Procopy and asked her if, she could find me a bed in the nurses' dormitories, as I felt happier being with the other nurses than I did at the royal's end of the palace. Although I had slept in the next room to the Grand Duchesses, I felt very much on my own and more than once I bumped into Rasputin coming from the Tsarina's private apartments. He looked at me as if he could imagine what I looked like, without any clothes on, which made my skin crawl. Once or twice he tried to touch me, just trying to hold my hand but I shook his hand off and told him to leave me alone. Moving in with the other nurses seemed to be the better alternative, as Nicky had telephoned to tell me that there was more trouble in St Petersburg, a couple of times or we were snowed in and the roads to Tsarskoye Selo were impassable. In my time at the hospital, I spent my evenings reading nursing manuals that Sister Procopy gave me, to improve my nursing skills. I did see the Tsarina and Grand Duchesses in passing but not really to talk to. I enjoyed the camaraderie of being with the other nurses, some who had also run into Rasputin. We would spend time sitting on each other's beds, exchanging stories and laughing a lot, which we needed as a form of light relief, after the trauma of working a day on the wards.

I was allowed a week off at Christmas, mainly because Mama's baby was due and I wanted to be with her at the birth. Sister Procopy had also leant me (among her many other books), some on midwifery. I had poured over these books, just in case the doctor couldn't reach Mama in time, either because of the riots, which seemed to be getting more frequent or the snow, which at that time of the year was always a constant threat. So far Mama's pregnancy had been text book, probably because she spent a lot of time with her feet up and resting. She seemed to have doubled in size over the last few months of her pregnancy but of course, I had never been subject to any pregnant women before, so it all seemed alien to me. Maria and Mikhail had settled in well and was busy setting up the nursery, under Anya's supervision, in readiness for my new little brother or sister. I couldn't believe that at eighteen years of age, I was finally going to be a big sister. I prayed that all would go well with Mama's delivery. Sometimes, when I was alone and thinking about the worst-case scenario and the thought that I might lose either my mother or baby brother or sister or both, I would shed a few tears. It would seem so cruel that now Mama had finally found true happiness with Gregor that she might lose it all, in death. Then I would give myself a stern talking to, telling myself not to be so pessimistic. I voiced my fears to Nicky, who told me that I should look on the bright side and not to worry until there was something to worry about. My husband to be always spoke words of common sense.

Because of Mama's impending 'lying in', we all congregated at Mama's and Gregor's town house for Christmas. Having a house full of servants who usually had very little to do, as the household consisted of just Mama and Gregor, she told us that they would be glad of something more to do. Even Nicky stayed over on Christmas Eve and Christmas day, with Mikhail acting as his 'valet'. Tanya came with me, as my maid and Ava came with Grand Mama, so for the first time since their marriage, Mama and Gregor had a house full of guests.

The house had been decorated in true Christmas tradition, with garlands of greenery tied up with red ribbons and an enormous Christmas tree with pretty baubles and candles. According to Mama, young Mikhail's eyes were as big as saucers when he saw his first Christmas tree. I had bought the little boy a wooden train for Christmas, which I had wrapped and put under the tree for him. Nicky had brought him some thick, warm clothes for the winter. I had bought his mother a thick winter coat, Nicky had bought her some winter boots. Grand Mama told us we were spoiling them but we both said that we still felt responsible for them and it did give us a great deal of pleasure just to see the looks on their faces.

Mama was waddling about like a penguin, with her big 'bump' as she called it. Gregor followed her like the doting husband and father to be.

Christmas eve we all sat playing 'gentle' parlour games, so as not to disturb Mama too much. Mama's chef provided us with beautifully prepared meals. We all attended midnight mass at the Cathedral on Christmas Eve. We had decided to do this instead of going in the morning, as Gregor insisted that Mama be allowed to stay late in bed.

When we returned, we placed all of our presents under the Christmas tree for ourselves and the staff. Young Mikhail had gone to bed early, being told by his Mama, if he wasn't a good boy and go to bed early then St Nicholas would not come. I think he had more presents under the tree than anyone else. Young Mikhail had endeared himself to everyone in the household and Maria had proved to be a good and willing worker, although the real work had not arrived, as yet. Maria, now having a paid position was able to buy her son a Christmas present, which was the first time in Mikhail's young life and she was so proud of herself, being able to save some money and also spend some of her wages on both herself and her little boy. They both seemed to have become an integral part of the extended family and integrated well with the rest of the staff. All was harmonious in the Pinegin household.

We all went to our bedrooms that night, Grand Mama's room was between Nicky's and mine (I presume that she had been elected to guard my virtue and not let Nicky come creeping into my room in the dark of night.) Nicky thought it was funny and made jokes about it to me, telling me that I must put a chair against my bedroom door to stop 'nocturnal raiders' he said twisting an imaginary moustache again. I laughed and told him that I was going to wear my sheerest nightdress in anticipation. Grand Mama scowled at us, as if we were preparing for a nocturnal tryst and we started giggling again.

When Mama went upstairs to bed, we all followed her. Lying in my lonely bed, my body ached with a need unknown to me, knowing that Nicky was so near to me, yet so far away. I did as I always did and turned my mind back to the night we spent together in Karl's shop, imagining Nicky's arms around me and finally fell asleep.

Christmas morning, we were all dressed in our best and downstairs by ten o'clock, by which time all the candles, on the Christmas tree had been lit. Fifteen minutes later all of the staff from the Pinegin household assembled excitedly in the massive gold and white hallway. Amongst them was, of course Maria and Mikhail, who was hopping excitedly from one foot to another and tugging on his mother's skirt whispering, "He came. He came, Mama." Everyone grinned, after all Christmas was mainly for the children. Gregor was the one to hand out all of the presents. As it was the first year of his marriage, he and Mama had been particularly generous to the servants. All of them had new uniforms, plus new shoes. He was deliberately making Mikhail wait until the end, until the poor little fellow's bottom lip began to tremble, thinking that St Nicholas hadn't brought him anything. He turned and with tears in his eyes, asked his mother if he had been a good boy. When Gregor heard this, he went around to the back of the tree where all of Mikhail's presents had been placed.

"And now, I think for the most important of all, Mikhail, I do believe these are all for you." He pulled out six presents for the little boy, whose face lit up at the sight of them all.

"I have been a good boy, Mama!" he shouted, "Look what St Nicholas has brought me."

He just stood there looking at his pile of presents, until Gregor asked him what he was waiting for and to go and open them. What took us a few minutes to wrap was torn apart in seconds. Each present made the little boy more and more excited.

I knew, seeing how Gregor was with the little boy, that he would make an excellent father.

When Mikhail had opened all of his presents and said thank you to everyone, Maria helped him upstairs to the nursery, where he was allowed to play with his new toys on the floor. I popped my head around the Nursery door, shortly after, to see Mikhail playing happily with all of his new toys.

His mother, when she saw me, asked me in. "Miss Thalia, I don't know how to thank you for all that you have done for us, for Mikhail's presents and my new coat. We have never been this warm, in winter and it is wonderful. I used to struggle to get him anything for Christmas but with working for your mother and step-father I have managed to buy him a proper present. Igor was right, you have been an angel to us, as well as to him. Thank you again, very much."

I could feel tears spring to my eyes and instinctively went and hugged first her then her son, then I told her that it was my pleasure. It genuinely was.

We all sat down to Christmas dinner at two o'clock, after the servants had had their Christmas meal, then afterwards we opened the presents that we had received. Mama and Gregor had brought me a new fur coat, to keep me warm. Grand Mama had asked Auguste Brisac to make me a new evening gown in a deep purple velvet. Nicky had brought me another ring. This time it was my birthstone ring, which he obviously had made by Karl's staff. Again, it was another beautiful stone flashing a rainbow of colours. I had brought him silver cufflinks and a silver cigarette case. For Mama, I had bought things for the baby, a silver teething ring and rattle. For Gregor I had bought a box of his favourite cigars and for Grand Mama, a pair of fleecy slippers. Gregor had bought Mama a beautiful diamond and emerald necklace, bracelet and matching earrings. I laughed, saying that obviously Karl had done well for business from our family this year. I put my new ring on my right-hand ring finger and went upstairs to change into my new gown. When I came back downstairs, Nicky looked at me with a look of adoration in his eyes. "You look beautiful, darling. That colour suits you." He helped me down the last stair and pulled me into his arms. He thanked me for his presents and kissed me deeply, until I heard Mama cry out.

We both rushed back into the lounge to see Mama standing in a small pool of water. I immediately knew what was going on. My baby brother or sister was going to make his way into the world soon. Keeping cool and calm, as my nurses training had taught me, I asked Gregor to carry Mama upstairs. Anya came rushing into the lounge when she heard Mama's cry. I told her to get clean sheets and towels for Mama's bed.

I followed Gregor and Mama upstairs to their bedroom. I told Gregor to go and call for the doctor, while I helped Mama undress and put on a clean night dress. I asked her if she had felt any contractions and she told me that she had had some niggling pains last night but they went away. I felt her stomach go hard with another contraction. I looked at her and told her to prepare herself, as this time they weren't going to go away. She smiled proudly at me and stroked my cheek. "Will you stay with me, Lia, through this? I know that as a young unmarried girl you wouldn't normally be expected in the room where a baby was being born but I know that you will keep everyone calm, including me. I hope that while you are here I won't scare you off childbirth with my crying out with the labour pains?"

I told her that of course I would stay and she could cry as loud as she liked. I tried not to think of the possible outcome. Anya came upstairs carrying clean sheets and a pile of clean towels. By that time Mama was sitting up in bed in her nightdress. I saw a look of pain cross her face and felt her stomach go hard with another contraction.

Gregor knocked on the door and said that he had left a message for the doctor who was attending Mass at the church, someone had gone to fetch him. He looked questioningly across at Mama. She smiled reassuringly at him, "I am fine, Gregor. I am in the good hands of Nurse Bobrov or as Maria and Mikhail call her, 'Nurse Angel'." She then shooed him from the bedroom and told him to go and read a book or keep Grand Mama from worrying, or something

He blew her a kiss and left. I asked Mama if she would like to lay back and relax, while she could.

It took quite some time before the doctor arrived, in the meantime, Mama's contractions were coming regularly and strong and before he arrived, I was beginning to think that I might have to delivery my baby brother or sister all by myself. I asked Anya to bring me some scissors and twine and a bowl of hot water, just in case.

I must admit, I gave a great sigh of relief, when I heard the doctor arrive downstairs. Shortly after, I heard him knock on the door to Mama's bedroom and enter. He looked across at me, as if to say, 'what are you doing here?' Before he had chance to ask that question Mama introduced me and told him that I was a nurse in Tsarskoye Selo. His countenance changed then, to one of respect. "You have a very trying job, Nurse…"

"Bobrov," I told him.

Mama moaned as another contraction swept over her body. I told him that the contractions were coming every three minutes. "Very good, Nurse Bobrov. Very good, Countess." He looked at me and asked if I wanted to stay, as his midwife had gone to visit her sister in Moscow. "I could do with another pair of hands; that is if you don't mind?" I told him that I would be pleased to help.

He told me to lay out his instruments on the bed. I took a folded clean towel, laid out his instruments and covered them with the other part of the folded towel. He nodded his approval at my methods. As Mama struggled with her labour, the doctor explained to me everything he was doing and everything that was happening. I could tell that Mama was tiring as her moans became weaker. I looked at her and asked her if she was all right. She nodded and smiled weakly at me. It wasn't long before she was using all of her strength to push my baby brother or sister into the world. As the doctor was working to help Mama give birth, he told me everything that he was doing. "The head is crowning now, nurse. Another push, Countess, and we will be able to get the shoulders out." I held her hand and gave her encouragement as she pushed. Finally, she gave one great push and my baby brother was born. The doctor told me to tie off and cut the cord. Once I had done this my little brother took a deep breath, filled his lungs and started to cry, lustily. Knowing that Mama had given birth to a healthy child with no endangerment to her life or that of her baby made me give a great sigh of relief. After cleaning up my baby brother, I wrapped him in a blanket and placed him in Mama's arms. Tears were streaming down her cheeks as she looked down at him. "I never thought to see a day such as this again."

"You have a perfect little boy, Countess. Congratulations," the doctor said.

I helped him clear away his instruments, then he left. Before he went the doctor looked at me and smile. "Thank you for your help Nurse Bobrov, you were very professional and efficient. If we get to see pleasanter times, I would be more than happy to have you as a midwife." I thanked him and followed him downstairs and to the front door, where he shook my hand. Gregor stood in the hallway smoking. "You have a son Gregor." I told him. "You can go up now and see Mama but finish your cigar first."

Grand Mama was sitting in the lounge a look of fear on her face. I went and knelt down by her. "Grand Mama, you have a healthy little grandson and Mama is fine. Let Gregor have a few minutes alone with Mama and their new son, then go up and meet your new grandson." I kissed her and looked over at Nicky.

"I do believe, Lia, you are in love with another male." He had his usual cheeky twinkle in his eyes as he spoke. I told him I was afraid to admit that I was total head over heels in love.

It was my first experience with a new baby and I found him quite exquisite, from his little fingers, down to his little toes. Anya came in crying unashamedly. "My lady has come through safely. I thank God and all his saints."

I think that the safe birth of my little brother and Mamas safe delivery of him was my best Christmas present ever, that year.

Ilia Dimitri Gregor Pinegin was christened on the first day of the New Year 1915 at Kazan Cathedral, with all of his family and staff around him. It was Maria that carried him to the font and handed him to the priest. Mama had bought Maria and Mikhail new clothes, especially for the occasion, much to their delight.

Grand Mama was as delighted with her new grandson. "I had no involvement with you when you were growing up Lia, but I am certainly not going to miss out on this little boy's life." she told me as she proudly held him when we went back to Mama and Gregor's after the Christening.

# Chapter 24

## The War Continues

I was working back at the hospital shortly after Ilia's Christening. I told Sister Procopy that her manuals on childbirth had been invaluable and told her of the role I played in Ilia's birth.

We seemed to be twice as busy as before on the wards. Not only did we have patients with war wounds but also terrible cases of frost bite, in the soldiers out in freezing cold temperatures with inadequate clothing. Amongst my duties, I was also studying hard to become a fully qualified nurse. I know that I didn't have to but it was something that I wanted, to prove to myself and those around me that I was more than competent at something and not just some empty-headed debutant. Much as I loved going home to my family and Nicky, I wanted to study and I thought that my friends, the other nurses, would be able to help me with that task. My friends Katya Patenko and Olga Procopy helped me greatly with my studying; firing questions at me, asking me what I would do for this or that. I had a lot to thank them for. I poured over the books that Olga had leant me, making notes, to review later. Finally, the morning came for me to sit my exam to become a fully qualified nurse. There were another four girls with me taking the exam. We had also studied together in our own time. We all looked as nervous as each other. The only consolation was that because we were so short staffed, even if we failed, we could still go back and work on the wards. The hospital needed everyone they could get. Young girls from the village had been recruited to keep the wards clean, to stop the spread of infection. Their duties were mopping floors with disinfectant and wiping over other surfaces as well. That sort of help allowed us nurses to spend more time with our patients. I heard that the royals had also been recruited for writing letters home for some of the soldiers, as well as doing 'observations', and making beds. The Tsarina couldn't make beds any more due to her bad back, but could still do observations and writing on the behalf of the soldiers. It was rare for the poorer people to be able to read and write, but usually there would be someone in their village or town that could read and write like the village priest who would read the letters from the soldiers to their family and also write on the family's behalf back to the soldiers. This is where the Tsarina and Grand Ducheses contributed.

The nursing exam took three hours for written and an hour and a half for practical. At the end of it, I felt as exhausted as if I had done a full shift on the wards. We would be told two days later, whether we had qualified as nurses or not.

On the Friday Nicky arrived to take me home. Just as we were leaving Olga Procopy handed me an envelope. Nicky asked if I was going to open it. All I could do was shake my head. I viewed the envelope with trepidation. I hoped that I had passed my nursing exam but I didn't know and I was scared to find out, in case I had failed. I hated the thought of failing. I wanted to prove that I was more than an empty-headed debutant that relied on her looks rather than her mind, to everyone who thought that I was playing at nursing, similar to the 'Royals.' I said that I would wait until I got home.

The roads were clear, travelling back to St Petersburg, with packed snow piled up like a long white wall on the side of the roads. On the other side of that wall were fields of virgin white snow. It was still bitterly cold weather. The frozen rivers and streams cutting through the, white, fields, like a snake, lay frozen and still. I asked Nicky if the river near Grand Mama's was frozen and were people skating on it? He told me they were and the vendors had set up stalls on the banks selling hot chocolate and hot food for people.

By the time we drove through the outskirts of St Petersburg, a weak sunlight was breaking through the clouds, promising a sunny but freezing cold afternoon. Nicky stopped by his town house first, to collect his skating boots, then drove me to Grand Mama's.

I ran upstairs to change into something a lot thicker and warmer and to get my ice skating boots, leaving my unopened letter on my bedside table, to read later.

Grand Mama was at a friend's house having afternoon tea and catching upon local gossip, which she had not done for several months. It seemed that for a short while, at least, peace reigned in St Petersburg. Even the crowds were more concerned about the war. Many of the men had been conscripted into the army to become more 'cannon fodder' and so, many of the protesters, were now being sent to the front.

I was looking forward to going skating, which I hadn't done for well over twelve months and never with Nicky. I had seen couples linking arms and skating around and had envied them. Now it was my turn with Nicky. He stooped down in front of me to tie my boot laces, then sat down next to me to tie his own.

"Right Miss Bobrov, are you ready?" he asked.

"As ready as ever, your Highness."

He took my arm and helped me down to the frozen river. Other couples were skating past us, as well as young men on their own and young women, in the hope, maybe, of getting a young man to put his arm around her waist and they skate off together. It was good to feel Nicky's arm around my waist and his hand holding my hand. So much had changed over the two years since I first came to St Petersburg. I never thought that I would integrate so easily into St Petersburg society or my new life but I had. I had arrived there as a shy young girl from the country and been turned into a social young lady, soon to become a princess, also a good nurse or so I hoped.

It was as if Nicky could read my thoughts, "Who would have thought over two years ago that I would be marrying the young lady who fell on the ice and hurt her pride. It was a lucky day for me, even if it wasn't so lucky for you, darling. I still can't believe that you walked all the way up the bank and on to your grandmother's with a badly sprained ankle. Everything that has been thrown at you, you have overcome. Do you know how proud I am of you, my darling Lia?"

I smiled up at him, "How could I not be when you are always telling me so. I am proud of you as well, Nicky. I don't know what you did those times when you left St Petersburg but whatever it was, I am proud of you too."

"Maybe one day I will be able to tell you," he said. We skated for an hour, then went and had a mug of steaming hot chocolate, to warm us in the cold of the day.

We arrived at Mama's and Gregor's so that I could have a cuddle with my little brother and see Mama and Gregor as well, of course. Our noses and cheeks were rosy red from the bitter cold.

Mama and Gregor were in the lounge when we arrived. We spent a while talking to them. Nicky told them that I had taken a nursing exam and Mama immediately asked why I hadn't said anything about it. I told her that I didn't tell her in case I failed. Both Mama and Gregor confidently said that I would never fail anything that I put my mind to. Then they asked me when I would know if I had passed. Nicky told them that I had already had my letter but wouldn't open it. I punched him playfully on the arm. Mama looked at me, "Lia, why not?"

I told her that it was for the same reason. She told me that when I left them that day, I was to go home and open my letter and ring her, immediately, to let her know whether I had passed or not.

Suitably scolded, I told her that I would, then Mama turned to Nicky and told him to make sure that I did.

After we had finished discussing nursing, Mama rang a little bell that was on one of the side tables and Maria came down carrying Ilia and young Mikhail was following her. It seemed that Mikhail had grown very attached to Ilia and called him his little brother, although Maria blushed and told him that Ilia wasn't really his brother and he shouldn't call him that. Mama and Gregor didn't seem to mind, so everywhere that Ilia went, Mikhail followed.

Until Ilia was born, I never realised that babies had a smell all of their own and I loved it. Every time I held him, I would nuzzle his little neck and smell his, 'baby-ness'. I looked forward to the time when I would be able to hold the baby that Nicky and I had made together in my arms and smell that same baby smell.

Two hours later we left my family and went back to Grand Mama's house. Grand Mama was upstairs, dressing to go out to the theatre that evening. I ran upstairs to my room and picked up the envelope which I had left on my bedside table. Tempted as I was to open it, I wanted Nicky to open it for me and if I had failed, to break it to me gently.

When I went into the lounge where he was sitting, I handed him the letter. "Please, Nicky, will you open it for me?" I asked.

He mouthed 'coward' at me, although I knew that he never thought it, (he was always telling that I was the bravest person he knew), then tore the envelope open, unfolding the paper and reading, his face not giving anything away. I was beginning to get impatient now. "Nicholas Ivanov, tell me. Have I passed or failed?" I blurted out.

"I thought that you didn't want to know, Nurse Bobrov," he teased me.

"Well, now I do."

"I thought that I told you, Nurse Bobrov," he continued.

I went to say 'No' but then realised that with him calling me 'Nurse', he had told me.

"I've passed?"

"Did you ever doubt it, Nurse Bobrov?"

I shook my head, tears in my eyes, although Gregor had taught me well back in Smolensk, I had never been put to the test. Now I finally had been tested on something and I had passed.

Nicky thrust the paper in front of me. "See for yourself, darling." He picked me up, swung my around and then kissed me deeply.

When he left me breathless, he put me down and ordered me to ring Mama and give her the good news.

Grand Mama came downstairs then asking what all the noised was about?

"I have just passed my nursing exam, Grand Mama. I am just going to telephone Mama and give her the good news."

When I told Mama, she sounded so pleased for me. Grand Mama said that we should celebrate and asked Peter Abramovich to bring us a bottle of champagne to celebrate. She also said that she was going to the theatre to see Tchaikovsky's Nutcracker and asked Nicky and I if we would like to accompany her. Nicky said he would have to go and change, he looked at me for approval. Anything to do with Tchaikovsky I would be pleased to go to, so I nodded to him in agreement.

Nicky left shortly after that and said that he would come back for us. I still had a couple of hours to prepare to go out, so ran upstairs and asked Tanya to run a bath for me. I dressed in my purple velvet gown that Grand Mama had bought me for Christmas, put on my pearl choker, matching bracelet and earrings and touched the perfume that I kept for evening wear, behind my ears, between my breasts, my neck and at my wrists. I felt almost human for the first time in ages. We hadn't been out for, what seemed like, such a long time. I was either, snowed in at the hospital or too tired to go out. After the last time Nicky and I went out to Minsky's and had people shouting abuse at us, we hadn't gone out in the evening for a long time after that. Short notice that it was, I was really looking forward to it. I was looking forward to seeing Nicky in evening dress again. I thought my fiancé was so handsome, especially in evening dress.

As usual the theatre was packed, we sat in Grand Mama's box, waiting for the curtain to rise. When it was dark and the orchestra had started up, he took my hand and placed a kiss on it. Could my life get any better? When the dancers started, we both sat with a smile on our lips, hearing the familiar 'thump, thump, thump' of the dancer's pointes. That had been what had really started us talking that first time at the theatre, watching 'Swan Lake'. I thought that Swan Lake was beautiful, but The Nutcracker was magical.

It was the perfect way to celebrate my success. In the interval Grand Mama ordered a bottle of champagne to our box and toasted my success in my nursing exams.

# Chapter 25
## A Visit from Our Patron

Nicky collected me the next morning to take me to the hospital. In my changing room, I took my outdoor clothes off to change into my uniform, which had been washed, pressed and folded neatly, waiting for me on the little table as it always was but the difference was on my nurse's cap, which now sported a thin blue band around the top, denoting that I was now a fully qualified nurse. Proudly I put it on my head and secured it with two hairpins, to make sure that it stayed secure.

I jumped when I got out of the room, to find someone waiting for me. Without even looking, I knew who it was from the odour of alcohol and unwashed body. It was Rasputin.

"Ah Bella Thalia. As beautiful as ever. I had to come and congratulate you on passing your nursing exam. Now you are a fully qualified nurse and still unmarried." He made a move to grab me I was about to move back into the safe confines of my dressing room when an authoritative voice behind him spoke sternly.

"Rasputin, leave that nurse alone and remove yourself from this hospital!"

I couldn't see who it was standing behind his tall, skinny body. I stepped around him to see the Dowager Empress standing with Sister Procopy and some of the Doctors. I could feel myself blush to the roots of my hair.

Rasputin began mumbling about why he was there but was cut short. "You may be welcome in certain quarters of the palace but not in the nursing quarters. Now remove yourself immediately," the Dowager Empress re-iterated.

He made a quick bow, then all but ran off, to the private royal quarters.

The Dowager Empress came over to me, her face full of concern, "Are you all right my dear? He didn't hurt you at all, did he?" She put a finger under my chin and made me look into her eyes. "Thalia, did he touch you?"

223

"No, your Highness but if you hadn't come in time, I don't know what would have happened. Why are you here?" I asked my saviour. (Not that it was really any of my business I thought afterwards).

"Didn't you know, my dear, that I am patron of the Red-Cross?" She looked up and saw the blue band on my cap.

Olga Procopy told her that I was one of the newly qualified nurses. "Nurse Bobrov passed with the highest marks, Your Highness," she explained.

"Congratulations, my dear. Very well done," she said. "I will have a word with my daughter-in-law and tell her to keep that man away from the wards and the nurse's quarters."

Olga said that she would be pleased if the Dowager Empress could intervene on the behalf of all her nurses to stop Rasputin being a nuisance to all the female medical staff.

I curtsied to the Dowager Empress and excused myself saying that I needed to get to the ward.

Katya was the first to see me with my new cap and congratulated me. Even some of the patients, that were lucid enough, commented on it.

I told Katya, that the Dowager Empress was on the premises and it looked like she might be inspecting some of the wards, so we should make sure that everywhere was ready for an inspection.

Katya and I did a quick look over the ward, to make sure that it was presentable for our distinguished visitor. There were a few beds that needed bedclothes straightening but that was all. We quickly tidied the offending beds, then went on our rounds doing the temperatures and blood pressures, then went around again with the medications. While I was going around with the medications, the Dowager Empress appeared at the door to our ward, along with some of the doctors who I had seen with her, when she had disciplined Rasputin. Sister Procopy, who was also with the group, called me over.

"Nurse Bobrov, would you be kind enough to take our guests around the ward and explain to them more about your patients?"

I nodded and started the round of the ward, explaining who the patient was and what was wrong with them. I explained that some of the patients weren't suffering war wounds, but from the freezing cold temperatures and frost bite, one of the doctors then asked me, what we were doing for them. I told them as best that I could, then moved on to the next patient and went through the same thing, until I had covered all the ward that I dealt with. Then I explained that because the ward was so large, I didn't cover all the patients, that the other three quarters of the ward was covered by other nurses. Sister Procopy, thanked me and asked if they wanted to see any more of this ward or move on to another ward. They all thanked me and moved on to another ward. Just before they left, the Dowager Empress just stopped behind and asked again me if I was all right after my encounter with Rasputin. I nodded and thanked her for her concern. She touched my shoulders in a friendly gesture and smiled at me. "I will have a word about him. Well done, my dear."

Before the end of my shift, some of the nursing staff were called into the main hallway to pose for a photograph with our patron. The Dowager Empress insisted that I and some of the other nurses stand at the front with her. Some of the patients that could be wheeled from the ward, were placed in front of us to also pose for the photographer. I looked around to see if the Tsarina and Grand Duchesses were there for the photograph and was surprised to see they were nowhere to be seen.

Once all of the photographs had been taken, we were dismissed to return to our wards or finish our shift.

There was a lot of chatter back on the ward after the photograph session, also a lot of talk about the Dowager Empress going around the various patients and talking to them. The patients felt honoured that she would actually talk to them. I could tell from their voices that they had a lot of love and respect for the Tsar's mother, if not his wife.

# Chapter 26

## Our Wedding Day

Once the spring days came, the atmosphere in the wards seemed to lift a little with the temperature. Just to see blue sky and the sun shining would lift anyone's spirits. Sister Procopy said that the patients who could walk, could go out into the grounds. Those that were fit enough to go out in wheelchairs, could be wheeled out into the grounds and we opened some of the windows to let the fresh air circulate around the wards.

Outside the sculptured gardens, which were still kept in immaculate order by an army of gardeners was a riot of colourful spring flowers and shrubs. Their perfume filled the air. Normally the royals would be at their summer residence in Lavardia but the Tsar had 'gone to war' so the rest of the family stayed at Tsarskoye Selo. The two Older Grand Duchesses and the two younger ones were either wheeling patients around the gardens or reading aloud to others. The Tsarina, I noticed was in a wheelchair pushed by Gregori Rasputin, not far from where I was walking with one of the patients who had lost both of his feet to frost-bite, along with some of his fingers. It was a week before my wedding day and I was excited, nervous, apprehensive and I suppose even a little scared, of what, I didn't know. It certainly wasn't Nicky that I was scared of. Maybe the fact that being a virgin, I might disappoint him on our wedding night.

On a day where the sun was shining, my mood was so much lighter. I laughed and joked with Peter, my patient. We stopped and chatted with other patients and nurses, about the weather and the war. Some even said that on a day like this, regardless of their injuries, it was good to be alive.

Peter and the other patient noticed the Tsarina talking with Rasputin.

"What is she doing here, the German bitch and with him?"

The other patient said, "We can't get away from her, even out here. Maybe it is true what they say about her and Rasputin. They say there is no smoke without fire and with her husband out of the way..."

The other nurse bent down and scolded him, telling him that he must not say such things and that she and the two older Grand Duchesses were nurses too, trying to help the soldiers, who had suffered for their country.

The soldier snorted, "Helping us soldiers, more like spying for the Germans! After all that's where she comes from, Germany, not Russia. Look at how she is looking at the 'Mad Monk, she's even touching him. I didn't believe what they were saying about her and him but seeing them together..."

Peter, who was my patient, joined in then, "They say that between her and Rasputin, they forced Germany to go to war with Russia. We go to the front totally unprepared. Look at me. If they had provided a proper winter uniform and good sturdy boots, I wouldn't have lost my feet or my fingers. Some men didn't even have a gun to shoot but had to take scythes and pitchforks to the front to fight with. How are we supposed to win a war like that?"

I saw Rasputin look over to me and instantly I shivered. "Are you all right, Nurse Angel, you look like you've seen a ghost?" asked Peter.

Seeing Rasputin had brought a cloud onto what would have been a perfect day. I knew that he was a womaniser. It wasn't just me that he had tried to compromise. Other nurses, when we had been housed together in the dormitories, had been objects of his attention. He would try and single them out and then pounce. Some of the nurses said that he had managed to kiss them, others said that he had laid his hands on them inappropriately. They had immediately reported it to Sister Procopy, who had talked to the Tsarina, who said the he was just a tactile person and that he meant no harm. In other words, she made excuses for him. Things had been better since the Dowager Empresses visit, so maybe she had had a word with her daughter-in-law, about the man.

The day before my wedding, I had the day off. Three months before my wedding, I had asked Katya Patenko, my good friend among the nurses and Olga Procopy, to be my bridesmaids. Olga said that she had to work on the day of my wedding but told Katya that she could have the day off. I asked, Auguste Brisac, if she could make a bridesmaid's dress for Katya, which she did and was now hanging up next to my wedding dress in my bedroom. To make it easier, I asked Nicky if he could drive me to the hospital, when Katya's shift finished, the night before our wedding, to pick up Katya and drive us both back to Grand Mama's.

I had worn my wedding dress at my final fitting but not since it had been delivered and certainly not with my wedding veil. This was deemed to be unlucky. I wanted to see the finished product on the same day that Nicky would.

When Katya stepped into my bedroom, she was awestruck. It was certainly a big step up from the nurse's dormitory. Tanya showed Katya to her room, which had been Mama's, next to mine, again Katya was too stunned to speak, which was a first. When she had put her small bag with her toiletries in her bedroom, she came back to mine, knocking on the door before she entered.

"Thalia, I never knew that you lived in a house like this. I didn't even know that your Nicky was a prince, until recently. Why on earth did you become a nurse when you didn't have to?"

It was hard to explain. I told her that I had seen so much poverty and unfairness in the country, which I couldn't help, so I thought if I did nursing, it would somehow help some of the poor. Hearing me say it, sounded patronising and lame but it was the only way I could explain it. I never told her that I had joined up with the Tsarina and Grand Duchesses. The atmosphere at the hospital from the staff and the patients towards the royals was not good, at best and I must admit that, after the time when the Tsarina ignored Igor's raised temperature and he died, I don't think that I felt the same towards her. When we were training, I thought that we were getting on reasonably well but these days, I began to feel that maybe they were doing it for other reasons than my own.

Anyway, enough of thoughts of the royals, the next day was my wedding day, the one that both Nicky and I had been longing for, for what seemed to be a terribly long time. Now I should be concentrating on that.

Nicky, Mama and Gregor, came over to Grand Mama's the evening before the wedding, to meet Katya and have a meal, prepared by Grand Mama's wonderful chef Ivan, who had been with Grand Mama for as long as Mama could remember.

Katya dressed in her best dress and came down stairs with me, to meet Mama and Gregor. We adjourned to the main dining room, which, these days was rarely used.

Everyone made Katya feel welcome and we tried not to make her feel uncomfortable. The evening was filled with laughter and happiness. Most of all it was filled with happiness, that the next day Nicky and I would be man and wife and the next night all of my wants and needs, that I had felt and had to ignore over the last few months, would be assuaged. I could feel Nicky's eyes on me all of the evening and began to think that, maybe, he was feeling the same.

Katya commented on how beautiful the meal was and thanked Grand Mama for letting her stay the night. Grand Mama said that it was a pleasure to make the acquaintance of one of my friends from the hospital.

Mama and Gregor were the first to leave, as they wanted to get back early to kiss Ilia goodnight. They kissed, Katya, Nicky and finally me, saying that they would see me at the cathedral, the following morning.

Nicky didn't stay long after that, saying that he needed a good night's sleep ready for our wedding day, then he leaned over away from Grand Mama and Katya's hearing and whispered to me, "More so for the night ahead of us."

I blushed, "Miss Bobrov," he said with his usual cheeky grin, "I do believe you are blushing."

"That is all of your fault, your Highness." I playfully punched his arm.

"You won't be able to call me that after tomorrow, as you will be one too."

I giggled, "It's infectious this 'highness' thing, isn't it?"

Nicky kissed me, then said good night to Grand Mama and Katya.

Tanya was there as usual busying herself in my bedroom. We discussed her duties for the morning and I asked her if she would run a bath for Katya in the morning and do her hair for her, before she came and attended me. She looked like she was about to argue but decided against it.

I asked her if she had packed her things away ready for attending me on my honeymoon at Tallin. That brought a real smile to her face, it would give her more time to spend with Rudolph, Nicky's man. I could see in the future that there might be two married couples living under one roof.

That night, both Katya and I went to bed early to get a good night's sleep and I thought that maybe Katya had never lived in such luxury before. It was my way of thanking her for helping me study for my exam. Becoming a qualified nurse meant a lot to me, probably more than she would ever know.

Katya asked me if she would have to call me 'highness' once I was married. I told her not to be silly. We were friends and friends didn't bother with titles. She looked at me unsure. "I don't want to be called Princess, Katya. I am just a nurse marrying a businessman, who happens to have a title of 'Prince'." We hugged each other, then went to our respective rooms. Peter Abramovich had said that he would drive Katya back to the hospital after the wedding had finished. Nicky told me that we would spend our wedding night at his (now our) town house, Chesmenskiy Palace, then, we would drive down to Tallin the next morning.

The amount of champagne I had drunk, that evening, seemed to relax me suitably, so that it didn't take me long for me to drift off to sleep.

Tanya woke me the next morning with her usual cheerful, "Good morning, Miss Thalia. It's a beautiful day outside," she said as she opened my bedroom curtains, after she had placed my breakfast tray across my lap. The sun streamed into my bedroom and caught my wedding dress hanging up ready and waiting for me.

She then went into Katya and ran her bath, opened her bedroom curtains and put her breakfast tray across her lap. Tanya told me that Katya said that she could get used to breakfast in bed. Once Katya had finished her breakfast and was soaking in her bath, Tanya came back in to me, to help me to bathe.

I asked her if she minded helping Katya as well. "No, Miss Thalia, she is a nice lady and thanks me for everything that I do for her."

I told Tanya that I would make it up to her.

I lay in my bath luxuriating in its warmth. Never in all my life in Smolensk did I think that this would happen, that I would be living in St Petersburg and marrying a prince, not just any prince but the cousin to the Tsar of Russia. I had travelled to St Petersburg wondering if I would ever find a man that could fall in love with me, certainly not in the first few weeks of arriving but I had. I felt truly blessed. No matter whether the Tsar was a good ruler or not, he always made me feel welcome. I had even had a kiss from the Tsar. He was a nice man, but a terrible ruler.

Tanya came back into the bathroom to wash my hair, "I asked Miss Patenko if she needed any help drying and dressing but she said that she could manage, so I have come back to help you." She washed my hair, then helped me out of the bath, into the waiting fluffy towel. I sat in front of the fire, while she dried my hair, then put on my underclothes and my dressing gown and sat down in front of my dressing table mirror. I touched some of my perfume which I usually used for evenings, to my neck, throat and wrists. Tanya began on my hair. I was to wear the diamond jewellery that I had inherited when I made my debut. When Tanya had finished my hair, she placed the tiara on my head.

While I was putting in my earrings, a knock came on my bedroom door. Katya poked her head around the door, apologising profusely, "Erm… Thalia, could I have some help with doing all of the buttons up on my dress? I can do them so far, then I would need to be a contortionist to finish them off." I laughed and told her to come in and sit down. I put the diamond bracelet around my wrist and Tanya put the matching choker around my neck.

"Oh, Thalia, even without the dress, you look beautiful." Katya said. Tanya asked her to turn around, while she finished doing up the rest of Katya's dress.

I handed a small box to Katya. "It's just a little something to thank you for agreeing to be my bridesmaid, Katya."

She opened the box to find a single string of pearls, matching bracelet and earrings. "Oh, Thalia, how can I thank you for…" – she moved her arms around in the air – "all of this. I know that it's only for today but I will remember it forever."

I told her to just enjoy the day… "You never know, you might find a prince today, who will whisk you away."

"If only!" She laughed.

Tanya finally helped me into me wedding gown, with tiny crystal buttons running all of the way down the back of the dress. The style was very simple. It was the materials that made my wedding gown look elegant.

"Oh, Miss Thalia," Tanya cried, "you look so beautiful, even more so than the night of your debut." Similar to my debut ballgown, my wedding dress had shots of silver running through the material, which of-course was virginal white, so that when the light hit it, it shimmered.

She finished the effect by putting on my Brussels lace wedding veil, which again was shot through with silver thread and went the full length of the six-foot train on my dress. Whenever I moved I seemed to sparkle.

I stood and looked at myself in my full-length mirror. I truly felt beautiful. I hoped that Nicky would be suitably stunned by my appearance.

Peter Abramovich, drove Grand Mama and Katya to the Cathedral, then turned around and came back for me. He helped me into the motor car, after which Tanya was busy arranging, my train and veil around me.

I sat in the back of the motor car on my own, looking up at the clear blue sky and the rainbow of colours of the flowers in the park as we passed by. I held my bouquet of Freesias on my lap, occasionally lifting them to my nose and taking in their beautiful perfume. We pulled up outside Kazan Cathedral and Peter came around to the rear passenger door, to help me out. The same photographer who had photographed me in my debut gown had been hired to photograph my wedding. I stood outside of the car for a couple of photographs then moved towards the cathedral.

Gregor and Mama, Grand Mama, Katya and Nicky had all been waiting in the entrance to the Cathedral. When Gregor saw me get out of the car, he came to me, to walk me to the entrance, for the first part of the ceremony, which was the exchanging of rings. Again, the photographer took a couple of photographs, then allowed us to carry on.

I think when Nicky saw me, he was suitable stunned. Gregor handed me to Nicky.

We finally stood together in front of the priest, as we placed the wedding rings on the ring finger of, each other's, hand. The priest then took our hands in his and led us to the centre of the church, with Gregor, Katya, Mama and Grand Mama following.

Once at the centre of the church, where all our friends and relatives waited, the Dowager Empress stood nearest to the central table, where Nicky and I stopped. He bowed to her and I curtsied. She smiled at us and we moved on. I handed my bouquet to Mama to hold, while Nicky and I declared that we entered into marriage of our own free will. The Priest then gave us a candle each, to carry through the rest of the Ceremony.

The priest said prayers on our behalf and then placed a crown over each of our heads. Gregor took the crowns from the priest and continued holding them over Nicky's and my heads, while the priest read, the Epistle then the Gospel, about the marriage in Cana, where Jesus turned water into wine. This was then followed by more prayers.

The priest blessed the cup of wine, which he handed to Nicky and me to drink. After that, the priest held the cross and our hands, while Gregor still held the crowns over our heads and Katya followed behind us as we walked around the central table three times, counter clockwise. I don't know about Nicky but I seemed to go through the ceremony in a daze. Nothing really seemed to register with me. I know that I should have been taking notice of the symbolism of the wedding ceremony but my mind just didn't seem to register anything except that the day that Nicky and I had been waiting for so long was finally here and within a matter of moments I would become Princess Thalia Ivanov. More importantly Nicky's wife.

The priest then took our crowns from Gregor and offered them up to God.

At last, with the religious ceremony over, Nicky and I stood at the front of the Alter and faced the congregation. This was the signal for everyone to come over and congratulate us and give us their best wishes for a happy and fruitful marriage.

"Well, Your Highness, how do you feel?" Nicky turned and asked, grinning at me.

"Very happy, Your Highness," I told him.

He lifted the hand with my wedding ring on and kissed it, "As I am, very happy, Princess Thalia Marguerite Titania Ivanov."

There were more photographs, even one with the Dowager Empress, who reminded everyone that she too was part of the family.

We went back to Grand Mama's for the reception. The photographer arrived to take more photographs of the bride and groom, while Mama and Gregor had gone home to collect Ilia, who, when he saw me, his little face broke into a great big smile.

I had seen as much of him as I could, considering that I was working but when I did see him, I played with him, so that by now, he was getting to know his big sister. Of course, wherever Ilia went, so did Maria and Mikhail, who had both been transformed in the months since Nicky and I had brought them to live with Mama and Gregor, to become Ilia's nanny, plus one, as Nicky used to call them. Nicky and I circulated around our wedding guests, who, obviously told me that I looked beautiful and asked where we were going after the reception.

Nicky seemed to be holding my hand all of the time and I could feel him rubbing my wedding ring, as if he needed to re-assure himself that we were now husband and wife. Katya came over to me, just before we were about to leave for Chesmenskiy Palace.

"Thalia, I can't thank you enough for such a wonderful day and my present. When I go up and change, I'll leave my dress in my room."

I told her that the dress was hers now. She smiled, "I don't know when I will have the opportunity to wear it again."

I told her that we would make an opportunity, kissed her and thanked her for supporting me throughout the day.

Nicky came over to me and said that I should go up and change as we would be leaving soon. I felt reluctant to take off my beautiful wedding dress, after all, this day had been a long time coming. I had worn my wedding dress for about five hours and now I had to take it off. It seemed such a shame.

Tanya and Rudolph had already gone to Chesmenskiy Palace, ahead of us, to prepare for our arrival, so I went up to my room alone. I took off my tiara and veil, then tried to undo all the tiny crystal buttons down the back. Someone knocked on my bedroom door. I told whoever it was to come in. I was pleased to see Mama come through the door.

"I thought you might need a hand getting out of your dress." I thanked her as she began the task of unbuttoning all of the tiny crystal buttons of my wedding gown.

"I'm going to miss you, Lia. It doesn't seem long since you were Ilia's age. Now here you are, a married woman and a Princess as well." She finally managed to undo all of the buttons, "I think it's a good thing I came up to help you. I don't think you would have managed all on your own."

"Yes, it is rather impractical," I said smiling at her. I felt sad that this would be the last time that we would be together for a while. Not only had my life changed so much since that first journey to St Petersburg but Mama's life had changed from a loveless marriage to my father to a happy and fulfilled marriage with Gregor.

"Oh, but you looked so beautiful, my darling," she hesitated struggling to find the right words, "About tonight…" she started and I could tell from her look that she felt uncomfortable talking to me about something so intimate.

I thought that there must have been another reason why she had come upstairs

I laughed and held her hand. "Mama, you forget that when I read those manuals on giving birth, it also told me how babies were made; so, you don't need to try and explain."

She gave a great sigh of relief and sat down on my bed. "I don't know whether it is the world we now live in or just Russia but you seemed to have grown up so fast over the last few years."

I said that I thought that it was just a sign of the times and the fact that I had been trained as a nurse. "You can't be naive after that."

I put on my blouse, skirt and jacket and matching hat, checking myself in the mirror. "You look beautiful. I won't tell you to be happy with Nicky. I can see by the looks on your faces that you will be. He is a good man, Lia. I am glad that you met him."

And there I was wondering if we could marry, being related, but it didn't matter after all. "So am I, Mama." I kissed her cheek and then we went downstairs, arm in arm. "I am glad that you married Gregor too Mama. He is the perfect father and stepfather."

Mama agreed with me. Nicky was waiting for me at the bottom of the staircase.

"Are you ready to go now, darling?" he asked, the light of love shining in his eyes.

I nodded. After we had gone around kissing and shaking hands with everybody, we finally left and started on our journey to Chesmenskiy Palace; just the two of us, Prince Nicky and Princess Thalia Ivanov.

Nicky reached over and clasped my hand, "You looked stunning today darling. An absolute vision, and your wedding dress...I am the luckiest man in the world." He raised my hand to his lips and kissed it.

"Tell me that in the morning," I teased him.

A wicked grin came on his face then, "Oh I will, Lia. I will."

We both laughed.

# Chapter 27

## Chesmenskiy Palace

It didn't take us very long to drive from Grand Mama's house to Chesmenskiy. Nicky held my hand nearly all through the journey. For some reason, I felt nervous about the night ahead. I didn't know whether Nicky was experienced and if he was, with how many other women. I didn't want to know. That was all in the past. I told myself. This was now but I was so totally inexperienced, if not totally ignorant. I just hoped that my instinct would show me the way or Nicky would.

Nicky drove us into the courtyard and pulled up outside the main entrance. I looked around at the outside of my new home in St Petersburg. From the first time I saw it, I thought Chesmenskiy Palace looked more like a prison than a palace. It was only when you were inside it that it looked more like a palace, with its marble hallway and high vaulted ceilings and small windows but it lacked the beauty and charm and brightness of our other home in Tallin. Kadriorg Palace had beauty and elegance from its beautiful manicured gardens to its fountains and beautiful ground floor rooms opening out onto a large patio and the upstairs rooms leading through double doors to balconies overlooking the gardens.

Nicky came around and opened my door for me. "Welcome to your new home, darling," he said kissing me. I looked up at the Palace. It was of an unusual shape in the form of a triangle but I still didn't like it as much as Kadriorg Palace where we would be making the five-hour journey to the next day.

Tanya, my maid and Rudolph, Nicky's man servant, would follow on behind us when we went on honeymoon to Tallin and Nicky's home there. It would be the second time a couple had spent their honeymoon at Kadriorg Palace.

He linked his arm through mine as we entered the main hallway, Rudolph and Tanya came out to greet us. "Welcome home, Your Highnesses," Rudolph said, as he and Tanya took our coats.

"The chef has arranged a cold collation in the small dining room, Your Highness," he continued.

"Would you like to go upstairs to change, Your Highness?" Tanya asked me.

Nicky told them both that we wouldn't be needing them for the rest of the evening, "We will take care of ourselves. Thank you."

Tanya looked like she was going to say something but with a look from Rudolph kept quiet.

Arm in arm we went into the small dining room. The food that Nicky's chef had prepared for us was delicious and having not eaten since breakfast, which was hours ago, I was starving. I didn't feel like eating back at Grand Mama's, I was too busy circulating among our guests. Nicky opened the bottle of champagne and poured it into two crystal glasses, handing one to me. "A toast, to us, Lia. May we live a long happy life and love as long as we live."

We chinked glasses and I looked at him over the top of my glass. I could not believe that finally Nicky was my husband. We had come a long way since the day I fell over on the ice and Nicky rescued me.

He looked at me, then took my hand and lead me upstairs to our bedroom. Already, it was dark outside. Our bedroom curtains had been closed and a fire had been lit in the marble hearth. The bedroom was beautifully furnished but lacked the homeliness of Grand Mama's or even the room that I slept in when we went to Tallin. It seemed so much more austere, with its burgundy colour scheme and dark wood.

Nicky took my glass of champagne from me and placed it on the bedside table. I looked at him. Just his look started the butterflies in my stomach and the wanting within my body. He kissed me deeply, setting my body aflame with wanting 'more'. His fingers deftly undid the buttons of my blouse and then my skirt. I didn't just want to stand there and let him make all of the first moves. That was not how I felt or how I wanted it to be, so I pushed his jacket from his broad shoulders and began undoing the buttons on his immaculate white shirt.

Beneath his shirt his broad chest was warm beneath my fingers. I let my fingers run through the dark hairs that I had seen from afar when we went swimming in the sea but never had we dared to touch each other for we might start something that we wouldn't be able to stop. Now nothing was stopping us.

He slipped my blouse off and let me lean on him as I stepped out of my skirt to stand before him in my underwear. Slowly he kissed my neck, my shoulders, my breasts, as he began removing my underclothes.

237

He carried me over to the bed, where I lay, watching him undress. Of all of the male patient's bodies I had seen, while nursing, none looked more beautiful, broad and strong as Nicky's did to me. My breath caught in my throat as he stepped out of his trousers and my body began to betray my feelings.

He lay down beside me, his warm body close against mine, I could feel his need for me and my body responded.

"Lia darling, I am not going to hurt you." He looked deep into my eyes. "You trust me, don't you?"

I nodded. I would trust Nicky with my life as well as my love.

He cupped and kissed my breast, then began trailing kisses all down my body. I could feel my body responding in ways that I never expected and my passion was matching his, as I arched my body enjoying the delicious feelings that were now exploding through all of me at every move, he made within me and I couldn't stay silent as we finally exploded together in one trembling moment of love.

When it was over, we lay wrapped, in each other's arms, sated, happy and content. Now I knew what 'More' was and it was wonderful. Nicky covered my face with his kisses. "I love you, my wife," he said.

"My heart is overflowing with love for you, my Nicky."

We slept curled up against each other, both of us had a smile of satisfaction and happiness on our faces.

The next morning, after we had eaten breakfast, we set off on the final leg of our journey to our other home in Tallin. Again, the weather was a perfect summer's day. Rudolph and Tanya had left while we were having breakfast to get to Kadriorg Palace before we did and unpack our trunks, for the month of our honeymoon there.

The journey was long and I wished that our motor car could take wings and fly us there.

As we drove up the long driveway to front entrance, I noticed that all of the downstairs windows had been opened to let the gentle sea breeze blow through the rooms, keeping them cool, in the heat of the summer's day.

Nicky turned towards me, in the car, "Welcome home my darling."

I told him that I thought that Kadriorg Palace felt more like my home than Chesmenskiy Palace ever would.

Nicky helped me from the car and looked around the grounds, especially the beautifully manicured gardens and the playing water fountains. "I can see our children running around here laughing," he said.

"I could imagine them here, the first time we stayed here." I said.

I could imagine Christmases and summers here, with Mama, Gregor, little Ilia and Grand Mama.

Then a dreadful thought hit me. How many Christmases and summers, would we be able to have here? I pushed, the unwanted thought from my mind, telling myself to enjoy each day as it came.

Tanya met us in the grand hallway, welcoming us home. She told us that both of our trunks had been unpacked and asked us if there was anything more, she could do for us.

Nicky said that she could tell the chef that we would eat on the patio outside the dining room that evening. She curtseyed to us and disappeared in the direction of the kitchen.

We went up to our bedroom to change into something more suited to the hot weather, then walked hand in hand down to the beach, where a changing tent had been set up for us to change into our bathing suits.

We swam in the sea, splashing each other playfully, then diving under the water and swimming. When we were suitably tired, we lay on two large towels on the sand and let the sun dry us.

Every day we spent down on the beach, swimming and reading one of the many books in Nicky's vast library. In the evenings we would have our evening meal either out on the terrace or inside in the dining room, if the temperature outside was too cool for outside dining. After dinner we would go into the music room and Nicky would either play the piano or put a record on the wind-up gramophone and we would dance. We played chess or just sat holding each other while we listened to the music on the gramophone. Then we would go to our bedroom to bathe and to make love. While at Grand Mama's Tanya had always wrapped one of the big fluffy towels around me, from the bath. Now that Nicky and I were married we acted as maid and valet to each other but Tanya always came to do my hair.

Our honeymoon was everything I could ever have wished for. We didn't read any newspapers while we were at Kadriorg Palace. This was our own little haven and the troubles of the outside world was not allowed in to ruin it. We would occasionally stop in the village and walk around the shops where Nicky introduced me as his wife. The people there would bow or curtsey to me, then I would talk to them about their shop, their goods and usually buy some small thing from each. In return one little girl brought me a little posy of flowers. I thanked her and bent down to kiss her. I think that I had endeared myself to them by taking and interest in them. Nicky seemed pleased by my actions, and once back at home would compliment me on showing a genuine interest in them.

By the end of the month in our own peaceful place in Russia, we were rested and tanned and feeling reluctant to leave our haven to go back to Chesmenskiy Palace and the real cruel, unfair, world that we lived in.

When we got back to 'Chesme', as Nicky fondly called it, we still had another couple of days until I had to go back to the hospital. I had missed the hospital but I would miss being with Nicky more after being together every day and every night for a month.

As soon as we arrived back in St Petersburg, we went to visit Grand Mama, Mama, Gregor and little Ilia who seemed to have grown in the month we had been away. I held him and cuddled him, burying my nose in his little neck and smelling his 'baby-ness'. Everyone commented on how well we both looked, tanned and relaxed.

Mama looked at me, as if to ask, if I had conceived on our honeymoon, which fortunately or unfortunately hadn't happened. I didn't know whether I was sad or relieved. I wanted Nicky's baby but I wanted to have Nicky all to myself a little longer before I had to share him.

Nicky and I went to Minsky's that evening to dine and dance, the next night we went to the theatre to see Tchaikovsky's ballet of Sleeping Beauty. It was a beautiful end to a wonderful honeymoon. We went back to Chesme, our town house, for our final night, before I returned to work. Our lovemaking was gentle and loving. Nicky held me tightly in his arms, whispering words of love in my ear, making me feel the most cherished and loved woman in the world.

I knew that I didn't have to go back to nursing but it was something that I had started and I did feel that I was making a difference, in my own small way. Olga Procopy had told me that I was a good nurse and to me, that was praise indeed. Nicky, although he hadn't told me in detail, had done his 'bit' for our country and now I was doing mine and Nicky didn't try to stop me. I think he knew the need that I had to prove myself. Mama had also said how professional I was with the doctor when Illia was born and also he had said that if I wanted to leave nursing at Tsarskoye Selo he would have been happy to offer me a position.

Why would I want to give it all up when I had so many people telling me that I was good at nursing?

# Chapter 28

## Nurse Ivanov

I was back at Tsarskoye Selo by seven thirty the following morning. I went to the ward where I had been working before I left to get married. Sister Procopy was on the ward, with another new nurse. Whether the nurse was new or she had just been moved from another ward to cover my absence from the hospital, I didn't know.

"Nurse Bob... Ivanov," Olga Procopy said, "Welcome back. I trust that you are ready to get working again?" It was back to business and Olga was forever the professional.

"I am reporting for duty Sister."

"Very well then. Follow me. You are to start work in the theatres to broaden your experience. I trust that you have removed your rings, nurse?"

"Yes, Sister." I had once again put my engagement on a chain and now my wedding ring joined it on the gold chain around my neck.

The operating theatres were in another wing on the ground floor of the palace. This was even more sterile than the wards. It had a smell all of its own, of carbolic and anaesthetic. I noticed this the first time that I walked into the area but soon after you had been working there for a while, you didn't notice it.

A nurse came out from one of the rooms and walked over to me.

"Nurse Ivanov, I am Sister Nadia Kuriakin. You will be under my supervision while you are working in theatre." She said. She was a lot older than Sister Procopy. She wore a tight fitting, cap, under which was scraped all of her hair, to stop it falling loose. Over her grey nurses dress she wore a long white cotton gown that seemed to cover her from neck to ankles and special theatre shoes.

Olga said that she would leave me in Sister Kuriakin's capable hands and wished me good luck. Then she turned and left us.

"I have seen you here down in the theatre suites before, haven't I?" she commented.

I told her that I had come down a couple of times with patients that were due to have operations.

She asked me if I had seen an actual operation before and I said that I hadn't. "Right, then we must rectify that first. I want you to gown up, scrub up and then meet me in theatre three." Each theatre was numbered by a large number on the outside of it. She showed me where to find a theatre gown, mask, cap and theatre boots, also where to wash and scrub my hands, before entering the theatre.

When I entered the theatre, Sister Kuriakin came over to me and introduced me to the doctor, the anaesthetist and the other theatre nurse, called Sacha Sharapova, who also looked quite a lot older than me. She called us nurses by or Christian names but just referred to the doctors as "Doctor." I must admit that I was nervous as to how I would get on working in theatre.

Sister Kuriakin told me that I was to stand back and just observe the first operation. She told me that if I felt faint, to leave the room, "The doctors have enough on their hands without pandering to a hysterical nurse." She warned me.

I felt that that certainly put me in my place. I heard the anaesthetist tell the doctor that the patient was ready. I felt my heartbeat increase as the doctor made the first incision. I thought that I might faint but I was too interested to see what the doctor was doing to think about anything else.

The operation was another amputation, which apparently was quite a common operation during the war, as well as ones removing bullets or shrapnel from soldiers. I saw nurse Sharapova put the patient's severed arm on a metal tray; cover it and carry it from the theatre. Sister Kuriakin told me that amputated limbs were sent to a furnace in the palace to be burnt.

"It's a terrible thing to say but we keep the furnace pretty busy." She saw the doctor cauterise the wound and finish up, then turned and congratulated me. "You didn't faint. Well done. Theatre work isn't for everyone, Nurse Ivanov. We have had nurses new to the operating theatre either pass out or vomit. You did neither, so now we will begin your training."

Nurse Sharapova explained all about keeping sterile surroundings and sterilising instruments used in the operations.

I watched another three operations that however bloody or gory they were, my stomach held fast and I retained a cool head. I found it very interesting, watching two men holding a person's life in their hands; the surgeon and the anaesthetist. The surgeon and the theatre nurse, worked in unison, with the nurse practically knowing the surgeons next move, before he made it and had the correct instruments ready to be slapped firmly in his hand.

I was told to take a break from the theatre and to go out and enjoy the sunshine in the grounds for half an hour, then return back to the theatre.

I took off the long white theatre gown, cap and mask, put them in a large basket and left the theatre suite.

The beautiful sunlight made me shade my eyes for a while, until I got used to it. The theatre suites had no windows in them. I walked around for a while, then sat on one of the benches, just enjoying the fresh air. I jumped when I felt a hand on my shoulder.

"Bella Thalia, where have you been hiding yourself."

I should have known by the odour that preceded him, who it was but it was being masked by the perfume of the late blooming flowers.

I stood up, to move away from him and brushed Rasputin's hand from my shoulder. "I have been away on honeymoon, now if you will excuse me, I have to go back."

He tutted mockingly, "But you have only just come outside. I saw you." He tried to take my hand but I shook him off. "You don't like me, Bella Thalia. Why is that?"

"I am choosey who I mix with and you are not the sort of person…"

"But I am only a simple man and you are a beautiful young woman," he interrupted me.

"The Tsarina and the Grand Duchesses might enjoy your company but I don't. Now leave me alone."

"I only want to be your friend," he said, moving closer. I could smell spirits on his breath and his unwashed body and I felt like retching.

"I chose my friends very carefully and you would be the last person that I would ever want for that position. Now leave me alone or I will tell my husband."

He began to laugh. His whole skinny, bony frame shook with his mirth. "And what will your husband do Bella Thalia, call me out… Don't you know that I am a peaceful man and a man of God."

"Then you will know when your advances are not welcome. Leave me alone."

Out of the corner of my eye I saw the Tsarina coming towards us. Would I be able to complain to her about this uncouth man?

"Father Gregori, I was wondering where you had got to," she said as she reached us. "Thalia, how good it is to see you."

I curtseyed to her.

"Matushka," Rasputin replied, "I was just here, making the acquaintance of Miss Bobrov," he said in a quiet, simpering voice.

"It is not Miss Bobrov now, Father Gregori. Thalia has married my husband's cousin Prince Nickolas Ivanov."

Again, he moved to take my hand to kiss it. I took a deep breath, "Your Highness, this man is being and has been a nuisance to me. I have made it quite clear that I am not interested in making his acquaintance but he persists in pestering me whenever he sees me. Please will you instruct him to stay away from me?"

I was shaking with suppressed anger and disgust and also fear of what the Tsarina would say to me having pointed out that her 'friend' was not to my liking.

"Thalia, I am sure that Father Gregori didn't mean any harm but I am sure that he will not bother you again if I ask him," she said.

"I would appreciate your intervention, Your Highness, not just for myself but some of the other nurses as well, who he has also forced his attentions on."

"Matushka…"

The Tsarina held her hand up to silence him. "Father Gregori, I am sure that your intentions are perfectly decent towards Thalia and the other nurses but if they do not want your company, then you must not force yourself on them. Please leave them alone to go about their very important work." She looked over at him. His head was lowered like a small child that had been suitably scolded.

"Do I have your word, Father Gregori, that you will leave Thalia and the other nurses alone?"

He nodded his head sullenly, "Yes, Matushka. You have my word that I will leave Thalia and the other nurses alone."

Rasputin and the Tsarina moved away and left me on my own. During their conversation, I had been holding my breath, scared of what might be said. When they moved away, I released the breath that I seemed to be holding and sat down again on the garden seat. My legs and hands were shaking. Never before had I ever thought that I could stand up against someone like Gregori Rasputin, a known drunk, womaniser and probably other rumours about him were true, as well.

I saw Olga Procopy coming over to speak to me. "My dear girl, are you all right? The theatre is not for everyone. You look absolutely white as a sheet."

I told her what had just happened. "That man has no right to be here in the hospital, for a start he is unclean and secondly, he disrupts the smooth running of the wards, by making himself a nuisance with the other nurses. I have mentioned it to the Tsarina but obviously not as strongly as I should have."

I told Olga that I had told the Tsarina and she made him promise to leave the other nurses and myself alone.

"That is good news, Thalia. So, tell me, how is it going with you in theatre?"

I said that I hadn't fainted or vomited and I found it fascinating. She asked me if I would like to continue with theatre work, after my three months of working there was up and I told her that I wasn't sure. Already I was missing the chatter of the patients but I didn't say this, as I wanted to give theatre work a good try.

I looked at my watch. My half hour break was nearly up and I didn't want to be late back to theatre on my first day there.

We parted and I went back to theatre, scrubbing my hands viciously to rid them of Rasputin, then putting on a fresh, clean, long white theatre gown, cap and mask. Nurse Sharapova began showing me how to lay out a tray for the next operation. She allowed me to take notes in a small notebook, for future reference.

After the third operation of the afternoon, I was told by Sister Kuriakin, that I could go home. I went back to my room to change from my uniform into my every day clothes and waited outside for Nicky to pick me up. As usual he was on time and once in the car, heading back to Chesme, asked me how my day had gone.

I told him that I had been moved to theatre and was there for three months.

"You've actually seen an operation?" he asked me surprised.

"Six actually but I was only observing. I think they wanted to find out if I would faint or not."

"Did you?" Nicky asked, concerned.

"No. I found it fascinating but I miss being with my patients though," I said without really thinking what I was saying.

"You mean, they don't have patients in the operating theatre?" he teased me.

"I meant talking patients, that aren't asleep all of the time."

He took my hand in his and kissed it. "Do you realise Princess Ivanov, that, I am very proud of you and what you are doing and achieving."

I laughed at him, "You are just biased, Your Highness, because you are married to me."

"That could be part of it but whatever you set out to do, you give it your best. There are no half measures, with you."

I kissed his hand, "No, no half measures with me. I love you totally and completely, Prince Ivanov." I looked across at him and saw that look of love in his eyes. "Do you want to be more impressed?" I asked him.

"Can I be any more impressed than I am already?" Nicky raised his eyebrows and looked at me.

I told him of my meeting with Rasputin.

"One of these days he will take a step too far and someone will stop him." His face had become a dark cloud of anger. I had never seen my husband angry before. Nicky always seemed mild tempered to me.

"Well, he won't be bothering me or any of the other nurses again. I had a word with the Tsarina, in front of Rasputin and said that he was being a nuisance not just to me but other nurses as well. She made him promise to leave us all alone."

"That was very bold of you."

"Your love makes me bold, Nicky."

When we arrived back at Chesme, after I had bathed and Tanya had dried and styled my hair, we sat down to our evening meal in the small dining room. This was the routine that our married life, would take. After dinner, we would sit in the lounge reading the newspapers and commenting on certain reports that piqued our interest.

"The Tsar has decreed the conscription of Central Asians," I said.

"More cannon fodder," Nicky replied.

"Nicky when I was on the wards, the soldiers there were saying that in the winter they had insubstantial clothing for the weather. Some of them had amputations, not from the war but due to frostbite. They lost feet, toes, because they didn't have proper boots." I pointed out.

"You need money to clothe and feed an army," was his reply.

"Doesn't the Tsar have money?"

"If he didn't, he would not own several elegant palaces with hundreds of staff. Nicholas has money but Russia doesn't, well none that he will release to help the soldiers and the war or his subjects."

"But surely the Duma could make him release the money."

"No one can make him release money. He is the Tsar. If the Duma did try to make him release the money, he dissolves the Duma and the Okrana take over the running of the country under the Tsar's orders. Then the student's revolt about the way the country is being run and the Tsar re-instates the Duma."

"Some of the soldiers said that they weren't even given guns to fight with but had to use scythes and farm forks. How can he win the war like that, Nicky?"

Nicky sighed and put his newspaper down. "Darling, he can't win the war like that or any other way. I have read that in some places, those that do have guns, are only allowed three rounds of ammunition a day. We cannot win a war like that. He has created an impossible situation. He is a weak man, who doesn't know how to govern or run a country. His mother is ashamed of the way he lets his wife govern him and of course his wife is governed by Rasputin."

"I know she makes excuses for Rasputin's behaviour. Today, when I mentioned it to her, she said that she was sure that, Father Gregori meant no harm. Nurses, not myself but some of the other nurses have had to literally fight him off. He knows exactly what he is doing and he thinks that because he is the Tsarina's 'advisor', he can get away with it."

"I should imagine that nurses know enough about the male anatomy to stop him."

"Yes, I think they do." I laughed, then said on a serious note, "But if they did that, they are scared that the Tsarina will step in and discipline them. In the Tsarina's eyes Rasputin can do no wrong. I don't understand the hold that he has over her?"

"No one does darling only the Royals themselves." He stood up then and pulled me into his arms. "Enough of them all. You are here with me now and I want us to forget about the Tsar, the Tsarina and Rasputin." He took my arm and we left the lounge.

We went into the room that housed his piano and he played for me, Tchaikovsky knowing that I loved the composer's music and also some Rachmaninov which he had introduced me to on our honeymoon. I sat in a comfortable chair and let the music wash over me. After the rigours of the day, I felt soothed.

Working in theatre wasn't as physically exhausting as working on the wards was, so that I wasn't as tired as I used to be, but working in theatre brought its own kind of exhaustion; an emotional and mental exhaustion.

When Rudolph and Tanya had finished preparing us for the night and had closed the bedroom doors behind them, Nicky took me in his arms and made love to me so gently and lovingly, whispering words of love. When we were sated, we would curl up in each other's arms and sleep until morning.

Every day I worked in the theatre, first observing, then preparing the trays for surgery. I was told the nature of the operation and looked at my notes to see what instruments, I should lay out. Once I had done that, I always double checked, to make sure that I had everything, before I took the covered tray to the operating table. Nurse Sharapova would then hand the instruments to the surgeon.

Apart from Nurse Sharapova and Sister Kuriakin, I didn't know the names of the Doctor or the anaesthetist. They were both addressed as 'Doctor'. Also, I had never even seen the faces behind their mask, so didn't even know what they looked like out of their theatre scrubs. In fact, they hardly ever spoke, only to ask for instruments to be passed and their voices were muffled behind their masks. It all felt very surreal.

# Chapter 29

## Peter

After I had been in theatre a few days, as I was finishing my shift and was heading from my changing room to wait for Nicky to arrive. I heard someone running behind me. (At first, I thought that it might be Rasputin again but I wasn't sure, as Rasputin usually had an odour of alcohol and unwashed body which preceded him).

"Nurse, Nurse Ivanov." I heard my name called. I stopped and turned around to see the doctor who had been working in the theatre with me. I recognised the face at once, barely believing that such a coincidence could happen.

"Peter. Peter Urvanski. Is that really you?" I said, unable to believe my eyes.

He reached me and stood standing with his hands in his pockets. "I apologise for not recognising you before Thalia but with your theatre gown, mask and hat on, I think that I would find it difficult to recognise my own mother, also, you have changed your name."

"I married recently," I explained still in a state of disbelief. "I am sorry that I didn't recognise you for the same reasons."

Peter laughed, "Who would believe that I would meet you again in a hospital of all places. The daughter of a Baron. I thought that you were destined to marry a rich husband and lead the life of a lady of leisure?"

It felt so good to see my old friend from Smolensk who had left our village to train as a doctor, like his father.

"I went back to Smolensk to see my father after I had qualified," Peter continued, "and he told me that your father and mother had divorced. He didn't know where you and your mother had gone. Have you returned home recently Thalia?"

I shook my head.

"I know that things were never very good between you and your father but I thought maybe you might have returned there."

"Once we moved to St Petersburg there was no reason to return to Smolensk" I told him.

I didn't see Nicky's car waiting for me, so we walked over to one of the benches in the grounds and sat talking. I told him about my life since I had gone to live with my grandmother, how my father had tried to keep us in Smolensk and how Mama. Anya and I had finally left our home one day, when my father was out visiting someone in another village.

After we had been talking for only a few minutes, I saw Nicky parking his car on the driveway. I waved to him as he alighted from our car and then he headed over to us.

Immediately I introduced him to Peter, explaining who Peter was.

Nicky shook hands with Peter, "I am pleased to meet an old friend of Thalia's."

Peter told Nicky that he hadn't recognised me until he saw me without my theatre cap and gown on until today and as soon as he saw my hair he realised who I was.

"I am sure that you two would like to talk some more, why don't you bring your wife over to us for dinner tomorrow evening if you are not working and we can all catch up with what we have all been doing the last few years." Nicky said.

"I am not married but I am seeing one of the nurses here." Peter told us.

I told Peter to bring her with him. When Nicky told him where we lived, I saw Peters look of amazement.

"You live in a Palace, Thalia?"

"Yes, I am afraid so," I said grinning.

"Then you are titled?" Peter asked me.

"Thalia is now Princess Thalia Ivanov," Nicky told him proudly.

Peter looked surprised, "Well, who would have thought? Do I call you both 'Your Highness?' I am not very well versed in 'court etiquette'."
Nicky told him that we were quite happy to dispose of titles, "Just call us Thalia and Nicky please Peter."

I told Peter to come to Chesme with his lady friend and we could chat more.

Peter said that he would like that and thanked us, asking what time they should come at.

I told him to be there by seven o'clock. We all shook hands again and Nicky and I walked back over to the car.

Once inside Nicky took my hand in his and kissed my fingers. "I am so pleased that you have met your old friend again Lia. You used to have a crush on him when you were younger, didn't you?"

"That was long before I even knew you existed and I was still quite young when Peter left Smolensk to go to Moscow to train as a doctor, like his father. After he left, I never saw him again. Peter was the only child that I could have as a friend because he was the Doctor's son. We did have other friends that we played with when we were younger but if Mama had known, it would have been frowned upon and I think if Mama had known she would have stopped me going out altogether."

This was the first time that Nicky and I had entertained since getting married, so I wanted everything to be perfect. I spent quite some time with our chef going over the menu for the next evening. Chesme only had one dining room rather than the formal and informal one at Grand Mama's but our dining room was big enough and I didn't want to make my elevated position seem like I was 'showing off' to Peter and his lady friend.

I wore one of my evening gowns, then thought that that might give the impression that I was showing off again, so I changed into one of my afternoon gowns and restricted my jewellery.

Nicky laughed at me making all this fuss over having guests to dinner.

"I am sure, Lia, that Peter and his lady friend won't notice whether you are wearing an evening gown or a ball gown!"

"Peter might not but his lady friend might," I said. I looked at Tanya. "What do you think?"

"I think the lilac afternoon dress will look well on you, Miss Thalia," she said as I sat in front of my dressing table while she did my hair. "Your cameo broach and earrings would go very nice with that dress they are not too … dressy," Tanya said.

At seven o'clock we heard someone knock on the door. Nicky and I were in our lounge waiting for Peter's arrival.

Shortly after, Rudolph walked into the lounge to announce Doctor Peter Urvanski and Miss Katya Patenko. Life was full of surprises. I didn't know that my friend Katya was even seeing a doctor.

Rudolph showed them both into the lounge, both Nicky and I rose to greet them. I flung my arms around Katya. "You never told me that you were going out with one of the doctors, Katya?"

"Peter asked me to go for a meal with him while you were away and I haven't seen you since you arrived back from your honeymoon."

Peter looked surprised at my greeting of his lady friend.

Nicky shook hands with Peter and gave Katya a kiss on the cheek and invited them both to sit down.

Katya explained to Peter that she had been my bridesmaid and laughed, "What a small world, who would expect that my doctor was the childhood friend of yours?"

"And who would expect my nurse had been my childhood friend's bridesmaid," Peter said.

It was a lovely evening with much reminiscing from my childhood and my early days in nursing.

Nicky seemed to enjoy Peter and Katya's company and it was decided that we would all go out to dinner and dancing on our next day off so that Katya could wear her bridesmaids dress again.

Our chef did us proud with the meal. Both Katya and Peter commented on it. Talk was lively around the dining room table, then we went back into the lounge where Nicky and Peter stood having a brandy and a cigar and Katya and I sat talking 'women's talk' as Nicky called it. Rudolph came in to the lounge again after the meal and Nicky and Peter had finished their brandies and cigars, to pour us all a glass of champagne.

"To old friends and long-lasting friendships," Nicky said raising his glass in a toast.

We all joined him and touched glasses. Life felt good. I had renewed my acquaintance with my old friend and I hoped that we would be seeing much more of Katya and Peter.

They left just after midnight and when they left Nicky and I decided to go up to bed. While Tanya was taking down my hair and brushing it, Nicky turned to me and said, "I have thoroughly enjoyed this evening, Lia. I hope that we see a lot more of Katya and Peter."

I told him that I did too and said that in my first few days in St Petersburg during my 'Transformation', I often thought about Peter and wondered what he would think of me as I became part of the St Petersburg society.

"Were you in love with him, Lia?" Nicky asked me after Rudolph and Tanya had left us and we lay in bed cuddled up together.

"I suppose I was, in a child's way but I think that I was only ten or twelve when he left to start his training and he had really just been the only boy that I spent time with. Yes, at that time in my life I thought that Peter was the one that I romantically dreamed about. I kissed him once, on the day he left Smolensk to go to Moscow to train as a doctor. I gave him a kiss on the cheek."

"And now you have met up with him again?" Nicky asked me.

I sat up and looked down at my husband. "Nicholas Ivanov, when I met you that night when we went to see Swan Lake, I never thought of any other man but you since then."

Nicky put his hands behind his head and grinned at me.

"Are you looking for a compliment from me?" I said and lay down next to him again and snuggled closely.

"Well, he's a good-looking, man," Nicky said and kissed the top of my head as it lay on his chest.

"Firstly, Your Highness, he seems very fond of my best friend and secondly I am a very, very, very happily married woman and every man pales into insignificance compared to my husband," I told him, kissing him on his chest where the dark hairs tickled my nose.

Nicky lifted my chin and kissed my lips and so started our lovemaking, gently, lovingly to confirm our love for each other.

I hoped that we would see much more of Peter and Katya socially.

After three months I had finished my time in theatre and left with a glowing report from Sister Kuriakin and, Peter, as the surgeon that I had been working with. I had moved from observing, to preparing the surgical instruments, to handing them to the Peter, who re-iterated that I had an instinct for theatre work. I was asked if I wanted to stay and for I while I did feel torn, between the technology of the theatre and the talk and banter with patients that were awake. In the end I decided to go back to the wards.

Sister Procopy welcomed me back and Katya, away from Sister's prying eyes, flung her arms around me and hugged me, telling me that she was glad that I was back on the ward with her again. "Of course, I didn't like you spending time with Peter." She said with a twinkle in her eye. I assured her that much as I liked Peter, I was very much in love with my husband. "We will have to all get together again when our days off coincided," I told her.

Before I started work Sister Procopy called me to her. "I understand that you had a word with the Tsarina about Rasputin pestering the nurses, after you had moved to theatre duty?" Sister Procopy said.

I asked if it had worked and was told that it had to a certain extent but the Tsarina had said that he wanted to come onto the wards to bless the patients, and give them spiritual guidance.

"So, we have not got rid of him, then?"

"As yet, no."

I started back, working on the wards again, with the shadow of Rasputin hanging not just over me but the other nurses as well. I was always on the lookout for him on the ward, but thankfully he stayed clear of the ward that I was on. Maybe my little talk to the Tsarina had partially worked. At least he was leaving me alone and I also think staying well away from Olga Procopy. It seemed that he had restricted himself to blessing men on the other wards. Soon enough even the sisters of those wards were complaining about him. In fact, I had heard on the hospital grapevine that Rasputin he been caught wondering around the nurses' dormitories in the nude. When challenged he said that he had been sleep-walking. Someone did suggest that he should be locked in his bedroom at nights.

# Chapter 30

## Another Birthday

October came again and my birthday. Nicky and I had invited Mama, Gregor, Ilia and Grand Mama over to dinner that evening. Of course, where Ilia went, so did Maria and Mikhail, who we had put in the nursery that was waiting for our child to occupy it, if or when I got pregnant. As the weather was getting colder, we invited them all to stay the night and opened some of the guest bedrooms. Peter and Katya were both working so couldn't attend, although I had asked them.

I had instructed our Chef on the menu. This was the first time that we had entertained my family as husband and wife and I wanted to make a good impression. We had all the best crystal, table linen cutlery and crockery out for dinner and Nicky had ordered two bottles of our best wine to be brought up from the cellar.

When Mama and Gregor arrived for my birthday, they also brought little Ilia who was progressing well. He was now standing on his strong little legs and pottering around, enjoying his new-found freedom. Of course, he was doted on by his loving parents, Grand Mama and Nicky and me. Maria was doing a brilliant job looking after him and I do believe that young Mikhail was also aiding his progress in some small way, as well.

The talk around the dinner table was about Ilia and his antics, now that he was nearly ten months old. Already he had a cheeky laugh and grin when he saw me and Nicky, who always tossed him in the air and played with him. I wanted so much for it to be our baby that Nicky played with but after four months of marriage, there was still no sign of a baby in the offing. Nicky didn't seem to mind, he kept telling me that he wanted me to himself for a little longer and I wanted my body to stay slim and attractive for him for a little longer too.

Our dinner went very well. The food was cooked to perfection and the conversation at the table was scintillating. There was a lot of laughter, as usual, once we all got together. Because Mikhail was of an age for schooling, Gregor had taken it upon himself to teach him. He said it was to give the boy a good start in life and Mikhail had an inquisitive mind. Gregor said that it kept him occupied, as his estates more or less ran themselves. He and Mama had visited his hunting lodge a few times during the summer and his estate manager seemed to have everything under control. It was suggested that Gregor should arrange a hunting trip but Gregor had never fired a gun in his life, so that idea was put on hold. Nicky had said that he had been taught to hunt and when he was younger, he and the Tsar used to go on hunting trips. Gregor's hunting lodge was two hours' drive from St Petersburg, so they could make it there and back in the same day, if he wanted. "Then when you are proficient enough, I could give you a few names that you could invite for a weekend hunting party."

Mama and Grand Mama encouraged Gregor to take Nicky up on his offer, which after coaxing and coercing, he did. It was agreed that while I was away working at the hospital, Nicky would collect Gregor and they would go to the hunting lodge and start on Gregor's tuition. I was so pleased to see how well my step-father and husband were getting along. From the look on her face, I could see that Mama was pleased as well.

I always enjoyed the company of Mama, Gregor and Grand Mama and was sorry to see them leave the next morning. They all kissed me on the cheek and thanked me for a lovely time and then kissed and thanked Nicky. Outside the sky threatened snow again and it had turned bitterly cold overnight. (Our summers never lasted long enough). Nicky and I stood at the entrance and waved everyone off, then went inside again.

"I have a birthday present for you that I didn't want to give you with everyone around." He took my hand and led me into his study. He went over to the safe and opened it. I don't think I had ever been in this room, every other room in the Palace, over the months of our marriage but Nicky just pointed out where his study was and walked on. I am sure that he would have taken me in to his study before, if I had asked him but the thought never occurred to me. It was a relatively small room, with one window overlooking the courtyard. Besides the safe was a writing desk and chair, a cabinet for papers and ranged along one whole wall, a glass case housing a range of rifles and hand guns. I looked closer at them. There must have been half a dozen rifles and another half a dozen hand guns.

"I see you are interested in my gun case. Have you ever fired a gun, Lia?" He asked, as he stood behind me and put his arms around my waist. He began to nibble, playfully at my earlobe, which sent an excited tingle running all through my body.

I shook my head. "The only person capable of teaching me to shoot was my father and as you know, we had nothing to do with each other, so, no, I have never learnt to shoot."

I saw, a tiny mother of pearl handled gun, small enough to fit into a small reticule. "That one looks pretty." I pointed it out to him.

"That one is a lady's reticule pistol, small enough for a lady's hand but just as deadly as any other gun."

I asked Nicky who had it belonged to.

"My mother, I do remember that. I can remember my father teaching her to shoot. She became quite good at it, as well. Would you like to try it, darling?"

I nodded. Nicky drew out a set of keys from his desk drawer and unlocked the gun case. He picked up the gun and handed it to me. Although relatively light it felt solid in my hand.

"See these little things at the end of the barrel?" He pointed to them. "They are the sights. When you want to aim at something, you line it up against the sights."

I lifted the gun and lined up the door handle to his office. "Once you have them lined up with your sights, then you slowly pull the trigger…" I looked at him, worried that the gun was loaded and I would damage the door. He smiled and kissed my ear, "You don't have to worry, darling it's not loaded and the safety catch is still on."

"It is so pretty to do so much damage. Could it kill someone Nicky?"

"Loaded and the safety catch taken off, it could certainly injure someone."

"I presume that your parents didn't have these…"

"On the day they died? No, they had no reason to. They didn't think that their lives were in danger." I placed the gun down on his desk and put my arms around his neck. "I'm sorry Nicky, bringing up the past."

He kissed my nose, "It was a long time ago now."

I asked him if he missed them. "There are times when I wish they were still alive; like when we were married. They would have approved of a "spirited" girl like you. My father taught me to shoot and when I went to live with Nicholas and the Dowager Empress, Nicholas and I used to go hunting together as I think that I have already told you. But, I didn't bring you here to give you gun lessons, I brought you here to give you these." He had placed several leather clad boxes on his desk. "These were all of my mother's jewels. They have been locked away here since their deaths. I should have given you them when we first married but never got around to it. I'm sorry darling."

"It doesn't matter to me, Nicky. You have given them to me now. Thank you, darling."

I lifted the lids of one box after the other. Inside were jewels of every colour; sapphires, rubies, diamonds, pearls, emeralds; necklaces, bracelets, rings and tiaras.

"All of the trappings of a true princess, Lia. Now you will not be restricted to just the diamond set that you wore for your debut. My time with Karl Faberge taught me that these were quality stones and what woman would not like beautiful jewellery?"

I kissed Nicky and thanked him. "Now we need to find somewhere to go that I can wear some of them," I teased him.

As Princess Ivanov, I did receive plenty of invitations with Nicky but many of them coincided with my work, we had to decline quite a few. I had to organise my diary to keep the days that I was at Tsarskoye Selo, free. I even had to arrange dress fittings with Auguste Brisac to coincide with my free time. Whenever Nicky and I did go out, I could never wear the same dress twice. Since my marriage to Nicky, I had to have new calling cards printed and I now had a gold card case to carry my calling cards in. (A birthday present from Mama and Gregor.) All suitable accessories for a young princess.

# Chapter 31
## December 1916

December came and with it, heavy snows. In my free time Nicky and I went shopping for Christmas presents for our staff and the family. Ilia would be a year old at Christmas and growing fast. He was talking; not always what he said could be understood but he was so enthusiastic in what he was trying to tell you. He was the apple of his parent's eye, also his Grand Mama and big sister.

Nicky had seen a rocking horse, which he fell in love with, whether it was for him or Ilia, I wasn't quite sure. Mama and Gregor were looking at a red tricycle for him but decided that he was too young to ride and Grand Mama was looking at a wooden train set. He was a thoroughly spoilt little boy but he was also taught to behave and have good manners even at his young age. Gregor said that you could never start young enough with teaching good manners. So, Gregor taught their son and Mama gave him all of the kisses and cuddles, not to say that Gregor didn't give him those, but he and Mama had their own tasks for bringing up their young son, with the help of Mikhail and Maria.

I was back with my patients on the ward again and still being called 'Nurse Angel', by many of the patients. Often moving about the hospital, I would see the Tsarina and Grand Duchesses, who sometimes would stop and ask how I and Nicky were.

"We don't seem to see much of you and Nicky these days but I suppose since you are still working, you don't have much free time. We are having our usual ball, this Christmas Eve. I will be sure to arrange for invitations to be sent to you and your family. It should be a lovely time, as my husband, the Tsar will be back from the front for a month."

I thanked the Tsarina and curtsied to her and the Grand Duchesses, before returning to the ward.

Katya saw me talking with the Tsarina. I explained that we had first trained together but as a Princess, we would be invited to the Christmas Eve ball at the Winter Palace. "Oh that must be wonderful, Thalia. I envy you. You will have the chance to wear a beautiful gown and after wearing this," she tugged at her uniform, "it must be wonderful. I haven't even had chance to wear my bridesmaids dress from you wedding yet."

I told her that I hoped we could all get together before Christmas and go for a meal and dancing at Minsky's. I asked her how things were going between her and Peter.

"Oh, he is so nice, Thalia, he is very kind and handsome. What he sees in me, I will never know but I will make the most of it." she laughed.

I told her that she would make a brilliant doctor's wife. "He has invited me to go out to dinner with him at some time over Christmas and he did say that there would be dancing as well."

"There you are then, that will be your excuse to wear your bridesmaids dress. So now you will have two occasions to wear your dress."

She smiled, "I never thought of that and there I was wondering what to wear. Thank you Thalia."

We went back into the ward for the afternoon's medication and observations.

More riots and shootings were reported in the newspapers. It seemed to me that there seemed to be more riots during the winter months, when it would have been so much better in the spring and summer months, rather than standing around, chilled to the bone in the freezing cold.

It wasn't the riots that took precedence in the newspapers on 19 December but the murder of Father Gregori Rasputin, "Royal advisor, who disappeared on Saturday, 17 December, and his body was dragged out of the Malaya Nevka River on Monday, 19 December. After much investigation over the following days, it was reported that he had been shot once, which did not kill him and then shot again and finally a shot at point blank range to the head. His body was then wrapped in a broadcloth and thrown from the Bolshioy Petrovsky Bridge. Unfortunately, whoever threw Rasputin's body from the bridge forgot to weigh the body down so that it would never be found. The police found one of Rasputin's galoshes stuck between the pylons of the bridge."

The Tsarina was distraught, with grief over her 'friend'. She instigated a full investigation into Rasputin's murder.

She need not have bothered. Not long after, Vladimir Purishkevich, one of the men that was with Rasputin on the night of his death, boasted that he had killed Rasputin. It was at Prince Felix Yusupov's Palace, where Rasputin had an apartment, as well as his rooms at Tsarskoye Selo. It was reported that his murder took place in a cellar that had been converted and soundproofed. Why this had been done was not reported.

Reports varied widely on how Rasputin was killed. Some said he was poisoned, others that he was shot, others, that he was drowned but however he was killed, I didn't care. The man was dead and I as well as my fellow nurses was greatly relieved. No more would I or any of the Nurses at the hospital feel under threat from the terrible man ever again.

The Tsarina and Grand Duchesses didn't report for work on the wards for some time after Rasputin's death, which, I am sorry to say was another relief but because the ward was three staff short, I was transferred to cover for them. The patients on the ward all talked about the departure of the 'German Bitch', and her puppies, which I felt was very unfair but could understand why they felt that way. We were fighting Germany and she was from Germany before she married the Tsar...but no more would she be under Rasputins influence.

Covering for the Royals was like going back to training again, sterilising beds, making them up, changing the bedclothes with patients in them, which I did with another nurse called Irina, then going around, taking temperatures and blood pressures.

The ward was full of talk about the Tsarina and her daughters, not just from the patients but also from Irina, as well.

"You know why you've been moved here, don't you? The Tsarina and her daughters are in mourning for that horrible man, Rasputin. Not that the daughters did much work, they seemed to spend more time flirting with the patients, than working. The Tsarina tried to work but she would only do certain chores because of her bad back, so she said. I just think that she didn't want to dirty her hands. When she was on the ward, you could cut the air with a knife. She is not well liked, you know." Irina whispered to me. "I never believed the flyers or rumours that have been circulating about the Tsarina and the Grand Duchesses but seeing how they are mourning the horrible man, maybe they were right."

I didn't need to reply, Irina did all the talking for the two of us.

One patient, who I was taking his blood pressure, asked me, "You're the one they call Nurse Angel, aren't you?"

I just smiled.

"I know why they call you that, now, with your hair colour."

Once he started calling me Nurse Angel, the whole ward started calling me it. Not that I minded but I was trying to stay professional, while they flirted outrageously with me. I told them that I was married and many of them said that he was a lucky man, whoever my husband was. I made sure that no one knew that I was a princess. I was just Nurse Ivanov or Nurse Angel.

Although Chesme was nearer to the hospital than Grand Mama's house was, when the snow came down, it still blocked the roads and I had to stay at the hospital overnight again. I didn't mind, now. I was getting to know more of the nurses and I enjoyed all of the chatter and banter that went on at the end of our shifts. I rang Nicky to tell him, not to risk the roads in the dreadful weather. He told me that he could get the Troika out and collect me but it would have taken ages to get here and ages to get back again. I told him that they would probably have the road cleared by the next day and I would be home then. He told me that he would miss me curling up to him. I knew that I would miss it too. My throat ached with trying to hold back the tears. I told him that I loved him and he said that he loved me too. Then the telephone went dead.

Olga Procopy came to my room later that night. "I am sorry that I had to move you again Thalia but with the three Royals being off, I needed someone who was a hard worker and who I could rely on. You know why they are off?"

"Rasputin's death. Apparently, it has upset them greatly."

She made a sound of disgust. "I wouldn't waste any energy on that man, let alone tears. I do not know what on earth they saw in him."

"I understood that he was their spiritual advisor," I said.

"Him!" She scoffed, "He was nothing but a womaniser and a drunk."

"Well, at least we won't be bothered with him ever again." I said.

"No, thank God. All of the nurses can sleep safely in their beds from now on. Do you know that we found him wandering around in this wing stark naked? Not a pretty sight. He made out that he had been sleep walking. I told him then that I would tell the Tsarina that she should lock him in his room at night to stop such a thing ever happening again. He never did it again." I never realised that it was Olga that had found him and reported him. "Once again she tried to make excuses for the man." Then she said "Good riddance to the man. I won't lose any sleep over him. I don't suppose anyone else would apart from the Royals"

We both laughed. I did enjoy the time with my friends. Katya had gone out with her Peter that night, all dressed up in her bridesmaid's dress. Peter had hired a Troika to take them to a restaurant in the village. They had left under a bundle of furs to keep them warm.

It was eleven o'clock when she returned, bright eyes and red faced from the cold. Olga Procopy took out a bottle of vodka from a cupboard. "Here, have a drink of this, to warm you up. You look frozen to the core, in fact I think it wouldn't do any of us any harm." She pulled out three small glasses from the same cupboard and poured the vodka into them. "Prost!" she said and drank it in one gulp, then gasped. "It shows how often I drink." She laughed. Katya and I did the same. It was very strong stuff, which warmed you as it travelled down from your throat. Both Katya and I gasped after we had drunk it, then laughed.

"And how was Doctor Love?" I teased her.

"Peter complimented me on my dress. I told him that it was my bridesmaids dress from your wedding. I didn't want him thinking that I could afford to dress like this all of the time."

"No, it wouldn't be very practical on the wards, would it?" I joked. Again, we giggled. I think that after just one glass of vodka, we were all slightly drunk. I said that I needed to get to bed and wished them both goodnight.

It felt strange sleeping on my own again in the dormitories. I didn't have Nicky's warm body to snuggle up to, to keep me warm on a cold night like that.

It was another two days before the roads were clear enough for Nicky to come and pick me up. Which took me up to my Christmas Holiday. It was Christmas Eve, the night of the Royal Ball. When I got home, I asked Tanya to run me a bath. It was lovely to lay back and enjoy the warmth seeping into my very pores. Another year had passed and so much had happened in that year. Marriage, passing my nursing exam. Little Ilia would be a year old on Christmas day and was looking forward to St Nicholas coming and bringing presents not just for him but also for young Mikhail who was his playmate although three years older. Although Maria was employed by Mama and Gregor, to look after Ilia, she was more like our extended family, the same as Tanya, Rudolph, Anya, Peter Abramovich and his wife Ava. I was sad that I was still not pregnant. Each month I hoped that this would be the month but life carried on the same. Nicky still made light of the fact, taking any pressure off me. Russia was still the same, with its protesters and rioters and civil unrest but there was one aspect that was missing now and that would be Rasputin. I think several people sighed with relief when they read of his death. Maybe not the Royals but there were a lot of Russians whose lives had been negatively affected by the man, mainly women. No longer could the Royals be influenced by him, which must be a good thing.

A knock on the bathroom door, roused me from my thoughts. Nicky poked his head around the door, "I thought you might have fallen asleep in there."

The water had cooled somewhat. I asked him where Tanya was.

"I told her that I would call her when you needed her," he said with a devilish grin on his face. "Are you going to get out then, Mrs Princess?"

"You have to hold the towel open for me to wrap around me when I get out of the bath." I told him.

"Yes Mam." He picked the towel up and wrapped it around me. He kept his arms around me and kissed me deeply.

"Now I know why I married you." I whispered against his cheek as his hands move possessively over my body.

"And why is that?"

"Because you make a lovely lady's maid," I teased and ran naked from the bathroom as he still held the towel in his hands.

He stood at the bathroom door grinning devilishly at me, "I know why I married you, Mrs Princess. You look delicious naked."

We arrived at the ball later than we should have done. It was my first opportunity to wear some of Nicky's mother's jewels. That night I wore sapphires and diamonds to match the ice blue velvet of my gown. I noticed that the Tsar was on the dais minus the Tsarina and the two older Grand Duchesses. The young Tsarevich was sitting on the chair where his mother should be and his grandmother, the Dowager Empress was sitting on the other side of the Tsar.

When she saw Nicky and me, she signalled for us to come over to her. When we approached Nicky bowed to the Royals, while I curtseyed. Then Nicky went and kissed his aunt on both cheeks and the Dowager offered her cheek to me, to kiss.

"My dears, it seems ages since we last met. You will have to come to dinner one evening and then I will also arrange a family dinner with my sister and your mother and step-father Thalia."

We thanked her, then she asked Nicky to dance with her, which of course he did. The Tsar seeing me standing on my own asked me to dance.

"I understand that you are, now, a full-fledged nurse Thalia and you have passed your nursing exam with flying colours. Congratulations, my dear."

I thanked him.

"Have you been working on the wards all of the time?"

I told him about my three months in theatre.

"And how did you enjoy that?"

"It was extremely interesting, Your Highness."

"Do I detect a 'but' coming?" he asked.

"I prefer my patients to be awake, sir."

He threw back his head and laughed. "I can understand that, my dear. And how is life treating you?"

"Nicky and I are very happy together. Of course, my nursing takes up a lot of my time."

"I am very pleased you are both so happy together. A good marriage is very important to one's happiness," he said.

The dance ended. The Tsar handed me back to Nicky, who bowed while I curtseyed to him, then Nicky whisked me onto the dance floor again.

"You seemed to be having a good conversation with the Tsar," Nicky said. I told him that we were talking about my nursing and also about our marriage.

"I hope you didn't give away any 'trade secrets'?" He grinned down at me, "I would hate my cousin to feel an inferior man compared to me."

"Nikolas Ivanov, you are incorrigible!"

"And you, my darling wife, are beautiful. The most beautiful woman here tonight but there again, in my eyes you have always been the most beautiful woman."

"And you, my darling husband, are biased but I am not complaining." We continued dancing for a while, "What did the Dowager Empress want to talk to you about, Nicky?"

"You, for one thing and how happy we looked together. She has heard many words of praise for 'Nurse Angel'. She has taken a particular interest in your career."

"I am very flattered."

"We are invited to dine with her, the day after tomorrow."

I wondered why that was but let the thought move to the back of my mind, as Nicky waltzed me around the floor.

The young Tsarevich danced with his grandmother, then sat down while the Tsar danced with his mother. They seemed to be having quite an animated conversation, which must have been enjoyable, as they were both smiling throughout the dance.

It was gone midnight, when Nicky and I drove back to Chesme. It had been a lovely evening. I had worn one of my new ball gowns from Auguste Brisac. I was glad I had decided that it was the ideal time to wear my mother-in-law's jewels. Nicky had looked at me before we left for the Winter Palace and had smiled when he saw me looking in the mirror at me wearing his mother's jewels.

"You look like the 'Snow Queen', out of one of the children's fairy tales." He commented. Looking at myself in the mirror with my platinum blonde hair and the blue of my dress and jewels, I could understand what he meant.

Tanya and Rudolph were waiting for us when we arrived home, ready to help us prepare for bed but Nicky dismissed them, saying that we could manage, ourselves. When we were alone, I commented that they would be thinking that we were making our personal staff redundant.

"I would never do that to them, although they are staff, I still look on them as our extended family. Wherever we go, they would come with us." He assured me.

I did feel relieved, as I would hate to let Tanya go. Over the few years that I had been in St Petersburg, we had become friends, much as Mama and her maid Anya. We had been together through emotional trials and tribulations, Tanya and I and I would hate having to lose my friend rather than my maid.

Nicky helped undo my dress, with all its tiny crystal buttons running down the front of the gown. He cursed at how long it took him to undo them all and I giggled at his frustration, telling him that he shouldn't have dismissed Tanya.

He laughed as well, "I wonder what Madame Brisac would say, if I tore it off you."

"She would be absolutely horrified, after all of the work her seamstresses had put in to sewing all of those buttons on."

"In that case, I will respect their work and carry on with my task."

As last the final button was undone and Nicky helped me out of my gown, flinging it over one of the arm chairs. Slowly he began to peel off my undergarments, kissing each bit of my body as it became exposed. By the time I lay on our bed naked, I was wanting him to hurry and divest his own clothes to lay with me.

Christmas day was spent at Mama's and Gregor's as it would need a small lorry to carry all of Ilia's presents and Mikhail's, to wherever we would spend

Christmas day. Also, when Ilia was tired, he could go to sleep in his own bed. As well as it being Christmas, it was also Ilia's first birthday. That alone was a great celebration, especially as we never thought Mama could have any more children. Peter Abramovich had driven Grand Mama over for her grandson's first birthday.

When Ilia saw his dapple-grey rocking horse, he shouted, "Horsey!" and held up his arms to Nicky, to pick him up and put him on the horses back. He started to rock immediately on the horses back, although it was still a little too big for him. Mama, all concerned, told him to hold on tightly and be careful.

Mikhail was also allowed to play downstairs with all of us, as was his mother Maria, who supervised the boys at play.

I told Grand Mama that Nicky and I had been invited to dinner with the Dowager Empress, two days later and told her that her sister said that she would invite all of us all over to dine, at a later date.

"I can appreciate that my older sister has a busy diary but I do miss being with her. It was such fun, the last time we were all together, talking about old times, when we were young."

Although Grand Mama never said it, I knew that she missed me living with her as well. She also missed Mama living with her. When I thought of all the years, that both Mama and I, lived in Smolensk, with Grand Mama never seeing us, the couple of years that we had spent with Grand Mama was very little, but very precious. I also missed her. Grand Mama's home must be very quiet since Mama and I had left, no dramas, no laughter, no fun as we were 'all girls together' as she used to say when we went shopping or to the theatre with no men around. Now all that had changed, certainly for me as with all of my nursing and Mama with Gregor and Ilia. Now Grand Mama was on her own most of the time at home. I knew that she had plenty of invitations from friends that she had made in the years Mama and I were in Smolensk.

After our dinner, Maria brought out a beautiful birthday cake for Ilia, with a candle on, which Gregor helped him blow out. We all clapped him, when he blew the candle out.

After Ilia was put to bed, exhausted after his first birthday and Christmas, Mikhail went upstairs with Maria to their own room. It was left to us adults to talk. Gregor had brought a bottle of champagne up from their cellar and we toasted my little brother and his first birthday.

"I am glad that we are all together this evening," Nicky said, he had a serious look, on his face. I began to wonder if this look had anything to do with what the Dowager Empress said to him the night before.

"The Dowager Empress is concerned about the state of the Country, she has invited Lia and me for dinner the evening after tomorrow, to discuss things further but I am thinking that we may have to be prepared to leave Russia soon."

The room was deathly silent, as we were all thinking of the implications of what Nicky had said.

"What do we need to do, Nicky?" Gregor asked.

"I think we should start thinking about moving things out of St Petersburg."

"Move them to where?" Grand Mama asked.

"It must be away from St Petersburg. I thought that we could all go to Tallin. It's on the coast. I could, maybe, secure a boat for us all. It would be easier to get out of Russia from there. I need to speak to the Dowager Empress to find out more but I am just warning you."

"I am sending my man Rudolph to Kadriorg Palace, with some of our things after tomorrow night. Aunt Lilia, would you allow Peter Abramovich to take some of your things to Tallin?"

Grand Mama nodded.

"Gregor, what about you?" Nicky asked.

"I could drive down to Tallin myself. Marguerite, you could stay here with Anya and Ilia. The more room we have in the cars, the more things we can move."

"We can't take large heavy things. I don't know what size of boat I can get hold of yet but you will need clothes, if you have some false bottom cases, then we could put jewellery and money in them, otherwise, just fold valuables in clothes, in trunks."

"Oh, Nicky, I can't believe that this is happening." Grand Mama cried. I had never seen her so emotional, scared even.

"It's not happening yet, Aunt Lilia. Please, don't get upset. I am just preparing you for the worst. It still might not happen but the more prepared we are, if it does happen, the better and easier the transition will be."

"Grand Mama, the main thing is, if we do need to leave Russia, we will all be together."

"Think of when you left Denmark, Mama, you were on your own then, now you will have all of us to help you."

"Babushka, I am an old woman now, not a young girl."

"All the more reason for you to let us help you." Nicky said, then with more of his old self, "You are not old. You are younger than your sister and she travels all over the world."

"She has a huge, luxurious, yacht to do it in."

"Well, I will try to find one to compare with hers for you."

"I would also suggest that you start withdrawing money from your bank accounts. Not all in one go but a bit at a time, to stop any suspicion. If anyone does ask, which really is no one's business, tell them that it is for a business venture of mine in America."

"How many of us will be going, Nicky?"

"Obviously, all of us here and hopefully our personal staff, who will suspect that something is going on, with the movement of goods. I thought, probably, a total of thirteen or fourteen."

"That's going to need to be a big boat," Gregor commented.

"It has got to be a sturdy, sea faring, boat, as we will have to cross the oceans. Don't worry Aunt Lilia, I will find one, so that you won't have to take turns in rowing." That lifted the atmosphere, somewhat.

After more light hearted chat, we finally all made our 'goodbyes' and went to our respective homes.

Grand Mama still looked worried, which worried me. It was true what she had said earlier, she wasn't a young woman. When Nicky and I were in the car, driving back to Chesme, I voiced my concerns.

"I know darling. I will try and make the transition as easy as possible. Gregor will be a great help as well and so will Rudolph and Peter Abramovich. Also, if your Grand Mama is taken ill on the journey or anyone else for that matter, we have a fully qualified nurse with us." He reached across and squeezed my hand. "Don't worry darling. I already have matters all in hand."

I was surprised at this. "You do?"

"Ah, I am so subtle that you didn't even know. Whenever we have travelled to Tallin, Rudolph's car has carried something ready for the move.

"I have had a lorry move larger things to Tallin and if asked why, I would simply say that we preferred to live at Kadriorg Palace when the children come along."

"If they come along," I said, "I feel that I am letting you down, Nicky. I am still not pregnant."

"I know, darling, which means that I have you all to myself a little longer. Stop worrying, Lia. I am sure that it will happen. In the meantime, we are having fun practicing."

"Oh, Nicky!" I said, feeling a blush covering my face in the darkness of the car.

On the appointed evening, Nicky and I were announced to the Dowager Empress, who came to greet us, enthusiastically.

Nicky and I bowed and curtsied first, then she offered her cheek to both of us, to kiss. I felt that, the relationship with her was subtly changing to a more personal standing. Whether it was because of the fact that I had married Nicky or I was her sister's granddaughter I didn't care. I just felt very honoured.

"And how is married life treating you both?" she said, inviting us to sit down.

"I highly recommend it, Your Highness," Nicky said.

She laughed.

"And your nursing, Thalia, are you still enjoying it, now that you have been moved back to the wards?"

"Yes, Your Highness, I prefer working with patients that are awake." Again, the Dowager Empress laughed.

"I understand that you were moved to the ward that my daughter-in-law and my two grand-daughters were on?"

"Yes, Highness."

"They are still in mourning for that stupid man, Rasputin. Why they should mourn for such a man is beyond me. He was a drunk and a womaniser. Some even say that he practiced Black Magic, although I am not sure that I believe that. You had some experience of that, I remember, Thalia?"

"Unfortunately, yes. I have you to thank for stepping in at the right time, Your Highness."

"He should never have been allowed on the premises. It was the Tsarina who insisted on that. What she saw in the man, I will never understand…

"I do know why. She believes that the man can cure my grandson."

"Cure the Tsarevich?" Nicky asked.

The Dowager Empress sighed, "Only a few close families know this but young Alexi is a very sick young man, he has a blood problem, where even the slightest knock can cause him to bleed… You being a nurse must know what it's called Thalia?"

I thought back over my medical textbooks, "Haemophilia, Your Highness?"

"Yes, that's the word. Clever girl. If you had been a man, you should have trained as a doctor, Thalia."

I blushed, "I don't think that I am that clever, Your Highness."

"Well, it is of no matter, as you are a young woman. My daughter-in-law thought that this Rasputin could heal the young Tsarevich, when he had these… episodes. That is why she kept him close to her. Enough of this though, I brought you both here on another matter. Thalia, you know that Nicky has been… working for me, in the role of an unofficial ambassador."

I never realised, that I would ever be entrusted with such confidences from the Dowager Empress. I nodded.

"Nicky is not the only person that I have working for me, there are a select few others. They act as… spies… for me. They infiltrate areas that no one of our standing can get into."

I felt uncomfortable being entrusted with such things. "Your Highness, would you rather talk to Nicky alone? I could go into another room."

She touched my hand, "No my dear, a husband, a good husband, should have no secrets from his wife and I trust your discretion, Thalia. I feel that I can trust you as I trust Nicky, with such confidences."

I thanked her for her faith in me.

"My 'spies' are telling me that the unrest in our country is getting worse, there are talks of forcing my son to abdicate. I have had words with him and told him so. I told him that, for his family's safety, they should leave Russia. He is either too stubborn… My son believes that he is the answer to Russia's problems. He says he knows what his people think and they love him, unconditionally. His is wrong Nicky but he will not listen. He has not listened to me since he married that woman. Over the years she has turned him against me. She has poisoned his mind to the needs of his country."

Nicky interrupted her, "Your Highness, if he were stronger willed…"

"He is strong willed Nicky but about the wrong things. I hate to say this but you would have made a better Tsar than him."

"Your Highness," Nicky whispered, "that is treason."

"I know but you are the only one that I can talk to openly, Nicky, with such candidness. I have been troubled for so long… I try to help him but he won't help himself. He can't help himself, because of her and that dreadful man Rasputin.

"Now Rasputin is dead. I had hoped that he would finally see sense… Well, I have washed my hands of him. I can do no more. I have decided that I am leaving Russia. I have seen others do it, now I must leave."

"When do you intend to go, Your Highness and where?"

"I still have things that I need to do. I will make one last plea to him.

"I like Copenhagen, it reminds me of St Petersburg. I will ask the Tsar if he will allow his children to come with me, if he will not leave. That is all that I can do."

"Your Highness, it must be terrible for you, for what you are going through," I said.

Again, she touched my hand and held it for a short time.

"Thank you, my dear. You are so kind… I feel that I am a terrible mother, to be like this but he gives me no choice. I cannot stay in Russia and see him…"

Nicky said that he was sure that the Tsar would make the right decision. The Dowager Empress said that she doubted it.

While we ate dinner, our conversation turned to happier things. The Dowager Empress asked me about my little brother, she also asked about her sister.

"I shall have to have a family meeting. Next week would be a good time. I shall send an invitation to my sister and your parents Thalia and of course you and Nicky." I told her of the days that I had off. "Of course, my dear, I wouldn't take you away from your nursing. I will arrange it for one of your days off."

Shortly after that, we took our leave and drove home to Chesme. "I cannot believe that I was privileged to so much, Nicky. I can understand her talking to you that way but not me."

"When we were dancing on Christmas Eve, she told me that she had a great deal of respect for you. She said that the Tsarina and Grand Duchesses were just 'playing' at nursing but you had immersed yourself wholeheartedly."

"I am honoured that she has so much faith and confidence in me," I said.

"You deserve it, darling. You understand now why I told the family that we must leave Russia. I think that when the Dowager Empress invites us all to dine with her, she might say something about leaving."

With the Dowager Empress saying that she was going to leave Russia, I felt a sadness come over me. What would happen to all of the beautiful Palaces, all of the beautiful houses? Would they be left to go derelict or would they become overrun with the everyday Russians, living in their palatial rooms. Russia had masses of beautiful buildings, an amazing history, just looking at the three hundred years of Romanov rule, let alone all of the beautiful churches and cathedrals, the architecture of Russia was extravagant but beautiful and I felt sad.

# Chapter 32

## 1917

When I had gone back to the hospital, the day after Nicky's and my visit to the Dowager Empress, I found Katya on the ward with a broad grin on her face.

While we were tidying and changing some of the bedclothes, we could talk.

"You look very pleased with yourself, Nurse Patenko. Did you have some free time over Christmas?" I asked her.

"Yes."

"And why the big smile?"

She lifted a gold chain from around her neck to show a diamond engagement ring. "Peter asked me Christmas day. I am going to be a doctor's wife, Thalia. Doctor and Mrs Peter Urvanski." She said as she quickly hid it beneath her uniform again.

I was so happy for her and Peter. A doctor would find work anywhere and she, as a nurse would also be welcome, anywhere.

I told her how pleased I was for her. I asked her if they had named a day to marry and she told me that they would wait for a while and get to know each other better. I said that I hoped they would be as happy as Nicky and I was.

"I shall want you to be my bridesmaid, Nurse Ivanov."

My heart dropped. I probably wouldn't even be living in the same country. I smiled and said if I could do, then I would. Then a thought hit me, "As my wedding present to you, how would you like a wedding dress made for you, by Madame Brisac?"

Katya stared at me in disbelief, "Do you mean that, Thalia?"

I told her, that of course I did. "Auguste has all of your measurements from making your bridesmaids dress, so all you will have to do is discuss material and style." I thought that even if I couldn't be at her wedding, I would still be there in spirit, with her wedding dress.

I told Katya that I would contact Auguste Brisac and tell her what we had arranged.

"If I wasn't on duty and making this bed, I would kiss you, Thalia Ivanov."

Mama, Gregor and Grand Mama received their invitations from the Dowager Empress the day that I returned to work. Ours was waiting on the hall stand when I returned from the hospital.

It was New Year's Eve, when we were invited to dine with the Dowager Empress. We all dressed in our finery, to be presented. In the meantime, Nicky, Gregor and Peter Abramovich had already made one trip to Tallin. Nicky had used the hunting trip with my step-father as an excuse to teach him to shoot and Gregor now carried a gun with him all of the time, with the safety catch on, of course.

When we entered the room of the Dowager Empress, we all observed court protocol and bowed and curtsied to her, then she went to Grand Mama, kissed her cheek and Mama's, then came over to me and kissed my cheek. She went to Gregor and held out her hand for him to kiss and kissed Nicky.

"I am so glad, that you could all come this evening. We do not get to see enough of one another and I have a special reason for inviting you all but we will talk of that later."

She complimented me on my gown, which was an emerald green velvet and I wore Nicky's mother's emeralds. "I am so glad to see that you are wearing Nicky's mother's jewels Thalia. It would be such a shame not to wear them. They are so beautiful."

She began talking to Mama, Gregor and Grand Mama about Ilia, then the subject moved to when she and Grand Mama and Nicky's mother were young Princesses in Denmark. It was interesting to hear more about their youth.

The meal was delicious, as would be expected from a senior member of the Royal family and the conversation was cheerful, which was a change from the way our family conversations had been running over the last week since Christmas day and the previous meeting with the Dowager Empress.

When the meal was over, we all retired to the beautiful lounge. When we had all been served drinks, the Dowager Empress dismissed the staff, saying that we could help ourselves.

When she was certain that we were quite alone and none of her staff could hear, the Dowager Empress spoke to us all in confidence. "Besides having a family get together, I did have an ulterior motive for inviting you all here. You are close family to me, other than the Tsars family and I feel that I should let you know that I will be leaving Russia soon. There is nothing for me here anymore. My son has his own ideas on how to run the country, so I thought it best for me to back away."

She didn't talk as openly to my family as she had done to Nicky and I but she said all that they needed to know.

Grand Mama asked where she was going.

"I have a property in Copenhagen, already there are Russians living over there that have already left this country when there were rumours that we might be going to war. Other Russians have fled to America and some to England."

"I don't mean to be rude Highness but why are you telling us this?" Grand Mama asked.

The Dowager Empress nodded, understanding what her sister meant.

"Lilia, you are my only sister now, you are widowed, as I am and I would like you to accompany me back to Denmark. Also knowing how fond you are, naturally, of your daughter and now your baby grandson and of course Thalia and Nicky. I would like you all to come along. My yacht, the Polar Star is large enough to accommodate, you all."

"Your Highness, we have staff that are like an extended family," Mama said, "There is Ilia's nanny and her little boy…"

"Highness," Nicky said, "We have been thinking the same as yourself. Including us all, there would be a total of thirteen or fourteen, plus we have luggage…"

"I totally understand Nicky. When I have had the Royal family on board with their retinue of staff and all their luggage, I am sure that we could accommodate you all."

"Surely, it cannot be known that you are leaving the country for good, your Highness and with us coming along with all of our luggage," Gregor added.

The Dowager Empress said that people were used to seeing her off on her 'travels' as she put it.

"My home in Copenhagen is already set up. I have been adding to it over the years. It was a plan of mine to retire there, at some stage but it has turned out sooner, rather than later. It has enough rooms to accommodate you all until you can get yourselves organised."

"We have already moved some things down to Tallin but we still have some more to move, Highness." Gregor told her.

She told us all that she still had things that she needed to do. "Nearer the time, I could get the captain to sail down to Tallin and anchor offshore from Kadriorg Palace. We could then get the launch loaded and make several trips until it is all moved, then we could get you all transferred to the launch and onto the Polar Star but what about your staff there Nicky, how can we do this without them knowing what was going on?"

"I have told my staff that we are moving into the Palace permanently, which is why we are moving so much down there. I could give them some time off, before we 'move in'." Nicky told her.

"That could work. Thalia, what about you and the hospital? How could you get away from there without drawing any attention to yourself?"

"I could say that I am sick or that Ilia has been struck by some childish ailment and I am looking after him."

It looked like fate had stepped in to help us leave our country but I never expected it to be in the guise of the Dowager Empress. She told us that as soon spring came and the snow had melted, then would be the time for us to leave. "So, you still have a few months. Obviously, if we need to move earlier then I will contact you, so get your things down to Tallin as soon as possible Just in case. Because we are living in such uncertain times, nothing can be etched in stone don't mention this to anyone else, not even the staff that you are bringing with you. The men will have to know, as they will be helping you move your things down to Tallin and also coming with us but keep this from everyone else," she said finally.

She touched Nicky's clean-shaven face, which he had now kept, for quite some time. "I am glad that you shaved off your beard, my dear boy. You looked too much like your cousin, with it. I would hate for you to be mistaken for him."

Grand Mama, who had kept quiet while we were discussing our plans, finally spoke. "I can't thank you enough, Minnie, for what you are doing for me and my family."

"Lilia, you forget, they are my family too and it is nice to hear my nickname spoken again."

"I am sorry, Highness, I forgot myself," Grand Mama apologised.

Her older sister smiled. "I think when we are all together like this, I would like to be reminded of our youth and happier, carefree times."

The ormolu clock on the mantelpiece chimed midnight. Nicky said that he thought that it was time for us all to leave, as it was getting late. The Dowager

Empress nodded. "I am sure that you will have a lot to talk about and think about."

We all wished her a 'goodnight' and left for our respective homes. Nicky told Grand Mama, that we would visit her the next day. She smiled and kissed his cheek. "I am glad that you came into all of our lives my dear."

# Chapter 33
## Preparation

After the meeting with the Dowager Empress, the whole family were busy in preparation. It was made known to our staff that Nicky and I were preparing to move down to Kadriorg Palace permanently and we were moving things down there ready for our move.

Grand Mama had told her staff that as we were moving out of St Petersburg, we had invited her to live with us, as we felt better knowing that she was away from all the rioting. Peter Abramovich and Rudolph were moving our things and Grand Mama's things down to Tallin. It was mainly trunks of clothes with false bottoms made in them, which held jewellery and money for our new life. It was no use moving furniture it would be much too bulky and heavy. Nicky had already opened bank accounts in New York for us.

Gregor was doing the same. He was telling his staff that he was moving Mama and Ilia to the hunting lodge, to get them away from the riots. Rudolph was moving between helping Peter Abramovich and Gregor. I had told Tanya to pack away all of my summer clothes.

Nicky had already stored the majority of my jewellery, money and the guns in the false bottoms. When we were lying in bed one night, I posed the question to Nicky as to how we would get everything down to the beach from the house?

He kissed my nose, "I am glad that you have brought that up. I have asked for one of my men to make some trolleys, so that we can easily move unwanted furniture from the house and store it in one of the store houses, away from the main house. I am afraid darling I said that you wanted to put your own stamp on the place, as would your grandmother."

I asked him if we were going to take any furniture with us but he said no, then he thought again and said that that it was a good reason to explain why he wanted the trolleys made. "I am also having a pier made out into the water so that I can go fishing. It will have a path leading down to it."

"I do believe, Your Highness, you have thought of everything." I was snuggled up close to him as we usually fell asleep this way.

"It would be impossible to move heavy laden trollies over sand and I want it to be moved pretty quickly."

I went back to work, as if nothing had or was happening. The Tsarina and the two older Grand Duchesses had come back to the ward and I had been moved back to the same ward as Katya, again. Sometimes I would look at her and wish that I could bring her and Peter with us but knew that it would be impossible. I just hoped that they would be able to find a safe harbour. Also, Olga Procopy had been a great friend and colleague to me. I would miss her too. As long as the hospital survived, she and all of the staff would survive. I was, maybe, looking on the black side, regarding their future and also the future of Russia. Things might not change that much. The war couldn't go on forever and when the war finished, they would still be needed in hospitals, hopefully not nursing amputees all of the time but the general things that hospitals dealt with, maybe even midwifery.

In February Katya had told me that they had found a nice home in Tsarskoye Selo and were intending to marry in the summer. "I never thought that it would be this year but when Peter found this house, he said that he couldn't see why we couldn't get married in the summer. The house is nothing big or fancy but it is clean and solid and was the village doctor's house before but he died and it became free, so we took it. There are enough rooms so that when we want, we can start a family, we have enough space and one of the downstairs rooms, if Peter wanted could be turned into a doctor's surgery."

I told her that I was very pleased for them both. "Well, the future Mrs Urvanski, I think when we next have a day off together, we should go and visit Auguste Brisac's premises and get that wedding dress sorted."

Katya's eyes lit up, "Oh Thalia, that would be great fun and we can get your bridesmaids dress sorted out as well."

I told her that she need not bother with a bridesmaids dress for me, "I have a whole new summer wardrobe with dresses that I have not worn yet. You tell me what colour you want me to wear and I will sort through my vast wardrobe for a dress of that colour and if I haven't got one, then I will ask Auguste to make one for me."

"Are you sure that you wouldn't mind that, Thalia?"

"Auguste's prices are rather extravagant; I wouldn't expect you to buy my dress for me. I know that you will be a doctor's wife but I don't even think that Peter's wage would cover Auguste's charges. I want you to astound him on your wedding day, just as I did with Nicky, on ours."

She finally agreed and said that we could make a day of it and go for a meal after. I agreed. "If you are buying the dress, then I will buy the meal. Oh, Thalia, you are such a good friend to me. I never would have thought that I would become great friends with a princess."

I told her that it was just a title and that I was just a country girl who happened to have a handsome prince fall in love with her.

"Just like a fairy tale. You have never made me feel that there was any difference between us," she told me.

"There isn't. We both have two arms, two legs and two eyes; just the same."

I could see Sister Procopy watching us, so we parted and started doing the rounds of temperatures and blood pressures.

It was a few weeks later that our day off coincided, so we went together to Auguste Brisac's workshop to discuss Katya's wedding dress. Katya's face was flushed with excitement as we poured over styles and then materials for the dress and her veil.

Rather than Katya wearing a tiara of gems, she said that as it was a summer wedding, she wanted a circlet of summer flowers. Auguste suggested that rather than have real flowers that would wilt through the day, she would be better off having silk flowers. "That way you will be able to keep it long after your wedding," Auguste explained. She and Katya discussed what flowers she wanted and what colours and settled on a circlet of peach roses and ivy.

"You could have your bridesmaid dress of the same colour Thalia." Katya said.

"I do believe Auguste that you made me a summer gown in a peach colour, didn't you?"

"Indeed, I did, Your Highness, it would be ideal as a bridesmaid's dress."

With everything sorted, I gave Auguste my card for her to send me the bill and she told us that Katya's dress and veil would be ready for a final fitting in two weeks.

I was mentally calculating when that would take us to. I had to be sure that I paid Auguste's bill before we left.

From Auguste's we found a small restaurant that was advertising good food at reasonable prices. We went inside and ordered the beef stroganoff, followed by coffee. Around us were everyday workers that had come from the banks or offices or shops for their lunch. There was no gold leaf or crystal chandeliers, like Minsky's or the other restaurants I would normally frequent with Nicky or Mama and Grand Mama but the place was neat and clean and tidy and the food was delicious.

After Katya had paid the bill, we left and went our separate ways; she back to Tsarskoye Selo and me back to Chesme.

Nicky was waiting for me when I got home. "Did you have a good time with Katya, darling?"

I told him that it was great fun. "When we get Auguste's bill, Nicky, I want it to be paid straight away. I don't want to leave Katya or Peter to pay for it, after we leave here."

Nicky agreed. He was sitting reading the daily newspaper when I came down from changing. I asked him if there was anything interesting in the newspaper.

"Not unless you call workers at the Putilov plant in Petrograd going on strike, interesting."

I sat down beside him and snuggled up close. "You're going to miss, Katya, aren't you, darling?" he said, kissing the top of my head.

"Katya and Olga, although Olga isn't so fun loving as Katya, well she's not as young as Katya... Oh I wish that we could take them all with us. Katya and Peter, Olga, Karl and his family..."

"I know, Lia, but being practical, we couldn't. The Dowager Empress is being extremely generous in allowing us all on the Polar Star as it is, besides our friends are not at risk of losing their freedom if not their lives, because they are not close members of the royal family."

"I know, Nicky," I said and snuggled closer to him. "I am trying not to think about the possible threat to our lives, maybe not so much Mama and Gregor, but to Grand Mama and us." He kissed my forehead.

"You know your problem Mrs Princess, you have too good a heart."

"Can anyone have too good a heart, darling?" I asked him.

"I wouldn't want you any other way but we have to be practical."

I sighed, "I know."

"To transport all of the people you want, we would need to get another ship, probably twice the size of the Polar Star, and that is not exactly small, besides that, we can keep this quiet with the people we have, if we had any others, it would attract attention and suspicion. With the Dowager Empress inviting us on the Polar Star, it has solved a massive problem for us. I was getting a little worried about finding transport for all of us, without attracting attention."

When we went upstairs later on and were on our own, our lovemaking was sweet and gentle.

The next morning we went over to Grand Mama's to see how she was. I was worried about her health and the stress that this move was having on her. The Dowager Empress was used to travelling all over the world, no one paid much attention to her leaving again. Grand Mama had been in Russia for over forty years now, after travelling to Russia to marry my grandfather but since then Tallin had been the furthest she had travelled and she wasn't getting any younger. For her sake, I would be glad when we were all safely onboard the Polar Star, making our way to Copenhagen. She was scared about us leaving, although she tried not to show it. I was glad that Peter Abramovich and his wife Ava were there to give her support but there again, Peter and his wife were not young themselves. I presumed that he was of a similar age to Grand Mama. It was a good thing that Nicky, Gregor and Rudolph were there to help them both.

When we arrived at Grand Mama's, we found her sitting in the lounge reading the newspaper. When Igor announced us, she folded the newspaper, stood up and came over to kiss us.

I asked her how she was.

"Oh I am fine my darling, how are you both?"

I told her about my day out with Katya and choosing her wedding dress. I said that we were working on the same ward again and told Grand Mama about Katya and Peter finding a house in Tsarskoye Selo.

"I am glad that she has found someone. I liked her from when we met at your wedding.

"I was just reading in the newspaper that Petrograd was having problems with strikes and demonstrations. They say that they want Russia to pull out of the war and the Tsar to abdicate but I don't understand how that would happen. Who would rule Russia?"

"The Okrama would, Aunt Lilia, the same as the Parliament in Britain the Monarchy are only a figurehead there, but the political decisions on how to run the country are left up to the government to decide. The government has been voted for by the people in the hopes that the ministers then make the right decisions for the country.," Nicky told her.

"What would happen to the Tsar and his family if he abdicated?" she asked.

"I presume they would retire to somewhere like Livadia, until the Tsarevich was old enough to take over as a figurehead of Russia; very much like the British Queen."

"That doesn't sound too bad, if they could all retire to Livadia. The weather is so much better there than here, I should imagine." Grand Mama said with a sigh of relief. In all of this we seemed to forget that although Nikolas was Tsar he was also Grand Mama's nephew the same as Nicky, so it was understandable that she would be concerned.

"Are you all ready to move down to Tallin with us Aunt Lila?" Nicky asked.

"I think Peter has another couple of trunks to move. He said that he would take them down tomorrow."

"Do you want me to get Rudolph to come and help him?"

Grand Mama said that she would be grateful for that, "After all Peter is not as young as he used to be. It will be good for him and Ava to take things easier, when we get there and let the youngsters deal with the heavier duties."

I felt that Grand Mama seemed to be taking it all in her stride and I breathed a little easier.

"I am sure the sea air will be good for me, don't you Thalia?" she said to me.

This was Grand Mama the actress coming to the fore, again and mentally I was applauding her. We stayed for lunch, then moved on to Mama and Gregor's.

As usual, as soon as Ilia saw us, he lifted his arms up for a cuddle from me. Willingly I obliged my little brother and smothered him with kisses, which made him giggle.

"More Lia, more!" He would shout and I would do it again.

Once he had had enough of me kissing him, he would then wriggle in my arms and ask Nicky to 'Throw' him.

"Hello little Count," Nicky would say to him.

"Throw Nicky, throw me up and catch me," my little brother demanded.

Nicky was so good with him. I loved to watch them play together.

When Ilia had finally had enough and had laughed so much that he was exhausted, Nicky put him down. Ilia sat down and played quietly with his toys until Maria came to tell him that it was time for his afternoon nap.

I think Nicky had worn him out, as he took Maria's hand and walked, quietly with her upstairs to the nursery.

When the 'adults' were on their own, the conversation changed to more immediate things.

"Petrograd is suffering at the moment, I see," Gregor said.

"It makes a change from St Petersburg," Nicky replied. "I am going to help Peter Abramovich to take some more of Aunt Lilia's things down to Tallin tomorrow. She said that that is the last of her belongings and she will be ready to move in with us."

I felt that everything we spoke of these days was in a code of some sort. It felt very strange, that we were, more or less, talking of everyday things but really talking about a monumental change in our lives.

"When we decided to move down there, why don't you come and spend some time with us. I am sure having you and little Ilia around will help Aunt Lilia settle in that much quicker. What do you say, Gregor?"

"Well, I suppose we could do that, before we move to the hunting lodge, if it won't be too much trouble for you?"

"I have a couple more things that I want to sort out here first but I can ring you and let you know when we are going down Gregor."

Oh, it was all being done so smoothly. It was as if we were all actors in a play and that play was being acted out in the here and now.

We talked for a while longer, then went home.

Back at work, reality hit back, as more patients were brought in, the peace that had been our ward was suddenly shattered, by the moaning of men in pain.

These men weren't soldiers but men of St Petersburg, caught in the crossfire.

The time flew on the ward, as we were kept so busy. When Nicky picked me up, after my shift had finished, I was exhausted, more than I had been for a long time.

"Have you seen the papers today Lia?" Nicky asked me as I got into the car.

"I have been too busy darling. We had an influx of patients, not soldiers but the general public."

"You look exhausted. I think a nice soak in the bath and early to bed is my prescription, Nurse Ivanov."

We drove towards home in silence, until I remembered that Nicky had asked me if I had seen the newspapers.

"What about the newspapers, Nicky?"

"Sorry darling, I did not mean to…" he started to say.

"Nicky, I am all right now. I was just exhausted, by the work and the noise but now I have had a bit of peace and quiet, I am all right now. What do the papers say?"

"The Tsar has ordered the disbanding of the Duma again but apparently they won't go. They ignored his order and has demanded that they organise a provisional government."

"It's starting then?" I said.

"Darling, it started a long time ago. This is the beginning of the end of Russia, as we know it."

"Oh, Nicky," was all I could say.

"The Dowager Empress spoke to me today and told me that she will be leaving on 'one of her trips', in three days' time. She said that she would be anchoring off down south for a few days before sailing to Europe."

"Is this more code Nicky? Is it time?"

"We will all drive down to Tallin in two days, time." He explained that he had telephoned Grand Mama and also Mama and Gregor, who told him that they were ready.

"I am due to go with Katya for her wedding dress fitting tomorrow, can I take the money to pay Auguste? I could tell her that because it's a wedding present for Katya, I want to pay for it straight away, so that her bill doesn't get mixed up with the others. Does that sound convincing enough, Nicky?"

I was now being drawn more into the lies that we had been laying down for the last few weeks and months.

Nicky suggested that after I had been with Katya to try on her wedding dress, I should make out that I was feeling unwell and come home, then the next day he could ring the hospital and say that I was unwell and wouldn't be in for a few days.

It was all so simple if all went to plan. What could go wrong? I didn't know why but somehow it all felt too easy.

When we got home, we ate in the small dining room, then I went upstairs for a bath. After Tanya had run the bath and added perfumed oils to the water, Nicky told her that she wouldn't be needed for the rest of the night. Tanya wished us both 'goodnight' and closed the door behind her.

Nicky undressed me and helped me into the bath, then sat down on the floor.

"I like this," he said, "just you and me. I like to be able to wash all of the stress of the day from you and then wrap you up and dry you off."

"Well, Mr Prince, when we get to the new world and you don't have a job, I could always recommend you as a lady's maid." I joked with him.

"You wouldn't like me doing this to other women, would you?"

I shook my head, suddenly serious. "No, I would hate the thought of you with another woman, Nicky."

Suddenly the joviality had disappeared and it was my fault. "I'm sorry, Nicky," I apologised, "I didn't mean to ruin our time together."

He kissed my neck, "You haven't ruined anything darling. You've had a hard day. It's good that you have finished work, unofficially, of course. You need a rest. Just relax while I wash your hair."

He washed my hair as gently as Tanya ever did and when he had finished, he helped me from bath and wrapped me in one of our big thick fluffy towels. He picked me up and carried me over to the chair by the fire and sat down with me on his lap. "You are my princess and I could never love anyone else Lia. You are still the light of my life."

He dried my hair and gently combed it, then carried me to our bed. All the love that we felt for each other was poured into our lovemaking that night and we fell asleep curled up in each other's arms. Nicky had laid out the money to pay for Katya's dress on my bedside table.

Tanya woke me up the next morning, somehow Nicky had risen and bathed without waking me. "Good morning, Your Highness, did you sleep well?" She asked in her usual cheery way.

I had slept extremely well and felt full of energy. Tanya dressed and styled my hair and had laid out a skirt and blouse for me to wear that day.

I had arranged to meet Katya outside Auguste Brisac's workrooms. When I arrived, she had already been waiting there for ten minutes. "I was so excited Thalia."

Arm in arm, we walked into Auguste's workrooms.

"Princess Ivanov, Miss Patenko, welcome. Are you ready to try on your wedding gown, Miss Patenko? I have it right here. Come this way please."

She led us through to the back where there was a curtained off changing room and many tables with girls either cutting out material for dresses or sitting at sewing machines, sewing the gowns together. The work room was a hive of activity amidst all of the colours of the rainbow fabrics.

Katya went behind the curtains with one of Auguste's girls to help her into her wedding dress. After a while, the curtain opened and Katya came out grinning from ear to ear. She looked absolutely stunning as she stood and looked at herself in the full-length mirror.

Auguste brought the finishing touch, her veil and circlet of flowers and put it on her head. She looked so lovely, I felt tears well up in my eyes.

"You look wonderful, Katya," I told her as tears began to trickle down my cheeks.

"It's all thanks to you, Thalia. How can I ever thank you for," she opened her arms, as if to encompass her figure in the dress, "all of this. It is more than I ever dared hope for. How can I thank you Thalia?"

I hugged her, "Just be happy Katya and if you have a daughter, you could name her after me." I laughed through the tears. We ended up both crying and clinging to each other. I stood up and moved away from her, "We don't want to get tears all over your beautiful wedding dress," I told her.

When Katya went back behind the curtains again to take the dress off, I had a quiet word with Auguste, while Katya was getting changed. "Auguste, I want to pay for Katya's dress now, in cash. We have so many bills coming in at this time of the year and I want her to be wearing a dress on her wedding day that has been paid for and not payment pending."

"Your Highness, I know that your credit is good, you needn't bother."

"No Auguste," I insisted, "It's a wedding present, so I would rather pay for it now."

Auguste blushed. I could see that she was embarrassed to talk about money face to face. "Please, Auguste."

"Very well then, Highness, here is my bill." She handed me the headed invoice. I reached into my purse and drew out the money that Nicky had left for me.

She thanked me and made a note, that the invoice had been paid in full. By the time Katya came out dressed as normal, the transaction had been done. She asked Auguste if she could have the outfit delivered to the nurse's quarters at the hospital in Tsarskoye Selo the day before her wedding.

August acknowledged her request and said that it would be delivered as Miss Patenko wished.

I felt that I had done what I promised to do for Katya. We got out of Auguste's workshop and stood on the path outside, Katya flung her arms around me again.

289

"Thank you, Thalia. I really appreciate what you have done for me. Shall we go for a meal? My treat."

I had never felt so sad about leaving my friend and the tears began to flow again.

"I'm sorry, Katya, I'm not feeling very well. Would you mind if I just went home? I think I am coming down with a cold or something."

Her face was all concern, "Of course not, Thalia. You go home and get to bed. I will see you at work, the day after tomorrow." I kissed her and thanked her. "If you don't feel any better when you are due to come back, stay in bed."

I smiled at her. "Yes, Nurse."

As I arrived home, I felt like I carried all the problems of the world on my shoulders. I decided there and then that as soon as we were settled, I would write Katya and Olga a letter.

Nicky was not home, so I went to the library and picked myself a book to read, then curled up in one of the big armchairs and tried to read but my mind kept going back to the big move. Why did we have to move, we had nothing to do with governing the country and although Nicky's mother and my grandmother were sisters to the Tsars mother, we posed no threat to the country. Looking back on history, I realised that the last big revolution was in Copenhagen where they killed all of the Aristocrats, surely that wouldn't happen here, would it? Tears were not far away when Nicky came in and saw me. Immediately he came over to me and wrapped his arms around me, kissing the top of my head, as I rested it against his chest. I could hear his heart beating with a steady rhythm, safe, strong and reliable, just like Nicky.

"How did Katya look in her wedding gown?" he asked me.

"She looked so beautiful and I won't be there to see her." The tears began to flow again. What was wrong with me? I was never this emotional usually. The soft life of a princess was making me soft. I scalded myself. Nicky handed me a handkerchief.

"At least you saw how she will look on her wedding day and she wouldn't have been able to afford such a beautiful dress if it hadn't been for you. Was she pleased with it?"

I nodded, unable to speak still, scared that if I did, I would start crying again. I didn't want Nicky to think that I was a baby.

I noticed that Nicky held the daily newspaper in his hand and asked him if there was any news of note.

"I think we are getting out just in time, Lia. You know there have been riots?" I nodded, "The soldiers that went to deal with the rioters have defected and joined them. Even the Tsar's own armies are defecting now!"

"Are you really surprised, Nicky, knowing the conditions that they have been fighting in?"

"Darling, the protesters were women and the soldiers refused to shoot women, so they joined them instead. The Cossacks didn't even try to stop the protesters. Also, they have released the Menshevik leaders from Peter and Paul fortress. There is no stopping them now. Sooner or later, the whole army will turn."

For our last night at Chesme, I asked chef to prepare us a special meal. Over the months of our marriage and the time we had spent at Chesme, much as I disliked it at first, I had grown quite fond of Chesme Palace. It was where Nicky and I spent our evenings making love and curling up together, finally sated, to sleep until the next morning. It would never compare to the beauty of Kadriorg Palace but I would have fond memories now of Chesme.

Nicky opened a bottle of champagne and we toasted our 'new life' at Kadriorg Palace. Between us we finished the champagne off before going to bed. I must admit that I floated to bed that night. For the last time, we made love in our big bed at Chesme, falling asleep in each other's arms.

# Chapter 34
## The Journey

The next morning after breakfast, Nicky and I drove in his car, leaving Rudolph and Tanya to follow behind in Nicky's other car. We had a small case with some of our everyday clothes. All the rest of our clothes were already down in Tallin, waiting for our arrival. I laughed when I thought of the meagre belongings that Mama and I had arrived with when we first came to St Petersburg. Now to travel I had four large trunks; Nicky had three, then there were clothes for Tanya and Rudolph. Then there was Grand Mama's trunks and Peter and Ava's then Mama's trunks, Gregors trunks Ilia's trunk, then Maria and Mikhail's belonging

Mama and Gregor were travelling down separately with Anya, Maria, Mikhail and Ilia. The boys had been told that they were going on holiday, not that the weather seemed like holiday weather. It rained for the majority of the journey down to Tallin.

Nicky and I had stopped at Grand Mama's, so that Peter Abramovich could follow us down with Grand Mama and Ava, her personal maid, who was also Peter's wife and my personal maid, Tanya's mother. At least we were keeping their family together and with Gregor and Mama, bringing Maria and Mikhail with them, they were keeping another family together. It seemed that troupes of Cossacks had been deployed, going to villages where aristocratic families lived. For what purpose, we didn't know.

Some of the smaller villages had already been ransacked and burnt for what reason, nobody knew. We could see dark clouds of smoke rising up from the ruins. Nicky drove straight past in an effort to reach Tallin before the Cossacks reached it. Peter Abramovich kept up a close pace to our car and the one driven by Rudolph. No one wanted to stop, now until we reached what we all thought was our safe haven of Tallin. We stopped briefly to refuel but quickly got on the road again.

"Lia darling, look in that compartment." Nicky told me. I did as he asked and found two guns and boxes of ammunition. One of the guns was the small mother of pearl handled one that Nicky had showed me, sometime ago. "The safety clip is on but as yet they are unloaded. Do you think that you could load them both if I tell you how to do it?"

I nodded.

He told me how to load the guns. My hands shook as I placed the bullets in the chamber of the guns, then Nicky told me to keep the mother of pearl handled one on my lap and the other, he put down by his side.

"We won't have to use them, will we, Nicky?" I asked. Fear was gripping my stomach and I felt sick.

"I hope not, darling, but better to be safe than sorry."

I asked if Rudolph and Peter also had guns. "Yes. We had to be prepared for any eventuality."

Fear of being stopped by the Cossaks increased my heartbeat and I had to keep swallowing to keep my mouth from drying out. I was not used to putting myself in harm's way, I thought, then remembered the incidents that I had encountered since arriving in St Petersburg over two years ago. We travelled along in silence for a while, both caught up in our own thoughts, before Nicky asked me if I remembered what he taught me about lining up the sights and squeezing the trigger.

"I don't think I could kill anyone Nicky," I said, my voice beginning to tremble with fear

"I am sure that if our lives depended on it, darling, you would be able to."

"Nicky, I am used to nursing people with gun wounds, not inflicting them," I told him.

"I know darling but you seem to forget we are aristocracy and prime targets for the Cossacks. I am just hoping that because they are burning villages, it might slow them down and we have time to get away from Tallin.

"If we do get stopped, we are travelling to Tallin to work in the hospital there."

"But what about Grand Mama and Peter and Mama and Gregor?"

"Don't worry darling we have all got stories prepared. We even managed to get Aunt Lilia into some plain clothes, so that she wouldn't stand out. She has surprised me"

"Grand Mama can be quite the actress when she wants." I told Nicky, which seemed to lighten the atmosphere in the car.

"I haven't known her that long but I have a great deal of love and respect for her. Your mother and Gregor have welcomed me into the family so readily as well. I like Gregor. He may be old enough to be my father but I look on him as a good friend.

"I am part of a family again and I love it."

I asked why he felt part of my family, what about the Tsar's family?

"Court protocol, darling. Even the Dowager Empress very rarely let her 'guard' down. Very rarely was I kissed or hugged before I met you. I think Karl Faberge and Auguste were the nearest thing to friends that I had before then."

"After all of this time, you have never mentioned that before, Nicky."

"It never really bothered me. I was travelling all over the world buying gems and selling them to Karl. I suppose I didn't really have time to make many friends."

I asked him if he found it hard leaving Karl and Auguste.

"To some extent but I know they will be all right and maybe we will all meet up again, when this lunacy is over."

The weather slowed us down, as well as the fact that we drove around some of the villages, where we saw smoke rising from them in the distance rather than bump into the Cossacks.

It was already getting dark when we finally drove through Tallin to Kadriorg Palace. Nicky, Gregor and Peter had decided not to go into the Palace, as the lights would draw attention. We drove down the private road leading to the palace with the car lights off.

Nicky had told his staff at the Palace prior to our move, that as we weren't moving into the Palace for a few days, they should make the most of it and have some time off. We would instruct the staff with the unpacking of our cases, once we had moved in. So, fortunately for us, the palace was unusually empty.

We parked the cars in some of the outbuildings and immediately everyone, except Grand Mama, started loading trunks onto the trolleys that Nicky had had made. When we had the four large trolleys fully loaded, we all pushed and pulled them down the path, leading to the new path that led down to the wooden pier, which Nicky had had made. We unloaded the piled trunks on the end of the pier.

Luckily for us it was a night where the moon lit our way.

Nicky pulled out a torch and signalled out to sea. I couldn't see anything out there but shortly after, a light flashed on the horizon. Not long after, a launch came into sight with four of the Dowager Empresses crew on board. It pulled up at the end of the pier and the crew began loading the trunks on board. While they were loading up, we all pulled the trolleys back to the out buildings and loaded them up again. It was hard work, much harder than even I had ever known (even at the hospital) but the fear and the threat of the Cossacks set the adrenalin flowing through our veins. We pulled the trolleys back to the pier and unloaded them at the end again. The launch was fully loaded and turned back to go out to sea again, to be unloaded onto the deck of the Polar Star.

By the time we had dragged the trolleys back again, Gregor and Mama had arrived and parked their car in the outbuildings along with the other three. We told Maria to stay behind in the car with the children, who were fast asleep. Grand Mama went and sat in the car with them. We told them that once we were ready for them, we would come and collect them to take them to the launch.

Mama and Gregor helped loading the trolleys again and pushing them to the pier. It was only a few minutes before the launch pulled up at the end of the pier again. The sailors began loading again and we made another trip back to the outbuildings. We kept going, not even stopping for a drink to quench our thirsts. There was little talking as we were worried that our voices might carry in the silence of the night and alert someone.

The launch made another three trips and all of our luggage was safely on board.

We went back the outbuildings to get Grand Mama, Maria and the boys, Gregor carried a sleeping Illia in his arms and Nicky carried Mikhail, then hurriedly went back to the pier.

We heard an almighty bang, followed by another. Nicky hurried us on, "The Cossacks have reached the town. We need to all get on board the launch now." When we reached the end of the pier, the launch was waiting for us, with just one of the sailors at the wheel. I asked him, where the other three were?

"They must stay with the yacht Highness." We helped Grand Mama, Maria, Mama and the two boys into the launch, then Peter Abramovich, Anya and Ava on board. The launch was nearly full. The night sky now was lit with an eerie orange glow, as buildings in the town were set on fire and we saw torches in the distance, as Cossacks marched towards Kadriorg Palace.

Rudolph helped Tanya on board the launch and I was about to follow.

"I am sorry, Highness," said the sailor, to Nicky, "there is no more room. I will come back for you and the other two."

Tanya said that she would get off to allow me in but I looked back and saw torches not too far away.

"There is no time to change or come back. The Cossacks are already at the gates of the palace," Nicky said, glancing briefly back over his shoulder.

I looked at him, what could we do? I could swim but not as far as the yacht.

Tanya again said she would get out to let me onboard but Rudolph told us that she couldn't swim.

"I will go as fast as I can and come back for you," the sailor said.

"No, no, that won't work," Nicky said. He began looking around the pier for inspiration.

I told him that I could swim but not that far. "I know, darling." He looked at the sailor. "Would you be able to get us all over to the yacht if we didn't get inside the launch but hung on to the thick ropes on the sides?"

"It might slow us down somewhat, Highness, but it could work," said the sailor, who kept looking behind us at the ever advancing, torches of the Cossacks. "Yes, I am sure it would work." I looked at Gregor, Rudolph and Nicky and looked at the launch.

"There are ropes running along the sides of the launch," Nicky said. "We can hold onto them but it would mean us getting wet and the sea is very cold at this time of year. The men can do it. What about you, Lia, can you manage?"

Peter Abramovich said he would get out to allow me in but I told him no. He was too old. The cold water would probably kill him. I squared my shoulders, took a deep breath and nodded.

"That's my brave girl. You can do it, now let's get in the waters," Nicky said encouraging me as we could hear shouting not far behind us.

We could see flames coming from the downstairs windows of the palace. "They have got in. We must go now," Nicky said. In the launch Ilia woke up and started crying. His cries carried in the open.

I jumped off the pier and hooked my hands around the rope. Gregor followed by Rudolph and Nicky did the same. The shock of the cold water made me catch my breath. We could see the torchlights as the Cossacks were approaching the beach, probably hearing Ilia's cry.

"Go. Now," shouted Nicky.

The launch engine roared into life and it pulled away from the pier. Two Cossacks ran to the beginning of the pier, shouting, "Halt or we will shoot!" From the launch a shot rang out, bringing the first Cossack to his knees. The other soldier shot but it fell short of the launch. A second shot rang out from the launch and the second Cossack fell forward. The shooting brought the other Cossacks running to the beach and firing at the launch but by now, thankfully, we were out of range as the shots, pinged into the sea, not too far behind the launch.

I don't know how long it was before the launch pulled alongside of the Royal Yacht, Polar Star. It seemed like hours but in fact was just minutes. I was freezing and lost all sense of time and place, probably through the shock of the freezing cold water. All I knew was that I had to keep holding on to the rope, no matter what. My teeth were chattering, so hard against each other, that I thought I might break them. I couldn't even look to see if Gregor, Rudolph and Nicky were still hanging on.

Semi-conscious, I was pulled from the water onto the landing stage of the yacht. Someone wrapped me in a blanket and carried me up to the deck. Gregor, Nicky and Rudolph, all managed to walk from the landing stage up to the deck, where people held out blankets for them. Once we were on deck, everyone in the launch began to, climb up the steps to the deck, where the Dowager Empress was waiting. She went and hugged Grand Mama and Mama, then came over to me. "Thalia, my dear girl, you are safe, now," I cried like a child, with the bitter cold but also with relief. All of the planning and arranging had finally paid off. Nicky had been proved right about our lives being in danger. That alone was scary. I tried to look back and see what was happening on the beach. All I could see was the orange glow of our beautiful home in flames.

The Dowager Empress instructed that Nicky and I be shown our cabin, then the others were shown theirs. Tanya followed us, ready to help me get undressed but Nicky told her to go and look after Rudolph. She disappeared leaving Nicky and I standing in our cabin, wrapped in blankets and shivering.

I began undoing Nicky's wet clothes, saying that we should get out of them before we caught pneumonia. He began doing the same for me. Once out of our cold, wet clothes, we started rubbing each other's limbs, with the blankets that we wrapped around ourselves again, to get our circulation going.

A knock came at our cabin door, as Tanya came in with a tray carrying two bowls of steaming hot soup, with large chunks of bread and butter.

"How is Rudolph?" I asked her.

"He is cold, Your Highness but the Dowager Empress has ordered bowls of hot soup delivered to those who were in the water first and then to those in the launch."

I told her to tell him that he must get out of his wet clothes, straight away. She nodded and left us to the borscht. Never had it tasted so good. I could feel it warming me as I drank it.

"Rudolph won't need telling a second time." Nicky laughed, "That will be the last we see of them tonight. Are you feeling better, darling?" Nicky asked me as I finished off my soup.

I nodded, then thought of the sight we must make, both stark naked, wrapped in a big blanket, drinking soup. I started to giggle. "I like this attire for dining, Mr Prince."

"Yes, Mrs Princess, we must look a terrible sight but I like it as well," he said, hugging me. "Oh, I thank God that we are all safe. It got a bit too close for my liking" Nicky said trying to make light of the situation. "If it hadn't been for the crack shot that Peter Abramovich was, some of us might not have made it."

Another knock came at our cabin door. Nicky wrapped the blanket tightly around him, then opened the door.

Two sailors stood with two of our trunks. "I understand that these are yours, for the voyage, Highness." Nicky motioned them into the cabin, where they put the trunks on the floor. They bowed and then left us.

"Thank heavens for Peter, yet again. Gregor, Peter and I tried to prioritise which trunks could go in the hold and which trunks we would need immediately and he remembered."

"Not only a crack shot but highly organised. No wonder Grand Mama values him." I said, then went to one of the trunks to get out some dry clothes to wear.

"Where do you think you are going Lia?" Nicky asked as I pulled out a dress and some underwear.

"I thought that I would check everyone was all right, especially Gregor and Rudolph," I said.

"And who is going to check on you? Into bed with you. I am sure if anyone needs medical attention, then the Dowager Empresses has her own physician on board who will see to them."

He held the bedclothes open for me to get in bed then joined me. Someone had warmed the bed for us. We curled up together and went to sleep with the gentle rocking of the yacht.

The next morning, I woke with a start and rushed to our bathroom. What with everything going on, I never even considered that I might get seasick. I suppose that had been the least of my worries. After I had washed my face in cold water, I went back to bed exhausted. Nicky was awake and leaning on his elbow. "You're not sea sick are you darling?"

I told him that I had never been at sea before, so I didn't know.

"Poor darling, you just stay in bed and rest. You will soon get your sea legs." He said. "Is there anything I can get you, Lia?"

I told him that I could do with a nightdress, if I was going to stay in bed all day.

Nicky went to one of the trunks and brought out one of my nightdresses. "I can't have Tanya seeing her mistress naked."

"That's ridiculous, Nicky, after all of the times she has helped me out of the bath."

"I never thought about that," he said, and grinned at me.

I got out of bed, to put on the night gown, then climbed back in bed. I lay back against the pillows. Apart from the sea sickness, it was nice just to rest and have nothing more to worry about now.

Nicky got up and dressed and told me that he was going on deck for some fresh air. I asked him to check that everyone was all right after the previous night."

He gave a mock salute and left our cabin. Tanya came in later and asked if she could unpack my trunk and hang my clothes up. "Do you want me to lay out some clothes for today?"

I told her that I was sea sick, so I was staying in bed for the day. She asked me if she could get me anything. I said that I was just going to go back to sleep for a while. Quietly she emptied both Nicky's and then my trunk and hung up the clothes, then left me. I went back to sleep for a while.

Throughout the day Mama called in to see how I was, then Grand Mama and Nicky popped back, several times.

In the late afternoon, I decided to get up and go on deck with Nicky. He told me that the sea air might make me feel better and it did. The sea air was bracing but it felt lovely to feel it on my face. I began to feel much better.

The next morning, I woke up early, deciding that I would spend the day on deck, then all of a sudden had to make a dash to the bathroom again.

I had never known anything about sea sickness, so didn't know how long it would last or what to do to help me over it. I climbed back into bed again and snuggled up to Nicky. "Are still feeling ill Lia?"

"I'm sorry, Nicky. I wanted so much to go up on deck with you today."

He told me not to worry, "You'll soon get over it, darling."

By lunch time I was feeling much better again, so dressed and went up on deck, to stand arm in arm with Nicky at the rail, looking out to sea.

"Nothing but sea, everywhere you look," he said, "Nothing or no one can hurt us here. We are starting a new life now away from St Petersburg. Are you happy, darling?"

"Very happy and relieved. I never realised that it would get as bad as it did. I never realised that we were, literally having to flee for our lives."

"I am still a member of the Royal family as cousin to the Tsar." He kissed the top of my head, "Well it's all over now darling." We can spend the next few weeks, busy doing nothing on board."

"Won't we get bored Nicky? It's a long time since I have been just sitting around."

"Oh, there are plenty of things to do. There is a library, we can play chess, deck quoits," he said, then bent down and whispered in my ear, "and of course we can make love."

"That would be nice." I said and leaned against him. "It will be like a second honeymoon."

The Dowager Empress came towards us then smiling. "Thalia, my dear, you are looking better. The fresh air will help you feel better. You've been through so much, child, recently. Just relax and enjoy the peace and quiet."

I asked her about the library. "You may help yourself anytime, my dear. We have plenty of other things to keep you occupied, as well. When I have had my son and his children onboard, we have had to find plenty to keep them all occupied."

I spent the afternoon on deck on one of their loungers, covered in plenty of blankets to keep me warm. I dozed off to sleep occasionally or just at watching the sea. It was mesmerising.

Mama came and sat down with me, holding Ilia on her lap. As soon as he saw me, he wanted to come onto my lap. Mama told him that he must sit still because I was not very well. Ilya came onto my lap and reached up to kiss me. "Poorly Lia. I kiss you better." He always brought a smile to my face as he gave me one of his open-mouthed wet kisses.

Mama said that I was looking better. I told her that I felt better. Grand Mama came and sat down with us. "Oh, I love the sea air, it's so bracing," she said.

She had only been there a few minutes, when the Dowager Empress came over to us. She looked ill.

"Are you all right Highness?" I asked her. I gave her my seat so that she could sit down.

"I have just had some news on the telegraph. Nicky, the Tsar has been forced to abdicate. They have all been placed on house arrest." She said wearily.

"All?" Grand Mama asked her.

"The Tsar, Tsarina and all of the children are on house arrest."

I didn't know what to say. All of what Nicky implied was coming true.

"Do you know where they are, Highness?" I asked her.

"They were all at Tsarskoye Selo at the Winter Palace, so I presume they will be kept there."

I sighed with relief. "At least they are safe," I said.

"Yes. Thank God. They are no worse off, except that Nicky won't be ruling the country. He was never cut out to be a Tsar," she said sadly.

I think the Dowager Empress had time to think it over, as when she arrived in the dining room that evening, she seemed a lot happier. After a delicious dinner, that was as good as any served in the Palaces, The Dowager Empress suggested we retire to the salon and have some music, provided by a gramophone.

"Nicky chose something that we can dance to, there's a dear. We have to celebrate, that, although the Tsar and his family are under house arrest, at Tsarskoye Selo, they are all alive and well."

Nicky found some Waltzes by Strauss and he put one on the gramophone.

He came over to me and held out his hand. I looked over to the Dowager Empress to make sure that it was appropriate. She nodded and smiled. Nicky put his arm around my waist and we waltzed around the floor.

"It's a bit like home from home isn't it darling. All the creature comforts. They even have a piano on board. Later, we will wrap up warm and I will take you out on deck so that we can look at the stars. They all seem so much brighter and clearer at sea."

"Very romantic, Nicky."

"Have you only just realised that?"

We wrapped up warm and went over to one of the doors that lead from the salon onto the deck and we stood at the rails. Apart from the lights of the yacht, everywhere around us was darkness but I lifted my eyes to the sky, which was like one of Karl's jewel trays lined with black velvet, on which sparkled, an array of diamonds. I took a deep breath. "It's beautiful." I whispered in awe.

"Are you feeling better now, Lia? I hate to see you ill. In-fact you are never ill. You are normally so brave and strong but the sea sickness really lays you low for a while. I'm going to see the physician, on board and see if he can give you something."

I told him there was no need, as I as feeling much better.

"If you start feeling…"

I told him to stop worrying and being bossy.

"I can't help but worry, my Lia. You are the most important thing to me in the world."

"I know. As you are to me my Nicky." And stroked his cheek.

He wrapped me in his arms and I just stayed there looking over his shoulder, at the night sky. It was so beautiful. Life was so beautiful to me.

We went back to our cabin, arm in arm.

After we had made love so sweetly, we curled up together and let the rhythm of the waves lull us to sleep.

Early the next morning I was in the bathroom again, quietly cursing this sea sickness.

I crawled back into bed.

Nicky got out of bed as soon as I got it.

"That's it, Lia, I'm going to have a word with the physician. You can't carry on like this, darling." Before I had chance to stop him, he was dressed and out the door.

I curled up and went back to sleep.

The next thing I knew, Nicky was standing at my side of the bed with the doctor, who asked him, if he would leave us while he examined me. Nicky was reluctant to leave me but I told him to stop being such a 'fuss', as I was in safe hands.

The physician took my pulse, blood pressure and temperature.

"I understand that you are a qualified nurse, Highness?"

I told him that I was. He asked me where I had been nursing. I told him at Tsarskoye Selo.

"Oh, with the Tsarina and the young Grand Duchesses. Were you on the same ward as them?"

I told him that we had started together but then I was moved.

He examined my stomach and "Hmmmm".

"When did you last bleed, Highness?"

I had to think hard. "I'm not sure. After Christmas I think but I have been under so much stress and worry, what with work and then leaving Russia…"

Once he had examined me thoroughly, he grinned, "My dear Princess Ivanov, can't you tell the difference between sea sickness and morning sickness?"

I sat up in bed shocked. "Are you sure?" I asked him.

"Believe me, I have seen a lot of sea sickness over the years and also a lot of breeding women and I am pleased to say that you are one of the latter."

"I'm pregnant?"

"Yes, and I would say about three months. Your baby should be due in about September, if I am not mistaken."

"I'm having a baby. At last," I said.

"Do you want me to tell the father to be or will you?"

I told him that I would tell Nicky. He packed his bag and before he opened my cabin door, he turned to me. "Congratulations, Highness."

I thanked him wholeheartedly.

As soon as he left me, Nicky came in, a solemn look of concern on his face.

"What did he say? Was it to do with you being in that freezing cold water?"

I shook my head.

"It is sea sickness then?"

Again, I shook my head.

"Lia darling, tell me what is it?"

"A baby," I said simply.

"A baby? Is he sure?" Nicky asked, trying to take in the meaning of our wonderful news.

"In the doctor's words, 'My dear girl, can't you tell the difference between sea sickness and morning sickness?' As I have neither been pregnant before or been on board a ship. I didn't know the difference."

"We're having a baby. Oh, my darling, I am so proud of you," he said laughing as he picked me up in his arms and hugged me.

I suppose on board ship, news travels faster than the telegraph. By the time I had dressed and gone up on board deck, it seemed everyone knew that the Princess Ivanov was expecting a baby. Mama, Gregor and Grand Mama, came and hugged me as soon as they saw me.

When I saw the Dowager Empress, she stopped and said, "I hear that congratulations are in order for you and Nicky, Thalia?"

I nodded. "That is wonderful news. Something to boost morale. I am so very pleased for you both."

Nicky was strutting around on the deck like a peacock and I grinned at him. "The proud father to be," I said to him as I slipped my arm through his. I told him that I never even thought about being pregnant, even though I had not bled since Christmas. I told him that the doctor had said that our baby would be due sometime in September.

"September. I wonder where in the world we will be by then?" he said as he held me tightly against him.

"Our baby won't be a Russian citizen, unlike us." I pointed out.

"No that's true," Nicky replied. "Once we get to Copenhagen, I think we might stay until after the baby has been born."

I thought that we might like Copenhagen, where English was a second language there and I would be able to put all the English lessons that Gregor had taught me over the years, in Smolensk, to good use. It would be good for me to see how much of it I had retained. It would also be good for Gregor to know that his teaching of me had not been in vain.

It seemed that once the doctor had told me what my 'problem' was, the sickness began to abate. Certain smells still made me feel queasy but as time went on, even that stopped.

Grand Mama said that I looked 'glowing'. Once the sickness abated, I did feel very well and with the sea air and rest I felt better than I had done for some time.

Although we were wrapped up against the cold, we would play deck quoits, in the mornings, after lunch I would read a book on one of the many sun loungers scattered around the deck. At five o'clock we would retire to our cabins to change for dinner. Drinks in the lounge at six o'clock, then dinner at seven o'clock. After dinner we would retire back to the salon to play back gammon, cards and other games., while music played on the gramophone or Nicky would play the piano for us.

After our time at sea, we arrived in Skagen in Denmark, where there were, lorries and cars to take us to the Dowager Empresses Villa in Copenhagen. We travelled in four cars and behind us followed several lorry's carrying all of the trunks we had managed to sneak out from Russia.

Hvidore Villa was so much smaller than the Palaces that the Dowager Empress usually lived in and so much less elaborate. It had a much homelier atmosphere. Right from the start, I realised that it wasn't big enough to accommodate us all for too long and our first night at Hvidore, while we were in bed, Nicky voiced my thoughts.

"Darling, I know that we were going to stay here until the baby is born…"

I sighed, this life as a gypsy, did not suit me, certainly not in my condition. "I know Nicky. It is extremely kind of the Dowager Empress to offer us a roof over our head but if we stayed here we would be living on top of each other and I don't think that would be right."

"Tomorrow, I will have a word with the Dowager Empress."

I told Nicky that I didn't want the Dowager Empress to think that we were ungrateful.

He kissed the top of my head, "Don't worry, darling, I will be the epitome of gratitude and diplomacy."

We fell asleep as usual wrapped in each other's arms but even after so short a time, I missed the gentle rocking of being at sea.

# Chapter 35

## The Nomads

Nicky had a word with the Dowager Empress, the next morning and said that before we left Russia, we had decided to move to America and although he appreciated her wonderful hospitality, he would start making enquiries about steamers travelling to America.

The Dowager Empress said that she understood and she had enjoyed all of our company over the past few days. "Could we write to you once we have found somewhere to live and hopefully, once we have settled, we could invite you to stay?" he asked.

She touched his cheek and told him that that would be very nice. "I won't be able to return to Russia to be with the Royal family or I will be put on house arrest as well," she said sadly.

The next thing was to talk to Grand Mama, Mama and Gregor. We were all sitting in the large glass conservatory enjoying the lovely sunshine but without the biting winds when Nicky broached the subject.

"We are free from Russia now but we cannot stay here for good. Certainly not here, with the Dowager Empress. This is just a just temporary solution. Lia and I are hoping to make it to New York, via Amsterdam. I want to buy some diamonds there and hopefully sell them to Cartier or Tiffany's."

"Who are they, Nicky?" Grand Mama asked.

"Similar to Faberge, Aunt Lilia," he replied.

"Minnie, the Dowager Empress has asked me to stay with her and be her companion." Grand Mama said.

"Oh Mama, No!" Mama said, "What about little Ilia and Lia's baby when it comes. Won't you miss them?"

"Maybe I could come over and visit or you could come back over here?" she said.

"Have you made up your mind, Grand Mama?" I asked her sadly. I had only known her three years and I wanted her to be part of our family still. "Please come with us, Grand Mama. I don't want to lose you yet. We have really only just met. I want to spend so much more time with you," I said, tears streaming down my cheeks.

Nicky put his arm comfortingly around my shoulders.

"I know you do, my darling, but leaving Russia was more than enough excitement for me, my darling. Denmark is mine and Minnie's home. We have been away from it for too long. Babushka, you have a new life with Gregor and Ilia and you Thalia have a new life with Nicky and the baby, when he or she comes. It won't be so hard to leave America and come to Denmark as it was to leave Russia. I have Peter Abramovich and Ava to think of as well. None of us are getting any younger. No, my darlings, this is your adventure, not mine. Go with my blessing. You will always be in my heart. All of you."

Mama was trying hard not to cry, as Gregor put his arm around her. "You know that the Dowager Empress, won't stay anywhere for too long and if she knows she has family in America, I don't suppose she will stay here for too long. But when she travels, everything is organised, where she will go, how she will get there and where she will stay. What you are all doing is setting out on a new adventure. I am too old for adventures but I know that you will both be in safe hands with Gregor and Nicky." Grand Mama said trying to justify her decision.

We had another two weeks before we left. In those two weeks Nicky and Gregor had secured passages for us all, plus Anya, Tanya and Rudolph, Maria and Mikhail on the steam ship, Aquitania, which stopped near Amsterdam for two days, then sailed across the Atlantic Ocean on to New York.

Anya bid goodbye to Grand Mama, for whom she had been keeping an eye on both Mama and me, in the years that Mama was away from St Petersburg, to when we returned. Tanya bid a tearful farewell to her parents, Peter Abramovich and Ava. I hated breaking up a family, but having a quiet word with Tanya before we left, she told me that her future was with me and Nicky and the baby. She could still keep in touch with her parents so it was not completely breaking her family up as she like us felt that we were all extended family to each other, plus the fact, (although she didn't say this outright, but she wanted to be with Rudolph).

Nicky and Gregor had also telegraphed ahead and booked us to suites at the Waldorf Astoria. Once in New York, we would spend time looking for new homes to suit us all.

Both Grand Mama and the Dowager Empress hugged us all, wishing us a speedy and safe journey, as we drove off in two motor cars with four lorry's following, carrying all our trunks of luggage for our new life. The Dowager Empress had also given Nicky letters of introduction to several Russian aristocrats already in New York.

Our suites on board the SS Aquitania were not quite as luxurious as onboard the Polar Star but still very comfortable. Getting on board was a lot less dramatic than it was getting on board the Polar Star. I don't think that I would ever forget that dreadful night, as long as I live.

It took us two days to get to Amsterdam. Nicky left the ship, early every morning and returned in the early hours of the evening with a smile on his face.

Nicky stored his purchases in the safe in our cabin. "I am preparing for our future darling. I want top quality gem stones to present to Cartier and Tiffany."

Every evening Mama, Gregor, Nicky and me dined at the same table in the dining room, then in the evenings there would be dancing in the salon. Our fellow passengers were a lively crowd. Our time on board was very enjoyable. Ilia, Maria and Mikhail shared a cabin and Tanya also berthed with them. Rudolph was berthed with three other single men on the next deck down.

I was no longer struggling with morning sickness and felt full of vigour. In the evenings Nicky and I would dance to the onboard band, it felt like another honeymoon but with the addition of another person waiting to join us.

While on the voyage to America, we found out that this would be the last trip the Aquitania would make as a passenger ship. Once it had reached America, it was to be commissioned as a troupe ship. It seemed such a shame that all of the beautiful décor and fittings would be stripped away.

We were all standing at the railings on deck when we passed Liberty Island with the Statue of Liberty on. "Welcome to our new home darling." Nicky said, as we saw the Statue.

We all caught two taxis to the Waldorf Astoria, while Rudolph and Tanya organised for our trunks to be put into storage. The trunks with our everyday clothes in were stored with us in the taxi's.

As we drove through the streets of New York, to the hotel, I was amazed at the height of the buildings; the 'Skyscrapers'. I thought that I would surely feel claustrophobic, as it felt like all of the buildings were closing in over me.

The two taxis pulled up outside one of the tall buildings, obviously the Waldorf Astoria as announced by the sign in large golden letters, 'Waldorf Astoria', which was situated at 301 Park Avenue. The doorman held open the main doors for us all to enter and after, what we found was called a 'bell boy', four of them, took our luggage from, the two taxis and went into the large, marble floored, reception hall. Gregor and Nicky went up to register our arrival. After both of them signing the register, the man behind the reception desk, pinged a bell situated in front of him and gave two of the bell boys the keys to our suites, both on the same floor. We all followed them over to the lift, which was completely new to us, inviting us into the small compartment. One of them pushed a button for the twelfth floor and slowly the compartment rose until it reached the correct floor. One of the bell boys held the door open for us to step out, then lead us to our respective suites. I thought that St Petersburg was elegant but the suite that we had been assigned was as beautifully decorated, with windows looking over the street below. Motor cars looked like toys, they were so far away. I think the highest any buildings that I had been in had only been three stories high, so being four times higher was quite scary.

Not long after, Tanya and Rudolph arrived in our room and Anya, Maria and Mikhail went straight across to Mama and Gregor's suite.

Our suite was all in golds, not too unlike like my bedroom had been at Grand Mama's. It consisted of a large lounge, master bedroom with an en-suite bathroom and then there was a hallway with two further smaller bedrooms leading off, that shared their own bathroom and a small living room and a kitchen.

Because Mama and Gregor had more staff, their suite was larger, with more staff quarters, plus another bedroom for Ilia. I could not believe that so many rooms could be on one floor. The staff quarters were usually on the third floor of the house but because we were housed in a suite, their rooms were closer.

Before the bell boy left, Nicky gave him a tip. The bell boy thanked him and left, quietly closing the door behind him.

Nicky and I stood in the elegant lounge looking around us. "Is this suitable for you, Mrs Princess?"

I thought that it all looked very nice. "It won't be for long, darling, staying here is only temporary. We all need to find our own homes, as soon as possible and get settled, into them."

I asked Nicky he if thought that we might ever go back to Russia. He said that he didn't know. He placed his hand lovingly on my stomach.

"I would have liked this little one to have been born in Russia but it wasn't to be. Let's just make up our minds to make the most of it here in America and hope that America will embrace us. Gregor and I will need to find employment, with him being a tutor and me dealing in jewels, I hope that it won't be too long."

"Are we poor now, Nicky?" I asked.

"No, darling, not poor but we must be careful with our money for a while. Both Gregor and I had transferred the majority of our money over here, a long time before we left. We will have to visit the bank tomorrow or the next day, to get the finances sorted. We also have money, icons and jewels stored away in the bottom of our trunks, which we might be able to sell as well, if needed. Obviously the longer we stay here the quicker our money will diminish. You shouldn't worry over this darling, not in your condition. We will be fine, honestly Lia."

"If we weren't, Nicky, you would tell me, wouldn't you?"

He assured me that we would survive very well. I later found out, that not all Russian immigrants fared as well as us but New York did embrace us. Some of our Russian friends who were down on their luck, having escaped from Russia with little but the clothes on their back, became waiters, worked in hotels, took any jobs, that would pay them enough to keep a roof over their heads. Some were lucky enough to be able to continue living in the manner that they had been accustomed to, some even started their own business. The Russian Tea Rooms was one of them, which was situated on West 47th Street.

On our first night at the Waldorf Astoria, we all dressed in the best clothes that we had in the trunks, that had been brought to the hotel and dined in the hotel's dining room. I think rumour of us being there had reached the other guests, as heads turned when we entered. I suppose when people knew that we were a Russian Count and Countess and a Russian Prince and Princess and as America didn't have any royalty, we were objects of interest. After dinner we went and sat in the lounge in comfortable armchairs and drank coffee, talking about what we would do the next day, when a woman, overdressed in jewels and furs came over to us and started to talk to us like we were idiots. I presume that she didn't think we spoke English at all. I thought that I would show Gregor that his tutoring in the English language had not been in vain.

"We do speak English," I said.

"You are really Russian royalty?" she continued. "Did you know the Tsar?"

I was tempted to say that I had actually danced with him and Nicky was his cousin but I thought better of it.

"Only by what we have read in newspapers," I replied.

Nicky looked at his watch and said that it had been a long day and we should retire for the evening.

I stood up, "If you will excuse us, it has been a rather very long day."

She gave a sort of bob and said, "Of course, Your Highness. Good night to you all. I hope we can talk another time."

She went back to the table where she was sitting with another five people and I was sure she was telling them who we were.

We all went over to the lift and went up to our suites. Outside of our suites, I kissed Mama and Gregor and wished them goodnight. Gregor looked at me and grinned, "So you did take notice of me in our English lessons. I am impressed Thalia."

Both Mama and Nicky said the same and I giggled.

"Good night," I said in English.

We all went into our own suites. Tanya and Rudolph were waiting for us when we entered. I went into the bathroom and Tanya undid my gown and helped me into my night dress, then she followed me into the bedroom. After I had sat down at the dressing table, she pulled all of the pins from my hair and began brushing it. Nicky came in from the bathroom wrapped in his dressing gown, while Rudolph collected his clothes.

When we were alone in our bed, Nicky turned to me, "I was impressed by your English tonight. I think we all must start to speak it, all of the time now."

"Well, I've already started. We will have to see how your command of the English language is?"

Nicky rolled over on his side and looked at me, "Ah Mrs Princess I have had to use the English language several times on my travels around the world."

On 6 April 1917, America declared war on Germany. It seemed that we could not get away from conflict of one sort or another. Luckily the war did not reach the shores of America but was fought in Europe, thousands of miles away.

# Chapter 36

## 5th Avenue

Within a few days, after Nicky and Gregor had meetings at the bank to discuss our finances, we were viewing apartments. We had found that Fifth Avenue overlooked Central Park, the same as the Hotel. Mama said that it would be good for Ilia to be able to go over there with Maria and Mikhail and play on the grass in the good weather.

We started viewing apartments that had enough rooms to cater, not just for us but household staff as well. I couldn't believe that we could own an apartment so massive but Nicky said that we could afford it.

The apartment that I fell in love with was at 1049 Fifth Avenue, which was, what the Americans called, a 'penthouse suite'. It had a large lounge, formal dining room, breakfast room; a library, five bedrooms, including the master suite plus four rooms for staff and a kitchen. What I fell in love with most about our apartment was that it had a terrace around the outside, with doors opening to overlooking Central Park.

Mama and Gregor found an apartment not far from us at 810 Fifth Avenue, large enough to cater for them, Ilia, Anya, Maria and Mikhail.

Mama and I had a wonderful time finding furniture to suit our new homes. When we finally moved into them, we had photographs taken, so that we could send them to Grand Mama and the Dowager Empress. I also decided that now we were settled I would write to Katya and Olga, apologising for leaving them without saying anything; also, the problems we had, to leave the country. (Being shot at by the Cossacks and having to spend time in the freezing cold water); but most of all about me expecting our baby. I gave them our new address and asked them to write back to me with news of the hospital, the Royals and of course Katya's wedding to her doctor. I addressed the letters to them, care of the hospital at Tsarskoye Selo and hoped that they would find their way to them.

In August, we read in the news-papers that the Tsar and his family had been moved from Tsarskoye Selo to Tobolsk in Siberia. We were all relieved that they were still all together and safe but the weather in Siberia was so much harsher and colder than the winters in St Petersburg. We hoped that the Royal family were being housed in suitable housing against the poor weather.

Everyone was preparing for the birth of our baby, which was due sometime in September. We had the nursery all set up and Nicky and I were busy interviewing for a Nanny. We hoped that we could find one as good as Maria had turned out to be.

Before we had travelled to America, we had never seen coloured people but when interviewing for staff, including a nanny, we had quite a few coloured people apply.

I was rather shocked at first but once we got speaking to them, we found that they were very polite, kind, helpful and hard working. We ended up with a coloured Nanny called Betsy and a coloured Cook called Bertha, plus a lady that was to come in daily to clean for us. I must admit that Tanya and Rudolph were shocked but they soon got on together with our new staff.

A couple of months before the baby was due to be born, Rudolph and Tanya came and spoke to Nicky and me, asking for our permission to get married. We were pleased for them both and offered to pay for the wedding.

Poor things didn't have any friends, as yet, in America, so the wedding was a very small affair, with Mama, Gregor, Anya, Nicky and me attending. We all arrived at the Court of Justices in New York and saw the two people of our extended family marry each other. Nicky told them that they could have a long weekend off for their honeymoon and paid for them to stay in a nice small hotel the other side of the park.

When we all went back to our apartment, I realised that, what I thought was just back ache through standing so long at Tanya's and Rudolph's wedding was in fact the early stages of labour. I was tired that evening and went to bed early, with Nicky acting in Tanya's position and helping me to undress and get into bed. At four o'clock in the morning, my waters broke and I woke Nicky up, telling him that the baby was coming.

The Prince Ivanov, who I thought was always so calm and in control was wandering around the bedroom, in a complete panic, asking me what he should do. I couldn't help but smile at him. I told him to call the midwife, whose telephone number was on the table next to the telephone. After he had called the midwife, he called Mama and Gregor, who within half an hour had dressed and walked from their apartment, to ours. I didn't know, until she turned up with Mama and Gregor that it had been Anya who had sleepily answered the telephone in the early hours of the morning. Because she had always been there for me as a child, although being Mama's maid, had insisted on coming with them. Nicky had also gone and woke up Betsy who was already installed in one of the staff rooms, near to, what would be, the baby's nursery.

Once Mama and Anya were there, poor Nicky was sent into the lounge to wait with Gregor for the arrival of Mama's and Gregor's first grandchild.

I do know that Nicky was getting impatient waiting for the midwife to arrive, so Gregor later told me. Nicky was worried that the midwife wouldn't arrive in time and was panicking that there would be nobody responsible enough to step in, if needed.

Apparently, Gregor had told him that he was sure that between, Mama, Anya and myself we would manage, if needs be. Much to Nicky's relief, the midwife arrived an hour after my parents. She apologised for taking so long but explained that first babies usually took a long time in arriving. She reminded me a little of Sister Procopy, back in Russia; all authority and no nonsense.

By the time she had arrived, Mama and Anya had changed me out of my nightdress into a clean one, with another clean one ready if needed, plus clean towels. Every time I had a contraction, Anya would rub my back while Mama held my hand. Nurse Mary McCabe moved them away from my bed and rolled up the sheets from the bottom of the bed, "To see how the little mite was doing." She told me that she had originally come from Ireland in 1900 and did her nurses training in America. I told her that I had been a nurse in Russia. As she was busying around, she said to me, that if ever I wanted to go back to nursing, she was sure that any hospital would be pleased to employ me. "They are crying out for experienced nurses." She told us. She asked me what I had been doing on the wards over in Russia. When I told her, she was very impressed. "Oh, those poor, maimed souls. With that sort of experience, oh, they would welcome you, with open arms. Have no fear of that."

I said that I might be interested when the baby was a little older, as I did enjoy working on the wards. There wasn't much more time for talking as my pains began to get really strong and close together. Nurse McCabe was such a cheery person, giving me encouragement and chatting about her life in Ireland and her journey to America.

At five minutes to five in the afternoon, my son was born, weighing a healthy six pounds and seven ounces. As soon as Nurse McCabe placed him in my arms, she suggested that someone should make us some tea. "I am sure I am gasping for one and I should imagine you are too, Your Highness." I told her to call me Thalia and I certainly could do with something to drink. Nurse McCabe cleaned me up and helped me into a clean nightdress, then said that, "The father can come in now and meet his son."

Not only did 'the father' come in but also our son's grandfather followed him into the bedroom.

Nicky looked down at our son as he lay in my arms. I think I saw moisture in his eyes, when I passed him our baby. Mama and Gregor were grinning with pleasure as they looked at their first grand-child. "It's a shame, it is, that I don't have one of those cameras to take a lovely photograph of you all."

I thought that once I was recovered, it would be a good idea for a family photograph, to send to Grand Mama and the Dowager Empress.

"Have you thought of any names for this wee little lad?" Nurse McCabe asked, as she finished packing her bag.

With everything that had happened over the past months, I don't think Nicky and I, had even discussed it. Then, looking down at his scrunched up little face, which was protesting, about being brought into the big wide world, his name came to me. "Nicky, could we call him Yuri, after my grandfather."

"Your grand mama would be pleased about that if you did," Mama said.

Then I looked across at Nicky, "Unless you would like to name him after your father Nicky?" I said.

"He doesn't look like a Frederick, more like Yuri. We could call him Yuri Frederick Dimitri Ivanov."

"What a lot of names for such a little thing," Nurse McCabe said. "Well, now that you are safely delivered of your son and I have had a nice cuppa tea, I will leave you all in peace. I will pop in and see you both tomorrow and check that you are both fit and healthy."

With that Nurse McCabe turned and left my bedroom, with Anya showing her out.

Betsy said that Yuri was probably crying, now, because he was hungry, so Mama shooed everyone from the bedroom so that I could feed my son. As he suckled, hungrily, I felt my heart swell with total love for this tiny little man. Surely this was the miracle of life, when I considered what he had come from.

When Nicky came back into the bedroom, after Betsy had taken Yuri from me and put him in his crib, in the nursery, Nicky said that he would put an announcement in the New York Times to announce the arrival of Prince Yuri Frederick, Dimitri Ivanov to Prince Nicholas and Princess Thalia Ivanov.

Mama, Gregor and Anya came back into the bedroom to kiss me and wish me good night, before they left to go back to their own apartment. It had been a long day for all of us and I was very tired.

"Do you want me to sleep in the dressing room, tonight darling, so you can get a good night's sleep?"

"No, Nicky. I don't ever want to be separated from you, even in your dressing room," I told him, "I have asked Betsy to wake me, when Yuri needs feeding, so I doubt that I will get a good night's sleep anyway. You might end up begging me to let you sleep in your dressing room."

"Never," he told. "I love seeing you and our son together. I think I am the happiest man in the world tonight and that is all because of you and Yuri." The clock on the mantel shelf chimed nine o'clock. I asked him if he would come to bed now, as he must be as tired as I was. He nodded and began undressing. I loved to look at his naked body. As soon as he got into bed beside me, he held out his arm to me and I snuggled up to him. "Well it's certainly been an eventful day Mrs Princess," he said kissing the top of my head and holding me tightly against him.

"It certainly has been Mr Prince," I said sleepily. I know that I fell asleep shortly after, feeling safe, secure and very much loved, in his arms.

At midnight Betsy knocked on our door and brought a screaming, hungry little prince to me to be fed. After he had been fed, she took him back into the nursery to change him and put him back to sleep. Again, at five o'clock, he was brought to me, hungry. I might have been tired but I felt such joy and love as I fed him. Each time Yuri was brought to me in the night, Nicky woke up and just leant on his elbow watching us. "Never has there been a more beautiful sight to me," he whispered as Yuri was nodding off to sleep at my breast.

# Chapter 37

## Prince Yuri

The first thing, the next morning, after Nicky had breakfast, he went firstly to the telegraph office to send a telegram to Grand Mama and the Dowager Empress, announcing Yuri's safe arrival and of course his name, then he went along to the offices of the New York Times, to put the announcement in the newspaper.

That announcement in the newspaper started an influx of letters of congratulations from members of the Russian aristocracy in New York. I never realised that there were so many. Other Russians had moved either to England, France or even Australia, where Nicky had his opal mines.

Already Nicky had sold the diamonds, which he had purchased in Amsterdam, to Cartier, who when they found out that he supplied gems to Faberge, who was the jeweller to the Russian Royals and aristocracy, they were more than happy to see him and his wares. The senior buyer at Cartier said that they would be, more than happy to take any other gems from him when he had them and would pay him a handsome retainer, so that he would supply them, exclusively. Nicky told me that what profit he had gained on the gems alone, would keep the roof over our head for quite some time, let alone the more than generous retainer.

Gregor found a position at the university as a lecturer. I never realised but when he was in St Petersburg, before he came to me as a tutor, he had received his Doctorate in the local University. I was surprised that he accepted the position as my tutor but apparently Grand Mama had made him 'an offer he couldn't refuse' and paid him a lot more than he would get as a lecturer in Russia. Of course, with Gregor also being a Russian Count, as well was very attractive to the University.

We all soon began to realise that America was indeed a land of 'milk and honey'. Wages were so much higher than in Russia and the cost of living was so much cheaper than in Russia. We aristocrats had to pay grossly inflated costs for food and things in Russia, so that we could eat to the standards, which we had been used to. Even the money we paid to our cleaner was infinitely higher than we would have paid to our cleaner in Russia. Rapidly we realised that we would have to pay our staff, including Tanya and Rudolph, more money, in line with the American wages. Of course, although we had looked after them very well in Russia, they were certainly a lot better off, financially, in America, than they ever were in Russia.

Tanya and Rudolph returned from their honeymoon, all dewy eyed and very much in love. They returned to find a new addition to the household. When Tanya saw Yuri, she fell in love with him and asked if she could hold him. I told her that she could and made up my mind that when they had children, their child would be brought up with Yuri, just as Mikhail was being brought up with Ilia.

Within weeks of Nicky telegramming Grand Mama and the Dowager Empress, we received a reply telegram, saying, "We are coming to America, to see the newest Russian/American. Please book a suite for us at the Waldorf Astoria for a month starting from 15 October."

I was so pleased that Grand Mama would be coming to see us all but was surprised that the Dowager Empress was coming as well.

As it happened, the Dowager Empress did not come to America but went back to Russia, to see if there was anything she could do regarding the detainment of the Royal Family in Tobolsk. She did give Grand Mama explicit instructions to have photographs of the whole family taken and to bring some back to her. Having an insight into the American press, if the Dowager Empress had come over, they would never have left her alone. We had had a small taste of it after Nicky had placed Yuri's birth in the newspaper. Luckily enough the interest in us died down after Nicky told them that we had never met the Tsar, I was just a nurse and he was a business man. We just happened to have a title.

Mama, Gregor and Ilia, who was now nearly two years old, went to the docks to meet Grand Mama, get her checked in at the Waldorf Astoria, then bring her back to our apartment to see her Great Grand Son. Nicky had booked for a photographer to come to the apartment to take some photographs of the four generations, then some of Mama, Gregor and Ilia and some photographs of Nicky, Yuri and myself.

The photographer was with us for over an hour taking various combinations of photographs of us all, then left, saying that the prints would be available the following week. Grand Mama was so pleased with how her two boys were doing, bearing in mind that they were really uncle and nephew to each other.

Yuri was two months old now and when I cuddled him, I could smell that same baby-ness that I had of Ilia when he was a baby, who would be two years old on Christmas day.

Several times the five of us visited the Russian Tea Rooms. It felt such a shame that we would never be able to dine like this back in St Petersburg but we had moved on now.

We took Grand Mama sightseeing during the day and some evenings we would go to the theatre.

We were all worried about the Dowager Empress going back to Russia to see if she could arrange for the Tsar's family to be released. We were worried that she might also be put under house arrest with them, but as we found out later that she had 'friends in high places' who insured that she posed no threat to the country and was allowed to return to Copenhagen on the understanding that she would not return again or try to remove any of the Romanov family. It must have broke her heart to leave her grandchildren in such perilous times but she agreed. She had no alternative and was insured that the Romanov family would be safe.

Although we tried very hard not to draw attention to us; because Grand Mama was the youngest sister to the Dowager Empress of Russia, there were times when other members of the Russian aristocracy came and spoke to her, firstly, then to the rest of us. She was even in the newspapers. *'Dowager Empress of Russia's younger sister visits America.'* So, any chance of remaining incognito was spoilt. Everywhere Grand Mama went, you could guarantee at least one newspaper reporter was present with a photographer.

One good thing about it was members of the Russian aristocracy came and talked to us, to invite us to afternoon tea, dinner or to a ball, held in her favour, of course.

It did give us time to make friends in our circle. I made friends with Princess Kitty Valenskiya, who was a few years older than me, with two little girls aged five and seven called Micha and Sacha. The girls were looked after by a nanny and a governess, so Kitty had plenty of time to, 'show me around' and get to know more about New York, also get to know more members of the Russian aristocracy that were living in New York.

Everyone who met us, fawned over Grand Mama, as she was the closest link to the Dowager Empress of their homeland.

Much too soon, it was time for Grand Mama to return to Denmark and the Dowager Empress, who she said had been making up for the lost time for when they were not together in Russia, which was many years. She said that it felt like when they young Princesses again in Copenhagen. They had an awful lot to talk about, including Nicky's mother who was the oldest of the three Danish Princesses. When Grand Mama left, a month later, she carried letters with her addressed to the Dowager Empress, plus photographs of us all.

As we all stood on the docks to wave to her, there were tears in Grand Mama's, Mama's and my eyes. When Mama and I would see her again, we didn't know, which made it even harder to say goodbye.

I took comfort from Nicky and Yuri, as Mama took comfort from Gregor and Ilia.

Luckily, a few days later, Kitty came to take me out shopping and then afternoon tea. I was happy to leave Yuri in Betsy's capable hands and also, I knew that Tanya was on hand as well.

So, Kitty and I went shopping at the large apartment stores. This was a totally new experience for me, buying 'off the peg' clothes, although they were haute couture. I did miss the times that I spent with Auguste Brisac, with material samples spread out across my bed and pouring over patterns and styles in her 'style book'. Kitty told me that eventually people such as Auguste Brisac would be out of fashion. So much for progress. Kitty dressed to the height of American fashion, with her dark hair cut in a short bob, which was all the rage. She tried to get me to get my hair cut and styled but I was happy with my hair style as it was. Everyday dress and skirt lengths were cut just above the ankles. In this I did agree to follow the fashion, with Nicky whistling (like young American men) at me, when he saw me showing my ankles. I did ask Nicky what he thought about me getting my hair cut but like me, he felt that was a step too far.

I was surprised that by the end of November, shops and department stores in New York were dressing their windows ready for the Christmas period. Macey's were exhibiting Christmas presents in their store windows. These were always crowded with children looking to see what they wanted for Christmas, even if their parents could not afford them.

Christmas was coming and as far away as it was, the New York Times, kept us updated on what was going on in Russia. Reading it, made us realise, how lucky we were to have got out of Russia when we did. Area's originally in Russia, were breaking away and declaring independency. First the country was being ruled by one government, then that government was overthrown and another party had taken over the running of the country.

Because we left Russia, in haste, having to leave furniture and other large items behind, the rocking horse that Nicky and I had bought Ilia the Christmas before we left had had to be left behind. We decided that we would give him another one for Christmas. This rocking horse was dappled grey, with a white mane and tail, with a black leather saddle and reigns.

We thought that Yuri was too young to enjoy Christmas, so we decided to buy new clothes for him, as he was growing fast and outgrowing the clothes that we had bought for his birth. Daily he was looking more and more like Nicky, with his dark hair and grey eyes. Betsy was very good and patient with Yuri and any fears that I originally might have had, employing a black Nanny, had disappeared very quickly.

I had to smile when I remembered Grand Mama's reaction when she first saw Betsy and Bertha our cook. She was concerned that we all might be killed in our beds and called them 'heathens'. After only a short while in our employ, Betsy and Bertha proved to be angels, the way they took care of us.

We let Rudolph and Tanya go and buy the Christmas tree, which was eight foot tall. We had to buy all new decorations to put on it, as Christmas decorations was the last thing on our mind, fleeing Russia. The four of us decorated the tree, with much laughter. Having had them flee with us from Russia, Rudolph and Tanya, were more like our friends, than employees. Nicky and I allotted one of the staff rooms as their own living quarters, with their bedroom next door and gave them furniture for their rooms. Bertha and Betsy got on well together and said that they would be happy to share a bedroom, to enable them to have their own living room as well. We saw no problem with that, so agreed to their proposal as well. If we entertained and needed extra staff, we would hire them in from an agency, who we found was very good. The agency was keen for our patronage, as we were labelled Russian Aristocracy.

We had been invited to a ball Christmas Eve by Kitty and her husband, who was in a high position in a Bank. Mama and Gregor had also been invited, it seemed, along with every Russian Aristocrat in New York. It was a wonderful night, which brought back memories of another Christmas Eve's in St Petersburg. Many people came over and talked to us and said that they would send out invitations to us for dinner or another ball in the New Year.

We arrived back home at two o'clock in the morning on Christmas Day. It had been a wonderful evening. Mama and Gregor had invited us for lunch that day and as Ilia was old enough to know that it was his Birthday and Christmas Day, I could imagine that he would be waking everyone up early that morning. Once I had fed Yuri at four o'clock, he went back to sleep until nine o'clock, so it gave us chance to catch up on our sleep.

We took Yuri with us to give Betsy some time off on Christmas day. Before we left our apartment we gave Tanya, Rudolph, Betsy and Bertha their Christmas presents and wished them all a Merry Christmas. We had also instructed Bertha to prepare them all a Christmas dinner, which they were going to eat at the big table in the kitchen.

As Mama's staff were working Christmas day, we invited, Mama, Gregor and Ilia to our apartment, on New Year's Day, so that, their staff, could have the day off.

Ilia was delighted with his new rocking horse and we had also replaced the train that we had bought Mikhail. Which again he had to leave in Russia, so they were both happy with their presents and played quite happily until it came time to eat, which was when they went back into the nursery for their own Christmas dinner, leaving us adults to dine in peace.

Christmas passed into New Year and 1918 was upon us. Mama, Gregor and Ilia came to our apartment for the day but Ilia was unhappy with the fact that Yuri was too young to play with him yet. Mama and Gregor brought some of his smaller toys with him, so that he was kept occupied but after lunch, he seemed to get tired, so we put him in the nursery with Yuri to sleep, for a while.

We read, later on in January that the Russian Royal family had been moved from Tobolsk to Ykaterinburg. I could not understand why they kept moving them around but Nicky told me that with the balance of power keep changing, they all had different ideas on where the Royals should be housed that would cause the least trouble. I asked Nicky if they would be safe. He just shook his head. "Darling I don't know. I hope they will be but under the rule of Tsar Nicholas, millions of people had died and I suspect that someone would have to pay for so many lives."

I never realised that so many had died but looking at the statistics of the war alone, millions had died, as 'cannon fodder'. The newspapers said that seven million people had died under the Tsar's rule, either through the slaughter of protesters or the ravages of war. Seven million people was a terribly massive number of deaths to lay at the door of one man. The Tsar that I had been privileged to know was nothing like the man they were describing but there again, I knew little of him. When I asked Nicky about this, he said that indeed the Tsar could be like that, when push came to shove.

It wasn't until after New Year, that I received letters from both Olga Procopy and Katya and Peter.

I read Olga's letter first, *"Dear Thalia, I am so glad that you managed to write to me. I am glad that you arrived safely in America. I do understand that your lives were in jeopardy from the Cossacks. I don't know if you know but the Royal family has been captured and kept under house arrest, here in Tsarskoye Selo, so as you can imagine there are more soldiers here making sure that they don't escape. The hospital is still extremely busy and the Tsarina and Grand Duchesses, wanted to come back to nurse but were told that they couldn't, so we have been short staffed again. We could do with a replacement nurse of your calibre.*

*I am so happy that you are expecting a baby. You will make a wonderful mother. I don't mean to tell you what to do but I hope when you are recovered from giving birth and your baby is settled, that you might consider going back to nursing. You are a good nurse and it would be such a shame to let all of that training go to waste.*

*I am well, although life here in Russia doesn't get any better. With the winter coming, we are expecting the usual influx of frostbite victims. I have to be careful what I write as, all mail is being opened and censored, so I apologise if there are any big black marks in my letter to you. Let me know that you have been delivered of your baby safely. You are greatly missed Nurse Angel.*

*Olga Procopy"*

I showed Nicky Olga's letter. He commented about how long it had taken to get to America.

While Nicky was reading Olga's letter, I opened the one from Katya. I never realised how much I missed my two friends. I also missed nursing, feeling like I was doing something useful.

Katya's letter was so much more light-hearted than Olga's.

*'Dear Thalia,*

*I am so sorry that you missed my wedding. I was very unhappy that you weren't there but I do understand. We had a wonderful day and guess who took your place as my bridesmaid? Olga Procopy. Did you know that she can actually smile! No, I am being unfair to her, she played her part perfectly. I think my next mission now that I am a married woman is to find her a husband. What do you think? Maybe a surgeon, who is used to dealing with unconscious people!!! Sorry, that was unfair too but I still think she needs a man. Enough of Olga.*

*The wedding was wonderful. I think that Peter was suitably speechless when he saw me in my wedding gown. Thank you so much for your generous gift. I think when my first baby girl is born, I will call her Thalia, after you, then there will be two Thalia's in the world.*

*Our house is lovely, we have managed to get furniture off the black market and when the war is over, Peter said that he would like to become a country doctor, like his father and I will be his nurse. The only thing is, how long will that be? Still as long as I have my Peter, I don't mind how long it will be.*

*It was wonderful news that you are pregnant. You will have to write back to me when you have given birth and let me know what you have, a boy or a girl.*

*What is it like in New York? Has the war affected America at all? Oh Thalia, I do miss you, life isn't so much fun with you gone or at least life on the ward isn't so much fun.*

*Do write again soon.*

*Lots of love*


*Katya Urvanski (Mrs)'*


Katya's letter left me smiling, as she always did when we had been together. I was glad that she was happy in her marriage and that Olga had been her bridesmaid. I could just imagine Katya trying to be a matchmaker for Olga and hoped that she had luck finding a suitable husband for her. One that could make her as happy as both Katya and I were.

When I next saw Mama and Gregor, I showed them the two letters from Olga and Katya.

The next letter to arrive was for Nicky from the Dowager Empress in Denmark, telling him that Grand Mama had arrived back safely, with all of the photographs from her stay with us in New York. She said that Yuri looked like Nicky and he looked a handsome little boy, just like his father had been. She also said that she had not received any letters from the Tsar or any of the family, although she had written to them all several times. She said that Grand Mama had told her that we had a good life in America and she was pleased that it had worked out so well. She said that she hoped that we would be able to visit her and Grand Mama in Denmark.

Nicky was pleased that he had heard from the Dowager Empress. "Of course, the Tsar should have listened to her rather than to the Tsarina. They should have left Russia when they could but the Tsar wouldn't listen. The Dowager Empress knew how to run a country, she had experience from when his father was alive but he would only listen to Rasputin's puppet." Nicky said.

It was the first time I had seen my Nicky angry, especially about the Tsar. It was becoming more and more evident to me that the Tsar had been a terrible ruler. A weak ruler, who never took the advice of his ministers or his mother and when his ministers disagreed with him, he would depose the Duma and carry on in his own sweet way. When he found that he couldn't control his country that way, then he would re-instate the Duma, until they disagreed with him again and he would get rid of them again. Would the country have fared any better with another Tsar or would it still be going down the same route? I don't think anyone would be able to answer that question.

In February Nicky had word from Cartier, saying that they were, 'in the market' for more gems and Nicky told me that he would have to make a journey to Johannesburg in South Africa, to buy more stones. He told me that he would have to leave with Rudolph within a matter of weeks and would be away a month or so. He asked me if I would be all right on my own. I told him that I was not on my own, I had Yuri and Mama and Gregor were not far away. I also had Kitty to take me out and about, so I had plenty to keep me occupied. At least our lives weren't in danger.

Yuri was five months old, coming up to six months. He was sitting up, smiling and laughing. He was such a joy to Nicky and me. I think Betsy, as his nanny had it quite easy, as I wanted him with me as much as possible. Sometimes, Nicky would play the piano, in the lounge, which we had bought not long after we had moved into the apartment. If Yuri was with us, Nicky would sit him on his lap and let him bang away at the keys, laughing, when Nicky used to clap him. I hoped that when he was older, he would follow his father and take up learning to play the piano but it was much too early to say. Nicky said that if he enjoyed making the noises, as he got older, they would begin to make sense to him and he would want to learn.

# Chapter 38

## Alone in New York

Yuri, Tanya and I went to wave Nicky and Rudolph off from the docks as they boarded the ship to take them to South Africa. Nicky had been commissioned to buy sapphires, rubies and emeralds for Cartier. Thanks to Karl Faberge, Nicky could tell superior quality gems from poorer quality ones and buying for Cartier, only the best quality gems would do.

I held Yuri in my arms and pointed Papa out to him as Nicky stood at the railings. I told Yuri to wave to Papa and lifted his arm to do so, which made him laugh. I tried very hard not to cry but as the boat slowly moved away from the docks, my throat closed with unshed tears. Tanya didn't even try to hold back the tears and sniffled into her handkerchief. We found a taxi and went back home. The apartment felt empty without Nicky and Rudolph around. It reminded me of when Nicky had left, when we were in Russia. Rudolph had left with him then, leaving Tanya and myself on our own for, what seemed ages. Now it seemed like the clock had been turned back and Tanya and I were on our own again. The difference this time was, we knew where they were going and we knew when they would be coming back or roughly when they would be coming back. I tried to keep Tanya occupied by asking her to try the latest hair styles on me but there were only so many hairstyles for long hair that was in fashion then. When Betsy took Yuri into Central Park, Tanya and I would go along too, really just to help pass the time while our men were out of the country. At least this time we did get letters from them, although they took a long time to be delivered but at least we knew that they were safe.

Kitty came and took me out to tea a few times at the Russian Tea Rooms. I spent time with Mama and Ilia, while Gregor was tutoring at the university. It felt like we were a family devoid of men; all ladies in waiting.

At the beginning of April, Nicky and Rudolph returned home, a little later than expected but they returned home safely to us and that was all that mattered.

Nicky hadn't sent us a telegram to say that he was coming home, so when he and Rudolph arrived at the apartment, we were surprised but delighted. Every night since Nicky had gone, I would go out onto the terrace and look up at the sky, wondering if Nicky was doing the same thing. Little did I realise about time differences in countries. When I saw Nicky standing in the hallway, I ran, crying, into his arms, holding him tightly and feeling his kisses on my cheeks.

"Why didn't you tell me when you were coming home?" I asked, still with my head against his chest, hearing the strong, rhythmic beat of his heart, which I had often fallen asleep with.

"I thought that I would surprise you." Nicky said kissing me. Rudolph appeared, most likely after seeing his wife, to take Nicky's hat and coat.

"Are you well, Rudolph?" I asked him.

"Yes, thank you, Highness, I am glad to be home," he said before disappearing.

"Are you well, my Nicky?" I asked my husband.

"I am glad to be home again, with you and Yuri. Which, speaking of my son, where is our little boy?"

I told him that Betsy had taken him into the park, as the weather seemed a little milder.

We walked arm in arm to the lounge where we sat close to each other on the sofa.

I asked him if his business trip had been successful. "I think my employers will be extremely pleased with our purchases. Would you like to see them?" he asked.

I nodded. "I will show you them later, then. At the moment, I just want to sit here holding you close."

After Nicky had been home about an hour, Betsy came back with Yuri, in his pram, from the park. Nicky went and picked his son up from his pram and held him up. "He's grown, Lia."

"Babies do that, Nicky." I laughed, watching him with our son.

"Do you remember your papa, Yuri?" Nicky asked as he kissed him. Yuri grabbed his nose and laughed. "You've certainly got stronger while I have been away. Ouch you bully!"

"Yuri," I scolded, "don't hurt your papa, otherwise he will go away again."

Nicky tossed Yuri in the air and caught him, which made Yuri laugh. "It will be a long time before I leave you both again. I missed you both too much."

"We missed you too, Nicky," I told him.

Before we went to bed that night, I went and had a word with Bertha, telling her that we would have a dinner party the following evening, in celebration of Nicky's return. I had telephoned Mama earlier and told her that Nicky had returned and invited her and Gregor to dinner the next night.

It felt good to be snuggled up to my husband again, that night. The ache I felt in my heart, when he was away was physical. Before we had settled down for the night, Nicky had gone to his trunk, lifted the false bottom, that at one time had held my jewellery and precious family heirlooms that we didn't want to leave in Russia, now held gemstones for his new employer. He opened three velvet bags, each one containing gems. One of sapphires, one of emeralds and one of rubies. I could tell from my training with Karl Faberge that they were gems of the highest quality. I told him that Cartier should be pleased with them.

"If I have to leave again, I want you and Yuri to come with me. I couldn't stand to be parted from you both again."

I kissed his soft warm lips and said that I hated to be parted from him too.

Our time together was as if we had made love for the first time, exploring each other's bodies and touching places that brought cries of pleasure from each of us.

Sometime after we had become settled in New York, Nicky read in the newspapers that Tchaikovsky's ballet of Swan Lake was to be danced at one of the theatres. It was at the Bolshoi Ballet of Swan Lake that we had really met for the first time and he thought that it would be nice to attend and bring back happy memories. It did bring back poignant memories even to the thump, thump, thump of the ballerina's pointes. Nicky looked across at me and we grinned.

I thanked God many times, that that day, on the river Neva when it had been frozen over and I had skated and tripped over a tree root. It was Nicky who had picked me up. Who would have thought it all started with that?

After our terrifying departure from Russia, where we were running from the Cossacks, our lives had settled down into a calm that we had not known in our homeland for some years. I realised how lucky we were having Nicky to pre-warn and organise us. We had been a lot luckier than some of our fellow Russians who had fled from their homeland. Nicky had a good position with a retainer for supplying gems to Cartier and Gregor now had a good job as a professor at one of the universities. We were all settled. After Grand Mama had made one journey from Denmark to America to see her first Great Grandson, we were sure that we would all meet up again. Nicky often had letters from the Dowager Empress. Sometimes he would read it out loud, other times he just folded the letter and stored it away in his office desk drawer.

Now in a new country and our son, having been born here was an American citizen, I often wondered if we would ever go back to Russia. If we did, would the Royal family be back in charge of the country or would Russia be ruled by the Duma or some other sort of rule?

When I was alone, I often thought of the royal family, now in Yekaterinburg. (I was relieved that they had been moved from Tobolsk in Siberia where it was freezing cold). I wondered how the royals were spending their time. Were they receiving any post from other members of the family? Was the Tsarina and Grand Duchesses able to do any nursing where they were or just passing their time reading?

I wondered how the young Tsarevich was. He always looked a sickly child. How had he managed with the cold in Siberia? How had the Tsarina managed with the cold and her bad back? No matter what the newspapers said, I still thought of them as a close-knit family, that didn't really need outsiders, when they had each other.

The Tsar may have made mistakes but why were the royal family moved from place to place? How long would it be before they would be allowed to finally settle down to some form of a normal life?

I know that I hadn't been close to the royal females, (apart from the Dowager Empress) but I would never have wished them evil. When I thought about them, I thought about when I had danced with the Tsar and Nicky had danced with his cousins, the Grand Duchesses. There had been happier times for us all.

I thought about the Tsarina and the Grand Duchesses and the hold that Rasputin had over them and wondered if any of the rumours had been true.

I looked across to my husband as he played the piano with Yuri on his lap. At one time I used to think that he looked like his cousin the Tsar and realised that, really, he looked nothing like his cousin. I realised that it had only been the facial hair that made them look similar but Nicky was broader shouldered and narrower waisted. His face was more open and cheerful, whereas the Tsar might have smiled but very rarely did his smile reach his eyes. Now that Nicky had shaved off his beard, I thought that it made him look younger and bore no resemblance to his cousin, the Tsar.

Nearly every day of our lives in St Petersburg we worried about riots and strikes. We had seen soldiers being sent to the front without the proper uniform or equipment. Someone called our brave soldiers, 'cannon fodder'. I think they were probably right. It was said that under the rule of 'Bloody Nicholas' seven million people had died or been killed. I had witnessed that from the massacre outside the Winter Palace, where men, women and children had been slaughtered. I had read those men had been killed without a trial and I had seen what the ravages of war did to men. It was horrific.

I wrote often to Katya and Olga and they wrote back, although there seemed to be long silences between letters. I also wrote to Karl Faberge as well, enquiring after his family and the business but again the length of time between letters was long and any letters sent out of Russia were strictly censored.

My biggest surprise was I also had a letter from my father, asking for money so that he could leave Russia I was glad that Nicky was with me when I opened it. I felt so many emotions as I read it.

*My dear daughter I am sorry that we have not been close over the years. I am not a man to show his feelings but you are my daughter and this is your father asking you for help. Things here in Russia are very bad and times for everyone is hard. I am having to share our home with five other families. Everyone is calling everyone 'Comrade.' There is no class system. Everyone is on the same level more or less. There are food shortages everywhere. The horses I had in my stable have been slowly slaughtered one by one so that we can all eat. I am hoping that you can send me enough money so that, like you, I can leave Russia and come to America. I know that you are married and to a Prince so I know that you have money. I look forward to hearing from you. Your father."*

When I had finished reading it, I was literally shaking with anger, how dare he even think I would send him anything. The letter had all been about him. He never asked about me or Mama or our life in America. He just wanted money. The thought that if I did send him money he would be in the same country as Mama and me again made my skin crawl as I remembered what he had looked like and how he had behaved the last time that I happened to see him. Never in my life had I felt such anger. When I handed the letter to Nicky I began pacing angrily up and down the room with my fists balled at my side.

"Well, that is a turn up for the books," Nicky said as he handed it back to me. "I know that you are angry Lia, what are you going to do? Whatever you decide you have my full support. I have never seen you this angry before." Nicky said

"I have never felt this angry before. Ever. I know that it wasn't for the love of me that he has written and all through my childhood he had ignored me, as if I never existed. But to write now and pretend that he had any feelings whatsoever for me. You note he didn't even say my name. He never asked how I was or how Mama was. He knows that I, we have money, and he thinks that just because he sired me, I should help him." I said through clenched teeth.

"So, what do you want to do darling?" Nicky said, putting his arms around me.

"Burn it, but I also want to write to him and tell him exactly what I think of him. Nicky, I have never felt violent in all my life until now. I could kill him!"

"I think you are justified in feeling that way darling. I really do." He said as he placed a kiss on my head.

"What do you think I should do Nicky? What would you do if you were me?"

"I think you have a lot of things you want to say to him, to get it off your chest. Write a letter, whether you send it to him or not is entirely up to you. You can either post it or burn it, but you need to get how you feel for him off your chest, then draw a line under it."

"I am certainly not sending him any money." I said resolutely"
"I am in agreement with you about that." he said. "I think you should maybe sleep on it darling. Think about what you want to say to him."

It was easier said than done. In the early hours of the morning, after much tossing and turning, I got out of bed, went into the lounge and sat at Nicky's desk with a pen and paper in front of me. It took me a long time to think about just what I wanted to say to him. How to even start it. Dear father? No definitely not!

*"Sir, I am in receipt of your letter asking me for money to get out of Russia. I am pleased to say that I am declining such a reckless action on my behalf. You have never been a father to me. I was dead to you from the day of my birth, and that is fine, because I feel that I owe you nothing and to give you money to live in the same country as me I would have to be stupid, (which I can assure you I am not). I owe you nothing; certainly not loyalty. The day Mama and I left for St Petersburg was the day Mama and I became totally free of you and neither of us regret that. I neither want to see or hear from you ever as long as I draw breath."*

I didn't even sign it. When I had finished the letter, I gave a great sigh of relief. I felt that I had been holding my breath all of the time that I had been writing the letter. I didn't realise that Nick had got up from bed and was standing in the doorway watching me as I wrote.

"Do you feel better now darling?" he asked as he came behind me and put his arms around me, "I knew that you wouldn't be able to sleep until you had got it off your chest."

I held his hands and kissed them. "Do you want to read it Nicky?" I asked him. "Only if you want me to darling."

I handed him the letter and sat quietly while he read it. "What do you think Nicky. Have I been too hard?"

He laughed quietly and handed me the letter back, shaking his head. "Not at all Lia. I know that you are not really like that, but I think what you are feeling has been festering inside you for a very long time. As you said, you owe him nothing. Now what do you want to do about it, now that you have said all that you wanted to?"

"Go back to bed and think about it another time." I told him. Arm in arm we walked back to the bedroom where we fell asleep wrapped in each other's arms. When I woke the next morning, I knew what I would do. I burnt both of the letters. I would do to him exactly what he had been doing to me for years. I ignored him. I think that would have hurt him more than me writing back to him and saying what I had done in my letter.

Some might think that I was cruel, others might think that I was justified. I never mentioned my letter to Mama, she had a new life now and I didn't want anything to spoil it. We had all moved on with our lives and he had no part in them.

I felt that, overall, I had lived a charmed life and had been lucky enough to be in Russia at the time of the Romanovs where elegance and luxury walked hand in hand with poverty and pain and unlike seven million Russians, I and my family had survived.

# Epilogue

On 18 July 1918, the American newspapers' front pages reported that Tsar Nicholas II of Russia and all of his family had been executed on 17 July 1918 in Yekaterinburg on the direct orders from Lenin. None of the royal family had survived and the whereabouts of their bodies had not been disclosed, and remained so for many years.

To all of us Russian immigrants, it was devastating news. Nicky, Yuri and I booked passage to Denmark, to be with the Dowager Empress in her time of grief. Mama and Gregor stayed in America, to attended Mass for the lives of the Russian family, which was attended by hundreds of Russian immigrants that had fled, the same as us. We stayed for a month in Denmark then returned to America, when Grand Mama promised us that she would take care of her older sister.

Just over ten years after the slaughter of her son and his family, the Dowager Empress of Russia, Maria Feodorovna, passed away in her sleep on 30 October 1928. To me, her death marked the end to the rule of the Romanov's, although it had really ended ten years before, with the death of her son and his family.

We all returned to Denmark to attend the Dowager Empress's funeral, also to give support to Grand Mama after the death of her older sister. After Grand Mama had organised and attended the funeral, she returned to her family in America to spend the rest of her days in a new country. In the Dowager Empress's will she had left her, *'Dearly beloved Sister the villa in Copenhagen with an annual sum of money for either the upkeep of the villa or to do as she wished.'* As Nicky was her nephew and Mama was her niece the rest of her estate was to be split between them with all of her jewels to be given to me.

After Russia had settled down to some form of normality the Winter Palace in St Petersburg was turned into a museum with many of the Romanov artefacts on show. Our Palace in Tallin, which is now in Estonia, suffered damage during the war being burnt by the Cossacks the night we escaped from Russia. It has been renovated to its former glory and is now open to the public. It will never be our home again.

Over the years St Petersburg has had its name changed to Petrograd in 1914, then Leningrad in 1924, returning to its original name of St Petersburg in 1991. To me and many Russians it would always be St Petersburg.

After years of change and trauma, Russia would never be the same again.